# A FORMULA FOR MURDER

### A NOVEL BY

### DAVE VIZARD

ISBN 978-0-615-68213-6

Text and cover design by Susan Leonard
Cover photo by Bill Diller

Printed in the United States of America

# Acknowledgements

I could not have completed *A Formula for Murder* without the help and support of plenty of wonderful, generous folks. They shared their time, energy, and immense talent to help whenever I needed it, which turned out to be A LOT.

My thanks to Diana Collins, Michele LaPorte, M. Theresa Calkins, and Tom Glide for their editing and proof reading help.

Authors Jackie Vick and Dennis Collins, and all the members of Huron Area Writers Group, provided enough positive encouragement and support to push this writing project to completion. I also need to thank Mary Rose Levesque and Sharon A. Vizard for their not-so-gentle prodding to "finish the book." I can't thank you enough.

I also need to extend special thanks to Dawn M. Doyen for her pharmaceutical expertise and positive support throughout the project.

Good friend and photojournalist Bill Diller created the photo illustration for the book cover. He also shot the portrait on the back of the book. What can I say? He did the best with what he had to work with...

And last, but certainly not least, I thank my wife and partner, Barbara, for her loving support. Our life together has been an interesting, wild ride, and she's stuck with me through every turn, twist, and bump in the road.

# Dedication

This book is dedicated to the loving memory of my late sisters Marilyn and Kathleen. My "big" sisters were largely responsible for my early upbringing. They were smart, funny, talented and wonderfully creative in addition to being beautiful women. They inspired me to write and encouraged me to become a journalist. I think of them every day. I miss them dearly.

*Marilyn Vizard Neumann*      *Kathleen Vizard Murray*

# Get up you bastard, get up ...

The favorite day of the weekend got underway like most Saturdays for the Johnson Family of 5th Avenue in Bay City, Michigan. The only difference for Tanya Johnson was a day she would never forget – the day she watched her father die a slow, painful and premeditated death.

Tanya pawed across shelves that were at the edge of her reach in the pantry behind the family's kitchen. It was just before noon and she was hoping to find her mother's stash of chocolates.

As Tanya's outstretched fingers danced in search of confection, her father, Robert Johnson, a respected principal at Central High School, set the dining room table for four.

His wife, Isabelle, sprinkled salt into the gray cast-iron kettle of soup that simmered on one of the front burners of the kitchen's electric range. The distinctive aroma of her chicken noodle delight wafted throughout the Johnson's four-bedroom house on the East Side.

"Tanya, what are you doing back there?" Isabelle said, lifting a ladle of soup to her lips for its twenty-third tasting. It needed a touch more pepper. Isabelle did not really expect her daughter to answer, but she hoped the question would stop Tanya from completing the raid on hidden treasures in the pantry. "I hope you're not going to spoil your lunch by snacking. Besides, your rear-end doesn't need any padding. You've really got to keep your figure. Somewhere out there, there's a man waiting to meet you and marry you. We're not getting any younger, you know."

1

"Thanks, Mother. I really appreciate your reminding me of my advancing age and my widening butt." Tanya sank her teeth into a chocolate peanut cluster and chewed each morsel while moving toward the kitchen. "I may need some help getting my ass through the pantry door. Could you call the gravel pit and ask them to send over a large bulldozer, or a crane? You know, something powerful enough to move a couple of mountains? Jeez, the way you talk it sounds like I'm packing the Himalayas in my jeans every morning. And I'm not even crowding 40, yet. Give me a break, Mother."

At 37, Tanya was the oldest of the Johnson children and home for a weekend. She had taken a sabbatical from her teaching position at Western High School and was working on her second master's degree at the University of Michigan in Ann Arbor. Tanya was an exercise fanatic who watched her weight as religiously as men eyeballed her distinctive, sleek curves. She had gotten used to her mother's not-so-gentle teasing about her age and weight. She knew it was because Isabelle wanted grandchildren and her daughter wasn't cooperating.

During her early 20s, Tanya had toyed with the idea of giving birth without a dad in the picture, but she decided, after much consideration, that it wouldn't be fair to the child. So, in her mind, no daddy meant no lassie and no laddie. Besides, the career teacher convinced herself that her students were her children.

Other members of the Johnson clan also were a tad unconventional. Tanya's brother, Tim, was a professional student at Michigan State University, commanding more majors than the United States Army. At 28, he often bragged that he was in no hurry to start a work life, though his parents had long ago tired of his carefree ways. The Johnson's youngest offspring was Bobby, a senior at Central who wanted his folks to quit calling him Bobby and refer to him as Spike, the name schoolmates had given him during ninth-grade when he showed up for class with his hair moussed into six long, pointy spirals in the center of his head.

Tanya's father, who hadn't said much to either woman and appeared tired, only made one verbal request during the morning. When the 59-year-old educator smelled the fresh bread baking, he rubbed his round, trash-can-sized belly and asked Isabelle if the heels of a loaf could become bookends for a nice big, juicy double cheeseburger for lunch.

"Absolutely not," Isabelle responded. "Your blood pressure and weight are out of control. And stop licking your lips when you ask for food." Isabelle's husband handled the rejection like a dog that had been swatted with a newspaper. Mr. Johnson knew better than to argue with Isabelle when she had her mind made up. Better to let it go, then try for what he wanted later. He disappeared into his refuge, the basement, to read the Bay City *Blade*. The main headline on the front page of the local rag blared: "Clinton denies affair with Lewinsky," the scandal that was dominating the news of 1998.

Once seated, he cleared his throat to give the family luncheon blessing. "Dear Holy Father, we thank Thee for Thy many blessings, including our good health and good fortune and good food. Now, stand back, Bub, while we tear into all this grub." Ah, yes. The family patriarch had a half-dozen or so similar blessings that he used intermittently when the urge struck. Robert Johnson was playful like that, a nice mix of the sensible and senseless.

After his blessing, she smiled even though she'd heard him recite it dozens of times before. She poked at the chunks of chicken in her bowl and wound the noodles into tight swirls around her spoon.

Out of the corner of her eye, Tanya watched her mother break apart her bread and dip it into the steamy broth. Gentle rock music, a Barry Manilow oldie that gave her almost as much nausea as the soup, drifted from a radio in the kitchen. Outside, a car horn blared as the vehicle passed screaming children who played too near the street.

Robert slurped the steaming chicken noodle concoction from his spoon, catching his breath each time hot broth passed his lips. *Schwoooop, schwoooop, schwooop.*

But on the fourth deep sip, his eyes widened, his throat tightened and his face grimaced as if he'd just taken a quick, direct shot in the gut. And then he fell over, face first, right into the bowl of soup, sending the hot liquid splashing across the table toward Isabelle.

"Robert, Robert, what is it?" she howled, jumping from her usual spot at the Johnson table and reaching to pull her husband's head away from the broken ceramic bowl. "Tanya, help. Tanya, call 9-1-1," she screamed.

As Tanya looked up, the scene before her made goose bumps rise amid arm hair already standing on end. Her dad lay face down on the table, his eyeglasses twisted to the side of his head, his arms hanging at his sides, his mouth open, noodles on his forehead. Tanya's mom was furiously yanking upward on the back of her dad's bathrobe, hoping to raise him from his dropped-dead position.

"Robert, get up, please," she said. "Don't you dare leave me. You can't leave me now. We have two more kids to get through college. Get up, you bastard, get up."

Tanya's chest tightened and she gasped for air as her fingers fumbled furiously to find the cell phone tucked away in the pocket of her sweat suit. How could this be happening? This was not real. Her dad was not dying right in front of her. Her mom could not be losing control.

"9-1-1 Dispatch. How may I help you?"

"Send somebody now," Tanya yelled into the tiny phone. "My dad's in trouble. My mom's losing it. My God, I've never heard her swear before." The dispatcher tried to calm Tanya while she culled more basic information from the frantic woman.

By now, Isabelle had pulled Robert back up into his chair. His head hung straight back with his eyeglasses still tightly twisted onto the side of his face, giving his left ear its best shot ever at 20-20 vision. Isabelle pounded on Robert's chest with both of her tiny fists balled into fleshy gongs. As she swung her arms downward, her red hair flailed wildly like a bullfighter's cape.

As Tanya approached to help, she could tell that her mom's frantic life-saving effort was taking a toll on the 56-year-old librarian. Isabelle was getting winded, but Robert was not coming around.

"Dad, Dad, please," Tanya said as she tried shaking his massive shoulders. "You gotta come back. We need you."

As the Johnson women continued working on the lifeless body of the man who was the central figure in their lives, they could hear the sound of an ambulance's siren growing louder, making its way through the East Side neighborhood. Paramedics rushed up and bulled their way between the harried women, going right to work on Mr. Johnson. For several minutes, they prodded, poked and pulled at his slumped body.

"Looks like a heart attack, better hit him with the paddles," said the elder of the two lifesavers, "Please, stand back."

The Johnson women stepped away, not believing what was happening in front of them. Even electric shock could not jolt the overweight, sedentary man back to life. The paramedics continued to work on him as beads of perspiration on their foreheads drained to their armpits, forming widening sweat rings. Finally, they decided to move him to Bay Medical Center where there would be more help. They wheeled him out of the house and into the ambulance waiting on the lawn with its engine running, lights whirling, and radio squawking.

A small crowd of neighbors and gawkers had gathered outside the Johnson home. They whispered, they pointed, they stared with hands partially covering their opened mouths. The Johnsons were such nice people. What a fine family. How could this be happening to them?

Isabelle jumped into the ambulance to go to the hospital with her failing husband. She was wild-eyed, shouting a list of commands to Tanya as the big rear doors of the ambulance closed. She pushed the doors back open, banging the tallest paramedic in the nose with the door handle. He covered his face with his right hand

and tried to blink back the tears welling in his eyes.

"Call your brothers," she said, "Tell them to come home now. But don't tell Timmy how bad it is. We don't need him getting in a car accident on the way here."

Still holding his nose, the paramedic closed the door again with his left hand. But Isabelle wasn't done issuing orders. A shove from her forearm drove the ambulance door open and into the back of the hand that was guarding the paramedic's face.

"Damn it, lady, that hurt," he said, shaking his hand up and down like someone trying to discard a wad of chewing gum.

Undaunted, Isabelle continued: "And call the school and tell them to send Bobby home from band practice, but don't tell them why. Now, get going."

This time, the paramedic pushed the door closed, but stood back from it about three feet. It's a good thing he did. Isabelle was on fire still acting as if nothing were more important than her instructions. She rammed the door back open with her knee. "And then call Uncle Louie. It's noon. You can find him at the bar. He won't be too trashed, yet. He can spread the word to your dad's family."

Instead of trying his luck with the door again, the paramedic, blood trickling from his nose and a nasty cut on the back of his right hand, tried reasoning with Isabelle. "Lady, we've got to get your husband here to the hospital now, and if you don't quit kicking that door open, then I'm going to be on a stretcher beside him. So, please, cool it, and let us do our jobs."

Isabelle sat down in the ambulance next to her husband and held his limp hand. She looked at his face and shook her head back and forth. "How many times have I told you, Robert, to quit calling God Bub? Dozens of times, maybe more. But you never listened." She broke into tears as the vehicle's doors closed for the final time and latched.

Tanya went back into the house, the only home her family had ever lived in. She took a deep breath, wiped tears from her eyes, shoved the long blonde strands of hair out of her face and started looking up telephone numbers. Tim was at M.S.U. It would be tough to track him down. He liked to party and never slept in the same bed twice while he was away at school in East Lansing.

Bobby would be easier to find. At 17, he was much more predictable, especially when it came to Saturday morning band practice. He would probably be where he was supposed to be, but the trick would be getting a message to him without alarming others at the school. She didn't want to say anything to teachers or administrators until she knew what was happening with her dad. It looked bad for him, but maybe a miracle would save the family from heartbreak. She closed her eyes and prayed for good news as she hammered away with her thumb at the numerals on the cell phone.

The next couple of days were going to be agonizing for her family. Robert Johnson might never return to the family home. Life was draining from his body as the ambulance roared across town. It looked like a sudden and massive heart attack claimed his life. Sometimes, however, appearances are deceiving.

# Should we give it to the Fossil? ...

MONDAY

Nick Steele tried to look busy, not wanting to draw attention to himself on Monday morning in the newsroom of the Bay City *Blade*, the daily newspaper that circulates to about 50,000 readers across Northeast Michigan. His head pounded and his nerves were raw. The soft clacking of computer keys echoed in his skull like machine-gun fire. His stomach rolled with the gushing efficiency of a dishwasher. His body cried out for sleep or, barring that, chilled vodka and anything. A nasty hangover gripped his whole body in the same way a barfly clings to her panties and what's left of her dignity. From head to toe, the reporter hurt big-time and hoped to avoid the daily deadline rush.

As 8 a.m. approached and the hands of the giant, old-fashioned clock in the newsroom ticked off seconds and then minutes to the paper's first morning deadline, reporters and editors kicked their energy levels into a higher gear. They scurried about the newsroom, muttering and cursing as they bounced through a tan and brown maze of cubicles crammed full of computers, desks and telephones. They jostled paper printouts, cups of stale, burned Maxwell House, and day-old bagels that were hard enough to substitute for hockey pucks.

The resulting tension often erupted into some shouting between frazzled reporters and copy editors.

"Hey, what's another name for marketing manager?" called out one scribe to no one particular as he bent over his keyboard like a question mark leaning over the last word of a sentence. "Gimme a good second reference."

A reply was swift. "How about asshole? Nothing's more fitting than that."

The response was soundly rejected and the reporter returned a verbal shot in much the same way a tennis player backhands a volley. "Oh, thanks a lot, Dickhead. I owe you big time for that one."

Just another day at The *Blade*, where the grinding, pounding and mixing of information resulted in the production of another newspaper in much the same way beef, fat and gristle are ripped, smashed and mashed into ground-round at a meat-packing plant. To observers, both are very ugly processes, but most of the time the final product is at least tasty enough to be swallowed.

That kind of banter used to amuse Nick, but now it was just another boring element of the newsroom routine. At 49, Nick had been talked into believing that his best reporting years were behind him. He was the oldest dog in a room full of frisky, young news hounds. The *Blade* had been taken over by a bevy of young, tech-savvy 20-somethings. Even Nick's boss was 11 years his junior.

In guarded references and hallway whispers, they referred to Nick with derisive nicknames. "Fossil" was one he despised. "Antique" made him angry. "Old Fart" enraged his sensibilities. "Gramps" made him want to throw up his dukes first and then his cookies.

*Blade* management believed snot-nosed youngsters were going to save the paper by leading it through the Internet age, which most managers viewed as simply another passing fad. But Nick's vision produced a different result. He believed that managers would simply end up with the newspaper continuing to head in the same direction as pay-telephone booths and their hands dripping with snot.

But all of that was really just a minor irritation to Nick. In fact, nothing had mattered much to him since his wife, Joanne, had been killed in a car accident a few years back. They had been together for

21 years, 19 of them married. Their only son, Joe, 20, had moved to California after Joanne drew her last breath in the emergency room at Bay Medical Center. She had lost control of her compact car on an icy road and hit a cement embankment. It was the saddest day of Nick's life. He also knew that Joe had passing thoughts of ending his.

The younger Steele couldn't bear hanging around town. Too many things reminded him of his mother. Every time he drove by Carroll Park, Joe could see his mom unpacking a picnic basket filled with homemade sandwiches, fresh-cut veggies and fruits and cookies. While driving down Center Avenue, he could see her in the crowd, smiling and chugging down a beer on a frosty March morning as the family waited for Bay City's annual St. Patrick's Day Parade. Whenever he drove over one of the city's drawbridges, he could see her silhouette on a passing speedboat, shouting encouragement to young water skiers trailing behind her.

Finally, Joe gave his dad a hug, and left town without looking back. He followed some old high school friends out West. He wanted to start a new life and leave the old one in his past. The young Steele didn't call his dad much. Whenever he did, both men broke down into fits of crying while on the telephone. Their hearts were broken.

Since his boy left town, Nick spent most of his nights – and some days – at one of the city's legendary saloons. In fact, on this day Nick was hoping to avoid detection in the newsroom and sneak away to Mulligan's Pub to pound down a couple double screwdrivers. Cheap vodka and orange juice in the morning started the day off with a bang. If he could just make it to 9:30, the booze and orange juice would make him right with the world again.

But, alas, his peripheral vision told him the newsroom kids were conspiring against him in muffled tones again. He tried to ignore them.

"Should we give it to the Fossil?" An assistant editor tried to cover his mouth as he directed the question to Drayton Clapper, the 38-year-old local news editor, who was growing through the top of his hair and over the edge of his belt at an alarming rate. "It's only an obit. He can handle it – even if he is shit-faced and reeking of booze again this morning."

"*Sh-h-h-h.* Don't say that out loud." Clapper said, looking over at Nick and then snapping his head in another direction. "That kind of thing could be viewed as creating a 'Hostile Work Environment,' a sure bet for helping the old-timer win an age-discrimination lawsuit. Stop doing that. Call him Nick, even if we all know he's the Old Fart."

Both men laughed out loud. What a riot. They're so funny. Nick wanted to give them both a quick shot in the nuts, and let them double over in laughter at that.

"Go on, give it to the Geezer," one of the younger reporters added, loud enough for most to hear. "It's a routine obit."

That was it. Nick could not hold his tongue any longer. He stood up from his desk, jettisoning his chair with a swift slam from the back of his legs. He faced the young reporter with the big mouth. "First, you know what my name is. Use it. And secondly, there's no such thing as a routine story, only routine reporters and unimaginative, boring writers."

"No offense meant here, Nick," the recent college grad said, backpedaling faster than an NBA guard transitioning to defense. "After all. We're just talking about an obituary – a story about a death."

The newsroom was quiet as a graveyard except for the gurgling of the coffeemaker. All eyes were on Nick as his stare cut to the rookie reporter's core. "An obituary is not about a death. It's a story about a life that was lost. It's a story about a person, who very likely had loved ones and friends who are now hurting. It's a story about a person who had hopes and dreams and accomplishments. It's a story about a person who probably made a contribution to this community – no matter how small.

"And good reporters don't jump to conclusions," Nick continued, lightening up a little. "They gather the information first, do their legwork, do the interviews – and then write the story. It doesn't work doing it the other way around. Now, give me that obituary call. I'll be happy to take it, and the story I file will be anything but routine."

Nick retrieved his chair from the other side of the newsroom where it had rolled. As he sat down, a quiet buzz returned to the newsroom. The young reporter he'd verbally spanked went to the restroom, muttering and whimpering.

Clapper delivered his usual command. "Steele, pick up an obit on line three. Keep it tight – about 12 inches, or whatever you think it's worth. And make sure we've got a head shot to go with it."

"Nick Steele," the reporter spoke into the mouthpiece of his headset, his head throbbing from the newsroom tension and the exertion, not to mention the seven doubles and six beers he'd guzzled the night before.

"This is Tanya Johnson. I understand that you're working on my father's obituary. I have the final times for the services and burial." Tanya had dreaded making this phone call. It was the last call in a nightmarish 36 hours that began when her dad seized up at lunch on Saturday. Calling the local newspaper for an obituary is not something she ever envisioned herself doing.

Morticians' assistants had already called in most of the information on her late father. Massive heart attack. Never knew what hit him. Instant death. Funeral service on Wednesday. Burial at Ridgemont that afternoon. An impressive list of surviving family members and a request for donations to the American Heart Association.

"I'm sorry about your loss," Nick said. "If you give me the final arrangements, I can include them in the story about your dad. I just need to call up the file with the basic info we already have on him. Which day did he die?"

The word "die" hit Tanya as hard as a runaway truck going downhill on a freeway. That made it final. This wasn't a bad dream. Her dad was really gone. A stranger said so. The word filled her with sadness again as she struggled to respond to the reporter's question.

Nick tried to tug a little more information from the distraught woman. "The background information I have indicates that your father was a career administrator at Central High School. I'd like to call some people from the school; maybe talk to some community leaders. Perhaps you could share the names of a couple of his former students who would be willing to talk about the impact he had on their lives."

"Oh, no problem. Dozens of them have stopped by the house. Some I haven't seen since I went away to college in Ann Arbor. I'll get you their names and numbers."

"Tanya, one more thing. I could be wrong, but what happened to your dad sounds very familiar. Didn't another administrator from Central die of a sudden heart attack – maybe three or four years ago?"

"Yes, as a matter of fact, we lost a good friend of my dad's five years ago. George Pepadowski was school district superintendent. He and my dad worked together for years. We were just talking about it last night. What a horrible coincidence."

"*Hmmm*. That is unusual. I wonder what the odds are of that happening? Oh, by the way, what about a photo? We have a picture of your dad, but it's at least 10 years old. Would you have a more recent picture – something fitting?"

"Yes, I'm sure we do. I'll have to look for it. How can I get it to you?"

"You can drop it off at The *Blade*, or I could swing by your house and pick it up, whichever you prefer. But we'll need it this afternoon."

"Our home is pretty chaotic right now. It would save me a lot of time if you could pick it up," she said. "Do you know where to find us? How about around 3 o'clock?"

"Yup, I've got your address. See you at 3." Nick quickly looked up at the newsroom clock and decided he would bang out the obituary and put off the screwdriver until lunchtime. The story would keep him busy and out of the crosshairs of newsroom managers.

But he looked forward to going to the Johnson home in the afternoon. Any reason to get out of the newsroom was a good one.

The Johnson home was on 5th Avenue, just one block off of the city's historic Center Avenue. The legendary thoroughfare was a five-mile stretch of Victorian mansions lining both sides of the street. The graceful, beautiful homes were built by lumber barons more than a century ago when pine ruled Michigan. They were the only painted ladies in town that the community bragged about.

It was an absolute delight for most people to drive down Center. Many of its stately homes had been rehabbed to their former glory. Whenever he could, Nick would pull into a driveway to ogle the architecture and fine craftsmanship of the aging structures. But today, he had to hustle. He had to stop at the Johnsons' house, pick up the picture, get it to The *Blade* production department and then meet a buddy of his at O'Hare's Pub, a watering hole on the West Side of town.

As Nick pulled his rebuilt 1972 Pontiac Firebird into the Johnson driveway, he could see through the windows that the house was filled with guests – family, friends and neighbors who had stopped by to comfort the stunned family. He sat in the driveway for a moment, hoping that someone would notice his arrival and have the picture sent outside so that he would not have to intrude. Nick didn't mind being a pushy reporter when he had to, but this was not the time or place for it.

He was relieved when the front door opened. Tanya stepped out onto the porch and motioned for him to come up. The University of Michigan graduate student caught Nick off guard. Ann Arbor women, as the stereotype goes, are more widely known for their brains than their beauty. Simply put, Tanya was stunning. Tall, slender, and shapely with sandy, blonde hair. As he approached, even the sight of red and swollen eyes could not mar her distinctive face. Almond-shaped eyes. High cheekbones. Full, pouty lips. Tiny ears, mostly hidden by a long, luscious mane.

"Hi. You must be Nick. I'm Tanya," she said, sticking her right hand out to greet the reporter.

"Nice to meet you. Thanks for helping me with your dad's death notice and the photo," he said, as he grasped her cold, delicate hand. Nick had been intrigued by her voice on the telephone, but he learned long ago not to trust the sound of a voice through a receiver. People almost always sound different than they look.

"Would you like to come in?" she asked, her voice soft and faint.

"No, I know this is a very difficult time for your family. I won't stay. I'll call you if I need anything else. Thanks again for your help," he said, as he shook her hand again and smiled.

The aging reporter backed up on the porch, unable to pry his eyes off of her. But he retreated one step too far too quickly, falling backward down the steps. The tumbling of his 6-foot 2-inch, 200-pound frame down the stairs startled Tanya and brought her relatives to the front door.

"Everything OK out there?" Isabelle Johnson asked.

"Yup, everything is okie-dokie," Nick, responded, picking himself up from the sidewalk. "New shoes. Still breaking 'em in, still a little slippery."

That brought a smile to Tanya's lips, the first he had seen. It made every hard bounce in the fall worthwhile. Slightly dazed from his trip down the stairs and smitten by the encounter, he headed for his souped-up wheels.

Tanya watched him from the front yard as he drove away from the Johnson home. He waved good-bye to her, swerving the Firebird at the last second to avoid sideswiping a pickup truck parked in the street.

Nick drove across town, but could not shake the image of Tanya from his mind. At every stoplight, he could see her standing at the top of her front porch steps. Her smile, which had flared only briefly, now stuck to his brain the way ink becomes a lasting part of a printer's hands. But having such thoughts about her immediately made Nick feel guilty. What about Joanne? How could he be true to Joanne and have the hots for Tanya? It made him feel like a creep. Even so, he wondered why he had been such a klutz in front of Tanya when he really needed to be cool?

"It was the dumbest, clumsiest thing I think I have ever done," Nick told his pal, Dave Balz, while hoisting a mug of draught beer to his lips at O'Hare's. He licked the resultant foam from his thick, graying mustache. "What a clumsy idiot. She must have really been impressed by the great reporter who's still learning how to walk."

"I got to admit that your dive down those steps sounds pretty damned funny," said Balz, who had recently retired after 35 years as a reporter and editor at The *Blade*. "I'd say you really fell for that chick, but I won't because I know you'd punch me for the felony torturing of a cliché."

They both laughed and ordered another cold beer. Nick had decided to save the vodka for a nightcap. He continued to tell Balz about the death of Robert Johnson and how it knocked his family off its feet.

"Two deaths. Two administrators. Same school. Same circumstances. That's a lot of coincidences, don't you think? How often is that going to happen? I'll have to check our files when I get back to the office."

Nick continued work on the next day's hangover, demanding a triple Ruskie Juiskie, Russian vodka with lime juice and sugar. He wanted to get good and numb so that memories of Joanne could not rob of him sleep again. Passing out in his living room was easier than dealing with his loneliness. He would worry about work later.

Nick didn't know it then, but The *Blade* files would reveal even more coincidences about the two deaths than he could have imagined. These two deaths were too similar, and not unlike another still in the planning stages.

# Her nickname is "The Castrator"…

As early morning, October sunshine peeked through a hall window and warmed Nick Steele's prone body in the entryway of his apartment building, a hot and wet tongue dabbed at his neck just under his right ear.

The sensuous activity aroused more than the slumbering reporter's mind. "Oh, baby, that's it. Go lower," he said, turning from being stretched out on his side to his back. "Yeah, baby, you got it going. Now, go further down. Lower, baby, lower. I'll help you with my belt buckle."

Nick tugged at the skinny strap of leather holding up his slacks as the tongue raked across his mouth three times, then wiped his nostrils clean with two quick licks. The activity pushed sleep out of his brain and his eyelids up.

"Jenny, go lay down," he said, moving his right hand from his belt to push away the drooling, chocolate Labrador retriever that straddled him in the foyer, his head resting on the "Welcome" mat in front of his door. "Get off me, go on. Go away. You smell, and you're dripping all over me."

Nick rolled over and wiped his mouth with the back of his hand. As he struggled to reach his feet, he could hear Jenny's owner, Mrs. Babcock, calling for the pooch and trying to alert Nick to the dog's presence in the entryway.

"Jenny, come here, you bad dog," she said from her living room through her open front door. "I hope she didn't get in your way or bother you, Nick. One minute I saw her sitting by the door licking her butt and then the next minute she was gone."

That tidbit of information prompted Nick to take another swipe across his mouth with a sleeve, and spit out what he was now sure was grit on his teeth.

"Obviously, she likes you," his elderly neighbor continued from inside her apartment. "When you came home this morning, she started whining and wouldn't leave the front door until I opened it to take her out. Sorry she got away from me."

But Mrs. Babcock wasn't half as sorry as Nick was about his sordid state. What could be worse than getting kissed by a butt-licking dog after spending the night passed out in front of his door? His apartment key hung from its lock, only partially inserted because it was upside down. Nick let out a low moan, which served as a summary of his being as well as the condition of the key that he had tried jamming into the lock.

"Mrs. Babcock, do you still have that extra key for my place? I think mine is pretty well trashed," he said, yanking it from the door.

His neighbor approached with key in hand. "Looks like the key isn't the only thing that got trashed last night. Nick, you look like hell, and I think I heard you comment a few minutes ago about Jenny's aroma. Well, I gotta say that Jenny smells like a bouquet of fresh roses compared to you. You stink of liquor and cigarettes. And look at your pants, Nick. Did you soil yourself again?"

"No, Mrs. Babcock, I did not. I'll have you know that the big wet spot on my slacks is from vomit. And not my own, I might add. I seem to recall coming to the aid of a good friend at closing time last night and the thanks I received was projectile barf."

"Some friend. Would this friend have a name?"

"Yes, she does, but it escapes me at this moment. In fact, you probably would have been saying hello to her right now if she hadn't gotten sick on me. Instead of her, I ended up with Jenny licking my face."

"Nick, you've got to take better care of yourself. What a mess. You're too young to let yourself go like this."

"Thanks, Mrs. Babcock. But that's not what they think in the office," Nick said, fingering the letters O-M-E that were pressed into the side of his face from lying on the doormat. "They think I'm too old to do the job, and they really don't care if I take care of myself or not. I guess I'm lucky to have you watching out for me."

Nick said good-bye and thanked his neighbor, checking his watch as he stumbled through his apartment door. He was already late for work and in desperate need of a shower, a razor and a toothbrush – not to mention some coffee and a fistful of aspirin. Nick hoped that he could get one of the few remaining friends he had in the newsroom to punch the time clock for him while he slipped into the building through a rear door.

The time clock in the newsroom was new. It came to The *Blade* when the newspaper's new publisher, D. McGovern Givens, took over in 1998. Givens was a pioneer in that she was one of the first women to break through the glass ceiling of an industry once solely the province of aging, neckless white men. Minorities and women rarely made it to the top, and those who did only made it with guns blazing. They rose through newspaper management by leaving the bodies of gutted, middle-level, incompetent, male Caucasians in their wake.

D. McGovern Givens scratched and pulled her way to the top of management at The *Blade*. Nobody gave her anything. Nicknamed "The Castrator" for the long line of men she emasculated on a campaign to become publisher, no one got in her way. Though the nickname was largely unwarranted and grossly unfair, she never discouraged anyone from associating it with her name. Like most of the things that she kept in her life, it served a purpose. It told every man she came in contact with to cover his nuts and watch his ass whenever she was within striking distance.

The tall, dark-eyed brunette got her start working in the circulation department of the paper when she was still in high school and everyone called her Diane Givens. In those days, she favored blue jeans and sweatshirts and burgers and fries to more sophisticated wear and fare. She drove an old pickup truck to cover her delivery route, stopping often to toss bundles of papers to eager teens ready to spread the news. At the end of the day, that same truck carried her to night classes in the business department of Saginaw Valley State University.

Before long, the newspaper moved her from the loading docks to the advertising department where a flair for words and a knack for closing the deal served her well. Diane Givens shot for the stars. Every time a sales agent left the department, the aggressive young upstart volunteered to gobble up the unattended customers, adding them to her ever-growing list of clients. In two years, she had become the newspaper's top-selling advertising agent, earning far more in commission than she did in base salary.

After graduating from college and earning Certified Public Accountant designation, Diane Givens was promoted to Controller of The *Blade*. As the paper's chief business manager, she set tough policies and guidelines. If you broke her rules once, you got a warning. If you broke them twice, you got suspended. If you broke them three times, you were out the door. Nobody walked on Diane. She wore the boots in her department and used them to kick ass – female as well as male – every day.

Diane Givens also went way out of her way to show the owners of the newspaper company that she knew how to pinch a penny and get every nickel out of a buck. One such policy required that every reporter and ad sales rep turn in their old, empty ink pens before they could be issued new ones. In addition, every page of their spiral notebooks had to be filled out – on both sides – and certified independently before new ones were issued. Waste was a word that could not be found in her vocabulary.

The final transformation for Diane Givens came when she was promoted to publisher and decided that her name was not distinguished enough. That's when she dropped Diane in favor of a first initial and brought her middle name, McGovern, which was actually her mother's maiden name, to the forefront. D. McGovern Givens had a certain ring to it. It was strong. It was tough. It was unyielding. And it gave no advance warning to the uninitiated that she was, indeed, a woman.

Nick and the other peons at the paper rarely had anything to do with Givens or the editor, who was largely viewed as the publisher's eyes, ears, and mouth in the newsroom. The paper's top brass went to Rotary and Lions and Kiwanis club meetings. They chummed up with members of the local Chamber of Commerce and sat on a bevy of advisory boards around town. Mostly, they stayed out of the way when it came to actually gathering and reporting the news and putting the paper out every day.

Even so, a device like a new time clock in the newsroom told all that a new honcho was running the show. Nick knew he had to be careful with the machine that kept track of his "ins" and "outs" because he could not afford to give his superiors new reasons to fire him. That's why he was so delighted when he was able to convince a colleague to clock him in to work that morning. It allowed him to slip into the newspaper building through a rear door, hang up his jacket in a janitor's closet and go to the newspaper morgue to sort through files. If he were lucky, no one would notice that he was late.

The morgue at The *Blade* was like a lot of daily newspapers around the country. Editors a few years ago decided it was time to move the paper into the current century by spending a few bucks and turning its ancient clip-file library into a modern digital archive. The problem was that they decided to do it "over time," meaning that the old clip files had to be maintained while time moved forward and the new digital archive was built.

This meant that Nick was likely to spend a lot of time sifting through the old files, hoping that what he was looking for hadn't been lost, tossed out or misfiled when it was put back into the morgue.

But luck was on Nick's side on this day. After several minutes of looking through old files from Central High School, Nick found a short article about the superintendent of the school district keeling over from a heart attack while at home. The article said George Pepadowski was 58 at the time and died early in the morning while in his bathroom.

"Damn," Nick muttered, "he probably kicked off while straining at the stool – the same thing that got Elvis! I've got to remember how dangerous that is." The article also indicated that Pepadowski's home was at 4th Avenue and Carroll Park, only about two blocks from where the Johnson's lived.

Nick jotted down a few notes: Johnson worked for Pepadowski, they were neighbors, they died at home, they had heart attacks, and they were roughly the same age, but they died six years apart. Underneath those notes, the reporter wrote down the word, "COINCIDENCE," underlined it twice and placed a giant question mark alongside it.

Both men were very high profile in town. Lots of people would know about them. Nick decided to get on the horn and make some calls. He knew that if he talked to enough people, he'd find out all there was to know about the two men and their deaths. He carried the files into the newsroom and made his way to his desk without rousing a whisper or a frown. He was 35 minutes late, but nobody was waiting for him, and, even better, nobody was screaming at him.

Three notes rested atop the pile of papers on his desk. The first was a hand written "Thank-you" note from Tanya. He opened it and looked at the neatly written words. "Nick, thanks so much for the nice article on my dad. It was beautifully done. Our whole family simply loved it. Tanya." Nick lifted the note to his nose and drank in the sweet, soft scent of a woman that he very much wanted to find out more about.

The second note was from Dave. "I've got something for you. You'll love this. I think we're on to something. Both these guys died exactly the same way. Meet me at O'Hare's at 7:30." Nick flipped the note back on his desk. That meant this night was going to be another head-thumper, and Nick wasn't sure he could handle another one so soon.

The third note was from his boss. It instructed him to cover the courts this week while one of his fellow reporters was on vacation. That meant he would be out of the office most of the week, which was good news in his book. Nick headed for the newsroom's backdoor and swung through the paper's production department and picked up the photo of Tanya's dad. He would drop it off at the Johnsons' home, probably Thursday, the day after the funeral.

On Nick's way out, he noticed a memo from The Castrator posted on the bulletin board in the hallway: "REMEMBER TO TURN OFF ALL LIGHTS AND ALL COMPUTERS WHEN NOT IN USE. OUR ELECTRICITY BILLS ARE SKYROCKETING. CUT THE JUICE WHEN NOT IN USE, OR WE'LL CUT YOU – D.M.G, The Publisher."

Nick just had to get out of the office before *Blade* management overwhelmed him. He figured that his supervisors were slowly killing him with a smothering amount of bullshit – much more than any normal human being was meant to swallow. Dave would help him numb his pain later that evening. A beer or two, or three, would be a good thing. They'd also push deeper into conversation that would help link the deaths of two administrators.

# The Finger Factory maimed employees...

As Nick pulled into the Johnson family driveway, he wondered how distraught its members would be. As a rule, reporters abhor walking into these kinds of family disasters. The whole scene would be awash in crying and nose blowing and hugging and hand shaking – raw emotion at every turn. An outsider showing up and telling survivors "sorry for your loss" never seemed like it was enough to provide solace.

Robert Johnson's funeral and wake had been yesterday. About 300 people said farewell to a man many admired and respected. Successful educators touch, and sometimes change, many lives during the course of their careers. The man students called, "Mr. Bob," was no different. They wrote and recited touching tributes to their mentor, sang mournful hymns, and offered up prayers before carrying him to his grave, all the while mopping salty, warm tears from cheeks chilled by the October Michigan air. They also tried their best to comfort a stricken and sobbing family.

Nick decided he would simply drop off the photograph of Robert Johnson, express his condolences and be on his way. As he sat in his hot rod and looked over her place, he thought the Johnson home seemed oddly quiet. Only one car rested in the driveway, one light illuminated the back of the house and one brightened the front. Gray smoke wafted in soft puffs from the two-story chimney and floated against a bright, blue sky. Light gusts of wind rattled red, orange and gold leaves on maple trees in front of the house.

Two young neighborhood daredevils whistled by on their bikes, challenging one another to jump a pothole in the street that was big enough to swallow a marching band.

As he walked up the sidewalk, Nick studied the front steps that had betrayed him during his first visit to the Johnson home. One step at a time, he made his way to the top and pushed the doorbell, peering into a living room picture window that looked out over the porch and front yard. The drapes were open about halfway, revealing a dark and lifeless sitting room. His second poke at the doorbell yielded the sound of soft footsteps that grew louder by the second, ending with the turn of the doorknob. Tanya answered the door with her teen brother peering from behind her left arm.

"Hi, Nick. Come in," she said, pushing the door open with one hand and gently nudging her brother backward with the other.

"Hello, Tanya. I just wanted to drop off this photograph of your dad. I know this is a bad time, so I won't stay or get in the way."

"Oh, no. Please come in. Everyone is over at Uncle Al's for dinner. Bobby and I just ran home to pick up some of his homework. He's been off school." She put her arm around her brother. "Bobby, this is Nick Steele, the reporter for The *Blade* who wrote the obituary on Dad."

Nick stepped into the entryway of the home. He could smell warm pizza coming from the direction of the kitchen where the muffled tones of a TV weather forecaster predicted a cool, light rain later in that evening. Nick pushed his right hand out in front of the gap-toothed, rail-thin senior. The two shook hands firmly, the young guy doing his best to grip and pump the large hand of the tall, older reporter.

"Hi. I liked your story about Dad, but I don't think our mom did," Bobby said. "It made her cry."

"Everything makes Mom cry right now, Bobby," Tanya said to her brother, cutting into the introduction before Nick could complete it. "Now, why don't you go gather up that homework so you can eat your favorite treat before we go back over to Uncle Al's."

"Nick, can I get you something to drink? How about a cold beer?" Tanya said.

"Oh, no thanks. Maybe I'll have one later," he said, turning toward the young man walking away.

But Tanya wouldn't let it go. "I thought I could smell beer when you walked through the door," she said, studying Nick. "I thought maybe you'd be ready for another one."

"Ah, yes. I had a couple of beers at lunch," he said, hoping that he didn't reek from last night's bender. "I'm sorry. I didn't realize you could smell it."

The teenager waved at Nick as he headed for his bedroom.

"Nice meeting you, Bobby," Nick said, waving back and stepping into the dining room.

"You, too. And call me, 'Spike.'"

Nick turned to face Tanya. "Here's that photo. I'm glad you liked my piece on your dad. His passing was so sudden. Had he been ill lately?"

"No, that's just it. The heart attack came out of nowhere. It caught all of us by surprise. Sure, he was a little heavy and struggling to keep his blood pressure under control, but no one thought it would kill him. I just can't believe he's gone. It all happened so fast. I guess we should have been paying more attention to doctor's orders, but the docs tell everybody to lay off all the good stuff in life."

"High blood pressure? That's it?" Nick stroked his chin with his right hand and then looked over Tanya's shoulder into the darkened living room where family snapshots sat atop every shelf, desk, mantel and table in the room. "No other heart problems? Anything else? When was his last medical checkup?"

"Last spring," Tanya said. "I know. I must have heard my mom tell friends that a thousand times during the funeral wake. Otherwise, I think he was OK. The only other thing is that he was drinking more heavily than I'd ever seen before – almost every day. My mom said he was just down in the dumps about getting old."

"Believe me, he wasn't that old. 59 is not old. That's only 10 years older than me. They call me the 'Antique' in the office, but it's really not ancient. The whole thing about your dad seems a little odd to me," Nick said. "Just like George Pepadowski's death six years ago. Maybe it's something in the water over at Central High School, or maybe it's just all those high school kids. I know that would be enough to drive me over the edge. One thing's for sure, I know I wouldn't have the patience to be an educator today."

"Funny you should mention Mr. Pepadowski. Several people brought up his passing during the wake. Dad and George were good friends and worked on a lot of projects together at school. George was a great guy and he absolutely loved the school. He worked all the time and my dad thought the world of him. They were always doing something up at school, something for the kids. I think they looked at it as a kind of crusade. A lot of the Central kids come from some pretty tough family situations and Dad and George looked at themselves as those kids' only hope in life."

"Well, if you don't mind, I'm going to ask around town a little about your dad and George. They sound like quite the duo. Maybe it would make some kind of retrospective piece. You know, a look back at both of their lives and what they were trying to do for kids at the school. Their legacy after all of that tireless work."

Nick turned and headed for the front door. "I have to get going. Supposed to meet someone shortly."

"Oh, well, you don't want to keep *her* waiting," Tanya said, as she opened the door and looked at Nick's face to see his reaction to her statement, which was really meant to be a question.

"No, no. It's a him. I mean, I'm meeting a guy, but not that kind of guy. No, I mean a friend, another reporter who happens to be a male," Nick said, turning away from the door to look Tanya squarely in the eye. "We're going to have a beer at O'Hare's."

With that, Nick turned and stepped squarely into the closed storm door, shoving his nose and chin flush into its glass. His right foot smacked the door's aluminum base like a drummer hitting his snare. His awkward exit pushed a smile across Tanya's lips again. Was it her charm or the beer that made him so clumsy?

"Oops. Gee, I guess I wasn't watching. Sorry." Nick opened the door and walked out on the porch, focusing on the steps.

"That's OK, don't worry about it. Thanks for returning our photograph," Tanya said, stepping out onto the porch with her new friend.

"No problem," Nick said, sticking his hand out in front of her for a so-long shake. He wanted to hold her tiny, soft hand for even an instant. "Say, I'm really sorry about your dad, and I'm really sorry to have met you under such trying circumstances. I'll call you if I need anything on that retrospective."

"Yes, I wish we could have met under different circumstances, too, Nick, but that's the way it works out sometimes," she said, taking his hand and squeezing gently. "I'll be here for a few days to help my mom and my little brother, but then I have to go back to school in Ann Arbor. I'm sure my mom can help you, though, if you need anything. I'll mention it to her."

"Oh, well. That would be fine, but could I have your number in Ann Arbor – just in case? You know. I wouldn't want to do anything that would upset your mother."

"Sure," she said, smiling and giving him her cell phone number and the number of the apartment that she shared with another woman in Ann Arbor.

Bingo. Nick had the magic digits and that made his day. No, actually, it made his whole week. Joanne would understand. Tanya was different. He decided he was going to toss himself into writing a story about Bob Johnson and George Pepadowski, two tireless educators who died young while giving their all to area youth. For a change, he would be working on a story of substance, something he could put his heart into.

Chasing great stories is what prompted Nick to pursue journalism. His interest in the craft began while he was in high school.

Back then, he saw it as a way to slay dragons and right great wrongs. Nick had a deep-seeded desire to root out injustice and shine the glaring light of public opinion on people who were going out of their way to hurt others.

That desire was seared into his heart at the tender age of 13 when he saw his father's life transformed in the blink of an eye.

James D. "Big Jim" Steele had been a part-time farmer who also worked in a small metal stamping plant in the tiny town of Sebewaing, located about 25 miles east of Bay City in the region of Michigan called the Thumb because it sticks out from the state's mitten shape like the thickest digit on a left hand.

The stamping plant was one of hundreds of small shops in rural areas that fed parts to the Big Three automakers in Detroit. Over the years, the Sebewaing plant had many owners and managers, but its nickname never changed. Everyone who worked there, or had relatives or friends, who worked there, called it the "Finger Factory" because of its notorious reputation for maiming employees.

During its 30 year history, the Finger Factory's giant metal presses took the arms, hands, fingers, feet, and toes of dozens of workers who were either inattentive or too slow to react to unforgiving and worn out machinery. Retirees often recalled with horror the plant's bloody toll.

One story many still repeat is the day when one of the plant's women employees got her pony tail caught in a set of rollers that were designed to separate machined parts. As the rollers wound up her pony tail and ripped hair and scalp from the top of her head, the woman's anguished screams rose far above the normal buzz of the machine shop. Every employee in the plant that day heard her painful howl, and most said her cries of agony were something they could not erase from their memories.

Big Jim Steele, who had taken the stamping plant job to supplement the income from his 200 acre farm and beef-cattle operation, lost his left hand to the fickle temperament of a press that had been misfiring and jamming every day that week. Despite Big Jim's complaints to management about the malfunctioning machine, it was not taken out of operation.

Repeatedly, he was told that if he didn't want the job, lots of guys standing in the plant's employment line were eager for work, hungry for any job that would pay bills and fill the empty bellies of a family. Forget about the state's health and safety regulations for factories. Only high profile, union shops had them. Out in the sticks, the workers were left to fend for themselves in plants that were often dark, smelly, dingy and dangerous.

Big Jim thought he had figured out how to handle the odd workings of the press when it caught him off guard. After completing a cycle where the giant cutting arm of the press stopped in the opened – or up – position, the machine jammed. Big Jim tried to free the cutting arm with the prodding of a crowbar in his right hand. As he leaned into the machine to pry the cutting arm free, he braced his body with his left hand on the surface of the cutting table. Suddenly, the cutting arm broke loose and slammed down, separating Big Jim from his left hand just below the wrist. In one thunderous thud, he was crippled for life.

Later, Big Jim told Nick that he didn't feel a thing when the press lopped off his hand. He only remembered holding up his handless arm and seeing blood spurting in every direction. He recalled that co-workers rushed to help him, but that they were more horrified by the gory sight than he was.

Big Jim received a workers' compensation settlement from the state of Michigan and benefits from the federal government. The Finger Factory was fined $200 by the state Department of Labor for using a malfunctioning machine that harmed an employee. Workers at the plant took up a collection to help Big Jim's family while he was recuperating in the hospital. The plant general manager, the man who had refused to take Big Jim's machine out of operation when it malfunctioned, declined to contribute anything during the collection, saying it might "set a bad precedent" in future accidents. A lawsuit against the company yielded a small financial settlement, but not nearly enough to compensate the loss of a limb.

A few years after Big Jim lost his hand, the Finger Factory went into bankruptcy and shut down. By the mid-1990s, it was discovered that the plant's owners had drained the company pension fund in what the local Chamber of Commerce described as a valiant, but failed attempt to save the company and jobs for the community.

Big Jim died at age 65, the same year he would have retired and started collecting Social Security. The doctors said he passed away because he did not take care of himself after catching pneumonia. But Nick believed he died from a broken spirit after what he went through while fighting and losing the battle against the Finger Factory. Nick buried his dad precisely 14 months before he said farewell to Joanne and laid her to rest in the same cemetery.

Nick pushed thoughts about Big Jim and Joanne out of his mind whenever they eased their way past his sensory sentinels. They were gone and nothing would bring them back. No use whining about it, he thought, you just had to keep moving. Regular visits to O'Hare's helped him along that path, blocking the pain and opening the way for short, restless bouts of glorious sleep.

# A Christmas tree dangled from the ceiling...

Nick pushed open the door to O'Hare's Pub and a warm wave of air tinged with the harsh smell of cigarette smoke and beer washed across his face. The rising buzz of conversation muffled the sound of 1970s rock music in the bar. Everywhere he looked inside the saloon, old friends and new acquaintances were tossing back beverages, telling stories and sharing laughter. Nick relaxed as he walked into the old watering hole. He was among friends. It had become his new home.

O'Hare's Pub is one of the great bars on Midland Street, a mile-long boulevard filled with buildings more than 100 years old. The antiquated, two- and three-story brick structures served as hangouts for the city's most nefarious past and present residents, including scalawags such as lumberjacks, sailors, insurance salesmen, and lawyers. These days, most of the buildings harbored quaint retail shops, craft and antique venues and restaurants or bars. Many of them housed apartments or condos on their upper levels.

Everybody – politicians, business leaders, doctors and the aforementioned attorneys – stopped by almost every day for a quick drink or a sandwich. It's where most deals were cut, decisions were made, and plenty of careers skyrocketed or died. If you were a player in the city, you stopped into O'Hare's whenever you could. The place had its own look, its own feel, and yes, even its own smell.

On one side of the establishment, a hand-carved, oak bar with two-story pillars and a rectangular mirror ran the entire 180-foot length of the narrow dive. The bar was so old that its foot rail had brass holders for spittoons, a necessity in any drinking establishment of the late 1800s or early 1900s. Now, the spittoons were receptacles for failed instant lottery tickets and cigar ashes. A large painting of a partially nude woman hung above the mirror. As Nick set his backside on a stool at the bar under the nude's sultry smile, he heard a couple of newcomers talking about her dark features and ample breasts.

"I heard one guy say that everybody calls her Mona," the tall visitor said.

His partner studied the large painting. "Is that because she looks like the Mona Lisa?"

"Nope," Nick said, breaking into their conversation. A smile spread across his lips. "They call her Mona because if you spend the night drinking under her gaze, you'll spend the whole next day moanin' from a hangover."

The visitors laughed and introduced themselves to Nick, offering to buy a drink. As he raised his first brew to his lips, he surveyed the landscape of O'Hare's.

Small tables and chairs dotted the floor. The wooden-plank floors had soaked up so much spilled booze over the years that they were sticky and stank of warm, stale ale with burned cigarette butts ground into them.

A 10-foot plastic Christmas tree, complete with decorations and wrapped presents underneath, hung upside down from the saloon's brass-colored, tin ceiling. The tree dangled over bar patrons year round, a tradition started by the previous owner that nobody had the heart to break. Old raffle tickets, music programs and a discarded brassiere, grandma-sized panties and an oversized jock strap were among other items of local interest that dangled from the ceiling, suspended by large thumb tacks.

The Stones and Bob Seger led a cast of old-time rockers wailing from a jukebox in the corner. But the music was kept low enough so that patrons could talk without screaming at each other. That simply would not do at O'Hare's. It's just one of the things that made it a different kind of place. People exchanged information and addresses and cell phone numbers and DNA here.

Nick waved to some familiar faces sitting at tables. Michael Davidson, an assistant prosecuting attorney, stood at the bar near the wait-stand. He leaned over a leggy brunette and chatted quietly into her right ear. He smiled and wagged a mitt at Nick as the reporter approached. Michael and Nick were about the same age and had become friendly. Their -alliance was one of convenience. Simply put, they needed each other.

Every good reporter likes having an "in" at the center of local law-enforcement power – the people who make the decisions on which laws to enforce and which ones to let slide. Sure, it's great having a pal in the police department, but the cops only push as hard on crime as the prosecutor's office lets them. At the same time, all good prosecutors – particularly those with ambition and a thirst for power – relish good relationships within the media. They want to buddy-up as much as possible with those who have enough pull to get them some high-profile publicity, or pubs, as those who crave it sometimes say.

In addition, Mickey and Nick shared much in common. They came from similar rural backgrounds. They grew up poor and hungry, always looking for where their next pair of second-hand shoes was going to come from. Growing up, they had to hustle their attributes like hawkers on late-night television infomercials. Both were the first in their families to graduate from college, and both had worked so hard that they were considered young prodigies in their respective fields. They also were old high school jocks, which sometimes became painfully obvious to those who overheard their conversations.

"Hey, Nick. How's it hanging?"

"Hi ya, Mickey. It's hanging quite well, thank you. It could use some of the attention you're obviously getting, but that's a story unto itself. Say, I've been meaning to ask you when the Ritowski trial is going to get started? I heard you're the lead guy on it?"

Nick stopped a few feet from the bar and stuck out his hand for the tall, lanky attorney to shake. They clasped hands. The brunette peeked over her shoulder, smiled at Nick, and then perched her puffy red lips on the rim of her wine glass.

"Should get started next week," Mickey said, leaning back against the bar and into his date. "I'm really looking forward to it. I think we've got a strong case. Stop by the office this week and I'll give you a little preview."

"Sounds great. I'll do that. Say Mickey, how are the wife and kids doing?" With that, the brunette pushed Mickey away with her left hand and swatted his dumbfounded face with the other. "You bastard," she said. "Call me when the wife and kids are no longer in the picture."

As she stormed off, the attorney rubbed the red side of his jaw and watched her head for the door. He turned to Nick. "Why in the hell did you say that? You know I'm not married and I don't have any kids."

"Yeah, but I figured I'd just stir things up a little. Besides that, it looked like you were having too much damn fun. Always good talking with you, Mickey. Catch you later."

"Hey, thanks a lot. I need more friends like you." The prosecutor sipped from his drink and surveyed the room for another young prospect, his next prey.

Nick turned and looked around the room for his pal. He quickly found Dave at his usual spot at the end of the bar – the perfect vantage point for any good reporter. Everyone in the joint had to pass Dave's spot in order to get to the restrooms

If you were a reporter bent on getting good, fresh information, then you had to pump everybody you knew every chance you got. That's how the better reporters worked their beats, even if it meant working the customers at a bar like a politician works a crowd at a Labor Day picnic.

"Hey, Dave, what's up buddy? I got your note," Nick said as he pulled up alongside the only guy he ever really trusted at The *Blade*.

Sally, a buxom bartender who enjoyed displaying her ample attributes in tight, plunging tank tops, brought Nick a frosty mug of beer before he could order it. "Thanks, Sally, you mind reader, you. You're just too good to me," Nick said as he hoisted the mug to his lips.

"I know it, Nick. For the life of me, I don't know why I put up with you two. It's sure not because of the tips. Reporters are tighter than a frog's ass – and usually not as pretty." Sally smiled as she sashayed away. They loved her, salty tongue and all.

Dave got right down to business with his friend. His voice was husky, the result of too many coughin' nails.

"I asked around a little for you about George Pepadowski. Hells bells, sounds like he ran a pretty tight ship as superintendent, kind of a control freak. When he was in charge, nothing happened without his OK. Everything, and I mean everything, had to go through George. If administrators or teachers stepped out of line, there was hell to pay with Georgie Boy. One of the office secretaries told me that he was very tight with Bob Johnson. They worked on a lot of big projects together. They got a huge funding proposal for the school district passed by voters. But they even socialized together – almost every weekend and holidays, I hear."

"What about his health?" Nick asked, as he took another sip of beer. "I know he kicked off from a heart attack, but what kind of heart condition did he have?"

"No, that's the odd thing," Dave said, turning to watch Sally shake it – fore and aft – all the way back down the bar toward them. "Everybody says he was a little overweight, but that's it. One day, he just keels over and leaves everyone slapping their foreheads trying to figure out what the hell happened. But the secretary did say he was taking something for high blood pressure, and she thinks he was drinking a barrel or two a week before he croaked."

The two stood quietly for a couple of minutes, watching a playoff baseball game on a TV at the end of the bar.

"So, what do you think? What kind of story do we have here?" Nick asked.

"Well, we don't have much. So far, the two of them kicking off just sounds like one heck of a coincidence," Dave said. "I think you just keep asking questions, keep talking to people, find out all that you can about them. If there's something there, it will surface sooner or later. One more thing. That secretary I talked to said the two of them had secrets, lots of talking in whispers."

"Secrets, huh? You know, I told Tanya I was going to work on a retrospective feature on her dad and Pepadowski. I guess I'll just keep going in that direction. Do you know, is there a Mrs. Pepadowski?"

"Yep, and she still lives in the same house, just around the corner from the Johnsons."

"I'll give her a call, maybe tomorrow," Nick said, as he downed the last of his beer. "It's Friday, maybe I can catch her at home before the weekend. See you later. Thanks a ton for the info. Hey, and leave a nice tip for Sally, OK."

"Yeah, right. I've got two tips for her. One is to bet in favor of the Lions on Sunday, and the other one is hankerin' to jump out of my jeans."

With that, Nick headed for the door. He planned to hit one more bar down the street, pound down a few and then head home to his apartment, which was only four blocks away.

# Where are your pants? ...

FRIDAY MORNING

The dull thud of aluminum tapping against the Firebird's driver's-side window did not rouse Nick from his deep slumber, but the blunt language of the cop with the metal flashlight in hand did.

"Wake up, you drunken son-of-a-bitch. You can't sleep on the street. Steele, what in the hell is wrong with you?" The police officer banged on the window again, this time with enough force to make Nick's resting head bounce against the hard glass. The side street behind O'Hare's Pub was dark despite the rising sun's early, feeble attempts at illuminating the town. "Come on, you're really testing my patience, Nicky boy. Wake up. Get up, and come on out of that car."

"Ah, leave me alone, Quinn. I need more sleep. Go away." Nick rolled away from the window onto his other side, his right arm propping his chin up from the Firebird's center console. He hoped his old friend, Patrolman Dan Quinn, would cut him some slack. "I can't come out, anyway."

"What do you mean, you can't come out? Why not?"

Nick's head hung down with his chin resting on his chest. His eyes were closed. His head bobbed as he spoke. "I can't come out because I don't have any pants on."

"What? You don't have any pants on? Why not? Where are your pants?"

"Don't know. Don't give a damn. Just leave me alone, OK?" Nick stirred in his seat some more, trying to find a comfortable spot after four hours of fitful sleep in his vehicle.

"Oh, no you don't. Come on out of that car, or I'm coming in after you – pants or no pants. What about underpants? Have you got shorts on?" The cop peered into the windshield of the street-rod. Under the steering wheel, he could see Nick's knobby knees, but not much else. He tapped his flashlight against the glass again.

That was enough. Nick decided to step out sans slacks. Though he was shaky and uncertain from another excruciating hangover, he pushed open his car door and stepped out on the street, revealing a baggy set of black boxer shorts adorned with a half-dozen green shamrocks. He was still wearing his jacket, shirt and necktie, but no pants. His hair was pushed flat and upward from where it had been smashed by the glass window. His eyes were as puffy and worn as a pair of old Harley-Davidson saddlebags.

"OK, that's enough, Mr. Leprechaun. Take your shenanigans, your bad hangover and your funky shorts and get back in your car or I'll arrest you for indecent exposure and decidedly poor taste. I can't believe it. This time, you've gone too far, Nick Steele. Now, where are your pants?" The officer helped Nick back into his car, but could not bring himself to lean inside the vehicle because of the smell of sour beer and spilled whiskey.

Nick settled back into his seat. "Well, make up your mind, Dan. Do you want me in or out?"

"I want you out of here, but I can't let you drive or walk home. If you can't find your pants, I'll have to take you," the officer said, looking down the street in both directions. A stray dog bobbed between trash cans in a nearby alley, but no people were in sight.

Nick looked around inside his Firebird. An empty beer can was tipped on its side in front of the passenger's front seat. The backseat contained old newspapers, four copies of True North Magazine, a man's winter coat and a bath towel. A pair of women's pantyhose was twisted and wadded up on the floor in front of the backseat. But no men's pants were anywhere in view.

"Well, occifer, uh, er, officer, I think I'm out of luck in terms of pants," he said. "You'd think these green shamrocks would have brought me a little luck, but no, hell no. Ju-u-st when I really need 'em, no pants."

By this time, the cop had retreated to his patrol car and searched his trunk. He returned to the side of Nick's car carrying a bowling jacket. As he opened it for Nick to step into, words stitched across the jacket's shoulders came into view: "Bill's Blind Alley Lanes."

"Thank you, Officer Dan, I'm much obliged," Nick said, wrapping the jacket around his waist and knotting its sleeves at his belly button. Still, his hairy legs were bare from his knees to the tops of his blue socks.

The cop led Nick to his cruiser and helped him get into the front seat. Nick looked at his watch – still plenty of time to get to work. He wondered if Jenny, the butt-licking dog, was still sprawled by her master's front door waiting for him to get home. Probably not, Nick thought. Nobody cared whether he made it home at night or not.

As Nick stepped out of the cop car in front of his place, the cop gave Nick a gentle scolding. "Nick, I know you're still missin' Joanne, but you've got to snap out of this. I can't take you home all the time, and you sure as hell don't want to be driving. Take care of yourself, man."

Nick thanked the cop, one of dozens he'd come to know on the force over the years, and made his way into his place where a hot shower, coffee, and four or five aspirin would help get him ready for work and the day ahead.

For a change, Nick was not the last reporter to show up in The *Blade* newsroom for work. As he nodded, "Mornin'," to the two clerks who sat perched and perky at desks in the front of the news office, he saw Drayton Clapper and his twin boot-licking lackeys heading into the morning news meeting, where the great minds of The *Blade* converged each day to decide which meaningless and pointless feature story would again dominate the front page and bore aging and thinning readers into their early graves.

On his desk, Nick stared at the slip of paper that had his next assignment on it. He was covering the courts for a vacationing reporter, but Clapper decided to slip him another feature to work on between robberies and rapes and muggings. The note briefly described changing weather conditions and suggested that the reporter go dig out a feature on an approaching fall heat wave. Temperatures, it seems, were expected to soar into the mid-70s during the week, something not unheard of but unusual for October in mid-Michigan.

Nick grimaced as he tucked the slip of paper in his shirt pocket. It was another routine assignment – kid features, lost pets, backyard-grown cucumbers that matured into a shape that strongly resembled the noggin of George W. Bush – which he would grind out like a lathe operator mills wooden spindles. The best part is that it would get him out of the office and keep his editors off of his back for another day.

Nick figured he would spend a good chunk of Friday at the county-owned golf course where he would talk to some old duffers about getting their last whacks of the year in out on the greens. After all, October in Michigan almost always meant some freezing temperatures and snow flurries. Retired golfers talking about their putting and shanking and past glorious fall weather would make a good little feature and some decent photos.

But before attacking the links, he rifled a city phone directory to find Mrs. Pepadowski's number. He punched in the numerals. She picked up the phone on the third ring.

"Hello, Pepadowski residence."

"Hi, is this Mrs. Pepadowski?"

"No, it's the queen of Lithuania," she said in a matter-of-fact tone, but then became playful. "Of course, this is Mrs. Pepadowski. Who's bothering me this early in the morning, and how did you know I wasn't rolling in the hay with a gentleman?"

"My name's Nick Steele. I'm a reporter with The *Blade*. I know it's early, but I decided to gamble that your thrashing about with a gentleman was complete for the morning and I was hoping to catch you before you started the day. Did you happen to hear about the death of Robert Johnson, the principal of Central High?"

"Oh, yes. In fact, I went to the funeral. Isabelle Johnson and I are still good friends. I felt so sorry for her, losing her husband like that. Well, as you probably know, I could empathize with her completely. I lost my husband the same way. She'll need lots of support to get through this."

"Yes, Mrs. Pepadowski, this will be a very difficult time for her. I wrote the obituary about her husband, and now I'm working on a retrospective about his work and his many accomplishments at Central. Of course, he did much of that work with your husband. I understand they were very close both professionally and personally."

"Oh, you're right about that. They did just about everything together – almost like brothers. Our homes were close to each other, so we did a lot of things together after school. We vacationed together. Why, we even had the same family doctors – M.D. and dentist."

"*Hmmm*," Nick said aloud. "The same doctors. That's interesting. Mrs. Pepadowski, could I schedule an interview with you to talk more about your husband, his work at the school district and his relationship with Mr. Johnson?"

"Certainly. I'd love to tell you all about George. I'll pull out the scrapbooks. Would you like to come over this afternoon?"

"This afternoon is perfect," Nick said. "How about 3 o'clock?"

"I'll see you then. And, one more thing. I was just kidding about rolling in the sack with a gentleman."

"I thought you were pulling my leg, Mrs. Pepadowski. You've got a good sense of humor. I'm looking forward to our visit this afternoon." Nick jotted down 3 p.m. in his notebook, and then wrote down: "Same doctors," and underlined it twice.

Bob Johnson and George Pepadowski shared plenty of things lots of people knew about through their professional and personal relationships. But they also shared much that almost nobody knew anything about. And it was the evil that they privately shared that put them in line to die.

# Gus blamed the school for not protecting his daughter ...

FRIDAY NOON

As Tanya walked toward her car from her final class on the University of Michigan campus in Ann Arbor, she couldn't shake from her mind thoughts about her family back in Bay City. They needed her almost as much as she needed them. The family had just placed her dad in his final resting place on Wednesday, and Tanya had hoped that burying herself in school would provide some solace. But her attempt to turn away from agony had failed, so she was heading home.

Tanya pulled her compact car out into heavy northbound traffic on US-23. As hunters of deer and fall colors hustled to leave metropolitan southern Michigan for the wilds and beauty of northern Michigan, Tanya cruised along in silence, oblivious to the rushing trucks, S.U.V.s, campers and R.V.s that swooshed past her. No radio, no headphones, no GPS. The dull, muffled sounds of her four-cylinder engine chugging along on the freeway broke the silence. She jerked the air freshener that hung from her rear view mirror and tossed it out the window because it's pungent citrus smell made her nauseous.

"Why did he have to die so young?" she asked out loud, tears once again welling in her eyes. The question echoed across her mind. Why? She and her mom and her brothers had so many plans, so many more things to do together. What did the family do to deserve this? What had they done that had been so bad that the person they all counted on had been summarily wiped out of their lives?

Nothing made sense to her anymore. Tanya's mind raced. Her dad had been an educator, her mom a librarian. They volunteered for every community fundraiser that popped up. The family regularly attended Sunday Mass and gave until it hurt when the donation baskets were passed. They visited neighbors and friends who became ill. They watched out for the elderly and minded the young and the aimless and the hopeless. They "adopted" less fortunate families at Thanksgiving and Christmas. They tutored and mentored and aided others every extra hour they could. Where had they gone wrong? What did they do to deserve this tragedy?

Tanya had no answers, just an empty feeling in her heart. Her dad was gone and her family would never be the same. As she pulled into her hometown, she wondered how her mom was holding up. A couple of terse comments from her mom about her weight and barren womb would even be welcome. They had talked and cried together on the phone Thursday night. That's when Tanya realized she had to get home as soon as she could. Hiding in Ann Arbor would not ease the pain, only her family could.

But before Tanya could go home, she had to make a stop at the neighborhood pharmacy for her mom. The family doctor had written Isabelle a prescription for some low-dose Valium. The nerve-taming medicine was supposed to calm the new widow enough to rest and to sleep.

The Easy-Med Pharmacy was just around the corner from the Johnson home. It was one of those gigantic, chain drugstores that carried everything on its shelves from high-priced pharmaceuticals to low-grade motor oil. But the people who worked at the pill palace prided themselves in providing top-notch customer service, the same kind of friendly help that could be found at any neighborhood establishment. Easy-Meds offered first-rate selection and the best discount prices for one reason – volume. They sold tons of merchandise and filled thousands of prescriptions every week.

As Tanya bounded down an aisle overflowing with condoms, cures for acne and relief from raging hemorrhoids, a supply cart coming the other way nearly hit her.

"Excuse me, didn't see you coming," said the man behind the cart. Their eyes met and locked. Instant, but awkward recognition.

"Hi, Gus. I guess I forgot that you worked here," Tanya said.

"Yup, still here. Ain't got no better place to go, Tanya," the aging, muscular man said, his eyes quickly diverting from hers to the cart, which had spilled a few boxes of tissues. "Sorry. Gotta go."

And with that, Gus Phelps picked up his boxes and pushed his cart past Tanya, who was still speechless from the surprise encounter. She turned and watched him shuffle his cart down the aisle, much slower than before. She wanted to stop him to talk some more, but decided not to just as the words rose to her lips. Not now, she thought, maybe next time.

Tanya and Gus had not really spoken in years, not since his daughter and her friend, Candace, ended her life by suicide nearly eight years ago. The troubled teen, who had just graduated from Central and had been accepted at Central Michigan University, crawled into the backseat of the family's Chevy Impala while its engine was running and parked in the garage. In less time than it takes to make breakfast, she let the vehicle's exhaust fill the garage with poisonous gas and put her to sleep forever.

Needless to say, Candace's death devastated Gus, and his wife, Ellen. They took a free-fall into depression in the months after Candace's funeral. Their despair got so bad that Ellen rarely got out of bed and Gus stayed awake night after night, pacing the length of their home again and again. They longed for the light of their lives back.

As Tanya waited in line for her mom's prescription, her mind filled with thoughts about Candace Phelps.

The free-spirited teen had been a popular girl at school, excelling in the classroom with near-perfect grades. She was a member of the National Honor Society and the drama club. She was also first-chair French horn in the school's highly acclaimed band.

Candace was not particularly athletic and she was very self-conscious about her appearance. Family friends often remarked throughout her young life that she looked more like her dad than her mother, who had been a high school beauty queen. Those kinds of comments cut into her psyche like a saber ripping through cloth. They made her feel inferior and kept her from developing self-confidence despite her many attributes.

While waiting, Tanya felt ill as she recalled the day when Gus discovered his daughter's lifeless body in the garage. Gus was awakened by the continuous barking of a neighbor's dog. When he checked on the mutt, he heard his car's engine running and found the body of his precious princess. He pulled her from the exhaust-filled death chamber and stretched her out on the grass in the backyard. His frantic attempts at mouth-to-mouth resuscitation yielded nothing but frustration and agony. Candace was gone, and there was nothing he could do about it.

The young woman left a note on the table next to her bed. "Mom and Dad: Sorry for all the shame I brought you, but I cannot live without him. Please forgive me. I hope you can find it within your hearts to remember me fondly. Love, Candace."

Ellen and Gus knew exactly what the note meant, but they had no idea that their budding flower was so distraught that she was considering suicide.

Gus blamed Central high school officials, including Tanya's dad. It was a terrible time for both families.

But Gus could not get over it. In his mind, the school had not done enough to resolve the problem. He would never forgive them or forget what they did.

While revenge hung over Gus's soul like honey bees swarming a hive, anger and hurt seared Ellen's. She and Gus grew apart. Their grief became a wedge. Their sorrow pushed them in different directions. Their emotions simmered for months. They did not talk. They did not comfort or confide in each other. Ellen wanted to move to another city to get away from the memories that she could not shake. Gus wanted to stay and get even.

Finally, Ellen left home without saying goodbye. Her note, left on a table next to their bed, indicated that she was going to live with her sister in Kalamazoo for a while.

That was seven years ago. Gus, who was focused on getting justice for Candace, rarely called her. He thought that maybe he and Ellen would get back together one day. But not now, not until he found peace with the passing of his beloved daughter. He vowed to not rest until the whole truth came out about Candace and what happened at the school.

So, Gus lived by himself and turned his home into a shrine to Candace and Ellen. Their photographs adorned the walls of every room. He kept the family's McKinley Avenue home in precisely the same condition it was when his women lived there. Their clothing and personal items were in the same dressers and closets the way they had left them.

Once a month he polished their jewelry and displayed it on their dressers. Every week, he did their laundry, even though no one had worn the garments. He enjoyed ironing the wrinkles out of their dresses. Ellen liked just a touch of starch, Candace none at all.

Gus doted over their belongings and remembered all the good years, the holidays, the special times in the life they shared. The life that had been shattered when a school romance between an adult and a teenager got out of hand.

When Gus was not at home tending to the shrine, he was at work. He would show up at the Easy-Med at all hours of the day and night. His boss loved his dedication and the fact that Gus never turned in any overtime hours. He was a valued and trusted member of the Easy-Med team. Gus had a key to every door, including the computer room.

The handyman had full access to the system and all of its programs and software. It was a vital part of the store's operation.

Gus, the jack of all trades who mastered some, did nearly everything. He stocked shelves, worked behind the check-out counter, waited on customers, handled photo processing, checked and reordered inventory, swept up, shoveled snow from the sidewalk in the winter and cut grass in the summer, emptied trash cans and kept the store's computer system up and running.

The computer system was Gus's favorite part of the job. Easy-Med paid for Gus to take computer-training classes at Delta Community College so that he could keep the system running as smooth as a cash-only checkout counter. Taking computer classes at Delta was no problem for Gus. He had plenty of time on his hands. Since retiring from General Motors, the handyman lived alone in a three-bedroom house on the city's East Side.

Life had been good for Gus Phelps until tragedy crossed the threshold of his front door. He and Ellen, the only woman he had ever loved, married young. They worked hard and tried to build a good life for themselves, living in a modest Cape Cod. The couple had only one child, Candace, though they had hoped for more.

Now that Candace and Ellen were gone, the handyman spent most of his time at the pharmacy. He had full access to its computer system and all of its programs and software. All of the drug store's business transactions were kept on computer hard drive, including all the files for customers. Once a customer's name and address were put into the computer system, a permanent file was established. Those files also included all current and past prescriptions for medicine. The system was so highly automated that a doctor's office could send or call in a prescription and it would update the patient's file within minutes. All the patient had to do was pick up the prescription once a month or have it delivered to the doorstep. It was very slick.

The prescriptions for George Pepadowski and Robert Johnson were among the hundreds of patient names in those files, and Gus knew all about the medications for both of the late educators. Plus, the handyman was watching over the file of one more former school district official, a former colleague of Johnson and Pepadowski who was still alive – at least for the time being.

The sound of a prescription number called over a loudspeaker at the drug store snapped Tanya out of her day dream of recollection about the Phelps family. As Tanya approached the counter, she caught a glimpse of Gus going back into the computer room. He stepped up to a terminal, logged himself in and watched files flip up on the screen.

"Excuse me," Tanya said to the clerk at the counter who checked her prescription against pill bottles that she was about to stuff in a sack. "Do you know Gus very well?"

"Oh yeah, everybody here knows Gus. He's our Mr. Everready."

"I didn't know that he had computer skills. I think he used to work on the line over at the Chevy plant."

"Gus has been in charge of maintaining our computer system for as long as I've been here. Now, you know that this prescription for your mother is Valium, right? Remind her not to take them on an empty stomach."

Tanya smiled and nodded at the clerk, then caught another glimpse of Gus, who was still pounding away at the keyboard in front of him. She left the Easy-Med and drove home where she found an empty house. A note on the kitchen counter indicated that Isabelle and Bobby went to a movie. The note also said: "Nick the reporter called. You can reach him on his cell phone. Don't hang around the house. Call a friend, have some fun."

# The band director bedded at least four students...

For once, Tanya took her mother's advice and decided to get out of the Johnson family home. She thought a little shopping in some of the quaint downtown stores might be just the right prescription to pull her out of a woeful mood. Browsing antique shops always proved to be a good distraction from things that were bothering her. She knew that she needed to stop thinking about the passing of her father, even if it was only briefly. Her good childhood friend, Cynthia Rowley, was going to join her for a burger and a beer at O'Hare's Pub later. They would gab about their teen years, laugh a lot, cry a little, hug when necessary and update their lives beyond the brief time they'd spent together during the funeral services for Bob Johnson.

She could hardly wait to meet Cynthia and ended her antiques tour early to head for O'Hare's. As she pointed her maize and blue car toward Veterans' Bridge and the West Side of the city, Tanya wondered what her old friend would be wearing. She hoped casual attire would rule the day. She wore blue jeans, a light beige turtleneck and a dark blue University of Michigan pullover. Her fears were relieved when Tanya spotted her friend walking down Midland Street toward O'Hare's. Cynthia looked stunning, but informal. The red and black checked Mackinaw jacket that she wore with blue jeans complemented her long, dark hair and coal-black eyes. The two women embraced on the sidewalk in front of the pub and then entered the West Side hangout.

But the doorway was partially blocked by an open 12-foot stepladder. Both women looked up and spotted an old friend, who was a bartender at the pub, wobble slightly on the ladder's top rung as he reached toward the ceiling with a staple gun in one hand and a pair of men's slacks in the other. Cynthia was happy to see the beer slinger.

"Mack, be careful up there. Your ladder is shaking like it's made out of Jell-O, and why are you stapling pants to the ceiling?" she asked, registering a visual note in her brain that the slacks were being hung next to a large, red bra and some fishnet stockings.

"Hi ya, Cynthia. These pants belong to us and Bay City now. Some idiot got totally wasted in here the other night and lost them in a bet. The night bartender said the guy staggered out the back door in his shorts, big green shamrocks and all."

Four cracks with the staple gun and the pants were suddenly part of O'Hare's history. "I never did hear what the bet was about," Mack said as he came down the ladder, two steps at a time. "But it really doesn't matter anymore, does it."

Tanya reached out to the bartender to give him a quick hug. "Mack, it's so good to see you again. Gosh, how long's it been?"

"Why, Tanya, I didn't see you come in," he said, pulling her toward him with his massive arms. "Long-time no-see. Five years anyway. Hey, really sorry to hear about your dad. He was a great guy."

"Thanks, Mack." She gave him a peck on the cheek and stepped back. "We came to catch up on old times with a drink or two, or maybe three or more." The three old friends laughed.

Mack carried his stepladder to the back of the tavern and the two women found a corner table. The Stones' "Brown Sugar" rattled loud speakers in opposite corners of the cavernous bar. The two former Central High School cheerleaders found a spot where they could talk and people-watch as the hangout began to fill early in the Friday afternoon. The spicy aroma of sizzling, steaming onions on the grill made them hungry.

"Tanya, how are you doing?" Cynthia asked, clasping her friend's hands on top of the table. "Are you holding up OK? How about your mom, and Bobby?"

"We're alright. It's just tough right now. Mom and Spike, that's what he wants to be called these days, went out to a movie. That's why I was so happy to hear that you were free this afternoon. Thanks for meeting me."

Mack brought his friends two cold beers and they started yakking, going way back to their childhoods and elementary school. Three hours, a couple of more beers and two legendary O'Hare's sliders passed as quickly as kids zipping down a playground slide.

"Oh, I almost forgot to tell you about running into Gus Phelps today," Tanya said. "It caught me completely off-guard. I guess I forgot that he was working at the East Side Easy-Med."

"I haven't talked to him in years," Cynthia said. "I heard that he's gotten really weird. What did he say?"

"Not much. We literally bumped into each other. He didn't say anything about my dad, just kind of walked away from me. And get this – he's the store handyman and runs the computer system. Can you believe that?"

Tanya and Cynthia reminisced about Candace Phelps. They missed her. Soon they switched to Candace's passionate romance with the school's band director, Darrin Appleton. Both women were glad that they had not been musical in school. Too many of Appleton's female students had become his victims. During his brief tenure, he was rumored to have had intimate relationships with at least four young women, probably more.

"I caught him making out in the band room with Candace and Sarah Evans on the same day," Tanya said. "It was incredible. My dad was furious when he found out."

"Sue Herndon told me that she finally gave in to Appleton," Cynthia said. "She said he wouldn't leave her alone. It just made me sick, and I know Sue still thinks about it after all these years."

"Who was the fourth girl? I always heard that there was

another, but I don't think I ever picked up on who it was. Did you?"

"No, after Candace died and it came out that she was pregnant, the whole thing just died down. Appleton was long gone and nobody wanted to talk about what had happened. It was all a complete nightmare."

"Did you ever hear what happened to Appleton?" Tanya asked as she shifted in her seat and leaned closer to her friend. "That bastard should have paid for what he did."

"Nobody talked about him anymore. I think people were eager to move on, which was easy for everyone except for the lives he ruined."

Tanya and Cynthia wiped tears from their cheeks and hugged.

Cynthia tried to change the mood. "No crying. You've had enough tears this week. Come on, let's get out of here and go for a walk. It's a beautiful day outside. How long since you've been to Sage," she said, referring to the limestone and brick, historic library and park that anchored the West Side of the community.

"Too long. Let's go." Tanya put two twenty-dollar bills on the table and the women left O'Hare's, passing under the hanging pants and assorted unmentionables dangling from the ceiling.

# Jimmy Hoffa is buried under a pool in Bay City...

FRIDAY AFTERNOON

At precisely 3 p.m., Nick pushed the black button that sounded the front doorbell at the home of Alice Pepadowski on 4th Avenue and Carroll Park on the city's affluent East Side. Alice and her late husband, George, had reared four children in the comfortable three-bedroom, two-story Tudor-style home. Each of the kids was now grown, married and producing their own offspring in other parts of the country. After George died from what appeared to be a heart attack eight years ago, Alice chose to live in the home alone, hoping its size and abundant memories would lure her children and grandchildren home for frequent visits. She was right. Though travel was expensive, the Pepadowski brood flocked home regularly, especially for holidays. Proud Polish families in Bay City were like that. They stuck together through thick and thin. It was one of the things Nick liked most about his adopted hometown.

The front door of the Pepadowski home swung open before he arrived at the top step. Nick figured the woman of the house must have been waiting for him. "You're right on time," she said, as a smile as long as the city's Liberty Bridge spread across her face. "I like people who are prompt. Please, come in and make yourself at home."

"Thank you. I'm Nick Steele from The *Blade*. I'm pleased to meet you. I learned a long time ago to be on time and make deadlines," the reporter said, stepping into the entryway of the home. As he did, a curtain of aroma fell on him so fiercely that it forced Nick's head to snap around to survey the dining room before him. His nostrils flared to pull in the sweet smell of simmering cabbage, tomato, onions, sausage and potatoes. Nick was certain some kind of bread was also baking in the oven. All of a sudden, his stomach barked out a message that it was empty and needed replenishment.

"Mrs. Pepadowski, what do you have cooking? It smells absolutely fabulous."

"Oh, not much. I just pulled some things together after you said you were coming by for a visit," said the tiny, graying woman who might be 5-feet tall if she stood on the tips of her toes. She reminded Nick of his grandmother. "Georgie Junior and his family were here earlier in the week, so I have plenty of food on hand. I hope you're hungry. I've got some Bigos (Hunter's Stew made from sauerkraut, fresh cabbage, sausage, fresh ham, onions and mushrooms), Pierogis (a cheese, onion, and potato filling, wrapped in a light dough crust), and fresh-baked bread. Sit down, Nick, you can look through our scrapbooks while you eat."

Nick lied, trying hard to be courteous despite the grumbling of his belly. "Oh, I couldn't possibly eat again today. Thanks, but I'll just look at the scrapbooks."

"Nonsense. If you come to my home, you eat. Nobody leaves the house of Pepadowski with a growling stomach. I'll fix you a plate."

Glad that his polite protestation was brushed aside, Nick sat down and scanned the Pepadowski dining room. Portraits of Pope John Paul (the only Polish pontiff), President John F. Kennedy (the only Catholic president), Martin Luther King (a preacher of peace) and Jimmy Hoffa, the late Teamsters' president, who was believed to have been killed by mobsters, hung on a wall over a large, oak hutch.

"Mrs. Pepadowski, why do you have a picture of Jimmy Hoffa on your wall? I get the other three, but why him? He was supposedly connected to gangsters."

The aging woman walked back into the dining room with two plates filled with steaming food. "Because my brother, Willie, was a truck driver and he absolutely adored Jimmy Hoffa. You know, he was one of the first labor leaders to try and boost up the middle class. Plus, he's buried under a swimming pool right here in Bay City."

"The cops dug up that pool, Mrs. Pepadowski. All they found were a bunch of dog bones. I'm afraid that's just another part of the Hoffa legend."

"The police just didn't dig deep enough,' she said, slipping a plate full of food in front of Nick. "Willie swears he's there. Willie's got connections."

Nick dug into the Polish delicacies before him. They were delicious. He moaned slightly as he chewed and savored a forkful of Bigos. "Wow, this is so go-o-o-d," he said, trying not to let the liquid from the chewed food drizzle down his chin.

While he ate, Mrs. Pepadowski only poked at her food. She couldn't wait to get started talking about the glory days at Central. After a few moments, she put down her fork and went to the wooden cupboard in the den and pulled out four scrapbooks, lugging the bound histories into the dining room for Nick. Oh sure, she could have pulled out another 10 scrapbooks of photographs, newspaper clippings and mementos from her late husband's years as superintendent. But she thought these four would be enough to show the reporter from The *Blade* what impact her late husband had on the school district and its 10,000 students. If he wanted more, she would be happy to pull out the rest.

George Pepadowski had worked at the district for more than 30 years. He started as a high school history teacher at Central, became its principal for eight years and then had been superintendent for the whole district for 12 years before his unexpected death.

"Of course, we were all saddened by Bob Johnson's passing. He was a good man. He and my George worked together for many years. We were great family friends, too. So, I must say that I am glad you are taking a look back at the wonderful things they accomplished. They were quite a team. They did so much for the kids. It seemed like they were always up at Central for one thing or another."

Nick, full from the delightful supper, slipped off his jacket and hung it on the back of his chair, pulling a long, slender notebook from a side pocket. "I appreciate your pulling these scrapbooks out for me. I've already looked over most of the news clippings from our files at The *Blade*. But some of the things you have here are irreplaceable."

Alice stood next to the seated reporter and started flipping the pages of the first scrapbook. "Now, tell me when you want me to stop. This is from George's early days at Central. Ah, those were such fun times. Some of these pictures have our own children in them. They were always part of the activities at the school, too."

The widow, who was in her late 60s, roared through the pages, providing a rich and colorful narrative to accompany the snapshots, news clips, school programs and fliers. Her enthusiasm soared with the rise and fall of her voice as she described the events unfolding before Nick. "This is from the year when the Central basketball team won the Class A state championship. You should have been there. Oh, George just loved those boys. He had coached most of them in junior high and he knew all of their folks." She continued at a frenzied pace, barely slowing to catch her breath. Nick wondered if he should go get her a glass of water. She was like a machine. Surely, he thought, she must be getting thirsty. But Alice continued right on through the second and third scrapbooks. Obviously, she'd done this before. Nick wondered if anyone was present during those historical tours.

Finally, when she opened the fourth book, Nick put the brakes on and slowed her down. It was a collection of items from the community-wide campaign to build a new field house at Central. George and Bob were right in the middle of this effort, but another prominent name and face started showing up in the news clippings and photos.

"His name is Charlie Joselyn. He was the president of the school board. He was very close to George and Bob." Alice slowed and the enthusiasm drained from her voice. She continued flipping pages, but now had grown nearly silent. Nick looked up at her face and could see that the pictures were irritating her.

"Was this not a good time?" the reporter asked. "You don't seem as excited about these clippings and photos as you were about the earlier ones. Is there something wrong?"

"Oh, no. It was just a stressful time. Charlie wanted to build the field house and it was a huge undertaking. There was no money for it and a lot of people at the schools wondered if it was such a good idea. He relied on George and Bob to see it through. It was very difficult. They had a falling out about it during the last year and a half of the building campaign. I don't know all the details, but it got pretty ugly.

"After the field house was built," she continued, "Charlie retired. By that time, Bob and George had quit talking to him. They never got along after that. And the field house, well, everyone kind of sees it as a huge white elephant. I know Bob and George regretted being so heavily involved in it, but they didn't have much choice. Charlie wanted that field house built, and nobody was going to get in his way."

"Where is Mr. Joselyn these days?"

"He lives just a few blocks over, but nobody sees much of him any more. I hear he's stuck in a wheelchair and mad at the world. Bitter, very bitter. He thought he was going to save the school district and almost ended up bringing it down. As far as I know, he didn't even go to Bob's funeral, which was a real shame. He was out of town during George's funeral – I was kind of glad about that. I thought all the stress hurt George. I think it was a factor with his heart."

Nick wrote furiously in his notebook as Alice recalled the difficult period. She was seated now, staring into the flames that flickered lightly in the living room fireplace.

"Did your husband have a serious condition with his heart? Were there other problems?"

"George was a little overweight and Doc Sheffield was giving him some medication for high blood pressure, but he'd never had a real problem with his heart. I think the stress had a lot to do with it. I think he was just wearing down. A lot of things were happening at Central. It's a big school with a lot of kids who had big problems. George had a tough job, and then you add the field house project on top of it. Well, I just think it was too much for him."

"What other things were going on at school? Can you remember anything specific that stands out?

"Well, I do remember they had a suicide. A lovely, young girl. It was tough on everyone. It happened over the summer, but the students took it hard just the same. George and Bob were shocked by it, and they were so afraid that there might be some copycats. They had special counselors come in to talk with the kids after school started up. No one talked very much about it. I think everyone just wanted it to go away."

"What was her name, do you remember her name?"

"Ah, yes. I think there's a picture of her right here in this one." Alice flipped through the pages of scrapbook number three until she came to a photo of a group of students at a varsity football game. "That's her. Candace Phelps. Just a wonderful girl. Nobody knew why. It was one of those things. Kids sometimes get so down in the dumps over the silliest things. It just tore her family apart."

Nick studied the photo of smiling girls who were furiously cheering for their team. In one picture, Nick noticed that Candace and Tanya mugged for the camera with their arms around one another. He jotted some more notes down.

"Hey, there's Tanya. She really doesn't look much different today."

"Tanya and Candace were very close. Candace's death left a lot of people scratching their heads."

"Well, you were right, Mrs. Pepadowski. There's just a ton of information in these scrapbooks. Thanks so much for sharing them with me. I've got to think through all this info, kind of digest it a little. Do you mind if I call you back later? I may have some more questions."

"No problem, Nick. Call me anytime. I'd be happy to talk with you."

Nick slipped his jacket back on and headed for the front door with Mrs. Pepadowski in tow. She continued talking about the old days and George as the reporter reached for the door handle.

"Thanks again for your help and the wonderful hospitality, Mrs. Pepadowski. I'll be in touch."

"Good-bye, Nick."

# Of the three, Charlie Joselyn was the only one left alive …

FRIDAY AFTERNOON

Nick walked quickly through The *Blade* newsroom, hoping to avoid detection. Nick could see notes dangling from every reporter's and editor's computer screen. More directives from The Castrator: "This is an official reminder that all telephone calls made from The *Blade* must be in regard to *Blade* business. Long-distance, personal telephone calls are strictly forbidden. We have hired a private firm to monitor all calls. Those who violate this policy will be reprimanded. Public flogging is not out of the question. The Publisher."

Ah, yes. Nick loved it when the publisher showed her warm, humorous side. What a riot. What fun she was. If she only knew how depressing her memos were to the staff. But he figured that was Drayton Clapper's problem, not his.

At his desk, Nick flipped open his notebook and quickly scanned the entries from his Pepadowski visit, stopping on the last page where he'd jotted down a reminder to call Charlie Joselyn for an interview. Nick found the Joselyns' telephone number in the newsroom's the city street directory, which sometimes carried unlisted numbers.

Before calling him, though, Nick ran to the newsroom morgue to check Joselyn's clip files. He found a half-dozen files fat enough to clog an industrial sewer pipe. Charlie Joselyn was a local legend – personally and professionally. The files documented a full and noteworthy life.

Nick examined news and feature articles that revealed a public life that spanned nearly half a century. As the reporter devoured one story after another, the community leader's bright and colorful life unfolded before him.

Charles Joselyn had made millions of dollars selling insurance and real estate in the region. Everybody in town knew Charlie. He'd been a star on the football, basketball and baseball teams at Central.

After high school, the rugged, handsome pitchman had spent two years in the Marine Corps and fought in Vietnam, earning a Purple Heart and Bronze Star. Shrapnel from a Viet-Cong grenade ripped into his back and legs and eventually bought him a ticket home from the war. Veterans' Hospital doctors were able to repair the damage enough for him to walk and live a fairly normal life, but the war injuries set the table for later back and leg woes that would degenerate into the arthritis and strap a wheelchair to his backside.

But, in his early years after the war, the injuries did not stop him from becoming successful and respected throughout the community. He was easy to talk to and bubbling with great stories, spewing them out like a comic doing standup. He was the kind of salesman who could sell sand to Egyptians. Wherever he went, folks wanted to shake his hand and say hello. They wanted to be his customers, and he and his blossoming businesses were happy to oblige.

In fact, when Charlie decided that he wanted to set his legacy in the community by becoming a driving force on the school board, all he had to do was announce that he was running for the office. Campaign workers appeared out of nowhere and spaghetti-dinner fund-raisers quickly filled his election coffers. No one doubted that he would win. Charlie Joselyn had always been a winner, no matter what he tackled. His first election was easy, and the successive campaigns were a breeze. He spent 25 years on the board – the last six of it at the helm as the president.

Those six years were as wild as a rodeo bull ride. School funding was down and the district was in need of major repairs, particularly Central, the mammoth high school with 2,000 students, mostly from middle-class and poor families. Central's buildings were shabby, giving the school a tattered image. Academics had slipped and the sports programs needed overhauls.

At the time, Charlie told all who gave him their ears that he believed in his heart that all of the school's ailments would vanish with the construction of a new multipurpose sports facility. Though his logic was flawed, he nevertheless was convinced that a top-notch field house would attract better athletes to Central, which would result in a better sports program, which would result in more alumni funding to patch up Central's other buildings, which would improve the school's overall image, which would – in the end – benefit all students and the district in general.

The grand scheme to rejuvenate the school started with a new $20-million sports facility that would, of course, be appropriately named Joselyn Field House. It would be the Taj Mahal of all sports facilities. It would be beautiful. It would be built with the finest brick, mortar and steel and it would stand tall for 200 years. It would be all Charlie, and nothing, would get in the way of the stampede he created to get it built.

Charlie conducted the massive fund-raising campaign for the field house like a maestro standing in front of an orchestra. He waved his baton and the Joselyn Field house shot out of the ground as quickly as a spring planting of field corn after a warm rain. It was his crowning achievement. In his view, it was the last useful thing he did before his health began to fail. Even the governor of Michigan attended the grand opening of the building.

Nick put down the last newspaper clippings and jotted down some final notes. Charlie Joselyn had accomplished much during his life and there was plenty to like about a man of action, a man who got things done. But Nick was also a little wary of an individual who had accumulated so much power. The clip files indicated that the businessman's activities went almost unchecked. Very few challenged him. No one questioned him or his actions. For decades, he pretty much did what he wanted.

Nick returned to his desk in the newsroom and decided to call Charlie Joselyn for an interview. It was late in the afternoon on a Friday, but he hoped he would catch him at home. He put on his headset and punched in the numbers for the Joselyn residence and let the phone ring. No answer. The phone finally went into its recorder. The message startled him.

"What the hell do you want?" The gruff-sounding voice of Charlie Joselyn filled the headset. "If you're a bill collector, go to hell. We'll pay you when we're ready. We're not home and we don't expect to be for some time. If you're calling to sell us something, then hang up and don't call back. If you're calling for me, then stuff it up your ass. If you want Doris, leave a number."

Nick chuckled and then composed himself to leave a message and number for Doris. "Hello, Mrs. Joselyn. My name is Nick Steele and I'm a reporter with The *Blade*. I'm working on a story about Central High School and the significant contributions Bob Johnson and George Pepadowski made to the school during their lives. I understand that Mr. Joselyn also played a major role at the school and in the district during their years. I'd like to arrange an interview with Mr. Joselyn. I'm not selling anything and I'm not a bill collector. I'm just looking for some information, and I wouldn't want to leave Mr. Joselyn out of my story if he belongs in it. Please call me at The *Blade* or on my cell when you have a moment."

Nick left his numbers and hoped he would get a return call from the crotchety old school board president or his wife. He really wanted to talk with Charlie Joselyn. He was the one with all the inside information. He had all the answers. He knew where the skeletons were buried. And, most importantly, of the Central High School threesome, he was the only one left alive – at least for now.

# Dave got caught under his desk with a creature from O'Hare's...

It was the end of long, hard work week and Nick was thirsty. He left The *Blade* building and headed for his car in the parking lot. But his screeching cell phone stopped him in his tracks. Nick checked the number of the incoming call. It was old friend and retired reporter, Dave Balz.

"Hey, man. Where are you?" A smile spread across Nick's face as he waited to hear his buddy's voice.

"I'm in O'Hare's, and I'm staring at something you've got to see."

"What is it, or maybe I should say, 'What's her name?' "

"No, not this time," Dave said. "Come on over. You'll see when you get here. I'll buy you your first beer, too."

"Deal. I'll be right there."

As Nick drove across Veterans' Bridge, he thought about Tanya. He wondered how she was doing and when he would see her again. She was sweet. JoAnne would understand. His late wife would have liked her, too.

Nick parked his car in a safe spot on Midland Street and watched revelers file into the bistros and taverns that lined both sides of the busy thoroughfare. One young couple beat him to the entrance of O'Hare's.

When Nick entered, he spotted Dave sitting at the end of the bar, chatting with a waitress. Out of the corner of his eye, Dave spotted Nick and stopped talking. He looked up at the ceiling and Nick followed his eyes upward.

Nick grinned. He was proud. "So that's where my pants ended up. Just a second, Dave, I've got to make a quick call."

Nick stepped back outside and pulled out his phone, calling up the stored number for Officer Quinn. No answer, but Nick left a message. "Dan, hey, I found my pants. They're up on the ceiling at O'Hare's. My pants are now legendary, and hanging with an extra sweet crease. Thought you'd want to know. Come on up and I'll buy you a beer."

Nick went back into O'Hares and joined his friend at the bar.

"When I came in, everybody was talking about your pants, man," Dave said. "They say you lost 'em in a bet. I'm almost afraid to ask what kind of bet, but I gotta know."

"Good question," Nick said, sipping from his first beer and turning to admire his pants on the ceiling again. "I remember coming back in here after spending a couple of hours drinking at Lucky's down the street. Lots of people in here, and I think I sat down with some folks from City Hall, but it's kind of fuzzy after that. I slept in my car out back, and Quinn gave me a ride home. That's all I remember."

Dave laughed and slapped his friend on the back. "It will all come out in the end. It's just a matter of time and we'll hear what happened."

"I can hardly wait," Nick said, chugging down half his beer in two gulps. "My memory's been a little foggy lately. The kids in the newsroom keep saying it's early Alzheimer's – the dirty, snot-nosed bastards. I think it's because I'm not getting enough sleep these days."

"Yeah, right. Alzeheimer's. Sleep. Maybe it's because of the full moon, too. Ever think it might be because you're drinking too much these days?"

"Yup, could be. I'll slow down one of these days, but not tonight. Ready for another, pal? Sally, we need a couple more beers and a couple of shots. Peppermint schnapps."

Dave changed the subject. "What are you working on that's good? Still poking around that Central High School story? I may have a little something for you on it."

"Well, I think it's going to be a good story no matter how it ends up. Right now, I'm working it from the perspective of how two dedicated educators gave the best years of their lives to making Central High School a better place for kids from some of the toughest neighborhoods in town."

"What about their deaths? The coincidences? What are you going to do with that?" Balz looked away from Nick and scanned the bar for women. "Is that part of the story?"

"Yeah. I think it's a fascinating part of the story. Here you have two friends, who share almost everything together, and they end up dying of the same thing – only years apart, but totally unexpectedly. They both up and keel over right out of nowhere. Hey, they even had the same doctor. I think that's interesting. I think readers would find that interesting."

"Well, here's a little something I picked up from one of the custodians at Central. He says there was a suicide. A girl, a junior or senior, and she was mixed up with one of the teachers who just up and disappeared. The custodian, who does not want to be quoted, says that the whole thing blew up at the school. He says it happened right when they were running that big fund-raiser to build the new field house. It would have been seven or eight years ago."

"Yup. Mrs. Pepadowski talked about a suicide. She happened to have a picture of the girl in one of her scrapbooks."

Nick whipped out his notebook and flipped through the pages. "Yeah, here it is. Candace Phelps. She looked real happy in the picture. The suicide is one of the things I want to ask Tanya about. But thanks, Dave, I really appreciate it. I don't know how it plays into this, but that's good stuff."

Nick looked at his watch and decided to try and call the Joselyns again. "Hey, I'm going to step outside and make a call. I'm trying to connect with Charlie Joselyn. You must remember him. He was a big-time player in town and at the school. I'll be right back."

"Oh, yeah. You'll have fun talking to that old, nasty son-of-a-bitch. He's snarly and mean." While Nick went outside, Dave hailed their favorite waitress. "Sally, bring me another tall cold one. Hell, I don't have to work tomorrow."

That, basically, could have served as Dave's philosophy of life. The short, bearded, heavy-set reporter never worried about much of anything. Work, being a damned good reporter, was everything to him. Nothing else really mattered. He was the kind of guy who shopped for his clothes at the Salvation Army and looked for dates among the women who prowled the aisles of Wal-Mart.

In fact, dating and women and a so-called normal social life were not his forte. Married four times – twice to the same victim – Dave never found the knack for successful matrimony. That's because the newspaper was his mistress, and, as everyone knows, wives and mistresses make very poor partners.

Before retirement, Dave literally lived at The *Blade*, chasing news stories night and day. While other reporters spent their personal time on the golf course or in the gym, Dave sat in the newsroom listening to the emergency scanner for cop or fire chatter that might make a good news story. He loved it so much that he gladly worked weekends and holidays because, as he often noted to the other reporters, "that's when you get all the really great human drama." It got so bad that editors had to make him go home when he was ill.

At one time, between wives number one and two, Dave moved into The *Blade* newsroom for about six weeks. He removed the drawers from his old Steelcase desk and slept on a mat and pillow under a tattered and faded green Army blanket. All other possessions were in the trunk of his car. Each morning, Ted, the janitor, would wake him up so that he could go into the men's room to wash and comb out his long, dark hair before the day got started. Often, sports copy editors, who were the first to show up at the newspaper each day, would find Dave standing in the men's room clad only in a T-shirt and shorts, vigorously brushing his teeth, a raggedy towel draped around his neck.

As legend has it, that all came to a sudden end when Drayton Clapper, the newsroom honcho, came into the office unexpectedly one night and discovered Dave sleeping under his desk with his arm wrapped around a creature he'd brought back from O'Hare's after closing time. Clapper found them by following a trail of women's clothes through the photo and sports departments to Dave's desk where her linen and his jeans and T-shirt marked the scene of the crime. As Clapper rousted them from beer-induced slumber, the editor thanked the stars above for that old Army blanket, which was the only thing that shielded his eyes from meshed naked flesh.

"Wake up you two, this is a professional newsroom," Clapper later told anyone who would listen.

Waking grudgingly, Dave supposedly responded: "I beg your pardon, sir. She's not a professional. I had to show her how to do everything. Hell, I offered her a 10 spot and she wouldn't take it. In my book, that makes this real love."

It was sad, but essentially the truth. Clapper yelled at him for about 20 minutes, banned him from sleeping in the newsroom, and added another note to his already bulging personnel file. Like all the other reprimands, Dave took it in stride and went back to doing what he did best–reporting and writing the news. That always seemed to smooth things over for at least a while.

That's what endeared Dave to Nick and the other purists in the newsroom. He was a newshound through and through. No more, no less. The copy desk referred to him as "Balz Out" when he wasn't around. They could always count on Dave to chase a story like a greyhound in pursuit of a mechanical rabbit at the track. All-out, all the time.

It's the reason Nick loved working with Dave and hooked up

with him on stories whenever he could. Even in retirement, Dave was still a better and more dedicated reporter than most of the full-time wannabes currently on The *Blade* newsroom staff.

As Nick stood outside O'Hare's and called the Joselyn telephone number, he kept thinking about how he could get Dave more involved with this story. Getting Dave hot on this piece would shove it into another, higher gear.

The telephone at the Joselyn household rang five times and Nick was afraid he was about to get a second dose of that nasty greeting from Charlie when he suddenly heard the sweet and friendly voice of Doris Joselyn.

"Hello, Joselyn residence."

"Hi, this is Nick Steele from The *Blade*. I called earlier and left a message. I hope this isn't a bad time to call."

"Oh, no. This is fine. My husband is taking a nap right now. He was at the doctor's office most of the afternoon and he's a little tired. We heard your message when we got home. He says he will give you an interview if your story is going to be a positive one about the school district. He said he's not interested in helping you throw mud."

"Well, so far it looks like it's going to be a very interesting retrospective piece about Mr. Johnson and Mr. Pepadowski and how they worked together for so many years to make Central a great school. I think Mr. Joselyn could really add some interesting perspective to it. When do you think we could get together?"

Doris Joselyn paused to think for a moment. "How about Monday afternoon – after Charles gets up from his nap? Would that work out OK?"

"Yes, that would be perfect. What time? Around 3 o'clock?"

"That sounds good. We'll see you then."

"Thanks, Mrs. Joselyn. This is going to work out just fine." Nick said goodbye and clicked off his phone. He was tickled to get the interview.

But Charlie Joselyn was not really napping. He simply didn't like fielding telephone calls and his wife, once again, covered for him. The crotchety old man was busy at home just being his miserable self.

Charlie turned his wheelchair around in his kitchen, struggling to get a glass of water to wash down his third – and last – batch of medicine for the day. The former president of the school board of Bay City Public Schools hated taking the medicine because it fouled his stomach and left him constipated. "A man who can't even take a decent shit isn't worth a damn," he said out loud to no one in particular.

During his last medical checkup, Doctor James Sheffield delivered the bad news to the Joselyns. "Charlie, your condition is worsening. Your blood pressure and diabetes are taking their toll on your heart. At the rate you're going, I don't know how much time you have left. I'm going to change your prescription to try and get control of your blood pressure. But you've got to help out, too. No more drinking and quit eating all that crap."

"Yeah, yeah, I know. You want me to give up all the good things. Anything I like is bad for me. Well, piss on it. I'm going to live like I want to – even if it means a fast checkout." Charlie's eyes narrowed as he turned a menacing stare from the doc to his wife of 52 long years.

"Who really gives a damn, anyway? Doris here has got our insurance agent's number on speed dial – don't ya, sweetie? Just waiting for me to go before you can cash in and spend your winters in Florida getting suntan lotion rubbed on your back by some young buck at 25 smackers an hour – you'll both probably be in the nude, laughing and splashing the oil in all directions and planning on how you're going to spend my money. Am I right, sweetie?"

"You're always right, Charlie. Only I plan to have two young bucks – in the nude – lathering my eager body with several hot, scented oils. I'll pay 'em both 40 dollars an hour and I'll give 'em each a big tip – right out of your life insurance fund. That's the only way you get good service in Florida, you know that, Charlie." She laughed out loud and Charlie grimaced.

"Now, forget all this silly talk and let's get going," she continued. "The afternoon soaps will be over before we get home." Doris winked at the doc with a wide grin on her face as she patted her husband, the only man she'd ever been in love with, on the shoulder. "We'll try to do better with his diet, Doc, and I'll watch his drinking. I've been doing that for a very long time. One of these days, maybe I'll get the hang of it."

Charlie's face remained squinched up in a sourful expression that made it look as though he'd just eaten a heaping tablespoon of ice-cold grapefruit. He didn't like it much when he baited Doris and she handed him back a spicy response – especially in front of other people. So, he said nothing as she nudged his wheelchair toward the examining room door. Charlie didn't even say goodbye to Doc Sheffield, who had been his healer for 30 years. He just stared straight ahead and stiffened his body in the chair as he and Doris left the office.

"Take care, Charlie. That new prescription should be at the pharmacy within an hour or so. You can pick it up tonight, or in the morning." Doc Sheffield shook his head, closed the examining room door behind him and jotted a note for Charles Joselyn's medical file. He would do his best to help his old friend by changing his medication, but he knew it wouldn't do much good if Chuck was bent on an early exit.

But the retired insurance and real estate tycoon had little choice. His 74-year-old body had been devastated by arthritis, diabetes and pole-vaulting blood pressure. The crippling ailments left the once-proud athlete broken and bitter as he neared the end of his life, which was already scheduled and coming sooner than he, his family or anyone connected to the man had realized.

# Candace Phelps did not die alone...

Nick guided his baby down East Side back streets toward Tanya's home, wondering about the family's grief. Only two days had passed since Mr. Bob's funeral, and Nick worried that it might be too soon to visit. Even so, he was glad when Tanya called from Ann Arbor that morning and invited him to come by to talk. Nick wanted to see her. He knew Joanne would have approved.

Nick slowed the Firebird and turned into the Johnson driveway. He let the 'Bird's massive engine idle and rumble for a moment before shutting it down. He looked up into his rear-view mirror to see if his hair was OK. Nick paused in his leather bucket seat because he did not want to appear too eager. He took a quick personal inventory. "Let's see, notebook? Here it is. Pen?" He felt the inside breast pocket of his jacket. "OK, what else? Hair? Check the hair again." He glanced back into the mirror. Not perfect but it looked OK. He smiled to make sure a chunk of O'Hare's munchies had not lodged between his teeth. "Everything seems OK," he muttered as he stuck a mint into his cheek, "let's go."

With that, he flipped open his car door and bounded out of the vehicle that still hissed from its run to Tanya's house. Nick turned to close the 'Bird's door and stepped to the side, squarely into a hole the size of a softball in the Johnsons' driveway. The awkward move sent the big reporter sprawling down onto the ground. His notebook went one way and his massive body went another, rolling onto the grass in the front yard. As Nick looked up from his tumble, golden leaves fluttered to the ground from the top of his head. He heard a concerned and soothing voice.

"Are you alright?" Tanya was standing on the front porch, looking down at the pathetic sight. Her fingers touched the bottom of her chin and a wide smile revealed gleaming teeth. "Nick, are you OK?"

"Yup. Stepped in a hole." Nick drew comfort from the glimpse of her smile, but quickly wondered how many more falls his body could take. Was he really this clumsy, was she that enchanting, or was it the three beers at O'Hare's that turned him into a tumbling buffoon? "No biggie. Just lost my footing for a second." The former high school basketball star sprang to his feet and brushed grass clippings from his sports jacket and jeans. He was so glad that the family dog did his business in the backyard and not the front. Suddenly, images of his neighbor's pooch, Jenny, flashed in his mind. The thought of her squatting and pushing and then greeting him with a wet tongue made him wipe his mouth with the back of his hand.

"Come on up, but watch the steps. They're tricky, too." Tanya muffled a laugh, which made it sound more like a squeal, and turned toward her front door.

The remark brought a huge smile to Nick's forlorn face. "I'll be careful. I know firsthand how dangerous those steps are. And your driveway is a bear, too. Just call me Grace."

The newsman made it up the stairs without incident and followed Tanya into the house.

"Come into the kitchen, I'm making some tea." Tanya walked ahead of Nick through the Johnson home. For the first time, Nick was able to study her form as she led him to the back of the house. He liked what he saw.

"Are you checking out my ass?" Tanya spoke as she walked and did not look over her shoulder at Nick. "You know, women can sense it when they're being checked out, and I could feel your eyes on my behind."

"Well, I guess you're pretty sure of yourself. Yes, since you asked, I was checking you out. But let me just say that I'm much more interested in the engine than the caboose. In my book, it's the total package that counts. I'm too old to get side tracked by shapes and sizes and appearances. You're a very attractive person in many ways, but that's prompted another question in my mind."

"Oh, really?" Tanya said, turning to face Nick. "What kind of question?"

"Ah, I don't know how else to say this, so I'll just shoot it out there. I'm kind of surprised that you're not attached – no significant other. What's up with that? You're such a catch that I'd think you'd have guys chasing you all over the place."

Tanya smiled and laughed lightly. "I've been close a couple of times, but the situation has never been right. I was seeing a guy for a few years and I thought he was the one. A TV sports announcer and a great person. I loved him dearly, but the Big C came to his door and rang the bell. Within a couple of months, he was gone. Cancer took him fast. Took me a long time to get over him. Not sure that I ever will."

"Oh, I'm sorry," Nick said. "I know what it's like to lose someone you love. My life has been one big, sloppy, drunken mess since I lost my wife. Not sure I will ever get over her, either."

The two looked into each other's eyes until the moment and the silence became awkward.

"Do you like tea, or would you rather have something else," Tanya said as she turned and walked toward the kitchen. "I think we have some beer in the fridge."

"No, I'm good with the beer for now," Nick said, wondering what she meant. Could she smell the beer on him again? Why isn't the mint working? "Tea is fine. I'm open to just about any flavor."

Tanya opened a cupboard door and searched for tea as Nick found a comfortable spot to sit down. The kitchen was massive, serving as a family gathering spot and a comfortable place to entertain company. Upper and lower cupboards surrounded the room. A two-way fireplace separated it from the open dining and living rooms. An eight-burner stove stood in one corner, simmering water for the tea. A solid wood cutting block dominated the center of the kitchen. Magnets on the refrigerator door held up Bobby's soccer schedule and photos from his last game. His most recent report card stood upright in a stainless steel frame atop the refrigerator, prominently displayed. It was an honor Mr. Bob bestowed on all his studious kids.

Out of the corner of her eye, Tanya spotted Nick looking at the frame. "All my report cards were up there, too. Tim's made it when they deserved to be on display, which was not nearly as often as my dad would have liked."

Nick smiled and fidgeted in his seat. "I'm afraid my grades were closer to Tim's than yours. But that's really a nice touch by your dad. He's in every room of this house, isn't he? Are you sure you're OK with me being here? Are you comfortable talking about the past right now?'

"Yes, I'm OK. It'll be good to talk with someone other than a family member. Every conversation with family is so emotional right now. I need something else. Please, let's talk."

Perfect. An open invitation to dive into the past. Nick started by recapping his visit with Mrs. Pepadowski earlier that afternoon. The only part he left out was the great food. He told Tanya about the scrapbooks and described the elderly woman's running narrative of family history at Central. He recounted the widow's view of life, including some of the turbulent times. Mrs. Pepadowski seemed to think that building Joselyn Field House put such a strain on her husband and Tanya's dad that it changed the men and their relationship with one another.

"Oh, it did," Tanya said. "My dad complained about the pressure, the stress they were under all the time. I think I was in junior high when they were raising money for it. My dad thought the whole thing was crazy and a waste of money and energy. He and George would sit out in the backyard and drink beer and grouse about it."

Nick asked about Charlie Joselyn. Background information about the former school board president and snarly old cuss would help him prepare for his interview on Monday. Nick pressed Tanya for details.

"Everything changed when he became president of the school board," Tanya said as she placed a cup of tea in front of Nick and sat at the table with him. "He had this big idea about the field house, and he became obsessed about it. I remember my dad and George talking about him arm-twisting everyone in town to contribute money, and then he went back and hit them up a couple of more times for contributions. It really caused a lot of hard feelings around town. People started to turn on Mr. Joselyn, but he didn't care. Nothing was more important than that damn field house."

Nick scribbled in his notebook and then flipped to a page where he'd jotted down questions. As he did, a half a dozen blades of grass and the flakes of ground up leaves fell out of the notebook, compliments of his tumble on the lawn. Sight of the refuse on the table lightened the moment, causing Nick and Tanya to laugh. She scooped the mess up and carried it to a trash container in the corner of the kitchen. The pause gave Nick time to change the direction of their discussion and bring up a sensitive subject.

"What about Candace Phelps? Can we talk about what happened to her?"

Tanya returned to her chair and studied Nick's face before she began. "Candace was a little older than me, but I remember how highly regarded she was. Everyone thought she was very cool. Smart. Good at about everything. Popular. But the high school band was her downfall."

Nick asked Tanya to continue. He thought it would be good to get background information from someone who knew Candace and experienced attending Central High School. He knew that a student's view of what happened would probably be quite different from the official report of the incident. Nick wanted all points of view.

"That's how she got involved with our creepy band director, Darrin Appleton. Cynthia and I were just talking about him. I'll never forget the prick. He was only a couple of years out of college. Real handsome, smart, and he'd played in a big time rock band to pay his way through school. Most kids liked him, especially the girls. He gave them extra attention. He offered all the pretty girls free instruction after class. I heard there was no shortage of takers, but it wasn't exactly free, either.

"Candace was one of them," she continued. "I never caught them in the act or anything, but the rumors flew. I remember kids talking about her coming out of the band room with her sweater on backward. Stuff like that. It got very steamy. They were seen together after school, on weekends. But nobody really talked about it out loud. Mostly whispers."

Nick was curious about the whispers. How far had the wind blown the muffled secrets of Central High School? Though Bay City's population numbered about 30,000, the neighborhood communities within it were small-town in nature. People knew each other and loved sticking their noses in each other's personal lives whenever they could. Rumors and gossip were almost like a sport – folks competed to see how much they knew and could reveal about each other. If someone had a dark side, it did not stay that way for long. Eventually, time would bring whatever was hidden out into the light.

Nick wanted to know who knew about the suspicious behavior and what they did about it. Nick figured that Tanya might not have all the answers, but he believed she'd have a pretty good idea about what other teachers and parents had heard about what was off-key in the band.

"We picked up all kinds of talk," Tanya said. "We even heard that Appleton was dating some of the moms, too! He even went after some of the old hags. Can you believe that?"

Nick did not answer. Instead, he walked over to the range and picked up the pot of steaming water. The break in their conversation gave both a chance to pause and think. Tanya looked for tissues in her purse. She did not need them at that moment, but fumbled for them nonetheless. Nick filled their cups. He dunked her tea bag with her spoon, and then drowned his in the same manner.

Tanya thanked Nick. He sat down and studied her face, trying to decide how much further he should go. Nick did not want his questions to hurt her, but his curiosity ached for more information, particularly about the suicide. The reporter checked his wristwatch and decided to edge ahead, asking her about it as she stirred the tea with slow, circling motions.

"What about the suicide? Mrs. Pepadowski said it happened over the summer. Do you feel like talking about it?"

Tanya stopped stirring and looked up from her cup. Light wafts of steam were all that separated Nick and Tanya's faces as they sat at the table. She leaned back in her chair and Nick quit talking. The kitchen was silent. Tanya looked down and folded her hands in her lap. She did not speak right away, but then blurted details in one gush, as if that would rid her of further discussion about the uncomfortable subject.

"Oh, Nick, it was just horrible. I remember that it happened right after the end of her senior year. Appleton finished his last day of classes, and then picked up and took off. He simply disappeared. No forwarding address. No goodbyes. Gone. What an asshole. He didn't say so long to anyone – not even Candace. It completely wiped her out. I saw her once after he left and all she did was bawl. That went on for days, and then I heard she went into her garage, started the car and just ended it all."

Anger filled Tanya's eyes and lifted her voice to a higher pitch. Nick pushed ahead, sensing that she might be on roll and eager to tell more. He floated a soft question, baiting her to continue. "Sounds ugly. How did your dad and George handle it?"

"Very badly. They were a mess all summer," Tanya said, leaning ahead in her chair and putting her elbows back on the table. She cradled the teacup in her hands. "George was getting ready to retire. I think that's what pushed him into it, and my dad, well, I've never seen him like that. He just got bombed every night all summer long and I know he didn't want to go back to school in the fall. My mom can tell you more. It was a horrible time. My worst summer ever.

"Nick, there's one more thing that most people don't know about. About a year or so after the suicide, I heard from some of the other girls at school that Candace was pregnant when she died, which means that she took two lives. They said her mom and dad found out about the pregnancy and the affair at the same time. They were told she was pregnant after the autopsy."

Nick scribbled with renewed fervor in his notebook and then took a sip of tea. He looked up at Tanya and noticed that her right hand was pushing a tear off her cheek. He reached over and touched her left hand with his fingers, hoping to comfort her.

"What a nightmare," he said, his voice just above a whisper. "It must have absolutely crushed her parents."

Tanya did not slow down, as Nick thought she might. The gloomy discussion did not open the floodgates and produce a tidal wave of emotion. Only a tiny trickle of tears ran down her cheeks and she mopped them up with a wad of tissue. Nick wondered if Tanya had ever openly talked about what happened before today. He sensed that she wanted to tell what she knew. He was relieved, and she kept going.

"It hurt them more than we can ever know. Her mom lost it completely. She ended up leaving town. And her dad went ballistic. He blamed the school – my dad, George, Mr. Joselyn. He went crazy over it."

The kitchen's sliding glass door opened and Mrs. Johnson stepped in carrying a paper grocery sack in her left arm. "I'm back, Tanya, and I see your reporter friend is here. I blocked his car in the driveway. I'll move it when he's ready to leave."

"That's OK, Mrs. Johnson." Nick said, standing up as the woman entered the room. He moved toward her and offered to help her bring in other groceries from the car.

"No, I only have one bag today. Just a little shopping after the movie. I dropped Bobby at a friend's." Isabelle Johnson saw the tissue on the table and could not ignore Tanya's red eyes. "Is everything OK here?" She looked at Tanya and then at Nick.

Tanya took the sack from her mother. "Everything is fine, mom. I was just telling Nick about some of the things that happened up at Central. You remember. The days when they were building the field house and how it stressed out dad."

"Those were difficult times," Mrs. Johnson said as she took off her jacket and draped it over the back of a chair. "Yes, very difficult, but I'm a little surprised that it made you cry."

"Well, I told Nick about Candace Phelps – her suicide. That whole story is enough to make anyone cry." Tanya poured her mother a cup of tea, squeezed a little lemon into it and then put it on the table in front of a chair next to Nick. "Please join us, Mom. Tell Nick about how it affected Daddy."

"Did you tell him the whole story?" she asked, sitting down. "Everything?"

Tanya nodded and sat down beside her mom at the table. Nick didn't say anything. He didn't have to. The women were spilling and he decided to sit down and let them vent.

"Up until that time, Bob had never lost a student," Mrs. Johnson said. "All those years as a teacher and principal and he'd never had a student die." The new widow stared intently at Nick as she stirred the tea, adding just a touch of sugar to the brew. "I don't know how to describe it. Her death knocked him off his feet. He told me several times that he did not know how serious the affair with the band teacher was. He could not believe what happened, and the idea that she was pregnant, too."

"What about Mr. Phelps? Did he confront your husband?" Nick flipped to a fresh page in his notebook. "What did he do?"

"You're taking notes. Before we go any further," she said, staring directly at Nick, "I have to ask you, is this going to be part of an article?"

"I'm planning to write a story about your husband and George and their impact on the school," Nick said, looking at Mrs. Johnson first, and then glancing in Tanya's direction. "Right now, the suicide does not seem like it would be part of that story, but I think it's important background information that helps explain why and how some things happened at the time. I'm taking notes so that I can keep it all straight. If I decide that I need to use this information, I will talk to you about it before I write it. Does that sound fair?"

"Yes, fair enough," she said. "Where was I? Oh, OK, back to Gus Phelps. He was so angry, and so outraged. He came to the house and demanded to know where the band teacher was. He did not believe that Bob was unaware of what was going on. I remember being scared to death. He grabbed Bob by the collar and pulled him out onto the porch. I was going to call the police, but Bob said no.

"Thank God you weren't here at the time, Tanya," she said, looking in her daughter's direction and searching for a tissue to dry her own eyes. "I remember screaming at Gus to leave us alone, to just go, or I would call the police. He shook your dad back and forth and then pushed him into the side of the house. He stormed off, saying: 'this is not over. The people who did this to my daughter, the people who let this happen, will pay for it.' I'll never forget that. It's so fresh in my mind that it was like it happened yesterday."

"Did Mr. Phelps ever confront your husband again?" Nick sipped his tea and quickly glanced at Tanya, who sat quietly staring out the sliding glass door. "Did he go after anyone else?"

"Yes. He did the same thing at George's house, but the family dog attacked him, bit his leg and he left. We tried to warn Charlie Joselyn, but it was too late. Gus was at his house before our call got through. The man was insane with rage. He thought we were all in on it together – a big conspiracy. He was convinced we all knew that his daughter was carrying on with the band teacher and did nothing about it.

"And that was not the case at all," she continued. "We were shocked when Candace took her life. Bob and George were never the same after that."

"What about Mrs. Phelps?" Nick looked up from his scribbling and stared at Mrs. Johnson. "Tanya mentioned that she thought Mrs. Phelps left town."

"It must have been a year or more after the suicide, but yes, she moved," the older woman said. "A neighbor told me she went to stay with a relative over in Kalamazoo. I tried to contact her once after that, but she never responded."

Nick closed his notebook and took a long sip of tea. Both of the women in the kitchen were weeping softly now. Talking about the past – especially a particularly painful part – had been more difficult than they imagined. Nick did not want to press them on it anymore. He was trying to think of a good way to conclude the discussion when Tanya broke the weighty silence that hung over the room.

"Nick, you said you wanted to ask about Daddy's illness. Mom knows everything. Ask whatever you like."

Tanya was making this too easy for Nick. He quickly shifted gears and asked Mrs. Johnson about her husband's health, or lack of it, in recent years. The widow said he had fallen into a depression since things went haywire at Central – the suicide, the construction of the new field house, and George's retirement and subsequent passing. She said he wasn't watching his diet or exercising and had been drinking too much.

"Bob lost his enthusiasm. The fire went out of him. The things that he loved so much – the school, the kids, and the teachers – didn't matter as much all of a sudden. He became very moody. Doc Sheffield tried to help him, but nothing seemed to work."

"What kind of medication was he taking?" the reporter asked, his notebook reopened now and the recipient of a good working over from his ink pen. "I'd have to look. I'm not sure off the top of my head. It was a couple of different meds. Something for his blood pressure, maybe something for depression. Tanya, go get dad's pills. They're in the top drawer of his dresser."

Great, Nick thought, they still had his medicine.

After a moment, Tanya bounded back into the kitchen with large plastic bottles in each hand. The amber containers were about half-filled with little pills. She handed them to Nick, who looked over the words printed on each bottle's label. He noticed that the pills were prescribed by Doc Sheffield and that they came from the pharmacy just a few blocks from the Johnson home.

"Gee, the names of these things don't mean anything to me. I have no clue what they are or what they are supposed to do."

"Go ahead, take them. We have no use for them now," Mrs. Johnson said as she sipped the last of her tea. "If I ever had a need for them, I'm sure Doc Sheffield and the pharmacy would have a record."

Nick thanked the ladies, closed his notebook again, and stuck the pill bottles in the side pocket of his jacket. He got up from his chair and started walking toward the sliding glass door. Tanya offered to walk him out. She motioned toward the back steps.

"Now, go easy. You haven't been down these steps yet," she said, smiling wide again.

Nick laughed and slid through the door, gliding down the steps without a miscue. "See you later, and thanks so much. Is it OK to call you if I have any more questions?"

"Call any time, Nick." Tanya flashed her easy smile at him. "See you later."

"Yes," Nick thought, as he jumped inside the 'Bird. "I'll have to think of a reason to call her tomorrow."

But Nick didn't have to wait to talk with Tanya the next day. When he got back to his apartment, a message on his recorder asked him to call her – right away. The journalist tossed his jacket on top of the heap of clothes piled in what served as his dining room. He grabbed his phone and punched in Tanya's number.

"Hi Tanya. Got your message. Did I forget something at your place?"

"No, Nick. But I've been thinking. There was one other girl at school who might have gotten involved with the band director. At least, she was part of the rumors. Her name is Sarah Evans – she's a year older than me."

"Can you talk to her and see if she'd be willing to tell us more about Darrin Appleton?" Nick said. He sat down in a dining room chair and pushed dirty plates away from the edge of the table so he could rest his arm while he talked with Tanya. "I know that might be difficult for her, but if she was involved with him, then she might be able to tell a lot about the band director and Candace. Besides, I'm curious about how many other 'girlfriends' Appleton had."

"I can try. Somebody told me she was going to Wayne State down in Detroit. I'll get in touch with her."

"Thanks Tanya. Good night."

# Nick's bedroom was just that – a room with a bed in it...

SATURDAY MORNING

Early morning sunshine warmed Nick's face as it edged through window curtains in his bedroom. Birds chirped from their tree-limb perches and squirrels raced across the roof of his apartment building. Nick rolled over in his bed and hugged his blankets. His left leg poked through the wad of sheets and covers. His eyelids flicked open and brushed away the remnants of a full night's rest. Nick felt good, and muttered to himself: "So, this is what waking up without a hangover is like... not bad. Not too bad at all."

The reporter rolled out of bed and checked his alarm clock – 8 a.m. Nick decided to go for a long walk before eating anything to break his fast. Walks along the old rail trail near his place sometimes helped him sort his thoughts. He flipped on the coffeemaker in his kitchen as he stumbled toward the bathroom. He wondered how cold it was outside. As he stood in front of the toilet, he glanced out the bathroom window. White, icy frost glistened in the sunlight, but still clung to the roof of a nearby apartment building.

Nick pulled the hood of his sweatshirt up over the back of his head as he whisked through his apartment door and walked into the crisp air. The rail trail stretched out along the Saginaw River in downtown Bay City for several miles. On weekend mornings, it bustled with activity. Joggers, roller bladers, bike riders and walkers converged on the narrow swath of asphalt paving. Walking allowed Nick to sort out the conflict that coursed through his head.

On this day, Nick needed to do a little mind wrestling with the Central High School story. Where was it going? Was he gathering too much unnecessary information? Was it worth the considerable time that he was now investing in the story? Was it time to tell his bosses that he was working on something that he thought would amount to more than a feature story? Should he tell them what he picked up about the band director who was supposedly abusing his female students? If the band director was, indeed, having sexual relations with students, then that's Criminal Sexual Conduct, even if he had their consent. It's rape, plain and simple. And what about all those who were aware of Appleton's activity, but did not report it? That's illegal under Michigan law, too. Was Charlie Joselyn so powerful that no one dared cross him and report this activity to the authorities? Did Charlie have that kind of influence with the cops and prosecutor's office? What did Nick really have beyond the perspective piece that he told the families he planned to write?

Questions piled on top of questions. Nick rolled the information over and over in his mind. He picked up his stride and pushed his body. The joggers on the rail trail were no longer pulling away from him. He could feel his heart kick into a higher gear and beads of perspiration formed on his forehead. Fear and apprehension suddenly flooded Nick's mind. Was this walk actually turning into exercise? What next, actual workouts and a healthy diet? He chuckled at the thought. The guys at O'Hare's would hound him unmercifully if they thought he had changed his ways. Rest. Exercise. Nutritious food.

And what about Tanya? Though they had just met, she was never far from his thoughts. He wondered if allowing his interest in her to grow was a mistake, personally and professionally. Was that interest clouding his judgment about the story? Nick rounded a slight curve in the rail trail and passed an older couple, which made him suddenly think of himself as one of those human workout machines in infomercials on late-night television. The couple, probably in their early 70s, strolled in the sunshine, holding hands and chatting quietly. They looked happy. The scene made Nick wonder if he would ever hold Tanya's hand like that. He knew that he was definitely attracted to her. For the first time since Joanne died, guilt did not block his thoughts about spending time with another woman. Joanne would be OK with Tanya, Nick reasoned. She seemed like the real deal – very much like Joanne and Nick's sisters, whom he adored.

Tanya was a beautiful young woman inside and out. He loved talking with her. She was a 90s chick, but still a little old-fashioned. Smart as a computer chip and as funny as a *Saturday Night Live* skit. She was pretty and shapely and he thought her thick mane of sandy blonde hair would look best resting comfortably on his chest between his shoulder and chin. But he knew he had to resist the urge to chase her while he was working on this story. Everything would have to be on the up and up – all business while he worked on a story that involved her family.

The cell phone riding on his hip vibrated as Nick finished the second mile of his walk. He slowed and pulled it to his ear. He figured Dave was trying to get his attention. He was right.

"Hi ya, Dave. What's up?" Nick swiped at the sweat on his fore-head with the cotton sleeve on his left arm and continued walking.

"Hey, man, have you had anything to eat yet? Wanna grab something?

"Sure, but Sally's not within reach." Nick knew the bawdy remark would get his old friend going.

"You got that right. I'd love to corner her just one time. Wouldn't she be a wildcat in the sack?"

"Yeah, too much for you or me. She is a wild one." The two roared at each other at the thought of getting to know Sassy Sally in a very intimate way. "I'm just about done with my walk, maybe another mile or so. Want to catch some lunch?"

"Walk? Another mile or so? What the hell is up with that? Have you got a fever, man – coming down with something? I can't believe my ears. Oh, I get it. You're probably draggin' a cooler of cold beer behind you, right? Got a flask in your hip pocket? Going to hit up one of those down-and-outers in the park for a doobie, right?"

"Very funny, Dave. I think better when I walk. You should try it some time. Thinking a little before you open your mouth is even better. Now, what about some lunch?"

"Sure, how about the Hub? I'm craving the chili. Noon sound OK?

"Sounds good. Hey, I've got something to show you. Are you still taking that blood pressure medicine?"

"Off and on. Right now, the doc says I don't need it. Getting out of that newsroom did wonders for my health and my temperament."

"See you at noon." Nick stuck the cell phone back on his hip and picked up his pace again. It would be good talking to Dave about the story. He hadn't filled him in on what was going on in a couple of days. The interview with Tanya and her mom had revealed a ton of new information. What they told him about Candace Phelps, the band director, the suicide, the pregnancy and the reaction of Gus Phelps had been nagging at Nick all night. Twice he woke from a dead sleep with it on his mind.

The newsman cruised around the last corner and bounded up the steps, two at a time, to his apartment. The two-bedroom rental was home to Nick, but really only fit for a Spartan. A slumping tan couch and an overstuffed green chair took up space in the living room. A television and stereo rested amid a stack of boards and cement blocks in a fashion that would have made any college dorm supervisor proud. No pictures on the walls. No plants. A large green and gold flag that hailed the prowess of the Wayne State University Tartars covered most of the front window but failed miserably as a substitute for curtains.

The dining room was not any better equipped. A sagging table leaned unsteadily just off the kitchen area with three chairs strewn around it. The fourth seat was the resting place for a stack of laundry that was in need of some detergent and water. A plate containing last night's leftovers occupied the only open space on the table amid a stack of newspapers, an old Sports Illustrated, a Playboy, and the latest David Morrell novel.

Just a towel's throw away stood the kitchen's gas stove, which had rarely emitted fire since Nick moved in. It was cluttered with used, mostly empty glasses and cups. Saturday was usually the day when he washed dishes from the week, but they would have to wait for another bath time. Nick brushed past the stove, making the cups and glasses quiver slightly. He grabbed a bottle of water from the fridge, which contained three oranges, a six-pack of Budweiser, a container of half-eaten yogurt, four slices of shriveling pizza and a jar of natural peanut butter. Nick loved ice-cold peanut butter, by the spoon or knife – never on bread.

The news junkie's bedroom was just that – a room with a bed in it. Clothing, about half of it on hangars, draped from every hook and nail in the walls. Disaster is not a strong enough word to describe the state of the place where Nick most often slept. The only thing in the room that was in its place was a large framed poster, which covered the wall above the bed's headboard. It depicted a scene from the 1930s. The poster showed a slender man with a pencil-thin moustache leaning into an old-fashioned telephone booth. A fedora with a "PRESS" card in its band was pushed back on top of his head. The old-style newsman, with an unfiltered cigarette dangling from the corner of his grimacing lips, spoke into the telephone's receiver. "Hello, sweetheart. Gimme rewrite," was the quotation that ran across the bottom of the poster. It had been a gift from Nick's older sisters, Kathleen and Marilyn. They had been his inspiration for going to college, and they gave it to him when he graduated from journalism school. He loved the poster and would never part with it. To Nick, journalism was all about getting the story, getting it straight and telling readers the truth about the things that were most important to them. Telling the story was as vital to his profession in the 1930s as it was today and would be in the future.

Nick found the last pair of fresh boxer shorts in the top drawer of his dresser and headed for the shower. He had to hustle if he was going to catch up with Dave at the Hub by noon.

# Doc Simpson's face was maize and blue...

EARLY SATURDAY AFTERNOON

The warm aroma of hot, greasy French fries seeped through the doorway as Nick walked into the Hub, a little saloon and grill in the Johnson Street Business District on the East Side of Bay City. The University of Michigan football team smacked helmets with the Penn State Nitany Lions on the big screen television as old gridiron warriors from the city's high schools hoisted cold beer and whooped and hollered with every back-cracking hit in the game. Nick spotted his old friend in his favorite booth near the back of the bar, just to the side of the restrooms.

"Hi ya, Dave. You beat me here again. Hope you haven't been waiting too long." He slid onto the bench seat across from the veteran journalist.

"Just got here. This is my first beer. You going to join me?" Dave asked, wondering if his friend's health craze was going to carry over to the bar scene. He handed Nick a menu and adjusted the place mat in front of him.

"No, I've still got a lot of running around to do. Dave, I think I'm on a really good story. I think I'll stick with ice water for now. Say, did I tell you that I had a really good interview with Tanya and her mother?" Nick opened his menu and scanned the lunch items. He pushed the menu aside and recapped his visit to the Johnson home on Friday. His pal listened carefully without interrupting. When Nick had finished, the old newsman had two questions.

"So, what happened to the band teacher? I think we need to track him down. And I'd be happy to deliver a little back-alley justice to that son-of-a-bitch if the courts won't." Dave had two daughters of his own, and did not like the thought of someone taking advantage of young girls.

"Just calm down there, buddy. We'll get to him at some point. Maybe you can nose around about him a little. The Johnsons say they don't know much about him or what's become of him, and Mrs. Pepadowski didn't have many details, either. I'm supposed to interview Old Man Joselyn on Monday. I'll buzz it past him and see what he says. But what happened to the band director is a very good question, and what he's doing for a living these days has to be answered before we're all done with this. I'm going to be very pissed if he simply moved on to another school district and started work on another harem."

Dave edged forward in his seat. "The other thing I'm curious about is the medicine you mentioned," he said. "What was Johnson taking?"

Nick reached into the side pocket of his jacket and pulled out the two plastic containers that Tanya had given him the day before. "These. Here, take a look."

Dave studied the labels on the two bottles just as a waitress, a young woman the two friends had never seen in the Hub before, pulled up at their table.

"What can I get youse," she said, looking at both men and butchering the language in an all-too familiar Bay City way. "The special today is a brat and sauerkraut on a hoagie bun with fries – all for four bucks. Can I bring youse a couple? And if youse say 'Go Blue' to me, then youse get one free beer."

The friends politely declined the delicious but artery-clogging entree and decided to save the "Go Blue" salutation until later. They asked for chef salads with light Italian dressing instead.

"I have no idea what the pills in this bottle are supposed to cure," Dave said, holding the larger of the two containers up to a glimmer of light that danced through the bar from the front door. "But this one, the one that indicates it's for high blood pressure, is very odd. My doc has had me on three or four different kinds of blood pressure pills, and they don't look anything like what's inside this bottle."

Dave took the cap off the amber bottle and poured two pills out into the palm of his hand. "These are a different size, a different shape, and a different color from what I've been taking. Maybe that means nothing, but it sure seems funny to me. Want me to show them to my doc?"

"Why not? He can probably tell you right away what they are. When will you see him the next time?"

"He's sitting right over there with that group of people watching the football game. He went to Michigan. He lives and dies with the Wolverines. Personally, I think the guy has got maize and blue testicles, but don't tell him I said that. I'll go ask him during the next timeout."

"Judging by how geeked he is about the game, maybe you better wait until half-time."

It was true. Wayne Simpson was a medical doctor of considerable standing in the Bay City community. In normal situations, he was considered an influential member of the medical fraternity in town and a stand-up citizen. But this was not normal times. It was a glorious Saturday on a fall day in Michigan, and the Wolverines were waging war on the big screen. And Doc Simpson was doing what any good fan would do – making a fool of himself and not caring a lick about it.

The M.D. was standing next to a table in front of the tube with a pitcher of beer in his right hand. One side of his face was painted bright yellow, and the other dark blue. His hair was greased and spiked in the shape of a large "M." As the Wolverines recovered a fumble, the rabid fans at the table went wild, including the doc, who was graceful enough to hug two of his buddies without spilling a drop of the beer. And when it came time for a toast, he simply hoisted the pitcher to his eager, puckering lips and gulped down three large swallows that made his Adam's apple bob up and down.

The two journalists watched the chaos that erupted from the group and then their eyes shifted to the Hub's front door as Tanya walked in with one of her schoolmates. The two beauties picked up on the football action in the bar and walked over to the wild scene.

"That's her." Nick was ready to jump out of his seat, but managed to maintain his composure.

"That's who?"

"That's Tanya, the one I've been telling you about. She's the blonde. I have no clue who her friend is."

Dave buttoned the top of his shirt and pushed his hair back away from his forehead. Nick was sure his pal had never seen lovelies like these wandering the aisles of Wal-Mart. At the same time, Dave swiveled all the way around in his booth seat to check out the delightful and intriguing Tanya, the first woman he had seen since Joanne to make his friend go gaga. Dave smiled and nodded without saying a word and turned to face his buddy.

"Wow, you're right. She is a knockout."

Nick jumped to his feet. He had to at least say hello. It was, after all, the polite thing to do. Something any gentleman would do. He skipped across the room, gently bumping an empty table with a thigh on his way. Tanya had her back to Nick and did not see him approaching, but she instantly recognized his voice – even in the noisy bar.

"Hi, Tanya. I see that you go to all the best places."

"And I guess you do, too." She turned and greeted the big reporter with her glacier-melting smile. Tanya reached back and tugged on her friend's arm.

"Cynthia, I want you to meet a friend of mine. This is Nick Steele. He's a reporter at The *Blade*. Nick, this is one of my best friends, Cynthia Rowley. I mentioned her when we talked yesterday."

Nick stuck his hand out and gently gripped Cynthia's small, soft hand. She, too, was gorgeous. Long, dark hair and big piercing eyes the color of coal. Slightly shorter than Tanya, she wore slightly faded jeans, a dark, fall jacket hid her form; Nick guessed that her shape was as striking as her smile. It had to be hot. She was Tanya's friend.

"Hello, Cynthia. I'm pleased to meet you."

"Hi, Nick. Tanya's told me all about you."

Tanya quickly stepped closer and wedged herself between Nick and Cynthia. She had no intention of letting them get cozy.

"We just stopped in to check on the game," Tanya said, glancing over her shoulder at the big-screen. "Cynthia thought her old boyfriend might be here, but he must be downtown at Mulligan's Pub watching it. I guess that means we'll be on our way."

"You're welcome to join us." Nick raised his right arm and gestured with a sweeping motion to the booth in the back of the Hub where Dave was patiently waiting for an introduction. "Why don't you at least come on back for a minute? I've got someone I'd like you to meet, too."

"OK, sounds good. We'll join you in a moment."

Nick turned and headed back to rejoin his old friend. It was great seeing Tanya. Suddenly, the day got a whole lot brighter. He wondered what she was doing with the rest of her afternoon.

"Bingo. They're coming back in a few minutes." The big guy sat down in the booth across from his pal.

"Great. Should I get our waitress?"

"I don't think they're going to stay. Tanya's friend is looking for someone. We'll see. Here they come now." The two charming women found Nick and Dave. Introductions only took a moment. Dave was impressed with both ladies, but he studied Tanya, watching her interaction with his friend.

"Would you like to join us? We've got a couple of salads coming," Nick said as he slid sideways on his side of the booth, making room for one of the women to sit down beside him.

"We'd love to, but we've got to fly," Tanya said, looking first at Dave and then directly into Nick's eyes. "I'm going to run Cynthia down to Mulligan's, and then I've got a couple of errands to run for Mom."

"So, you're just going to be running around town later?" Nick said, as his eyes waded into Tanya's.

"Yes. I've got to pick up a few things. Why?"

"Well, I've never been to Joselyn Field House. I've driven by it a lot, but I've never really checked it out."

"It's Saturday. I don't know if anyone would be there or not. I suppose there could be. Want to run by later and see if it's open?"

"That would be great. What would you think of swinging by here and picking me up after you've run your errands?"

"That'll work. See you in about an hour or so," Tanya said as she turned and reached out to shake Dave's hand. "Nice meeting you, Dave. I'm sure I'll see you around."

"No doubt. Catch you later."

The two women turned and walked away from the men. Dave looked at Nick and punched him in the upper shoulder.

"You dog, you. You set up a date right in front of my eyes."

"Oh no, this isn't a date. She's just going to show me around the field house a little. It's probably closed today, anyway. It's just some more background info. Not a date."

"Yeah, right. You dog, you." Dave punched his pal in the arm again, and they both laughed.

The Wolverines scored just before half time, sending a shiver up the spines of their fans at the Hub. Dave and Nick finished their salads. Dave asked to see the pill bottles again. He wanted to connect with his doctor before the second half started and the sawbones got too toasted.

"I'll be right back. Let me just run this by Doc Simpson." Dave jumped up and made his way across the room to where his doctor was regaling his friends with old stories about when he was a young man scouring the streets of Ann Arbor.

"Hi, Doc. How you doin'? Looks like your Wolverines are doing pretty well today."

"Hello, Dave. Yes, we're kicking ass and I love it. I absolutely love it. I guess I didn't know you were a Wolverine fan."

"I'm not, really. Just in here having lunch with a friend. Could I bother you for another minute or two? I've got something I'd like to show you and get your opinion on."

"Sure, no problem. What's on your mind?"

"These." Dave pulled out the two medicine bottles and showed them to his doctor. He tried mightily not to stare at the man's painted face and ridiculous hairstyle. "Are you familiar with these medicines?"

Doc Simpson studied the labels and nodded.

"These were prescribed for Bob Johnson. How did you happen upon them?"

"That was Bob's daughter who was just in here. She gave them to my friend, Nick Steele. He's a reporter at The *Blade* and he's working on a story about her dad. What do you think? The pills for blood pressure don't look like the ones you prescribed for me. Am I crazy or what?"

"I can't say for sure, but just from what I see in this light, the pills inside the bottles are what's on the label. But unless I'm mistaken and too buzzed to focus, there's some kind of mix-up going on here. I would never prescribe this combination of pills to someone with a heart condition. Bring them by the office on Monday, and I'll take another look. And don't forget – Go Blue!"

"Thanks, Doc. I'll talk to you later." Dave grabbed the pill bottles and turned to rush back to his table. "Go Blue, and go easy, Doc. You're scaring me a little. It's a long second half."

Nick was eager to hear what his friend had to report, but he had an idea that it was going to be good based on the smile ripping across Dave's face.

"You're not going to believe this," Dave said. "Doc Simpson says there's some kind of mix-up going on because of the combination. He wants me to bring them by his office on Monday when he can focus a little better. And judging by what's going on with his friends in front of the tube, I'd say that's a definite understatement."

"No kidding. That's very wild," Nick said as he took the pills back and returned them to his jacket pockets. "What the hell does that mean? Either we've got some kind of very weird screw-up going on, or we've got something very freaky happening. I'll have to ask Tanya about it when I see her later."

The two newsmen sat silently at their table for several moments, thinking about what they had just learned and trying to make sense of it. Then the younger man broke the quiet.

"One more thing, Dave. Tanya's mom says she thinks Ellen Phelps, the mom of the girl who killed herself, is living with a relative in Kalamazoo. Do you think you could track her down? I'd love to chat with her about what happened and tell her that we're going to find the band director."

"Let me see what I can find out. I'll call you when I know more. In the meantime, have a great afternoon with Tanya. And don't do anything I wouldn't do."

As Dave bounded away from the table, Nick suddenly visualized his friend sleeping under his newsroom desk in the nude, his limbs wrapped around a sweetie from O'Hare's with an old Army blanket as the last defense against revolting indecency.

"Somehow, I just don't think that's anything you need to worry about," he said out loud, rising from the table to use the restroom. When he moved, the pills in his pocket rattled against the sides of their plastic containers. Before long, those pills would reveal what happened to Robert Johnson and open a door that had been closed for years.

# Hey, it's beer-thirty...

## SATURDAY AFTERNOON

Joselyn Field House was a spectacular sports facility by any high school standard in the state of Michigan. In fact, it rivaled the sports houses of many small colleges throughout the Midwest. The massive three-story structure was built into the side of a man-made hill. Visitors walked up a steep incline to enter the front of the building while its back looked out over the Central High School football field, which had permanent bleachers built on three sides, giving the field a big-stadium feel.

The Jos featured an Olympic-sized indoor swimming pool and a half-dozen diving platforms. It sported racquet and paddleball courts, a complete fitness center with state-of-the-art weight-lifting machines and aerobic equipment. The facility also housed a basket-ball gymnasium that could seat 2,000 people. Every aspect of the building was first-class, from the locker rooms to the Jacuzzis. No expense was spared. The Jos had cost $20 million to build.

Nick pulled open the building's front door and held it for Tanya, who had slowed to admire the front of the impressive red brick and limestone structure. She had not been inside the field house since graduating from high school. The visit would be a trip down memory lane for her.

"Tanya, come on. I can't wait here all day." Nick let the door close slightly as Tanya scooted to slide through the small opening.

"Hold on there, big boy. I haven't been here in awhile. What's the big rush?"

Tanya grabbed Nick's hand and tugged him inside the field house's massive entryway, which also served as a Central High

School Hall of Fame. Pictures of the school's top athletes adorned the walls all the way to the ceiling. A trophy case stood squarely in the middle of the main hallway. It was chock full of glistening hardware from the school's glory days as a football, baseball, basketball and track legend across the state.

Nick was impressed. He had graduated from a small country school in the Thumb of Michigan. He had been one of his school's top athletes, but he would have had a hard time making any of the teams at a Class AA school like Central. The level of competition was that good. It was fertile ground that college scouts from across the country tilled regularly.

"What a great place," Nick said as he walked alongside the trophy case, pausing every few feet to admire an award or league championship. "After all the years I've lived here, I can't believe I've never been in this place. This reminds me of college. I've never seen anything quite like this for a high school."

"Come on, Nick. I can't wait here all day," Tanya said in the same tone that Nick had just used. And then she flashed her magic smile. "Let's go. There's a lot to see."

The Jos rarely closed. Athletes from throughout the school district trained in the facility night and day, weekends and over the holidays. As Tanya and Nick worked their way through the big field house, they watched boys and girls of all ages working out.

But their tour ground to a halt when they walked into the cafeteria. The walls of the eating and meeting hall were painted white and trimmed with the school's colors: purple and gold, which, oddly enough, is easier on the eyes than the ears.

"Let me buy you a pop." Nick pulled out a chair at a small table near the entrance for Tanya. They had the place to themselves. Dozens of tables sat empty. A single attendant was available to wait on customers. "What would you like? A Coke, or a Vernor's?"

"Orange. I'd like an orange drink with extra ice," she said, sliding into her seat. As Nick walked up to the cafeteria's counter to place their order, Tanya put her left foot behind the leg of the chair next to her and pulled it closer to her seat. She watched Nick closely. She did not want him to see her tactical move.

But when Nick returned with their drinks, he foiled her attempt to get chummy by sitting in the chair across the table from her. "Here you go. An orange with extra ice. Oops, I forgot napkins. I'll be right back."

Tanya waited until Nick was nearly back to the counter before she hopped up from her chair and scooted sideways to her right to land in the seat next to where Nick's drink has been placed. This time, however, she didn't try tugging his chair over with her foot. She just reached over with her hand and yanked it a foot closer to her.

Nick returned with the napkins. "Hey, I could have sworn you were sitting in that chair a minute ago," he said, pointing at the now vacant seat with his chin.

"I was, but I felt a draft sitting there. Must be an air-conditioning vent or something nearby. Here, join me." She patted the chair next to her and gave him a big smile while checking his eyes for clues to his thoughts. He melted, and dropped into the chair beside her, right where she wanted him.

"Is this a date?" she asked while he sat down and scooted the chair up to the table.

"No, this is not a date. This is simply a friendly outing between you and me as I gather information. You're just showing me around. It's an informational get-together."

"*Hmmm*. A friendly outing? Informational? I've been on a lot of dates, and this sure feels like one to me."

"Tanya, this can't be a date," he said with a tinge of regret in his voice. "I'm working on a story involving your family. It would be unethical for me to become personally involved with you while I'm writing about you. That's a conflict for me. I hope you understand."

"I know. I'm teasing you. This orange is delicious. What did you get? They probably don't have any beer."

The remark caught Nick off-guard, but he wasn't completely

surprised by it. It was not the first time that Tanya made a reference to his drinking. Nick decided to push back at her a bit.

"Coke. I'm drinking a Coke. Are you trying to say something about my drinking? I haven't had a beer in, well, one whole day," he said, grinning.

"Well, in the short time I've known you, it's pretty obvious that you spend a lot of time drinking," she said, stirring her orange drink. "It makes me wonder what you're hiding from, or what you're trying to avoid."

Suddenly, the conversation became uncomfortable for Nick. He shifted the weight in his chair and looked down at the table where his hands were locked at the fingers. He boosted his shoulders up and back by leaning on his elbows. He cleared his throat and glanced at Tanya out of the corners of his eyes. He studied his mitts and started to talk, his voice almost a whisper.

"I'm not hiding," he said. "I'm trying to forget. Oh, it's a long story. You don't want to hear it. Nobody does."

"I've got time," she said, "tell me. Tell me what's eating at you."

Nick paused a moment to collect his thoughts, then cleared his throat and vented. "First I lost my dad, then I lost my girl and then my son walked away from me. When I'm alone, which has been a lot for quite some time, Jim Beam and Mr. Budweiser are my friends. Having a few drinks makes things a whole lot easier. Sometimes, it's the only way I can sleep."

Nick told Tanya about the Trifecta that had knocked him off his game.

Watching the demise of his father – Big Jim Steele was never the same after losing his hand at the Finger Factory – is what prompted Nick to get into journalism. It was a story of tragedy and injustice that had to be told – like so many others. Nick missed his dad. They used to hunt and fish together and played softball whenever they could. At one time, the father and son tandem played on the same team together, making a great shortstop and second base combination. But the shop accident changed all that, and Nick was convinced that it led to the early death of Big Jim.

"You know, my dad could not deal with being crippled," Nick said, still avoiding Tanya's eyes. His shoulders slumped forward. He continued talking to his hands. Tanya put her right hand on his left arm. "He used to make jokes about it when we were out in public. We'd go into a hardware and he'd tell the clerk: 'I got to hand it to you, you know what you're doing.' Then he'd laugh and slap the clerk on the back with his stub. The clerk would be nervous and fidgety and I felt like crawling under a display. I guess that was Dad's defense mechanism. But every time he did that, it made me want to throw up. I felt so bad for him, and he just kept going downhill. Finally, he got sick and died a slow death. Pneumonia was God's way of putting him out of his misery."

The end of Joanne came much quicker. Nick told Tanya about losing the love of his life. Joanne and Nick had been mates since high school. They went to the senior prom together and coaxed each other through college. There was never any doubt in Nick's mind when he proposed marriage. They were a match and planned a long life together. Before long, their son, Joe, was on his way. The newest Steele's entry into the world changed theirs forever. But a drunk driver T-boned Joanne's car one evening, and her life ended before rescuers could even break out the jaws-of-life.

"She was the sweetest person I ever knew," Nick said, his eyes welling with water. "Joanne did not deserve to die. One minute she was here, and the next she was gone. Joe and I cried for a week straight. We didn't eat, we didn't sleep, we just cried like babies. That's when we started drinking. We'd make ourselves numb and then pass out from alcohol and fatigue. Joe said he had to go – he couldn't take any more. So, I gave him a hug and he left. Headed out West."

Nick searched his back pockets for a handkerchief. His nose dribbled moisture like a garden hose with a kink in it. His eyes were red and his cheeks were wet. He tried to blink away blurred vision without making eye contact with Tanya. She patted him on the back. Her gentle touch soothed and cooled Nick's emotional volcano.

"Do you ever hear from Joe?" Tanya asked, handing Nick some tissue and noticing that the two of them had captured the attention of the nearby cafeteria worker, who was now dabbing at her own eyes.

"Once in a while we talk by phone," Nick said, trying to sniff up the excess wet stuff and his composure. "But it always ends up the same way. When his mom comes up in the conversation, we fall apart and we're right back to where we were on the day he left. I gotta say that those talks are not much fun."

"Maybe it's time you two got together to help each other," Tanya said. "You're still grieving. You're still hurting. Why not take a break and go out West and spend some time with your son? It might be good for both of you."

Nick did not respond. The two of them sat at the table in silence. The cafeteria worker walked up to their table and placed a small pack of tissues in front of Nick. Without saying a word, she scurried away as Nick allowed a muffled, "Thanks," to escape from his lips.

After a moment, Nick looked at Tanya and said: "Where's the background music? You'd think a place like a cafeteria would have a little background music going, wouldn't ya?"

Tanya smiled and patted Nick on the back. "You'd think so. They seem to have everything else here."

"Not on weekends, no music on Saturday and Sunday," the attendant said, her voice rose so Nick and Tanya could hear her from her perch behind the cash register.

Nick looked at his watch. "Hey, it's beer-thirty. Want to go get a cold one some place?"

"Not just yet, maybe in a bit," Tanya said. She did not want Nick to start drinking while his emotions were so raw. Instead, she tried to shift the conversation back to business.

"So, tell me. How's the story coming?"

Nick was grateful for the subject change. He told Tanya that the story was coming along fine. He picked up new information for it every day with some very interesting twists and turns.

"And there's some things that don't make sense," he said. "They simply don't add up and I'm trying to figure them out."

"Like what?" Tanya sipped her soft drink through a straw that she'd been using to swirl the ice around in her cup.

"Oh, well, like the pills you and your mom gave me. I was wondering if you put the pills in different containers, or combined them."

"No, that's exactly the way Dad kept them. We didn't change anything. Why?"

"Well, my buddy Dave takes blood-pressure medicine and he said the pills in those bottles don't look anything like his meds. Plus, he showed them to his doctor at the Hub – you stopped at his table earlier today. He was the wild man with his face painted and hair spiked into a block M. And the doc indicated that it might be the wrong combination of pills for someone with a heart problem."

"That guy with the painted face was a doctor? That wild man. Remind me not to get anywhere near his stirrups. He seemed like he was pretty wasted. Are you sure he even knows what day it is?"

"He told Dave to stop by his office on Monday so he could take a closer look at the pills."

"So what does that mean?"

"I'm not sure, but it may mean he was taking the wrong medicine."

"The wrong medicine? How could that be? Dad was very careful about making sure he took his medicine every day. There must be a mistake somewhere. Maybe his blood pressure medicine is just different than what Dave is taking, or maybe the doc was confused. But what else? What other twists and turns are there? You've got me interested now."

"Well, the Candace Phelps suicide and her affair with the band director, and the fact that the band director just up and disappeared. I'm really surprised that those things didn't cause a lot of outrage. It's very strange."

"It was all very hush-hush at the time," Tanya said. "Not many people knew about the romance, and only a handful of people found out she was pregnant. Sometimes people would just as soon see a scandal go away. As cities go, this is still a pretty small town. By the way, I talked with Sarah Evans on the phone today."

"And what did she have to say?"

"Well, I told her about you and what we were doing. At first, she wanted nothing to do with it. In fact, she hung up on me twice. But, about halfway through my third call, she started to give in. One more call ought to do it. I think I can talk her into it, but I know it's still a touchy subject for her – even after all these years."

"Great. Let me know and I'll make time in my schedule to see her."

"What's on your schedule?"

"I'm supposed to interview Charles Joselyn on Monday. I plan to ask him about a lot of things, including the Phelps suicide and the band director."

"Uh, I don't think he's going to want to go there. I hope you're ready for rejection. He will probably shut you down when you ask about those kinds of things." Tanya looked at Nick and sipped on her soda.

"Oh, well. I'm used to getting the cold shoulder on touchy subjects. All he can do is refuse to answer my questions. But that's not going to stop me from asking them. I'll start out the interview by lobbing him some softball questions, and then I'll build up to the more sensitive ones. I'll leave the fastballs until the end. We'll see where it goes."

With that, Nick stood up from his chair and tossed his empty drink container in the trash. Tanya followed him. They walked out of the Jos and into the cool evening air.

"You want to go get that beer?" Tanya turned and looked at Nick as they walked.

"No, I'm good," he said. "I'm actually a little tired. It was a big day. I think I'll go home and crash."

After their heart-to-heart conversation, each felt more comfortable with the other. A light, cool rain started to fall as they walked toward Nick's car in the parking lot. Tanya wanted to grab his hand, but resisted the urge. Perhaps another time. She wished he would finish the story. But Tanya had no way of knowing that when Nick finally put the last pieces of the puzzle together to write that story, it would turn her family's life upside down.

# Appleton started grooming Sarah in ninth grade...

SUNDAY MORNING

Tanya knew she took a big chance by knocking on Nick's apartment door on Sunday morning. She felt that she had already been too forward in trying to advance their relationship, but she had exciting news and she wanted to tell Nick. When Nick did not answer the door, Tanya pulled a piece of paper out of her purse and scribbled a note on it. "Sarah Evans is going to meet with us tonight. I'll go back to Ann Arbor later. Call me. Tanya."

Indeed, that was exciting news. And it was no small feat on Tanya's part to swing the woman over to their side for a discussion.

From their conversations, Tanya knew the last thing Sarah Evans wanted to do was come out from the shadows and tell her story. The engineering senior at Wayne State University in Detroit was doing her very best to forget that part of her past. She wanted nothing more than to push her two years in the Central High School Band deep into the recesses of her mind. Her time as one of the band director's pet students was that painful, that hurtful, that heart wrenching.

That's why she hung up the telephone on Tanya when her old high school classmate called and asked her to step forward and talk about those dark days. Recalling the two years in high school when a trusted mentor violated her was something she wanted no part of – especially when Tanya suggested that she tell her story to a journalist.

"The past is the past," she told Tanya during a second telephone call. "And I'm not going there for you or your reporter friend. I'm really shocked that you would even suggest it. I thought you were on my side."

"In this situation, I will always be on your side Sarah, no matter what," Tanya said as she paced back and forth across her bedroom. "But this is something that you need to talk about not just for your own well-being but for others, too."

"I've never told anyone," Sarah said. "It's not something I'm proud of. I simply want to forget it. I don't want to talk about it, or think about it. Please, Tanya, don't ask me to do this."

"What about the others? If he was involved with you and Candace, then you know there's got to be others. That's the way creeps like him operate. They prey on young women. Don't you care about the other girls he's done this to? You can help stop him from hurting other young girls."

"I don't care about anyone else. Talking about it makes me want to hurl. Every time it comes into my mind, my stomach gets all knotted up and I start to have panic attacks. Whenever I think about it, I feel like it's going to happen all over again."

Tanya did not change Sarah's mind during their second telephone discussion. And it didn't happen when Tanya called back a third time. But, finally, after several tearful conversations, Sarah gave in to her friend's pleadings and agreed to meet with Nick for an off-the-record, or not-for-publication, chat.

Nick agreed to the conditional interview because he wanted to hear a firsthand account of the band director's suspected misconduct. So far, everything he had learned had come through second or third parties. But he also wanted to learn as much as he could about the band director and how he operated from a victim's perspective.

If Nick wanted to use the information in a story at a later date, he could always re-establish the ground rules for a new interview and talk with Sarah again. Even with those conditions, the young woman was nervous when she met with Nick and Tanya at the

Johnson home.

Sarah, who grew up in a middle-class South End Bay City neighborhood, had two older brothers. Her mother worked as a hairdresser out of a friend's home. Sarah had few neighborhood friends. At school, her grades were fair. The other kids liked her, but she was not wildly popular. Her friends considered her cute, but not pretty. She was slender, of medium height for her age. As she matured, nature shaped her figure with considerable care and detail.

Her dad, who laid bricks and took seasonal construction work when household bills screamed for attention, enjoyed watching his sons grow up. He liked to hunt and fish. Northern Michigan was made for guys, he often said. He didn't pay much attention to Sarah, who always believed that her conception had been an accident.

The dark-eyed brunette was as skittish as a deer when Nick started their conversation. Nick, Tanya and Sarah sat around the table in the Johnson's kitchen. The lights were low. Tanya turned off the radio when they started talking. Nick began the interview by going back in time to when Sarah was in elementary school. The reporter started by asking her about her first years in school, her friends, her interests, her joys, her disappointments.

Finally, he asked her about her interest in music. Sarah said her mother had a beautiful singing voice and could play a little piano. The family, however, could not afford lessons for Sarah. All their money went into hunting and fishing gear. That meant that every bit of training Sarah was to pick up had to come from public school or church. She told Nick and Tanya that she started by singing in the church choir and taking the rudimentary musical training offered all students in elementary school.

Sarah said she loved learning how to create music. Her middle-school music teacher, Kim Crawford, was a skilled musician who was enthusiastic about sharing it with young people. He encouraged her to play the flute, a difficult but wonderful instrument with which to develop a love of music. She threw herself into band. It offered her a place to immerse herself in something rewarding and creative.

But high school music and the marching band posed different challenges. Central's parading musicians held the distinction of being Michigan's longest-running high school marching band. It was legendary across the state and its leaders were held in high esteem. When Sarah tried out for the band, it had begun a transition period with a new teacher who had new teaching methods.

Darrin Appleton had only been working at the school for a year when he met Sarah during her freshman year. Immediately, she was drawn to him. The band teacher was youthful and easy-going. He had a light beard and shaggy hair. He was tall and slender with a medium build. Unlike the other teachers, he wore jeans and a sports jacket with an open-collared shirt to class. The guitar he played in his rock band was always on display in the music department. To the students' delight, he often ripped a few hot riffs of his latest project before or after class.

But it also became apparent that he played favorites with his students. Sarah told Nick and Tanya she knew that he liked her right away. She could tell by the way he looked at her. He singled her out for praise during class and practice. He offered compliments about her skill and practice habits. He greeted her with a warm smile and encouraged her to experiment. His criticisms were offered in hushed tones so that others could not hear of her shortcomings. He made a point of speaking to her whenever the two crossed paths outside of class. He teased her playfully and encouraged her to talk with him about the things that were important to her in school and at home. She told him things about her life that she felt she could tell no other. She said her mother was too busy for her and her dad was disinterested.

"In those days, I was miserable at home," she said, getting up from the kitchen table to look out the window as she spoke. "Like a lot of kids, I looked forward to the day when I could move out and start my own life with my own family in my own home."

By the middle of her freshman year, Sarah told Nick and Tanya that Appleton offered to work with her on her technique after class.

Private, personal instruction. She felt honored and fortunate. She never missed the twice a week, hour-long sessions. They started out innocently enough. He would walk her through his selections of music that others at the school were not practicing. Some of it was difficult and required extra effort, extra attention, and lots of repetition.

By the beginning of her sophomore year, the touching began. Sarah told Nick and Tanya that Appleton would put his hands on her to adjust her posture or the way she held her instrument. His fingers were soft. His touch was gentle.

"I didn't mind at first," she said, getting up from the table to walk off her nervousness. She started pacing back and forth in the kitchen. "I knew getting the technique right was important. His adjustments would make me a better player."

Soon, though, she said his hands lingered after the adjustments were made. One hand would rest on her leg, the other on her shoulder. When he stood in front of her and lifted her elbows higher to elevate the flute, the outside of his fingers would brush against her breasts. Sarah said his touch made her tingle. It also made her nervous and uncomfortable.

As time went on, he would stand beside her as she played, putting his right hand in the middle of her back, gently pressing against her bra strap. One day, Sarah said he placed his hand there and pushed the garment back and forth, causing her breasts to shake lightly. She looked up at him and saw him peering down into her blouse, watching the gentle sway of flesh.

"It scared me," she said. "Him looking at me like that gave me a chill. I stopped playing and told him that he made me feel uncomfortable."

The session ended. And so did his lavish attention. After that day, Sarah said he did not smile at her, talk to her or call on her in class. He was cool and distant. Sarah said he treated her like everyone else. Suddenly, she was average again. Nothing special.

During the next week, he did not invite her to stay after class for the special instruction. She cried every day. His actions toward her now made her feel small and worthless. She longed for his attention, his praise, his warm smile, and his gentle touch.

Finally, after two weeks had passed, the band instructor asked Sarah if she would like to attend a practice session after school on Thursday. It was a Monday. She said yes before he finished asking the question. Sarah told Nick and Tanya that she could hardly wait for the day to arrive. She could think of nothing else during the daytime hours and even dreamed about it at night.

On Thursday morning, Sarah recalled primping in front of the mirror. She wore extra makeup and spent an unusually long time brushing her long dark hair. She wore a black, short skirt held together on the side by a large decorative safety pin. Her top was bright red. It was tight and cut low enough in the front to reveal the edges of her black bra.

When the band director saw Sarah in the hallway that morning, she said he smiled warmly and said hello. Later, at lunchtime, he waved at Sarah from across the cafeteria. During class, he offered her high praise and special attention. Sarah told Nick and Tanya that at that moment, she knew the day was going to be one of the best in her life.

After school, Sarah went to the band room like she'd done before the rejection. The band director was not there. She waited, pacing the room. Did he stand her up? Was he only pretending to care about her? Didn't he want her, or not? Where was he?

When he finally arrived, he marched into the band room and quickly gave Sarah a long, warm hug and said that he had missed her. He patted her back gently and squeezed the back of her upper arms. He let his hands drop and they brushed over her bottom lightly. He asked her to sit down and play a special selection for him. She did. She believed it was the best piece of music she had ever played. Sarah said she felt like she was airborne with the man of her dreams at her side.

Then, he put his hands on the middle of her back. She recalled how he slowly rocked her bra strap back and forth. This time she did not complain. She stopped playing and looked up. But he was not looking into her top as she expected. He was waiting for their eyes to lock. He used his right hand to hold the back of her head and he leaned down and kissed her. She melted into his arms. From that day forward, she readily fulfilled his every command. He owned her heart and body.

"I couldn't say no again," she said, her voice breaking. "I loved him. I wanted him, and he wanted me."

Sarah told Nick and Tanya that she heard rumors about the band director being involved with other girls, but she refused to believe them. Mr. Appleton told her he loved her and they would be together one day. No more hiding. No more whispers. No more hurried encounters in the confines of a dimly lit band room. No more acrobatic sex in an overstuffed chair in his office.

But all that changed when her lover disappeared and Candace Phelps ended her life – almost at the same time.

"He ruined my life," Sarah said, reaching into her purse and fumbling for a tissue. Tanya quickly offered her one from her pocket. "That son-of-a-bitch took advantage of me. I was 16. He hurt me. He made me feel like a piece of trash. I can never forgive him. When I think of him and what he did, I want to throw up. Look what he did to Candace. She's dead, she took her own life."

Sarah wept. Tanya put her arms around her friend. Nick sat quietly watching the two hold each other. No words could make her feel better, he thought. No actions would help her right now. But he did make one vow loud enough for both women to hear.

"Sarah, that's why we've got to go after this guy," he said. "I promise you I will do everything I possibly can to find justice for you, and for Candace."

Eventually, Nick would learn that the way the band director played his students set the stage for death to visit three life-long educators.

# Touch my story and I will carve your eyes out…

## MONDAY MORNING

The *Blade* newsroom buzzed with activity on Monday mornings. Reporters and editors hustled to pull news stories and photographs and graphics together from the weekend shifts. Almost always, they could count on writing follow-up articles to weekend entertainment events as well as sifting through two days' worth of heavy police blotter activity – everything from traffic crashes to robberies, assaults and the occasional politician who ended up in the hoosegow for drinking too much and then displaying further bad judgment by getting behind the wheel of a car.

In addition, the city was a freshwater resort town, so The *Blade* generated a lot of stories out of escapades on Saginaw Bay. Fishermen always seemed to be in trouble on the water in the summertime as well as the winter. Their shenanigans, combined with wild boozing and partying by boaters or snowmobilers, often ended up making dramatic and sometimes tragic stories.

That's the kind of piece The *Blade* needed to pull together on this Monday morning. Drayton Clapper cornered Nick as soon as the veteran reporter walked into the newsroom.

"Nick, we've got a hot one going," Clapper said, walking alongside Nick as the journalist moved toward his desk. "I need you to handle this one – are you ready to jump on it?"

"What about all your snot-nosed wonders? Why not give it to one of them?" Nick stopped in front of his desk and turned to face his boss. "Are you sure you want the Old Fart to take it? I'm still the same guy – the Old Geezer – I was last week when your young, smart-asses were whispering about me."

"Nick, they're just kids trying to find their way. Look, I need you to handle this story. You've got the background for it. It's really got a lot of good angles to it, but it's going to take some doing to get it done. We've already got some people making some calls and working it. Will you handle it for me?"

"Sure. What's happening?"

The story carried a familiar theme, but each dramatic element of it was as different as a sunset. Three old high school buddies had gone fishing for walleye on the bay in a 16-foot aluminum boat on Sunday, a regular pastime for hundreds of people who live in the region. In this case, the threesome knocked down some shots of tequila with beer chasers while pulling fish into their small boat all afternoon. But the booze, fresh air and the water got the best of them.

One of them stood up in the boat to relieve himself over the side of the small craft. He was talking, drinking and urinating all at the same time. But a large wake from a passing pleasure boat rolled the small vessel high in the air and tipped it sideways. All three of the fishermen went flying into the water. Two popped up like bobbers and clung to the boat, which had capsized. The third fisherman, the urinator, however, hit his head on the side of the boat as he went overboard. The blow knocked him out and he inhaled more water than his lungs could hold. He drowned while his friends frantically yelled for him to surface and join them on the side of the boat. When the marine patrol found his body early Monday morning, his pants were unzipped and unbuckled, pushed down around his knees.

Nick interviewed the cops while three other reporters gathered information from the marine patrol, the survivors and witnesses on shore, and the new widow of the fisherman.

The woman agonized over the loss of her man. He was 45 and she 42. They had three kids, and were hoping the Almighty would grant them a starting five for a high school basketball team. The eldest was a freshman at Bay City All Saints High School. The youngest was 12. The mom hadn't told them yet, and was waiting for another relative to come and help her break the news. They would be devastated. Their dad was a great guy. He doted on them every day. Their pop flipped pancakes in the morning and helped with homework and other school projects in the evening. They loved him dearly. Mom adored him, too. He was the only man in her life.

The reporter who interviewed her said it broke her heart to talk with the widow because she was in too much shock to cry. The young scribe had basic information, but nothing that resembled a good quote – the kind of thing that would turn a routine story into a really good one. Nick asked the reporter for the woman's telephone number so he could call her for a chat.

When Nick connected with the distraught mother on the phone, she'd had a little time to think after her earlier interview with a *Blade* reporter. She thanked Nick for taking the time to call her back to talk some more. Nick knew she was eager to spill. Talking about her hubby eased her pain. She praised him.

"He was my whole life," she told Nick on the phone. "I went to sleep in his arms every night and woke up holding him every morning. I don't know what I'll do without him. This will crush the boys. He was such a good man, a loving and devoted husband and father."

The raw emotion in her voice pushed tears into the corners of Nick's eyes. As he scribbled notes during their interview, he thought about how much these two people loved each other. It made him realize that his love for Joanne was one of a kind, but not unique. Many couples were in love, and sometimes their unions were broken by tragedy.

Nick tried to comfort the weeping woman, but he knew his words were hollow. Nothing could ease her pain right now. He did his best to be gentle with her. And that included not telling her that rescuers found her husband with his pants down. There was no reason to share that information with her or anyone else. Some parts of a story never get told. Some things are better left unsaid.

As the big, round deadline clock in the newsroom ticked minutes away to the morning's final deadline, Nick finished writing his story, his fingers slapping at his keyboard so furiously that it sounded like the firing of a machine gun with a silencer.

All that was left was a final read and some tweaking, or polishing. Clapper rushed up to Nick's desk, the first signs of deadline panic working their way across his face. A deep furrow with a light bead of sweat stretched the width of his shiny forehead. His eyes were narrowed and twitched slightly. His voice was one octave higher than normal.

"Nick, how you comin' with that? I really need it now. We're right on deadline. I want to give the copy editors enough time to do it justice and I want to make sure we get a good headline on it."

"Just another minute. I'm almost done," Nick said. "I've got one more thing to add. You'll have it shortly."

Clapper pleaded for the story. "Good. What's the length? Are we still looking at about 15 column inches like we talked about earlier?

"Right now, I'm at about 27 and I've got a couple more paragraphs to add."

"Shit. You should have told me. We may have to cut it."

"You can't cut it. It's great stuff. It will be the best read in the paper today."

Whenever Nick was bold enough to say that out loud in front of the other reporters in the newsroom, he was usually right, which meant that Clapper would have to look for extra space in the paper to get it all in. But there was always something that could be cut or held in order to get a good read in the paper.

"We've got another Monica Lewinsky story inside today," Clapper said, more as a note to himself than an alert to anyone else. "We can cut it way down if we need to. Monica is an old story these days."

"No, don't cut the Lewinsky story," Nick responded. "Everybody loves reading about Monica. Cut something else. You've got to have a political story inside somewhere. Cut that. Everybody is sick of reading about political maneuvering.

"OK, you've got it." Nick pushed the send button on his computer and grabbed his coffee cup to get a refill. "Say, Drayton, can I get about 10 or 15 minutes with you on something after deadline?"

"Sure, but about 10 minutes is all I've got this morning," Clapper said. "My meetings are really stacking up today. Is it important? Does it have to be today?"

"Yeah, it really should be today. I've got an interview this afternoon and I should talk to you before then. Ten minutes will probably do for today, then we can recap tomorrow after I've had the interview."

The editor nodded his agreement at Nick and then dashed off to look at Nick's story over the shoulder of a copy editor who already had the piece on her screen. She scrolled through it, tightening it slightly on her first read. She told Drayton it was a good solid piece of work – sound structure, lively writing with a compelling lead. Two more reads for fine-tuning would send it onto a page, most likely in time to make deadline. Another copy editor did a back read and came up with three possible headlines for the story. The local news editor would select the one he believed would fit the story best and work within the front-page design.

"Good piece, Nick," the main copy editor yelled across the room so that everyone could hear the praise. "I hung on every word."

"Arf, arf," he responded. "Not too bad for an old dog, huh?"

One of Clapper's kiss-ass assistants spoke up. "Hey, I heard the victim's pants were down and he was taking a leak. That's what caused the boat to tip over. Why isn't that in the story?"

"It's not in there because it would only embarrass the family," Nick responded. "The guy has a wife and kids and other relatives in town. That tidbit doesn't need to be in the piece."

"Oh, OK. But I thought we were in the business of telling the truth," the assistant editor said to Nick. "This is an important element of the story and I think it should be included. We don't have to give every detail, but it's the cause of the accident. I want to add it to the story."

"No, the cause of the accident was three drunk guys in a small boat and a wave from a wake tipped them over. And if you touch my story, I will carve your eyes out of your skull with my belt buckle. Do you understand?"

"Yup, but what about the truth, Nick? Aren't we supposed to be pursuing the truth at every turn in what we do here?" Assistant Suck Butt stood his ground, pushing Nick's buttons.

"The truth? You want the truth?" Nick turned to his desk, grabbed his car keys and tossed them at the assistant editor. The keys hit his chest and dropped to the top of his shoes. "Take my keys, drive to East Lansing and enroll in a philosophy class at M.S.U. And while you're at it, ask the Dalai Freakin' Lama if he can also explain the meaning of life to you.

"We're in the business of assembling facts," Nick said, his voice rising. "We select facts from a news event and put them together in a compelling enough way that they will hold the attention of our readers and then enlighten and inform them so that they can make sense of what has happened. The fact that the victim may have been urinating is interesting, but it is not important enough in the string of events to hurt this man's reputation or harm is family or friends. Why add to their grief? I repeat, don't even think about adding it to my story."

At this point, Clapper stepped into the heated discussion. "OK, for today's paper we go without the details about the guy taking a leak. We can look at it as a possibility for a follow-up story. But right now, we're right on deadline and this story has got to move. Let it go as-is."

The photographs with Nick's piece were telling and sharp. The *Blade* photographer was at the dock when the marine patrol pulled up with the soggy survivors on board. One of the men was crying, the other was too shocked to talk or walk. They were draped in blankets and escorted by rescue personnel. As the foursome straggled up the dock with the marine patrol boat in the background, the photographer snapped off a stream of photographs. One would be the dominant image on the front page that day.

Nick filled his coffee cup and then headed for the local news editor's office. He waited for his supervisor and looked for a clear space to sit down. Back copies of the newspaper were piled in every open area of the tiny office, which was just big enough for a desk, computer, a filing cabinet and two chairs. Journalism awards filled one whole wall of the office. Another was lined with framed front pages, heralding the paper's past glory. A large window looked out over an alley and the backside of a large ugly, brick building that housed doctors' and dentists' offices.

Clapper was a fair man and a decent journalist. Nick liked working for him, except that he thought the manager was too lax with the youngsters in the newsroom. The best part about Clapper, though, was that he was still mid-level management and not high enough up the food chain to be a suck-ass company man.

Big corporations owned newspapers all over the country, and the publishers and editors who ran the papers were generally cookie-cutter business operatives who wore expensive blue suits and carried small, black briefcases. The men and women at the top were usually more worried about staying in position for the next promotion than they were about getting a better story or putting out a better newspaper for the benefit of readers.

So far, Clapper hadn't caught the top-brass disease, and Nick hoped he never would.

"Hey, good story today, Nick. Thanks for taking it. It was a gripper," Clapper said, tapping his pen on his desk. He stopped and paused, then added: "I was so glad to see you clear-eyed this morning – more like your old self than I've seen in quite a while."

"I had a quiet weekend, and spent most of Sunday sleeping

and reading and walking," Nick said, leaning back in his chair and crossing his legs. "Are you suggesting that I've been spending too much time partying?"

"Yes, specifically, too much time drinking," Clapper said, raising his chin and meeting Nick eye-to-eye. "You were back on your game this morning out in that newsroom – the old Nick Steele. Hope your back and planning to stay awhile."

Nick laughed at what he thought was a backhanded compliment from his boss. Discussion of the weekend gave Nick the opening he needed to introduce Clapper to what he'd been working on the last few days.

"I worked most of the day Saturday on my own time developing what I think could be a pretty good story," he said. "This one could have legs. I'll know pretty soon."

Clapper sat up straight in his chair, refocusing on his reporter. "Oh yeah, what's up? The clock is ticking and you've only got nine minutes left."

"I just wanted to bring you up to speed on a story I've been nosing around. It's moving in different directions from what I started with, and I thought I better update you."

"OK, shoot. Which story are you talking about?"

"Last week, you gave me a news obituary to do on Bob Johnson, a local educator who was very well-known and respected around town." Nick shifted in his seat, and pulled a clip of the obit out of his notebook for Clapper. "Since then, I found out that he and another educator at Central, George Pepadowski, who died six years ago in the same manner as Johnson, had a major impact on students. It seems that they were literally the dynamic duo at Central for years. So, I've been interviewing some of the folks who knew them for a retrospective piece."

"Sounds good. When will that piece be done? Do you have a target date for it?"

"Well, that's the problem. The story's changed directions a couple of times, and there are some elements to it that are getting kind of scary. That's why I thought I should tell you what's happening, and see how you want to move ahead."

"The clock on you is running. You're down to about six minutes now. Spit it out. What snags have you hit? What's so scary?"

"Well, the coincidences for one thing. Don't you think it's kind of odd that two old friends, who lived in the same neighborhood and did everything together and had the same doctor, died from the same thing six years apart?"

"No, I don't think that's so odd. They both had high-stress jobs, they probably didn't take care of themselves and they reached that age where people kick off all the time. What's so odd about that?"

"Here's the kicker. I've only made some initial inquiries, but it looks like there could be a problem with Bob Johnson's medication. I showed a doctor Johnson's pill bottles, and he said it looked like a bad combination – not something he or other docs would prescribe. I'm supposed to check back with him on it today."

"*Hmmm*. Now, that is kind of interesting. Anything else?"

"Yes, we've learned that a student at the school, a senior who had just graduated, died in a suicide seven years ago. Now, I don't have this completely checked out yet, but she apparently took her own life after she had an affair with the school band director, who just up and disappeared at the end of the school year."

"You said, 'We.' Are you working on this with somebody?"

"Yes, Dave Balz is making a couple of calls on it for me. Just poking around a little."

"Not Balz! He's supposed to be retired. Why do you keep hanging around that old bag of wind?"

"Dave knows everybody in town, and he's a good newsman. He has great instincts. I trust him. And, he likes to drink beer. I thought I better tell you that's he's helping me a little, because he might send you a small free-lance bill."

"OK, just don't let it run up too high. We do have a budget, you know. Now, tell me more about the suicide and the student/teacher affair. Did we carry anything about that in our paper?"

"No, it looks like we passed on it – probably because it was a suicide. The whole thing was very hush, hush at the school. The parents of the girl didn't even find out about the affair until after the suicide. And, there's one more thing. I'm told that the girl was pregnant."

"Oh, no. You said the band director just up and disappeared?"

"That's right. I may be able to find out more about that during an interview I have this afternoon."

"Anybody know what became of lover boy?"

"No. We don't know where he is, or what he's doing these days."

"Who are you talking to this afternoon?"

"Charlie Joselyn, the…"

"Former school board president," Clapper said, finishing Nick's sentence for him. "I know Charlie. He's a grouchy old son of a bitch. How is he connected?"

"Johnson and Pepadowski worked directly for him, and he's the only one left alive who knows exactly what was going on at the school seven or eight years ago. I'm hoping he can fill in a lot of the blanks – especially in regard to the band director. I figure he had to be right in the middle of that whole thing."

"Well, good luck getting anything out of Charlie. He's never been too fond of The *Blade*. The only time he's ever really talked to us was when he wanted publicity for some pet project. But be real careful with him. Charlie is still very powerful in this town. He can pull a lot of strings. He knows how to make things happen."

"Like the field house?"

"Yes, like the Jos," Clapper said. "You've seen the clips on what it took to get that thing built?"

"I've seen some of them. And the Johnson and Pepadowski widows filled me in on how big a deal it was at the time."

"OK, your time is up. I'd say you're heading in the right direction on this. Keep asking questions and pursuing this from the retrospective angle that you originally started with. But let's find out more about the suicide and the band director."

"And the pills? The mixed-up medication?"

"Yes, go ahead with that, too. But that doesn't sound like much to me. Check it out, though. And keep me posted on where you are with this thing. Let's start meeting regularly on it."

"Ah, one more thing. I'm supposed to drop by Michael Davidson's office some time soon." Nick stood up from his chair and stuck his notebook in his jacket pocket. He wanted Clapper to know that he had connected with the prosecutor's office. "He wants to give me a preview of his case on that big trial coming up. I thought I might just bounce some of this stuff past him."

"All right, but be careful. I don't like getting too chummy with the law, too early. You don't have any of this confirmed. It's all pretty speculative, and we don't know where it's going yet, either. We don't know if any laws have been broken. So, don't tip your hand too much."

"OK, I'll talk to you later," Nick said, as he opened Clapper's office door and stepped out into the newsroom. He was glad to have that over with. Now, he could push ahead with the story. He had just enough time to grab a quick lunch before his interview with Charlie Joselyn.

Nick stopped by his desk, picked up his phone and punched in the number for Dave.

"What's up, Nick?"

"I just got out of Clapper's office. I updated him. I told him you're working with me, and he wants us to chase the story."

"You told him that I'm on it, too? Oh, I'll bet that went over in a big way. How much swearing did he do? How many times did he use the F-word?"

"None. I think he's cool with it. We just have to keep an eye on your freelance charges. So why don't you go see your doctor and see if you can find out more about the meds. I'll leave the pill bottles here in my top desk drawer. I've got to see old man Joselyn right after lunch. Maybe we can touch base tonight."

"Sounds good. I also want to see if I can locate the band director. Do you have a problem with that? That's really been nagging at me. Let's find him."

"No problem. See what you can find out. Talk to you later."

"Nick, one more thing. Are you ready for this, are you listening? I'm going to sing something for you."

"Huh? OK, fire away."

"Oh, I got a gal in Kalamazoo-zoo-zoo-zoo," the retired writer crooned through the phone.

"You know, Dave, you can really be a geek sometimes. You're the only guy around old enough – besides me – to know a tune from World War II. If I weren't a big-band fan, I wouldn't have a clue what you're warbling about. Ah, let me guess. Does that mean you contacted Ellen Phelps, or are you just being an asshole again?"

"Actually, Glen Miller and his band were way before my time, but I still love those old, big-band era songs. And yes, I contacted Ellen Phelps. She's willing to meet with us whenever we can get over to Kalamazoo-zoo-zoo-zoo. Now, saying Kalamazoo-zoo-zoo-zoo and not singing it in tune constitutes being a real asshole."

"OK, I got ya. Kalamazoo-zoo-zoo-zoo is a long way away, all the way on the other side of the state. Maybe we can run over there on Tuesday or Wednesday afternoon. Let's check our schedules."

"Nick, you have a schedule. Me, I'm retired. Schedules are a thing of my past. Let me know when you want to go."

Nick hung up the phone and grabbed his notebook. That was great news and excellent work by Dave. He headed out of the newsroom for some quiet time before his interview with Joselyn. A bowl of Mary's chili at the Green Door Restaurant would taste good and allow him to collect his thoughts before his chat with the former school board member. Nick always ate alone before big interviews. Thinking and eating calmed him down. And Nick wanted to be totally focused and ready for this interview. He knew it could make or break his story.

# Prescriptions were altered by computer ...

MONDAY AFTERNOON

Office lighting in the computer room flickered every few minutes. Shadows from file cabinets hung on the wall as the computer operator clicked the mouse that sprung the machine into action. As the Mac whirred and clicked to life, the operator opened a notebook spilling with information gathered from one of the city's libraries. Background on medications and their uses, including information on fatal combinations of drugs, filled the pages of the spiral binder.

The operator used the computer's mouse to move the cursor down the long list of customers and patients, slowing through the "Js." Jacobs, Jackson, James, Janer, Johnson, Jones, and finally, Joselyn. The cursor clicked on the file for Charles Joselyn, opening his record of ailments and prescriptions.

The old real estate and insurance tycoon had a lengthy medical history that went all the way back to his recovery from wounds he suffered in Vietnam. During his life, Joselyn had swallowed more pills than Elvis, Jimi Hendrix, and Janis Joplin combined. He'd had problems with high blood pressure, hypertension, an irregular heartbeat, severe constipation and gout, just to name a handful of maladies. These days, Doc Sheffield was trying to get Joselyn's blood pressure under control, ease his anxiety and relieve the severe pain that he experienced from arthritis, which was exacerbated from his war injuries and kept him confined to a wheelchair. Making matters worse, Joselyn continued drinking liquor and smoking cigars. He also abused laxatives in a fruitless effort to relieve severe constipation, a result of poor diet, a lack of exercise and the mountain of pills he was ingesting.

Previously, the operator had noted Joselyn's main medications: Tenormin to cut high blood pressure; Buspar to help with bad nerves and agitation; and Celebrex, an anti-inflammatory medication to relieve arthritis. The operator knew what was going to happen, having carefully studied the medications, their histories as they were developed by the drug companies, their potential side effects and how they interacted when mixed with other drugs.

The research was tedious, but it paid off. The operator was able to observe a shuffling of drug combinations into a deadly formula – a formula for murder – that worked well for George Pepadowski and Bob Johnson, and would now work well for Charlie Joselyn.

Pepadowski had been on Accupril for high blood pressure, Zoloft to ease depression and stress, and the former superintendent was using Demadex as a diuretic. But the killer substituted Cordarone for Accupril. The Cordarone, when interacting with Demadex, resulted in a severe potassium and magnesium deficiency, which, in the course of just a few weeks, brought on a massive heart attack.

Then, Johnson had been on Tenormin for high blood pressure and Elavil for depression. Tenormin was switched to Tambocor. Once the Tambocor mixed with Elavil, the interaction brought on an arrhythmia that resulted in a massive heart attack.

In both cases, no one knew that the drugs had been substituted. Pepadowski and Johnson both died of heart attacks. No autopsies were conducted on either of them because their deaths were not suspicious. Because of their ages, poor diets and lousy physical conditions, heart attacks were not out of the question. In fact, Doc Sheffield had warned each of them to change their lifestyles or run the risk of dire consequences.

In the killer's original plan to exterminate the three educators, substantial time would lapse between each death. Separating each death by time would help disguise the nature of their deaths and the resulting coincidences. The original plan had more time lapsing before the disposal of Joselyn, but the war veteran's deteriorating health forced a change in plans. To achieve full revenge, it simply would not do for Joselyn to die of natural causes. So, the plan to kill him in the same fashion as his cohorts continued. The drug Methotrexate was substituted for Buspar. When combined with Celebrex, Methotrexate would cause a gastrointestinal toxicity, which would result in a slow bleed-out. It would be accelerated by Joselyn's abuse of laxatives. In less than two weeks, Joselyn would die from internal bleeding. His demise would be slow and uneventful. The only thing his wife might notice is a slightly darkened discoloration of his stools.

At Charlie Joselyn's age and general condition, any physician who examined his dead body would conclude that Joselyn had died of natural causes. He would be buried and the victims of the three educators – the girls who were abused by the band director – would finally find justice. At least that was the twisted thinking of the killer.

The computer operator smiled while looking at the Joselyn file before clicking off and putting the computer back to sleep. Later that afternoon, the latest prescription for Charlie Joselyn would be ready to be picked up at the local Easy-Med, and that would start the clock ticking on the crusty old bastard's demise.

# Teachers have been diddling their students forever …

MONDAY AFTERNOON

It was precisely 1 p.m. when Nick rang the doorbell at the front entrance of the stately home where the Joselyns lived on Park Street, a ritzy subdivision with big, manicured lawns, thick hedges, and as many flower beds as a commercial green house. The neighborhood oozed with the smell of another kind of greenery – money. Some of that dough came from banking, some from construction, and a whole bunch found its roots in health care as well as the sales of new cars and trucks. The Joselyns' impressive four-story brick and limestone home stood as a testament to the old man's ability to sell real estate and insurance.

Doris Joselyn answered the front door herself, though hired housekeepers scampered about just at the edge of Nick's view inside the home. Doris was tiny, maybe stretching to 5-feet-tall in the highest of high heels. She was as slender as a straw. She wore a bright blue, knee-length silk dress. She did not try to hide the real color of her hair. It was shiny and gray and spun into a big beehive, resting neatly atop her head. Nick wondered what held it so firmly in place. The reporter averted his eyes instead of looking for pins or bolts or screws on the sides of her noggin. A big, warm smile spread across her face. "You must be the young man from The *Blade*. You're right on time. Please come in."

Nick liked her immediately. Anybody who called him a young man these days was cool. She also reminded him of a distant relative who gave him cookies and patted him on the head when he visited her as a boy. "Yes, I am. I'm Nick Steele. You must be Mrs. Joselyn. We spoke on the telephone."

"Oh, call me Doris. Everyone does. Calling me Mrs. Joselyn makes me think of Charlie's mother, and she's planted over in Pine Ridge Cemetery, and that's something I'm not quite ready for just yet."

A grin spread across Nick's face as he stepped into the home's entryway, which was larger than his whole apartment. The room stretched more than 40-feet high. A large chandelier with more sparkling baubles than a belly dancer's costume hung from the ceiling. Its light gave the room soft but full illumination. The floor was polished mahogany. The walls were lightly textured. A deep cherry wood trimmed the doorways and windows. A spiral, wooden staircase rose to second, third and fourth floor balconies. One opening to the right of the staircase led to the main living room of the home, and another brought visitors to the den, secured by huge mahogany doors. Doris walked toward the doors and called for Nick to follow.

"Charlie will meet you in here. He's up from his nap and will be right along." She stopped at the den's entrance and pushed a button on a small remote control that she carried in her left hand. The giant door swung open. They walked into the lair of Charlie Joselyn.

Nick was impressed. An oak work desk with an overstuffed leather chair sat squarely in the center of the room, ready for duty. This is where the master sat when he was present, Nick thought. Trophies, awards, and certificates adorned the main interior wall. Photographs of Charlie with four former Michigan governors dotted the display. Books and maple shelving accented another wall. An entertainment center and full bar swallowed up another wall, waiting for thirsty guests. A limestone fireplace on the exterior wall dominated the room. French doors led to a courtyard. A painting of a much-younger Charlie and Doris hung over the fireplace. Joyous smiles lit their faces and the den. It was the only time Nick would see a smile on Charlie's face all afternoon.

"Please, make yourself at home," Doris said. "Can I get you a drink? Something with a little bite to it?" She walked toward the bar, but Nick's words stopped her as he slid into a chair that sat directly across from the work desk. "No, thank you. It's way too early for me to get started. But I appreciate your kind hospitality."

"Well, how about a soft drink or some water? You're bound to get a little thirsty when you and Charlie get going. Once he starts talking about the school, you two could go on for a couple of hours or more. I hope you're ready for this."

"Water would be good, thank you."

As Doris opened a closet and reached inside its refrigerator, the whirring sound of a wheelchair grew louder as it rolled closer. It stopped outside the doorway of the den, and then roared into view. Nick jumped up from his chair and turned to face the wheelchair as its occupant hit the brakes and made it skid sideways.

"I've always been partial to the grand entrance," said the master of all that surrounded him. He looked up at the younger man and lifted his large right hand from the chair's control panel and pushed it up toward Nick. "I'm Charlie Joselyn. Glad to meet you."

"Hello, I'm Nick Steele. Pleased to meet you. I've heard so much about you that I'm finally glad we're getting a chance to talk."

Nick sank back into the big, comfy chair and watched a ritual that occurred every day. Charlie maneuvered the chair next to his grand leather seat behind the desk. The Vietnam War veteran locked the wheels on the chair and then hoisted himself up onto wobbly, spindly legs. Once standing, the former school board leader rotated his body gingerly until his rear-end squared up with the leather chair. He then put his hands on the arms of the chair and gently let his backside slap softly against the leather.

"There, that's got it. Bet you thought I'd have a hell of a time doing that," Charlie said as his gaze shifted from the top of his desk to Nick. "I'm wearing out, but there's still plenty I can do for myself right, Doris? The old bull can still get it done, right?"

"Right, Charlie," Doris said as she put two coasters on the small table next to Nick and placed ice-cold bottled water on top of one and a chilled glass on the other. "I'm glad you said get it DONE and not get it UP."

"Oh, thank you, Doris. I really appreciate you pointing out to this young buck that I'm firing blanks from an unloaded pistol these days."

"Aw, come on, Charlie. You're not firing anything these days. For crying out loud, you're almost 80. Nick's not stupid."

Nick was a bit surprised by the salty exchange between Doris and Charlie, but he suspected they'd had many lively discussions during their 54 years of marriage. It actually amused him.

"I'll let you two alone to talk," she said, smiling at Nick and nodding toward Charlie as she headed toward the door. "Buzz me if you need me."

"That's right, Doris. You always have to get the last word in, don't you?" Charlie fidgeted in his chair and watched her make her way out."

"That's right, Charlie. You're right once again. See you two later."

"That woman is going to drive me crazy." Charlie looked over at Nick and reached for his hot tea, which steamed from a cup in a saucer at the corner of his desk. "Now, tell me again why you're here."

"I'm a reporter with The *Blade* and I'm working on a story about the legacies of Bob Johnson, whom I'm sure you know passed away last week, and George Pepadowski," Nick said as he pulled his notebook out of his sports jacket. "I requested an interview because the three of you worked so closely together in your last years at the school. I thought you could add perspective to the story that no one else could. That's why I'm here."

"Well, first off, let me say this," Charlie leaned back in his chair and cleared his throat, which resulted in a bark of half-choking, half-gagging sound that echoed across the den. "I will consent to an interview as long as your intention is to do a positive story about the school. I worked most of my adult life, and so did George and Bob, to build that school up and I won't have you or anyone else throw dirt on it. So, if it's muck that you're here to rake, then stuff it up your ass and take a hike.

"I've never trusted reporters," he continued. "You bastards are all alike and I'm sick of it, to tell you the truth."

"First off, Mr. Joselyn, I am not a bastard in any sense of the word and I am not like other reporters in any way," Nick said, trying his hardest not to raise his voice. "I'm an experienced, skilled professional who expects to be treated with respect and dignity. If you cannot muster a thimble of decency and civility, then this meeting is not going to go well, or go for very long.

"Like I said a moment ago, I'm here to talk with you about the considerable contributions that Bob and George made to Central High School and the school district. I expect this interview to cover their years at Central and most of the important events that occurred while the three of you were there."

"OK, before we get going, I've got to ask you a question," Charlie said as he looked squarely into Nick's eyes. "How old are you anyway?"

"I don't see the relevance of your question, but I'm around 50, if you must know," Nick said, shifting in his chair to look directly into Charlie's eyes.

"Fifties. *Hmmm*," Charlie rolled his eyes. "Why, I've got boxer shorts older than you."

Nick laughed and wondered to himself how long it would be before Charlie changed them and put on a new pair. He pushed that thought aside and turned up the charm. He knew it was important to get through this interview. "You're right, I'm just a kid, and I should be thankful anytime someone notes that. Central is full of rich history and you've been right in the thick of it with Bob and

George. You three have been through it all at the school. I know you can help me really pull this together."

"All right, then. Shoot. What do you want to ask me?"

"Let's start by going back in time. You grew up on this side of town and went to Central High School as a young man, didn't you?" Nick asked the question, knowing it was like dangling a worm in front of a hungry catfish.

That's all it took, and Charlie jumped on the hook and took off with it. Nick used all the skill of an experienced angler while trying to reel in information from the aging former school board president, and Charlie chomped on the bait, answering each question with rich detail and self-promotion. Nick took notes furiously, peppering the conversation with enough questions to keep Charlie moving through his whole personal history – Vietnam, his work as a real estate and insurance executive, his interest and devotion to the school and, ultimately, his relationship with Bob Johnson and George Pepadowski.

After more than three hours of steady chatter between the two, Doris poked her head into the den to check on them. "I could hear you two way down the hall. I guess that means everything is going well?"

Charlie looked away from the reporter and directed his voice toward the doorway. "Splendid, dear, just splendid."

"Do you need anything?

"No, we're fine. And, if we do, this big guy here can hop up and get it," Charlie said, his heavily jowled chin swaying in the direction of Nick.

"Well, I'm going to run a few errands, then. I've got to run by the pharmacy. They called and said your new prescription is ready. I'll pick it up. Anything else you need while I'm out?"

"If you're going to the pharmacy on Center, then pick me up a bottle of scotch. If not, we can pick it up later."

"That's where I'm going. I'll get it for you." Doris disappeared behind the mahogany doors.

Nick jotted down a note and circled it twice: "Doris and Charlie use the pharmacy on Center, the one where Tanya ran into Gus Phelps."

"Where were we?" Charlie asked, swinging his attention back to Nick.

"You were talking about how important it was to get the new field house built. You said you decided to make it your life's mission. Did you ever think that if getting it built was so difficult, maybe it wasn't meant to be?"

"What the hell kind of question is that? Of course it was meant to be. I decided it was. It was the only way we could turn around the fortunes of the whole school district. I knew it would work, but I had to sell it to every son-of-a-bitch in town. I worked night and day and weekends and holidays, twisting arms, kissing ass, threatening, pushing, pulling – anything it took to get it done. And then, after I did that, I went around and did it again.

"I literally begged for money," he continued. "We had to raise $4 million in cash, and then the matching grants and donations from foundations and the government would kick in. Bob and George helped. We worked on it all the time, and we finally got every last dime of it raised. That was one of the hardest things I ever did. Raising money in Bay City is as tough as fighting the damn Viet Cong."

"Didn't you run into problems? Were there any obstacles that popped up during the fund-raising campaign?"

"Oh, sure. It's a big goddamned school district. There are always problems, but we handled everything that came along."

"There's one thing that I've heard about that must have been very difficult to deal with."

"What's that?"

"The suicide of Candace Phelps. When a young woman takes her life, it's always difficult for the whole school. How did you handle that?"

"Oh, yes. That was tough, but suicide, as ugly as it is, is part of life. You have to deal with it and move on. We handled it just like we handled everything else."

"But her involvement with the band director must have made it extremely difficult. The other students. The parents. The other families. The media. Weren't there a lot of questions?"

"No, there weren't. We didn't let out all the details. We kept a lid on it as best as we could. Nobody really knew about the band director at first, that came out later. But we're getting off track here. Let's not talk about her. It's too depressing and doesn't really have anything to do with the school district and the construction of our field house."

"Well, I'm simply curious about it because some aspects of it don't make sense."

"What doesn't make sense?"

"There's a series of events that don't add up, and it must have been disruptive at the time. A young girl has a hush-hush affair with her band director, and then one day the band director up and disappears at the end of the school year, and then the girl kills herself."

"What's so difficult to understand about that? Teachers have been diddling their students – both boys and girls – since the beginning of time. Ever hear of Socrates and what went on in the ancient schools? Go look it up. It's part of history. It happened to us and it will probably happen again at some time in the future. It's human nature. You can't stop people from screwing."

"But don't you feel you have an obligation to protect your students from someone who would prey on them?"

"What? Why, you smart-ass. I had an obligation to look out for the interests of all our students and the school district as a whole. That meant making sure that our project stayed on track. I wasn't going to let a few young girls, tramps, really, wreck the fund-raising campaign."

"Tramps? A few young girls? You mean there were others besides Candace Phelps?"

"Now, wait a minute. Why are you asking me these things? We're getting off track again."

"There are a lot of loose ends here. This doesn't make sense. How many girls were involved with the band director?"

"Well, you've got the loose ends part of it right. Four girls all together had loose ends. They were knocking each other over to get extra attention and direction from that son-of-a-bitch band director. It all went to hell when those girls found out that he was banging each of them. The little bitches got jealous of one another. It looked like the whole thing was going to blow. I wasn't going to let some young tarts that can't keep their knees together get in the way of our fund-raising campaign. Can you imagine the scandal? So, we just called the prick into the office and told him we knew what he was up to and that he would have to leave the school district."

"You confronted him? Did he admit being involved sexually with the girls?"

"No, he didn't admit it. But he didn't really deny it, either. He just sat there with a big-assed, smug grin on his face."

"Why didn't you call the police when you found out he had become intimate with young girls at one of your schools?"

"So what? Why, this wasn't rape. The girls were all 16 or older. They were of age, and they were throwing themselves all over him. They begged to be banged. It was disgusting, and I wanted to be done with it. We thought it was best that he just go."

"We? Does that mean that George and Bob knew all about it?"

"Of course they did. It was their school. They'd heard whispers about the band director and his favorite students. But it was all just talk. He was too smart to ever get caught with one of the little snippets sitting on his face. They warned him about the whispers – several times."

"And did they go along with not calling the police?"

"They did what I told them to. We had too much at stake to get the police involved and let it get messy. I told them we had to get rid of the son-of-a-bitch, and get rid of him in a hurry."

"How did you fire him, then? Was there some kind of agreement made?"

"Bob and George got him cornered in a room and told him he would not be brought back in the fall. They told him he had to go, and we wouldn't make a stink about it if he went quietly and quickly."

"What about a job reference? What kind of job reference did you tell him you would give him?"

"We had a policy that we didn't give out any job references on any former employees. At the time, if you hurt someone's opportunity to gain future employment, they could sue you. Ask any lawyer who handles employment or personnel issues. Like everyone who's ever worked at the school district, we don't give a recommendation for or against. We simply tell the caller that the employee worked for us during a certain time period, and we do it without further comment."

"That means your band director walked away from here after taking advantage of four high school girls and didn't end up with a blemish of any kind on his record. I can't believe it. How could you let that happen?"

"By the time I found out about it, the damage had already been done. He was already screwing four of our girls and I wanted to get him out of here before he got his hands on any more. That was the cleanest way to handle it."

"But then one of his victims became distraught after he left and killed herself."

"No one saw that coming. She lost her head and went over the deep end. Really, there was no way of stopping it from happening. Once she became distraught, she got crazy."

"Do you think that being pregnant had anything to do with it? The man she loved, trusted, believed in and gave herself to decides to simply disappear one day. Do you think that could have pushed her over the edge?"

"Nobody knew she was going to pop a kid. As far as we knew, she was one of four young floozies who got carried away with one of her teachers. Sure, it was a tragedy, but those kinds of things happen all the time. Dying is part of living."

"But what about your responsibility to protect her? What about the responsibilities of her superintendent and principal to protect her? Who was looking out for her and her baby?"

"Now wait just a goddamned minute. How dare you talk to me in that tone? We had 10,000 students to look out for, and we did the best we could in a very tough situation. Don't you come into my home and lecture me about what's best for students. I did what was best for our students, and that was to get that field house built on time and within cost. And we did it. I couldn't have stopped what happened. I had to deal with it. Now, this interview is over. Please leave. And if you print any of this, I'll sue your ass."

Nick got up from his chair and headed for the door. He stopped suddenly and turned back toward Charlie. "But what about the Phelps family? What did you tell Gus Phelps and his wife?"

"I said that this interview is over." The old man was now barking at Nick.

"I'm leaving, OK? I simply cannot believe that you could look Mr. Phelps in the eye after you allowed the band director to leave town without being held accountable for what he did with those girls."

"I told him I was sorry about his daughter." Charlie's voice settled to a low roar. "I told him I wished we could have helped her. We didn't find out until later that she was pregnant." Charlie looked down at the polished floor, and swiveled his leather chair away from Nick, pointing it out toward the courtyard. "Now, please go."

Nick reached the large mahogany door and turned back toward Charlie, as the elder man slumped down into his chair. The top of his head was now barely visible above its back. "I'll be back in touch with you. I know I will have more questions for you about what happened."

Charlie didn't want any more questions. He didn't want to think about what happened. He simply wanted it all to go away. And he wanted Doris to hurry up and return home with his medication and the bottle of scotch. But the pills that were headed for the Joselyn home were much more than Charlie or Doris had bargained for. By the time those pills were all consumed, Charlie would be gone, too.

# I think your plan sucks and you're dip-shits ...

Nick tried to sort through his story while driving back to the newsroom. His instincts told him he was on the verge of pulling together a great piece. The Charlie Joselyn interview, which the aging school board president probably now regretted granting, guaranteed it. Joselyn revealed far more about the Phelps tragedy, the band director, and the school district's involvement than had been previously known. But the story still had plenty of loose ends and Nick had to figure out how to pull all the fragmented pieces of it together.

As Nick rolled into The *Blade*, he noticed two reporters and three advertising salesmen standing in the front of the men's room talking in muffled tones and shaking their heads. It seemed odd. Nick stopped and asked what was up. One ad rep responded by pointing at the door of the restroom and saying two words: "The Castrator."

Throwing caution to the wind, Nick marched into the lavatory – a place, until that moment, he'd always considered a safe haven for men. He looked high and low and side to side, fully expecting to see the publisher standing on the cool ceramic floor in the middle of the room with her hands on her hips, trying to figure out if she could use one of the urinals while standing up. Nick even peeked into the first two stalls, but the overbearing she-man was nowhere in sight.

Then he spotted the note taped to the room's single mirror. He read it quickly and understood why his co-workers were left muttering in the hallway.

"MEMO TO ALL EMPLOYEES: It's come to my attention that our usage of hand towels and toilet tissue is up 30 percent from this same time period a year ago. This is an additional and wasteful expense that cannot be tolerated. U.S. Department of Health standards indicate that one paper hand towel and two pieces of tissue paper are an appropriate amount of supplies to be used by each employee during each visit to the restroom. If you must use more than that, bring the items from home or go to the Personnel Department and sign a request form for additional supplies. And remember, this lavatory is not equipped with cameras, but I've always got my eye on you. Thanks you for your cooperation on this important cost savings measure. The Publisher."

Nick laughed, launching an echo that could be heard out in the hallway. As he walked past his co-workers still standing outside the men's room door, they stopped him to reveal their planned response to The Castrator's note.

"Nick, we're thinking of Tee-Peeing the whole building inside and out in protest of the bitch's latest outrage," said one of the ad men. "We also think we should clog all the toilets in the building with hand towels to show her how upset we are at her edict. What do you think? Are you with us Nick?"

Nick looked at each of the young men standing in the hallway. They each chuckled and high-fived one another, believing that they'd just hatched a grand plan that would convince the publisher that she was an idiot and persuade her to reverse her cost-saving order.

"I think you're all a bunch of fools and nitwits," Nick said, looking each of guys up and down like a rancher sizing up livestock. "What the hell good would your plan do? What does Tee-Peeing and clogging the toilets accomplish besides wasting more supplies?

"I think you should just be thankful that the publisher is still trying to cut costs and not cut your job, or cut your pay, or cut your benefits or cut your pension. Believe me, those cuts are coming and they will be painful for every one of us still lucky enough to have a job doing what we love. Why hasten the decline? Doomsday will be here soon enough. And just remember, every one of us can be replaced by a graduating college kid – someone who will work harder, know more about technology, and work like a demon for less money and benefits.

"So, I think your plan sucks and you're dip-shits. And don't call The Castrator a bitch. She's someone's daughter and doesn't deserve that. Stop wasting my time. I'm working on a great story. Don't bother me with your childish B.S."

When Nick popped back into the newsroom, he found a note on top of his desk. It urged him to call "Dave Balz as soon as you can." Nick pushed the note up near his phone and looked around the newsroom to see if he could see Drayton Clapper. The writer spotted him talking with another reporter at the other end of the newsroom. Nick waved his arms at Clapper while standing up at his desk. When he got his boss' attention, he mouthed: "I need you." Clapper indicated that he would be right along.

Nick picked up his phone and punched in the number for Dave. It took only two rings for the veteran reporter to respond.

"Dave, this is Nick. What's up?"

"I just left my doctor's office and he says the medicine in the pill bottles is what it is supposed to be, but he thinks the combination of the pills is wrong. In fact, he thinks that combination could be lethal. We've got to get them checked out."

"Hmm. I'll add that to my list to talk with Clapper about. I've got two questions for you, pal."

"Go for it. What's on your mind?"

"Look at the pill bottle and tell me which pharmacy it came from."

"Just a second. Let's see." Dave squinted at the bottle and struggled to read the fading print. "The Easy-Med on Center Avenue."

"I knew it," Nick said, instantly visualizing Gus Phelps working at the computer of the pharmacy. He jotted the fact down in his notebook.

"What's your other question?"

"Was your doctor's face still painted maize and blue this morning, and how badly was he hung over?"

Dave's chuckle rumbled up from his belly. "As a matter of fact, I think I did see a touch of blue behind one ear, and his coloring was more like the Spartans – green and white."

"Hey, I had a really good interview with Chuck Joselyn," Nick said. "He told me all about the Candace Phelps suicide and the band director. Sounds like they tried to keep the whole thing hush-hush while money was raised for the field house. Donations would have dried up if a big scandal erupted at the school. He says they told the band director to just leave town, though he was apparently having affairs with at least four girls. Can you believe it?"

"I think that means we've got to track down that band director," Dave said.

"I think that would be excellent," Nick said. "We've also got to run over to Kalamazoo to see Ellen Phelps. I'll see if Drayton will let me go tomorrow. I don't want to wait until Wednesday. Does Tuesday afternoon work for you?"

"How would you feel about interviewing Ellen by telephone and saving us a ton of grief, not to mention hours of driving?

"I would really prefer to do the first interview in person. It's way too easy to just hang up the phone if the questions get sticky. Besides, I think it's important to see the face and the body language during an interview on a difficult subject. Talking with a mom about her daughter's suicide and pregnancy, I think I want to be in that room easing her through it."

"OK, just thought I'd ask. Hope the Clap lets you go."

"I'm going to call Mrs. Pepadowski this afternoon to see if the Easy-Med was her family's drugstore, too. I'm betting that's the connection between the deaths and the families. All three families live near that place. I'll let you know what I find out."

"See ya, man."

Nick hung up the phone as his boss strolled up to his desk. "We're on to something pretty big here, Drayton. I interviewed Charlie Joselyn today and he confirmed that they pushed a band director out of the school district seven years ago when they found out he had sex with four teens at Central. One of those girls was so distraught over his disappearance that she committed suicide. She also happened to be pregnant."

"No kidding. But what does it have to do with the piece you were doing on George Pepadowski and Bob Johnson?"

"Joselyn says they both knew about the band director and the affairs. And now here's what we have to find out: Is that, in any way, connected to their deaths?"

"But that doesn't mean anything. You said they both had health problems. What connects them besides the fact that they used to work together?"

"I'm not sure yet, but I've got an idea. I need to make one more phone call and then I'll tell you what I'm thinking."

"OK, you know where to find me."

"One more thing, Drayton. I need to go to Kalamazoo tomorrow right after morning deadline. I've got to interview someone who can help us fill in the blanks on this story. Is that OK? I'll drive over, do the interview and come right back so that I'm in the newsroom Wednesday morning."

"Yes, but you're really starting to drag this thing out. You're spending a lot of time on this story. When am I going to see some copy? When am I going to get something I can print."

"Soon, soon. Trust me."

"My patience is starting to wear a little thin. I can't justify all your time on this. The paper just doesn't fill itself up with stories every day. That's why we have you around here. Let's pull this thing together.

"And another thing, Nick, put a tie on. I've warned you and warned you. You've got to wear a necktie."

Nick grabbed the phone book and looked up the Pepadowski number. He poked the number into his phone and hoped Mrs. Pepadowski would answer. Instead, he got her recording. He left his number and a short message: "Mrs. Pepadowski, this is Nick Steele. I've got another question about your late husband. Did you happen to keep any of the medicines he was using when he passed away? Please call me when you have a minute."

Nick hung up his phone and sank into his seat in one motion. Clapper was starting to put the pressure on for a story, starting to turn the screws. For the first time, he fretted about how this piece would turn out. The clock was ticking in more ways than one, and he had to make something happen.

# Candace kept a diary, and wrote about being pregnant ...

## TUESDAY MORNING

Kalamazoo is one of Michigan's great cities. With a diverse county population in 1998 of a quarter million people, it is home to Western Michigan University and a gigantic pharmaceutical industry that dates back to the early 1900s. It's also close to the fabulous beaches and the fresh water of Lake Michigan. Plus, it's just a few hours away from Chicago.

Nick loved visiting Kalamazoo whenever he could. It was a college town with lots of great restaurants and bars, trendy shops and beautiful neighborhoods. The western side of Michigan is also home to a significant number of Norwegians, Swedes and Finns, which results in the region earning a reputation for gorgeous blonde women. Mix in the facts that fall colors in Michigan were out in full display and that Nick was traveling with his friend, and the formula was set for a wonderful day.

The nearly four-hour drive across the state gave the two buddies plenty of time to talk. They solved world issues, kicked around the ups and downs of the stock market, comforted each other over another dismal season by the Detroit Lions, and talked about women. Nick yakked extensively about Tanya and her many attributes. And Dave mused about his latest Wal-Mart special, a former biker chick who now worked at Sage Public Library part-time and taught yoga on the weekends. She also enjoyed competitive beer drinking and musical farting. Clearly, she was Dave's kind of girl.

But more than anything, the lengthy trip gave them an opportunity to talk about the story and its varied aspects. Nick spilled out his theory to Dave. Someone at the Easy-Med Pharmacy, most likely Gus Phelps, poisoned Bob Johnson and George Pepadowski. No question, the handyman had the motive to do it. What Nick didn't know, yet, was how the men were poisoned. The two reporters hoped the interview with Ellen Phelps would reveal more information about her estranged husband, who she had not divorced after all these years, and the romance between the band director and her daughter.

Dave told Nick he connected with Mrs. Phelps after contacting former co-workers at her last place of employment. Her work associates had become close friends. They loved Ellen Phelps and tried to comfort her after the death of her daughter. But she did not rebound after the suicide and took an extended leave of absence from her company. After about a year, Ellen left the area for Kalamazoo without any fanfare, but she did leave her sister's telephone number with two close friends who were happy to share it with Dave.

"She was surprised by my call," Dave said, as the two pulled into the Kalamazoo city limits. "She clammed right up, but then relaxed and opened up a bit when I told her that we were trying to track down Darrin Appleton and that we knew he had hurt several girls at Central High School, including Candace."

Ellen told Dave that she did not want to be quoted in any stories about what happened years ago, but she would try to help the reporters. The idea that Appleton left Bay City without paying a price for his outrageous behavior still made her angry.

When the two reporters turned into Ellen's sister's driveway, they saw Mrs. Phelps waiting at the door. Tall and slender with light, shoulder-length hair, she bore a striking resemblance to Candace. Nick sensed that it was going to be a good interview.

Mrs. Phelps was at home alone in her sister's house. She greeted the reporters, offered them coffee, and took them through the house to a back-yard patio where they sat down in deck chairs around a large oval table under the bright yellow and gold cloak of an oak tree. It was a breezy fall day, but bright sunshine pushed off the day's chill to allow the foursome to sit outside comfortably.

Nick started the interview. He began by telling the woman that he and Dave were working on a story about the legacy of Bob Johnson and George Pepadowski at Central High School when they learned of her daughter's tragic death and the band director's escapades. He told her they were trying to find the band director.

"Did you or your husband ever learn what became of Darrin Appleton?" Nick said, as he took a sip of coffee from a large steaming mug.

"First, let me say that this whole subject is still very difficult for me to talk about," Mrs. Phelps said, looking at Nick and then turning slightly to face Dave. "I'm only agreeing to meet with you because I believe a terrible injustice happened and it upsets me to this day to even think about it.

"Darrin Appleton took advantage of my daughter, caused her to take her own life, destroyed our family and then disappeared. No, we never found out what became of him. Believe me, we tried. But, everywhere we looked, we hit dead ends."

"If you don't mind, let's start at the beginning, Mrs. Phelps," Nick said, leaning ahead in his chair and scooting it closer to her. "When did you and your husband become aware that the relationship between your daughter and her teacher had become inappropriate?"

"We didn't realize that she was having an affair with him until she took her life," Mrs. Phelps said, looking away from Nick's eyes and focusing on her hands as they fidgeted in her lap. "We knew that she had taken a liking to Appleton. Candace told us that they had developed a special bond, that he was unlike any teacher she had ever had. I thought it was merely a schoolgirl's crush. We had no idea it had become intimate, that it had become physical."

"How did you find out about it?" Nick asked.

"The suicide note she left was our first real clue, then I found her diary," Mrs. Phelps responded. "The diary tipped us off that she was pregnant. Later I found one of those home pregnancy test kits in her closet. There was also a notation of a doctor's office visit in the diary. So, we lost a daughter and a grandchild – all in one day. It was like we stepped onto the set of horror movie, only it was real and it was happening to us.

"We were simply floored by what we found," she continued, putting a hand on the right side of her head, as if to help hold it up. "We just had no idea. She'd been on anti-depressants right after she started high school, but we thought she'd grown out of all that. Sure, she had her ups and downs, but I thought she was doing fine. The diary was such a shocker. It was full of sordid details. It was very clear that Appleton toyed with her. He played mind games with her. He told her he loved her, for God's sake. He promised her a life together. He told her he wanted to marry her. And the whole time he was having sex with her – at school, in his apartment, even in his car – the bastard."

Tears rolled down Mrs. Phelps' cheeks. She hid her face in both hands and wept. Her muffled sobs tumbled out, echoing across the backyard. The reporters sat in silence, watching a mother's continued grief.

Dave pulled a handkerchief from his jacket pocket and handed it to her. She took a look at the wrinkled and soiled scrap of frayed linen, and said: "No thanks," flicking it back at him with two fingers. Then she excused herself and went into the house.

"Come on, man. That was gross. Giving her that nasty snot rag of yours was not cool," Nick said, shaking his head at the stunned reporter. Dave was indignant, rolling his eyes at the rejection. Obviously, the woman had no appreciation for real chivalry. He folded the handkerchief and put it back in his pocket. He then pulled a flask out of his breast pocket and poured a small quantity of golden liquid into his coffee mug, smiling smugly at Nick.

"I'm retired," Dave said. "I have no rules."

After a few minutes, Mrs. Phelps returned. She apologized for becoming emotional, and asked what else the reporters wanted to know.

"What about school officials? What was their response when you went to them?" Nick asked.

"Gus and I were completely wrecked," she said. "We totally lost it during the funeral. After we laid Candace to rest, it took awhile to figure out what was going on with the band director. So, it was probably a couple of weeks later before we went to the school. We talked to both the principal and the superintendent. They said they were sorry for our loss, but that they could not discuss Appleton or his departure because it was a personnel issue. Johnson and Pepadowski were uncooperative. Needless to say, those two S.O.B.s are not among my favorite people. They did not comfort us, they did not help us. We took it to the school board president, Joselyn, and he did the same thing. They gave us a snow job on the whole thing."

"What about the police? Did you call the cops?"

"Yes, we talked to the chief of police. I think his name was Bill Rochinski. He said he would look into it. Later, after about a month, he called and said there was no evidence a crime had been committed. Personally, I think the police were afraid of Charlie Joselyn. Old Chuck has always been a powerful guy in the community. He probably had something on the chief of police or the prosecutor, or both of them. It was pretty clear they weren't going to pursue this crime."

"What happened then?" Nick said.

"We were completely mortified. I could not believe what had happened to Candace, to us. The weight of it all was so crushing to me. I couldn't bear it. I couldn't face the reality of what had happened. Gus nearly went out of his mind. After the police washed their hands of it, he was livid. That's when he went to their homes – Johnson, Pepadowski, and Joselyn. He went after them, and quite frankly, I didn't blame him."

"Did the school administrators contact the police about your husband?" Dave asked, breaking his silence in the interview.

"They threatened Gus with a police complaint if he didn't back off, but I don't know whether they actually ever reported it. I think they just wanted the whole thing and us to go away."

"Did you try to get some counseling?" Nick asked.

"Are you kidding? What kind of counseling would help us after what we'd been through? Do you think some shrink who doesn't even know us or our family could offer us comfort? We talked to our minister, and he connected us with a social worker, but they, really, couldn't help us," Mrs. Phelps said, her face filled with anguish again. "I was so depressed I could not go back to work. I had trouble even getting out of bed. All I wanted to do was sleep, that was the only place I could find any relief – with sedatives. And Gus, he could not sleep at all.

"He went days and days without any sleep," she continued. "And then when he finally did get some rest, it was for only an hour or two at a time. He paced the house all night, back and forth, back and forth. During the day, he walked around and around the neighborhood – the whole time muttering to himself. It got so bad that I would wake up in the middle of the night and hear strange voices in the house. It was just Gus, asking himself questions and then answering in different voices. It was like he was trying to carry on conversations with different people."

"Did you try to find Appleton after that?" Nick asked.

"I didn't. I was too wiped out. I wanted so badly to quit thinking about it, to get it out of my mind. But Gus did. He went to the other teachers at the school, but they said they didn't really know Appleton very well and had no idea where he went. Gus kept saying he had to get even, he had to get justice for Candace."

"Did your husband ever say how he planned to get even, get justice?" Nick asked.

"We pretty much quit talking. Our lives were destroyed," Mrs. Phelps said, getting up from her chair and walking toward the backyard birdbath where two blue jays splashed in the shallow water. "I wanted to forget, and Gus could not forget. It consumed him. He made scrapbooks for Appleton, Joselyn, Johnson and Pepadowski. He compiled all the information about them he could get his hands on, categorized it and put it in the scrapbooks."

"Why did he do that?" Nick asked.

"I asked him what he was going to do with it, and he said something odd. I think he said something like, 'You have to know your enemy before you can defeat him.'" He even started following them around, taking notes about where they went, what they did, who they saw. He never got very much on Appleton, but he developed a ton of information about the other three."

"Why did you leave Bay City?" Dave asked, breaking into the interview again.

"I had to get away," Mrs. Phelps said, reclaiming her seat in the deck chair near the table. Everywhere I went, every thing I did, I saw Candace. All I did was cry. I thought my only hope was to walk away and try to start a new life."

"What about your husband? Why didn't he go with you?" Nick asked.

"Our marriage was shaky before Candace died. We had grown apart over the years. Really, she was the only thing that kept us together. With her gone, we had nothing. I tried to talk to Gus about it, but he said he would never rest until the people who had hurt Candace got what was coming to them. He said he was staying for Candace."

"Mrs. Phelps, I have to ask you this… do you think your husband is capable of violence? Did he hate Johnson, Pepadowski, and Joselyn enough to get revenge by trying to hurt them?"

"No, I don't think Gus is capable of physical violence," she said. "I think he wanted them to acknowledge that what they did was wrong, and that they should have been trying to help Candace, not covering up for the dirty piece of shit band director. I think he wanted everyone to know what happened to his daughter and why she took her life. The way they covered that up, it wasn't going to happen. I think Gus wanted them to pay for that."

"Now, I have a couple of questions for you," Mrs. Phelps said, adjusting herself in her chair so that she could see both of the reporters at the same time. "Have you found Appleton, and are you going to write a story for the newspaper about what he did?"

"We're looking for him now. We want to find out if he's still a teacher and talk with him about his tenure at Central," Nick said. "I talked with another young woman from Central High who said she had a relationship with Appleton at about the same time Candace did. We've been told that there may be others. Are you aware of others?"

"After I found the diary, I called other parents I knew. I asked them what the rumors were. The talk around the East Side was that four girls were involved with Appleton at our school. Besides Candace, I was told Sarah Evans and Susan Herndon were sucked in by that bastard. I never heard the fourth name."

Nick jotted down Herndon's name in his notebook, and thanked Mrs. Phelps for the interview. He asked if he could call her later if he had more questions.

"Yes, you can call me anytime," she said, before asking a final question. "Have you talked with Gus?"

"No, we haven't, but we expect to meet with him fairly soon," Nick said. "Is there anything you'd like us to pass along?"

"Just tell him I said hello, and that I hope he's OK."

"We'll do that," Nick said. "I'll make sure he knows that you asked about him."

Mrs. Phelps' life had been wrecked by what happened at Central High School eight years ago. The two reporters left Kalamazoo feeling sorry for Ellen Phelps.

Nick and Dave talked quietly on the way back home. Now, they had another good reason to finish putting this story together. They knew they had to give Mrs. Phelps some piece of mind and that meant shining a very bright light on Darrin Appleton and how he had harmed young girls and destroyed families. Predators like him never stop. They keep looking for their next victims, always preying on the vulnerable. He had to be stopped, and so did Gus Phelps. Nick and Dave talked at length about Ellen's hubby, wondering if Gus now had Charlie Joselyn in his sights.

# The publisher is really pissed this time ...

When Nick reported for work on Wednesday morning, he found two notes on his desk. The first was from Mrs. Pepadowski. It indicated that she would be happy to meet with him at 10 a.m. that day. The second note was from Drayton Clapper. It said Nick should see him right after deadline. It was urgent. Nick knew that because the note was written in red ink, a sign that meant Clapper was serious and hot as a $5 Glock.

Nick made his regular Wednesday morning police calls and filed two short stories for that day's newspaper. After finishing, he dashed off toward Clapper's office.

"What's up, Drayton?" he asked, collapsing into a chair in front of his editor's desk.

"You're in deep shit this time," Clapper said, his face as dour and forlorn as an unemployed undertaker. "Charlie Joselyn called the publisher yesterday. He said you went to his house, asked a bunch of rude, irrelevant questions, insinuated that he had done something wrong, and that you were dressed like a slob. He also said he had contacted his lawyer and would sue us if you wrote one word from that interview. You want to explain?"

"Wow, where do I begin?" Nick said, sitting upright in his chair. "I told you about the interview. I thought it went very well, but I can see how Charlie Joselyn might be upset. Some of the questions made him uncomfortable, but I don't think they were out of line. They were tough. I wanted to know why he didn't do more to protect some students who were being preyed upon by an animal."

"Nick, the publisher is really pissed this time," Drayton said. "Charlie Joselyn is a respected community leader, now considered an elder in town. The publisher does not like the idea of you going to his house and attacking him. Badgering community leaders is not good, Nick. Plus, Charlie said you were dressed like a slob – wrinkled jacket, scruffy shoes and no necktie. Please tell me you did not wear the jacket with the puke stain on the lapel. Did you go on that interview without wearing a tie?"

"I may have forgotten the tie, and the jacket, well I had sauerkraut the day before, so I suppose the lapel might have been a little messy." Nick said. "Monday was a crazy day. The tie thing may have slipped past me."

"Well, I've got to report back to the publisher," Drayton said. "She is not going to be happy. It sounds like you were accusatory in your interview and now we have the threat of a lawsuit. Please explain something for me. Why didn't you at least clean up for the interview? Would it really have hurt to polish your shoes, find a clean jacket somewhere in your closet and put on a necktie? You've received repeated warnings about the dress code, and you flaunt it. I don't know if I can keep protecting you on this anymore. That's all for now, but I will get back to you after I speak with the publisher. I'm telling you, Nick, you've waded into some deep shit this time."

The veteran editor watched Nick leave his office with his head hanging low. He hated seeing the talented reporter on the hot seat again. Clapper liked Nick and wanted to see him rebound from the funk that had shrouded his life since the loss of family members. Nick had good news instincts, he was a capable writer, and he had the good, honest intentions that can only come from a good heart. But, despite Nick's successes, his drinking problem was legendary and he continuously violated the company dress code while on assignment.

Nick left Clapper's office completely disheartened. Here he was on the verge of breaking what might turn out to be the biggest story The *Blade* had ever told, and his editor was giving him a ton of grief about how he handled an interview with a community leader and neckties.

Some days, Nick simply hated working at The *Blade*. So many policies, so many rules, so many procedures. Running the newspaper like a business really took the fun out of the job.

Nick looked at his watch. He had to hustle to make it to the Pepadowski residence on time. But, once again, his Firebird did not fail him. He pushed the rumbling muscle car through the back streets of the East Side, cutting through two alleys and across the lawn of the abandoned McKinley Elementary schoolyard.

At precisely 10 a.m., Nick rang the Pepadowski front doorbell. It did not take the lady of the house long to respond. She must have been standing right behind the door in her knee-length, flower-print, blue and white dress.

"Good morning, Nick. You're right on time. Please come in. I made a little mid-morning snack for us."

"Oh, Mrs. Pepadowski, you shouldn't have. I just had breakfast on my way into work."

"It's just some of my homemade jam on toasted fresh bread and some goat's milk."

"Goat's milk? I've never had goat's milk. Where do you get it?"

"From goats, you silly goose!" Mrs. Pepadowski roared with laughter. "Just teasing you, Nick. My next-door neighbor's son has a farm out near Munger, and they milk the goats every day. Some is used for milk, some feta cheese. Can you believe it? What fantastic luck we have. Please, come and sit down. The toast is still warm, and the milk, well, it's fresh squeezed."

Nick made his way into the dining room and got his first glimpse of Mrs. Pepadowski's mid-morning snack all laid out on the table. The woman was incredible. He knew his waistline would not have a chance if he spent very much time with her.

"Goat's milk, huh? Well, I guess it won't hurt to try it." Ever the good sport, Nick sampled the jam and toast. It was simply delicious. It brought back memories of when he was a youngster and his grandmother made him snacks of marmalade on fresh, warm, homemade crackers.

After two bites of toast, it was time to try the milk. Mrs. Pepadowski watched his every move, nodding approvingly as he munched away at the treat. She smiled as he put his fingers around the cold glass of goat's milk. She held her breath as he lifted the glass to his lips and let two small sips enter his less-than-eager mouth. He swallowed and Mrs. Pepadowski's eyes opened wide.

"Hey, not bad. I was afraid it was going to taste like chicken, or frog's legs. But it was actually pretty good. It's milk, but it just tastes, I don't know quite how to describe it, a little gamier, I guess. But thank you so much, Mrs. Pepadowski. What a wonderful treat."

Hurting someone's feelings was not Nick's thing, and he tried mightily not to whenever he could. He didn't want to upset Mrs. Pepadowski. She was sweet, and reminded Nick of his grandmother. But he sure didn't want to sample any more milk, either.

"Why, Nick. You've hardly touched your snack."

"I know, but I just can't eat any more. Big breakfast this morning. I really can't stay too long. Do you think we could take a look in your attic."

"Well, yes. I guess so. Follow me. I'll clear the table later."

Nick followed Mrs. Pepadowski up a winding stairway to the home's third floor. She opened a door and flicked on a light. They stepped into a room that was as full of memories and history as it was spiders and cobwebs. Nick gazed around the room. Every corner and crevice was packed with stuff. Clearly, this was a family that saved everything.

A makeshift clothing rack hung along one full wall. Coats, jackets, suits and dresses were neatly sealed in garment bags and dangled from a piece of pipe attached to roof rafters. Mrs. Pepadowski went to the end of the rack and unzipped a bag. It was her white, satin wedding dress. Her mother had it made for her in Poland. A tear welled in her eye as she held it up for Nick to see.

"It's beautiful, Mrs. Pepadowski. What a treasure."

"I can still fit in it," she said, holding her chin up proudly. "Over the years, I've only worn it for the big anniversary celebrations. You know, 20, 30, 40-year parties and, of course, photographs."

As she closed the garment bag, Nick looked around the room. Christmas decorations were stacked to the ceiling in a dozen large boxes at the back of the attic. Mrs. Pepadowski explained that the family always bought one Yule decoration during every vacation. The time, date and location of the purchase were noted in a family vacation book, which was hauled out at Christmas time every winter. As each item was placed on the tree, a member of the family recounted its history for all to hear and marvel at.

Garden tools, an old hammock, and children's toys lined another wall. Some appeared to be in good condition and other pieces were obviously there only for the memories.

A sea bag stood in one corner. It contained the uniforms, boots, covers and belts worn by George Pepadowski's father when he served under General George S. Patton in World War II. Grandpa Peppi had fought in northern Africa, Italy and France before a sniper's round hit slightly off center and took out a big chunk of his left shoulder. The wound took months to heal and rehab. It turned out to be a lucky shot, though. By the time Grandpa Peppi was ready to return to duty, the war was over.

Mrs. Pepadowski pointed to about a half-dozen large boxes near the front of the attic, just off to the left side of the doorway. One box at the bottom of the pile was marked with big block letters: GEORGE. The other, resting right next to it, was labeled: CENTRAL HIGH.

"The GEORGE box is the one you want. I tried to open it after you called and left the message, but I couldn't budge the boxes on top of it. Go ahead. Be my guest." The older woman stepped to one side to let Nick wrestle with the cardboard containers. He slid them sideways and then let them gently tumble to the floor.

Nick opened the box and found a large folder on top. It was full of photographs from George's funeral. Three photos of George showed him stretched out in his casket from different angles. He was decked out in his best suit. His hands were neatly crossed at his chest and the beads of a rosary interlaced his long, skinny fingers. The pictures were a bit jarring for Nick. He had heard of families photographing funerals, but the practice was foreign to him. He leafed through the other pictures. Lots of people crying, blowing their noses and hugging. In one photo, Mrs. Pepadowski hugged three young girls. Nick studied the picture.

"Those girls came from a horribly dysfunctional family. The father was abusive and the mother ran off with some Asian drug dealers. The poor kids were in trouble. George helped them put their lives back together. He found them a new place to live. He helped them find a real family, and he kept them in school. They absolutely loved George for that. I remember they cried all day during his funeral. In that picture, I'm trying to give them a little comfort."

A large, flat box, which originally contained pajamas, was wedged below the photo file. It contained all of George's eyeglasses. A notation on a little sticker labeled each pair with the years George had worn them. They were neatly tucked in their original eyeglass cases and placed in order in the box all the way back to when George first started wearing glasses in elementary school.

Nick pulled the pajama box out of the GEORGE box and spotted what he had come for. A large sealed plastic bag contained four amber-colored pill bottles. Mrs. Pepadowski picked up the bag and shook it gently. The remaining pills inside clattered against the plastic walls of the container.

"Ah-huh! I thought I saved them, but I wasn't sure." Mrs. Pepadowski held the bag up in the air and handed it to Nick. "This is what you were looking for, right?"

Nick opened the bag and pulled out the pill bottles. Their expiration dates indicated that they were the pills Mr. Pepadowski was using when he died. And they came from the Center Avenue pharmacy. "I think this is exactly what I was looking for. Mrs. Pepadowski, I could give you a big kiss. Thanks so much for helping me find them."

The older woman's face reddened slightly and she averted her eyes at the suggestion of a smooch. "Why, Nick. You're making me blush."

"May I take the pills with me? I promise to bring them back."

"Sure, Nick. But why are they so important? Why do you need them so badly that we're up here rummaging around, fighting off the spiders looking for them?"

"I'm not exactly sure yet. I'd like to have them examined, and then I can tell you what's going on. I hate to say anything until I'm sure of where this is going."

They placed the big GEORGE box back in the position where they found it and left the attic. When they got to the bottom of the stairs, Nick said he had two more requests of Mrs. Pepadowski.

"Would you mind if I came back here this weekend with Tanya Johnson and looked through the CENTRAL box up in your attic?" Nick thought the box might contain some notes about Candace Phelps or the band director. Tanya might be able to help him sort through the unfamiliar material.

"Oh, Nick, please bring Tanya by any time. I haven't seen her since her father's funeral, and we really didn't get much of a chance to talk then. Call before you come by, though."

Nick was a little afraid to do that. Calling ahead would give Mrs. Pepadowski time to get some more goat's milk and cook up a batch of who knows what.

"What was the other thing on your mind, Nick?"

"Instead of that kiss I mentioned upstairs, could I get a big hug?"

The reporter opened his long arms and the older woman entered like a boat being gently coaxed to its mooring. "Thanks for everything. You've been so helpful."

"You're welcome, Nick." Mrs. Pepadowski placed her head on Nick's chest and sighed. Nick held her tight, relishing the moment. The turmoil at work had made Nick anxious and uncomfortable, but the worst was yet to come.

# A pharmacist named Pillsworth will help ...

When Nick reported for work Thursday morning, he was asked to fill in on the copy desk for a line editor who was on vacation. The duty was a part of his job that Nick didn't really enjoy. He didn't like cleaning up the writing and reporting blunders of others. Plus, it was thankless work, unappreciated at all levels. He'd much rather put his energy and his skill into developing his own stories. But his desk assignment on this day was to do a first-read on raw copy coming into the local news desks.

Every day, some raw copy gets spiked, some gets boiled down to briefs, some gets combined with other news into roundups and sometimes a piece of work gets sent over to another reporter for re-write. Once in a while, a little news brief gets fleshed out into a big story.

As Nick bulldozed his way through one short story after another, he came across a report from one of the newspaper's older, most trusted writers. Her name was Jenni Thompson and she had covered every news beat on the paper over the years. Everyone at the paper loved Jenni, and her police sources out in the boondocks would call the paper and feed news stories only to her. The news story that Nick edited on this day was just such a report. It came from Michigan State Police post out in Bad Axe, the biggest community in rural Huron County and the hub of activity in the Thumb of Michigan.

The lead paragraph of Jenni's story went this way:

> "No one was injured in a fire that destroyed a barn outside of Bad Axe this morning, but the blaze killed 1,010 piglets. Fire department officials said they do not know what started the fire, which completely consumed the 10 ft. x 20 ft. outbuilding."

It's not every day that The *Blade* gets a news story where so many animals are killed. Nick edited the story, alerted the local editor to the destruction of livestock and put the story on the wire for the Associated Press to distribute to other news outlets around Michigan.

But something nagged at Nick. The story didn't add up. A 10 x 20 foot outbuilding, or small barn, is only 200 square feet of space. How in the world, Nick wondered, do you get 1,010 piglets in such a small space?

Nick quizzed Jenni about the apparent discrepancy in her story. Jenni checked her notes from the morning round of calls to police agencies outside of Bay City. "Yup, my notes are good on both numbers. 1,010 piglets and a 10 x 20 barn."

That reply, however, didn't satisfy Nick. "Jenni, it just doesn't make sense. Could you call your source at the police post back and double check your numbers?"

The veteran reporter rolled her eyes at Nick and picked up her telephone headset. Nick watched Jenni from his desk. Jenni talked with the desk sergeant in Bad Axe. Nick could see the older reporter chatting and laughing into the receiver on the headset. No doubt, they were having a good laugh at Nick's expense. Finally, Jenni took off her headset and came over to Nick's desk. "I just double-checked it, and my sources gave me the same info all over again. My notes are good."

"Thank you for checking." Nick appreciated the effort, even though it did nothing to clear up the conflicting information. After about 15 minutes, Nick could not stand it any longer. He decided to call the desk sergeant in Bad Axe himself. He looked up the number on the morning call list.

The desk sergeant answered and Nick identified himself. He said he was calling to double-check some numbers from an earlier news report. "I'm calling about the barn fire. The number of pigs and the size of the barn don't jibe. Can you help me figure this out?"

"Why, sure. What's to figure out?"

"Well, how do you get 1,010 piglets in a 10 x 20 barn?"

"Oh, no. I didn't tell Jenni 1,010 piglets. When she called this morning I told her one sow and 10 piglets died in the fire."

Now, that made sense. The fire claimed the mamma pig and her little ones. They could easily fit in that barn. Nick alerted Jenni to the miscommunication and called the Associated Press to get a "kill" on the wire version of the story. Everyone in the newsroom thought the mistake was hilarious, except for Jenni, of course, who was embarrassed that she had made such a basic error. It was also her wake-up call to get her hearing checked.

As Nick finished his morning desk duty, he motioned to Drayton Clapper for five minutes of the editor's time. "Drayton, I need you desperately."

"No you don't. Even my wife doesn't need me desperately. You can have three minutes. Meet me in my office."

The two newsmen met in Clapper's closet-sized office with freshly filled cups of coffee.

"I think it's time we connect with a pharmaceutical lab to get some pills analyzed," Nick said, pulling his chair closer to his supervisor's desk. "I was at the Pepadowski residence last night and Mrs. Pepadowski gave me her husband's pills. Now we've got the Johnson pills and the Pepadowski pills."

"Well, that's wonderful, but why do we have them and what does it mean?" Clapper flipped through his unopened mail as he talked with Nick. "You've got two minutes now."

"Lab analysis will tell us if there's anything fishy about the medicine. Remember, Bob Johnson and George Pepadowski from the school district? They both died under very similar circumstances but six years apart. They had the same doctor, used the same pharmacy, lived in the same neighborhood, worked out of the same school, worked on the fund-raisers for the big new field house and they helped gloss over a teacher/student romance that ended in a student's suicide."

"OK, humor me here. Again, why do you think there's something fishy about the medicine?"

"We had Dave Balz's doctor look at the Johnson pills. He said it was a bad combination, and he couldn't believe that a doctor had prescribed them. The doctor suggested the lab analysis."

"Oh, yes. You're working with Balz. I remember now. How could I forget? You're staking your reputation and your career on that loser."

"Dave is not a loser, and it's his doctor who believes that there's something fishy about the pills. Can I send them off to be analyzed?"

"How much is it going to cost? I need to know what a lab is going to soak us before I can authorize a big expenditure. Can't you have someone else take a look at the pills? My neighbor is a pharmacist. How about if we have her take a look at what you've got and then go from there?"

"That's fine by me. What's her number?"

"I'll call her and see if she'd be willing to give us a hand. What are you doing this afternoon?"

"Just waiting for you to call."

Drayton Clapper called his next-door neighbor, Pam Pillsworth, a registered pharmacist who worked for Evergreen's Pharmacies, a national chain that had a half-dozen stores scattered around Bay County. She worked at the pharmacy on Euclid Avenue and agreed to look at the medicine later that day.

Nick looked at the scrap of paper his boss had given him. "You've got a neighbor who is a pharmacist named Pillsworth? I suppose you're going to tell me you got a gardener who lives across the street from you named Jack Spade, too."

"Just go talk to her, smart ass," Drayton said. "She's very sharp and she knows her business inside and out."

"Thanks, Drayton. It will be good to find out if we're heading in the right direction on the pills." Nick stood up from his chair and walked toward the office door.

"Yes, it's time to either push this story or get off of it and go somewhere else," Clapper said as he finished emptying his mail basket. "You've invested a lot of time on this and, as far as I can tell, you don't have much to show for it. I can't justify keeping you on this without something more concrete. We've got lots of stories to cover out there, you know.

"Say, Nick, one more thing. I met with the publisher briefly yesterday and I tried to calm her down. I don't think I had much luck. I'm supposed to meet with her again this afternoon. She's very angry about your conduct. But I've got my fingers crossed. I'll keep you posted."

"Thanks, Drayton. I've been thinking. I suppose I really could have handled that whole Joselyn thing better. I just hope I don't get burned by a lapse in judgment."

Clapper hoped so, too. The local news editor did not want to think about the worst-case scenario regarding his reporter. And he was hoping that Nick would hit pay dirt on this story so that all would be forgiven and forgotten. But just as Nick's big story was heating up, his career was cooling way off.

# Pills are pills, they all look alike...

Nick pushed his hotrod west on Wilder Road. He hoped the pharmacist could help him confirm or reject his theory about the Pepadowski and Johnson pills, which rode along quietly with him in the car's front passenger bucket seat on the way to the West Side drug store.

The Firebird turned onto Euclid Avenue and Nick could see the big neon tree that marked the entryway for Evergreen's Pharmacies. As he parked his car in a safe area away from all the other vehicles in the parking lot, he wondered what Drayton Clapper's neighbor could tell him. He prayed that a lady named Pillsworth could tell him plenty about what was in the bottles he carried into the store. He found her immediately behind the pharmacy counter.

"Hi, I'm Nick Steele from The *Blade*. Drayton Clapper told me you might be able to help with a little mystery we have going on here."

"Glad to meet you, Nick. I'm Pam. Drayton said you'd be dropping by. What have you got for me?"

"These." Nick handed the two plastic bags of pills to Mrs. Pillsworth. "I got them from the relatives of the people the medicine was prescribed for. The people on the labels, they're dead. One died recently, and the other several years ago. The pills and the prescriptions are the mystery. We asked a doctor to take a look at them and he indicated that they're bad combinations, that they could be deadly under the right circumstances. In fact, he said he was surprised that any doctor would prescribe them in that combination."

Pam's eyeglasses dangled from a string of beads draped around her neck. The woman was short and stout with sand-colored hair. It was obvious that she did not spend much money on make-up – at least for work. But her pleasant smile made up for the lack of color in her complexion. Pam lifted the eyeglasses off of her ample bosom and put them on the top of her nose to study the pill bottles.

"*Hmmm.* These pills are very old," she said of the Pepadowski bottle. "I'm not sure if the pharmaceutical companies are even making these anymore. Cordarone, Zoloft and Demadex seems like an odd mix to me. And these others are newer, but I think your doctor friend may have a point about them. You never mix Tambocor and Tenormin. Of course, a lot depends on the conditions of the patients and their overall level of health. There are plenty of variables involved."

"Well, is there any way to check them?"

"Yes, we can take a look on the computer. All pharmacies today have computer software programs that allow you to instantly look up medications, check their side effects, and identify what their drug interactions are going to be. It all comes from a big database provided by the pharmaceutical companies. Follow me."

Nick scooted behind the counter into the back room of the pharmacy where huge canisters of pills, liquids and gels lined the walls. He followed Pam to a corner where the pharmacy's computer system whirred softly.

"The pills in the bottles match what's on the labels, so that hasn't been tampered with," Pam said as she stood in front of the computer but continued to examine the medicine.

"How do you know that? Pills are pills," Nick said, watching Pam's every move. "They all look alike to me. Some are just different shapes."

"That's right. They come in different shapes, different sizes and different colors. But almost all pills today are stamped in some way when they're made. Each carries an initial, or an abbreviation, or some kind of letter or number code that tells what it is. These pills all match what's on their labels. Let's see what the computer has to say about them."

Pam flipped on Evergreen's Gold Standard Pharmaceutical Cross-Reference software program. In seconds, she had the Johnson and Pepadowski drugs up on her screen. She checked their side effects and which drugs they should not be used with. After a few minutes, she flipped off the computer program and turned to Nick.

"Your doctor friend is right. These are very dangerous for the people they were prescribed for. You said both people died. What did they die from?"

"Heart attacks. They were in their 50s. They were overweight, no exercise, high blood pressure, and lots of stress from work. That sort of thing. They died and were buried and nobody seemed really surprised that they went the way they did."

"Well, I think this medicine should go back to the pharmacy it came from – the Easy-Med on Center – and the pharmacists there should check the prescription back through the doctor, the attending physician. This simply doesn't seem right to me, and I can't think of a reason why a doctor would give these to patients."

Pam was so helpful, that Nick decided to ask her about pharmacy protocol. "I've got a question for you. Is there any way the prescription could be tampered with? Is there a way it could be changed?"

"Most pharmacies today keep everything on computer file. Patient records, billing, prescriptions. Everything is in the system."

"So, if you had access to the computer system, you would have access to the patient files and the medicine that's prescribed. Is that right?"

"Yes, that's right."

"Well," Nick said, getting more excited at the flood of new information, "let me ask you this: If I had total access to this computer, could I get in there and manipulate the records, change the prescriptions?"

"Yes, you could. But the only people who have access are the pharmacists and the computer technicians. The technicians have no reason to really be in the files or to change them."

"But they would have access and they would have the ability to alter the files and the prescriptions, right?"

"Right."

"Then the technicians would also have access to the Gold Standard you just used to look up the drugs and their backgrounds, right?"

"True."

"Well, Mrs. Pillsworth, I can't thank you enough. You have been really helpful. I think you just helped solve our mystery. I think I know how these prescriptions were changed, and I think I know who did it. Thanks again."

Nick stuck out his hand to shake with a friendly and smart lady who had just made his day.

"Nice meeting you, Nick. And I must say something more about this. If you have information about prescriptions being tampered with, you should alert the authorities. This is serious business – not something to play with."

"Don't worry, I think the authorities are going to be in on this very soon."

# The prescriptions may have been tampered with ...

## THURSDAY AFTERNOON

Nick punched in the cell phone number for Drayton Clapper as he nosed his street-rod out into traffic on Euclid Avenue. No answer. Nick figured his boss must be out of the office by this time of the day on a Thursday afternoon, so he left this message: "Drayton, this is Nick. I know it's after hours, but I've got to talk with you right away. Call me on my cell when you can."

Tanya would be waiting for Nick at O'Hare's by now. Nick had been eager to see Tanya. She had left school a day early to join Nick in Bay City. He missed her. And he also wanted her to go to the Pepadowski home with him so they both could quickly go through that big CENTRAL HIGH SCHOOL box that was up in the attic. But now, Nick had a feeling of dread as he inched down Midland Street looking for a safe place to tuck away his 'Bird. He was going to have to tell Tanya about her father's medicine, that it had been tampered with in some way. He was not looking forward to breaking the news to her.

As he swung through the front door of O'Hare's, Nick spotted Tanya right away. She was sitting with a girlfriend at a table just to the side of where the upside-down Christmas tree hung from the ceiling. Nick wondered if she had done that on purpose, hoping the tree would serve as a substitute for mistletoe.

"Hi, Nick." Tanya stood up from the table and flashed a smile as bright as a laser beam at Nick. "Hey, I want you to meet an old friend. This is Sue Anderson. She's killing some time, waiting for her boyfriend."

"Hello, Sue, pleased to meet you." Nick shook hands with Tanya's friend and then turned in Tanya's direction. He wanted to give her a hug, but was afraid it would send the wrong message. It was still too early to go beyond the friendship stage in their relationship, yet he longed to hold her. Instead, Nick reached over with his left hand and gently clasped her right elbow. "Hi Tanya. It's great to see you. I missed you." He gave her arm a light squeeze with his fingertips and Tanya touched his hand with her left hand. Their eyes met.

Nick joined the women at their table. "Has anyone ordered food yet? I'm starving."

"No. This is our first drink," Tanya said. "It's not Friday, but we're ready to party."

"I know, I feel like partying, too, but I was wondering if you would give me a hand with something tonight."

"What's up?"

"Mrs. Pepadowski has a big box up in her attic that's marked CENTRAL HIGH SCHOOL. She says her late husband's papers and records from school are in it. I was hoping you could help me sort through it. It wouldn't take very long."

"No problem. Are we going to do this before or after we eat?"

"I don't know. Let me call her and find out if this is a good time."

Nick pulled his cell phone out and walked toward O'Hare's front door to place the call. He looked up at the ceiling and saluted his pants, which were still displayed neatly next to the granny panties. Luckily, he connected with the older woman on the third ring of her phone. He and Tanya could come over anytime, she said. When Nick returned to Tanya's table, she was alone. Sue had connected with her boyfriend and had gone. Nick was glad. It was too difficult to talk with Tanya when a third wheel was sitting at the table. A frosty mug of beer sat on the table in front of the place where Nick had been.

"Thanks for ordering that for me," he said, sitting down next to Tanya. "Mrs. Pepadowski says we can come over any time, so we could go right after we finish these drinks, if that's all right with you."

"Sounds fine to me. I haven't seen her in awhile. It will be nice to say hello."

"There's something I have to tell you, and I'm not quite sure how to go about it."

"Well, how about just spitting it out. What's up?"

"Your dad and his medicine. Remember the pill bottles you gave me?"

"Oh, yes. What did you find out about them?"

"Tanya, I don't know how to say this… But it looks like someone tampered with either your father's medicine or his prescription."

"What? What do you mean tampered?"

"We've had your dad's pills – and Mr. Pepadowski's pills – looked at by both a doctor and a pharmacist independently. They both said the drug combinations are not right. They think the prescription is wrong."

"Are you saying that there was a mistake at the pharmacy, or that Doc Sheffield made a mistake with the prescription?"

"I'm saying that it looks like something is wrong with the meds your dad was taking. It's got to be checked out." Nick did not offer his theory to Tanya. He didn't have the hard facts to support it, and he didn't want to upset her needlessly.

"Let's go see Doc Sheffield. He can tell us what's wrong right off the bat."

"I'm sure his office is closed by now. Maybe we can connect with him tomorrow. Do you know where he lives?

"Heck, yes. He's just a few blocks from our house. Wait until my mother and brothers find out. They will freak out."

"Maybe we shouldn't tell them until we know more. It's the same thing with Mrs. Pepadowski. Let's not say anything to her tonight about it. When we have solid information, we can tell her what we found out."

"You mean Mr. Pepadowski's medicine was wrong, too? How can that be? Nick, what's going on here? This sounds too... too crazy."

"I have some ideas, Tanya, but I don't want to say anything until I have more facts. Let's finish our drinks and then run over to Mrs. Pepadowski's house. This will all work itself out very shortly."

Nick paid the tab, left a nice tip for Sassy Sally and they left. Nick could tell that he had upset Tanya with his revelation, but she was handling it well. It wouldn't be long now before all the facts were out in the open.

# Nobody knew who Appleton's fourth victim was …

The front door swung open and Mrs. Pepadowski held her arms open to give Tanya a big hug. "Tanya, how are you? It's so nice to see you again. Come in, come in." The two women hugged and patted each other's backs for what seemed like minutes to Nick, who used the pause in the action to drink in the warm, spicy aroma coming from the Pepadowski kitchen. It was a familiar smell. When he was growing up, Nick's neighbors were Polish. Galumpkis, stuffed cabbage or pigs in a blanket, have their own distinctive smell. There's no hiding it, no getting away from it.

"Hello, Nick. I didn't think you'd be by this quickly. But I'm happy to see both of you." Tanya and Nick entered the house and shed the jackets that the nippy November air in Michigan required. The smell of hot food caught Tanya's attention.

"Mrs. Pepadowski, are you cooking what I think you're cooking?" Tanya closed her eyes and filled her nostrils. "It smells absolutely delicious."

"Yup. I'm making Galumpkis for Sunday dinner. The boys are coming home this weekend. I thought I'd surprise them with a homemade meal. They're almost done cooking. I'll dish some up for you and Nick. I made plenty."

"Oh, no, Mrs. Pepadowski," Nick said, trying to sound convincing. "We couldn't possibly impose. I was just hoping we could go through the big CENTRAL box in the attic. You don't have to feed us. Really."

"Nick, I wouldn't hear of it. Of course, you're going to eat a little something. I made some fresh bread, too. Go ahead and look in the attic. You know the way. When you're done, I'll have a plate on the table for you."

The two thanked her, and made their way up the back staircase to the attic. Tanya had been to the house many times over the years, but she could never recall going into the attic before. Nick opened the door and flicked on the light. Tanya was stunned by the amount of stuff in the big, warm room just under the roof.

"Now, what are we looking for again?"

"That big box over there, the one that's marked CENTRAL HIGH SCHOOL on the side," Nick said. "I want to know if Mr. Pepadowski kept any notes on the band director. I was hoping we might be able to find out more about what went on at the time. We know about Sarah Evans, of course. But what about the other girls he was involved with. Maybe it's in here, maybe it's not. I saw the box when I was searching for Mr. Pepadowski's pills, and I thought it was worth a shot."

"OK, let's see what we can find." Tanya pushed a box of books toward Nick and motioned for him to sit down. "Let's dig into this, and then go dig into those pigs in a blanket."

The box contained a wide assortment of school testing and grading documents, as well as dozens of manuals on teacher training and techniques. Nick and Tanya dug through the carton, pulling out smaller boxes and containers. Finally, at the bottom of the cardboard box was an 18" x 36" envelope bursting at its seal. PERSONNEL/CONFIDENTIAL was stamped on the front. Nick grabbed it, ignored the label and quickly opened it, spilling its contents onto the floor. Dozens of single files skidded around their feet. Each file had a staff member's name on it. Nick and Tanya pushed through the files, pawing the ones they were not interested in off to the side.

"Here it is." Nick picked up the file marked DARRIN APPLE-TON. It was thick with memos, notes, and loose slips of paper. He thumbed through the two-inch package. Two formal reprimands were at the back of the file. Each complained of inappropriate contact with a student. The descriptive detail in each account mirrored the others. Teachers reported that they witnessed too much touching, too much private contact between Appleton and his charges, and too much individual, personal instruction. The file notes also indicated that rumors and whispers flourished among staff and students about the teacher's affinity for his female students. The relationships between the band director and Candace Phelps, Sarah Evans, and Susan Herndon were noted as "concerns" by teachers. On both forms, under the area of the reprimand marked ACTION TAKEN, George Pepadowski had written: "Teacher warned, letter placed in personnel file, principal notified, special training recommended." The form did not indicate whether parents were notified of possible inappropriate behavior. Nick had the feeling that they probably were not called.

"Tanya, did you know Susan?" Nick continued to thumb through the file as Tanya read over his shoulder. "I knew her, but she and Candace were older, so we really weren't friendly. I was much closer to Sarah because she was only a grade ahead of me in school."

Sarah Evans was mentioned in one report. Her name also was underlined in a memo from the school nurse, who indicated that she found the young girl weeping in the hallway one afternoon. When questioned, Sarah told the nurse that she was crying because she walked into one of the band department's instrument storage rooms and found the band director kissing Susan Herndon, who was not wearing any clothing from the waist up. The nurse indicated that Sarah was more upset with the girl than she was with her teacher, referring to Susan as a bitch and a dirty slut. "I think something is going on here between Sarah and Mr. Appleton, and it feels dirty and disgusting," the teacher wrote.

No other girls were mentioned by name in any of the notes in the APPLETON file. It made Tanya curious. "This has really got me wondering who the fourth girl was. Candace can't tell us and

Sarah said she didn't know of any others beside Susan. Maybe we should track down Susan and ask her if she knows of others who were involved with this creep. I haven't seen her in years. I'll have to ask around about her."

"Yes, that would be good to find out. I was also hoping we might find something that indicated where Appleton was heading when he left the area. I don't see anything about reference calls, or calls requesting that the school transfer his teaching records, or anything like that."

"You're right, Nick. But I think I saw something at the front of the file." Tanya lifted the bulky folder from Nick's hands and flicked through its pages. "Here it is, Appleton's job application form. His home state is Florida. That's where he grew up and went to school. Maybe he went back home."

"Hey, you might be right. Good thinking. We'll have to check it out." Nick pulled the two formal reprimands and the Sarah Evans memo from the file, folded them neatly and stuck them in the side pocket of his sports jacket. Tanya and Nick put everything back in the box just as it had been before they flipped the attic light on that day. Nick could tell from the expression on Tanya's face that something was bothering her. He asked her if everything was all right.

"Well, yes, I am a little upset. If Mr. Pepadowski knew about Appleton and his exploits with girls at the school, then my dad must have known, too." Tanya turned and faced Nick. "It really bothers me to think that my dad and Mr. Pepadowski knew what was going on and didn't do more to stop it. This is going to shock my mother when I tell her everything we've learned."

When the two returned to the Pepadowski dining room, they found the lady of the house serving two heaping and steaming plates full of Polish delights.

"You're just in time. Please sit down. What can I get you two to drink?"

Nick quickly suggested water, hoping to head off an offer of milk. As Mrs. Pepadowski whirled back into the kitchen, Nick thanked her for letting them look through the documents in her attic.

"Oh, and I wanted to let you know that I took two forms and a memo from a file to get them copied," Nick said as he used his fork to gently pull back a leaf of cabbage so tender from cooking that it broke apart in small pieces. "I promise to bring them back on Monday."

"That's OK, Nick. Did you find what you were looking for?"

"It was very helpful, thank you," Tanya said, responding for Nick because he was chewing contentedly on a big piece of Galumpki. "Nick's chowing down. Don't get in his way. By the looks of it, I don't think he's eaten this week."

The two women laughed as Nick rolled his eyes and wiped his chin with his napkin. "But I think we're good," Tanya continued. "It was very nice of you to let us go through Mr. Pepadowski's things."

"I hope it helps. Nick said it was important. I believe him. But I wish I knew what this is all about."

Nick stopped chewing and looked up at the two women seated with him. "I'll be able to tell you everything very shortly. It will all be coming out very soon. Trust me."

# I found the bastard and he's teaching in Florida…

## LATER THURSDAY NIGHT

Nick poked the throttle of his beloved car gently as he turned into the parking lot of his apartment building.

"I hope you don't mind stopping here for a minute," he said to Tanya as he pulled the car into its resting spot. "I need to check my messages and change real quick before we go back out. Is that OK?"

"That's fine. I had no idea you lived downtown. Does this mean we're going out – out?" Tanya flipped open the door on her side of the car and hopped out.

"Well, not going out as in 'going out,' but there's a few things we should talk about tonight. I thought maybe we could kick them around a little bit, maybe have a beer or two. Did you have something else you wanted to do? Am I being too presumptuous?"

Nick turned toward Tanya and studied the expression on her face before bounding up the steps to his front door. He hoped he hadn't offended her. Suddenly, it dawned on him that she might have made plans to meet some friends, or go out on a date, or spend the evening with her mother that night. It was only about 9:30. "I could run you home if you're tied up tonight."

She followed him, using the railing to pull herself up the front porch stairs. "No, I didn't make any plans for this evening. But you hadn't said anything about going out. I should check in with my mother because she'll worry if I don't."

The duo walked into Nick's living room and he clicked on a floor lamp. Tanya was stunned by the filth. It stopped her in her tracks. She gazed around the small apartment. Not one thing was in its proper place.

"Nick, you live like a pig."

"Ah, come on. Pig is a little strong – don't you think?"

"No. In fact, I may have understated your living conditions. Good thing all my shots are up to date."

"Nothing in here will hurt you, including me. Come in, sit down for a minute. You can make your call while I change." Nick walked through his dining area and flipped on the kitchen light. He glanced at his telephone message recorder, hoping that Clapper had called him back. It was not blinking. He continued on toward his bedroom.

Tanya stepped through the living room and dining area gingerly, afraid that brushing up against anything would leave a soil stain on her jeans. If he just picked up and tossed out the empty pizza boxes, she thought to herself. But she could not hold her tongue for very long.

"You know, we just spent about an hour or so in an attic and I have no doubt in my mind that it was cleaner than this place," she said, elevating her voice so that Nick could hear her from his bedroom. "Nick, you make good money. Why not at least hire someone to clean this place once a month? The crud in here is unforgiveable."

"I know. I apologize. I don't really think of this as a place to live. It's a place where I keep my stuff and stop once in awhile. I try to wash the dishes every week or so, but I guess I've fallen behind a little on it. Did you make your call yet?"

Tanya was already punching in the number to her mom's place when Nick came rolling out of the bedroom. Instead of his work uniform of slacks, sports jacket, button-down shirt and the sometimes-present necktie, none of which ever matched particularly well – he had on his casual uniform – blue jeans, Detroit Pistons T-shirt and hiking boots.

"Hi Mom. I'm at Nick's. He's changing and then we're going

to go out for a bit," she said into her phone while eyeing Nick as he loaded his pockets. "No, this is not a date. I think that point has been made pretty clear. We're just talking and gathering information again."

Nick looked at Tanya and smiled. The grin on her face stretched nearly ear-to-ear as she listened to her mom. "No, I won't be late. Probably just an hour or two. If it's going to be later than that, I'll call." She said goodbye and clicked off the phone.

"Are you ready to go?" Nick said, all put back together and eager to leave the place that made Tanya so uncomfortable.

"You bet. Let's hit it." Tanya quickly made her way toward the door. When they were coming up the stairs, getting ready to enter the apartment, she'd wondered if Nick was going to use the occasion to try and kiss her. As they left, the idea popped back into her head, but only briefly. Perhaps another day, she thought to herself.

Nick skipped ahead of Tanya and opened the machine's passenger door and held it open for her.

"Your carriage awaits you, my lady."

"Thanks, but courtesy doesn't make up for your filthy apartment."

"OK, I'll make sure it's sparkling clean the next time you visit."

"Who says there will be a next time?" Tanya snapped her seatbelt into place and looked over at Nick as he entered the driver's side of the sports car.

"Oh, that was cold. Real cold," Nick said. But the reporter could not finish spitting out his thought because his barking cell phone interrupted. It was Dave calling. He clicked the call on.

"What's up, Dave?"

"I found him."

"Who? You found who?"

"The band director. I found the bastard. And get this, he's working at a school district in Florida."

"No kidding. That's great. Where are you?"

"I'm at O'Hare's. Swing by and I'll tell you all about it."

"I've got Tanya with me. We were at the Pepadowski place. Just a second, let me check with her." Nick put his cell phone down against his stomach and asked Tanya if she wanted to stop at the West Side bar to find out about Darrin Appleton.

"Dave says he found him in Florida. You were right on the nose. What do you think? Want to stop by?"

"Sounds good to me. This ought to be really interesting. Tell Dave I can hardly wait."

Nick pulled the cell phone back to his ear and told Dave they would meet him in about 15 minutes. He clicked off his phone and glanced at Tanya, who seemed to be as tickled at the news as a kindergartner hearing the bell for recess.

"Dave is a good reporter. I knew he would track Appleton down, but I'm kind of surprised he did it this fast."

"What else did you want to talk about?" Tanya asked, facing Nick. "We're probably going to spend most of the time at the bar talking about Appleton."

"You're right. Dave will have lots to tell us, so maybe we should kick this around now. I wanted to ask you about tomorrow. I was wondering if you would help me barge in on Doc Sheffield to ask about the prescriptions."

"I was hoping you'd say that," Tanya said, "I'm eager to find out what the deal is with those pills."

"Me, too. But because of doctor-patient confidentiality, I'm sure he wouldn't talk to me about it. But I'll bet he'd talk to you or your mom."

"So, what are you thinking here? Do you think Doc Sheffield prescribed the wrong medicine or that it somehow got screwed up, and that's why my dad died?" Tanya turned in her seat and faced Nick. She placed her left hand on top of his right hand as it rested on the gear shifter in the center console. She squeezed it gently. "Is that what you think happened? Is that why my dad is dead?"

"Tanya, I have a theory about what happened, but I don't have all the facts. What I do know is that a doctor and a pharmacist each have told us that there seems to be something wrong with the medicines prescribed for your dad and Mr. Pepadowski. Something is not right, something is out of whack. They said the medicines could be deadly combinations."

"Well, then what is your theory? Come on, Nick. I'm a big girl. I can handle it. Just level with me."

"All right then. Here it is. I think Gus Phelps changed the prescriptions for your dad and Mr. Pepadowski. I think he killed them both to get revenge for Candace. Your mother and Mrs. Pepadowski said Gus was outraged because he believed they didn't do enough to protect Candace from the band director."

"Oh, Nick, I don't know about that. Even if he wanted revenge, how would Gus change the prescription? Is he really smart enough to do that? He's a handyman. And what about Mr. Joselyn? If Gus went after my dad and Mr. Pepadowski, why hasn't he killed Charlie Joselyn, too?"

"I don't know. Maybe Joselyn is next. When I was at the Joselyn home last week I overheard Doris say that she was going to pick up a new prescription for Charlie. She was going to pick it up – along with some scotch – at the Easy Med. That's where Gus works. We should contact the Joselyns tomorrow."

"I don't know, Nick. This all seems so hard to believe. Murder? Three people?"

"Tanya, I know it sounds wild, but it's really not that far-fetched. All Gus would have to do is some research, which is within his reach, and then alter the prescriptions on the computer. Once you understand the system and the medications, it really wouldn't be that hard."

"If Gus is the killer, how does Doc Sheffield fit into this, then?"

"Well, we need Doc Sheffield to look at the labels on the pill bottles and then check his medical records for both patients to see if they match. My guess is that they won't match, and that will mean that someone at the pharmacy changed the prescriptions.

Everything at the pharmacy is on computer file – all the prescriptions for each customer. There ought to be a record of every prescription, indicating when it was updated or changed and by whom."

"How are you going to get into the pharmacy computer files?"

"I haven't figured that out yet. But I'm thinking we won't have to. I figure that once Doc Sheffield sees that his prescriptions have been tampered with, he will call the authorities. That's another reason I wanted to stop into O'Hare's tonight. If Mickey Davidson is in there, I think I'll pull him off to the side and give him a heads-up on where we're at with this."

Nick turned into the O'Hare's parking lot, circled it twice looking for a good place to rest his 'Bird. He couldn't find a safe place, so he pulled his beloved machine up onto the front yard of an abandoned house just down the street from the watering hole. They would have to walk a bit, but his car would not get banged up – at least on this night.

Tanya started to open her door, but Nick insisted that she wait for him. His thoughtfulness was another thing that she loved about the reporter. He lived like a slob, but he treated her with respect and dignity.

Dave motioned for Tanya and Nick to join him at a table in the corner of the festive saloon, which was jammed – as usual – on a Thursday night. Music from a live band wafted through a huge doorway in the wall. The owner of O'Hare's was a smart cookie. Years ago, he bought the building next door, which had been a ladies' dress shop. The two places shared a common wall, which the owner blasted a huge hole through. The maneuver allowed him to lawfully run both places with one liquor license.

"So, Dave, how did you find Appleton? I'm dying to know," Nick said as he motioned at Sassy Sally to bring the table a round of cold beers.

"I started by going to the public library and getting the Central High School yearbook for the last year that Appleton was at the school," Dave said as he hoisted his mug of brew and drained the contents in two massive gulps that scared Tanya with its suddenness and efficiency – not a drop dribbled down his chin or leaked out his nose. "I made a list of all his fellow teachers and just started calling the ones who are still in the area. I must have called 40 teachers before I found one who admitted being friendly with the son-of-a-bitch. He told me to check Florida."

"Ah-ha, Florida," Tanya said. She stood up and reached over to give Nick and Dave a high-five. "We were right. Sorry, Dave. Florida is a tidbit Nick and I came up with tonight while we were in the Pepadowski files. Please continue."

"From there, I went to the American Association of High School Band Directors Web site and checked its listings for Florida. And that's where I found Appleton's name in the first column. He was at a school district in Jacksonville. So I called the school and asked to speak to him. They told me he no longer worked there. They said he had been gone about two years. No other information available."

By this time, Nick couldn't contain himself. "Then you called the local paper, right?"

"That's right. The Jacksonville *Times-Union*. The education reporter knew all about Appleton. She said he had a great reputation as a music teacher, but could not leave the little ladies alone. A bunch of parents got together and went after him, and the next thing you know he up and leaves. The reporter says she heard he hooked on at the largest school district in Daytona Beach."

"Ah, that's excellent work, Dave." Nick looked at Tanya and winked. "I told Tanya I knew you'd find him. Anything else? Did you call the school in Daytona?"

"I called at 3 this afternoon and asked to speak with Darrin Appleton. Now, get this. The woman in the front office said he was busy giving instruction to a student and could not come to the phone. I said, 'Let me guess. Would he be giving individual instruction to a female member of the band?' There was a long pause, and then the woman wanted to know how I knew that. I told her it was just a guess and that I would call back."

"Oh, my God, he's at it again," Tanya said, and then she stole a line from Dave. "That bastard is going after more girls. We've got to stop him. Did you call back?"

"I waited about a half hour or so and then buzzed him back. This time, the woman in the office transferred me to his phone. He picked it up on the second ring. I told him I was from the Bay City *Blade* and that I was working on a story about Candace Phelps. He hung up without saying a word."

"We may have to go down to Florida, Dave," Nick said. "I haven't been able to get a hold of Clapper all afternoon. I hope he will go for it. We've got to chase this."

Just then, Nick saw Mickey Davidson come into O'Hare's. He waived at the attorney and asked Tanya to update Dave on their plan to find Doc Sheffield and contact the Joselyns. Nick jumped up from the table and headed over to the bar where the young prosecutor was waiting to be served a vodka martini with a twist of lemon.

"Hey, Mickey, I'm glad you stopped by. I've got something I wanted to give you a heads-up on."

"Oh, yeah? What's up, Nick? Is this a story you're working on, or just something you've come across and want to alert me to because you're a good citizen?"

Nick told Mickey – in very general terms – he was working on a follow up story about the death of a local educator and may have stumbled across some crimes – murder and possibly rape.

"Murder and rape? That's quite a bit to stumble across. I hope you didn't hurt yourself when you fell."

Nick and Mickey laughed nervously. Sassy Sally brought Nick a beer, but he did not drink it. He set the mug on the bar and told the prosecutor he would have more to tell him in a day or two.

"Nick, I appreciate your filling me in on this, but I need to remind you that you cannot withhold evidence if you know crimes have been committed," Davidson said. "You must come forward with it as soon as you have it. I hope you're not thinking of trying to write a story about it first."

"Mickey, I'm trying to be cooperative here. I have no evidence. I'm not in the evidence business. That's your thing, that's what you do. I have information and I'm trying to compile facts and share that with readers of The *Blade* – sharing what I know is my job, and I will be happy to share with you, too. I'm a news reporter, not a cop. I'm not sure exactly how this is going to end up yet. There are still a lot of blank spaces on this thing."

"OK, well, keep me posted."

"We may have something tomorrow morning, or the next day. I'll call you if it comes together." Nick went back to his table. He knew it was time to leave O'Hare's. Friday would be a big day, perhaps one of the biggest in his career. He had no way of knowing just how big the day was going to be in the grand scheme of things.

# Friday was a day Nick would never forget …

## FRIDAY MORNING

The last day of the workweek in the newsrooms of many daily newspapers in America is always a little spastic. That's when reporters and editors are putting together three days' worth of newspaper in the time usually allotted for just one.

It's also the day when most firings take place. Doing the dirty deed on Friday makes for an automatic cooling off period between management and the ditched, and it also allows separation to settle in on the staff over the weekend. Friday marks the end of the week, so it's really kind of appropriate when it, too, marks the end of a career.

Until Friday, Nick did not really believe that the end was near for him. In his nearly 22-year career at The *Blade*, he'd reported and written several great stories for the paper. He showed up and worked hard almost every workday, rarely calling in sick and often working nights or weekends without overtime pay. Only a handful of minor blemishes marred his personnel file. Two written reprimands for arguing with superiors about his work and two for dress-code violations, both noting that he failed to wear neckties when the occasion dictated that one was required. He'd also received two swats on his knuckles for drinking on the job (though he objected to both criticisms because alcohol was served by hosts at the press conferences where the transgressions occurred).

Nick figured his latest so-called screw-ups – the confrontational interview with Charlie Joselyn and his failure to attend the interview wrinkle-free and with a tie – would result in two more reprimands for the file. But he was wrong. The reporter sensed foreboding doom when he was summoned to a mid-afternoon meeting with his boss, Drayton Clapper, and the editor-in-chief of The Blade, Morton D. Richardson, whom the scribe had only spoken to three times in his tenure at the paper.

As Nick entered Richardson's office, a feeling of dread spread from the top of his head down to his toenails. The two editors were seated at a round, flat table in the middle of the office away from Richardson's massive, oak desk, which spread across the far corner of the room. The only objects on the desk were the editors' elbows and Nick's personnel file, which rested on top of another manila file. Right away, Nick noticed an empty cardboard box – one probably big enough to hold a 20-inch color television set and some stereo speakers – on the floor in front of the desk.

"Come in and have a seat, Nick," said Richardson, as he wriggled his large bottom into the back of a chair that was about to undergo severe stress. "These are meetings that I never enjoy, but, unfortunately, they are sometimes required."

Nick pulled out the remaining chair at the table and sat in it without saying a word. He searched Richardson's and Clapper's faces for signs of leniency and mercy. He found none. Clapper looked away, and then down at the table as Richardson began reciting a well-rehearsed script. Nick thought Drayton was about ready to throw up.

"Nick, in reviewing your personnel file and your recent conduct, I think it is very clear that we are going in different directions. The newspaper is going one way, and you have decided to follow your own path. Nick, that cannot continue any longer. I think it's in everyone's best interest that we part ways completely and formally. We're going to have to let you go, Nick."

Nick cleared his throat before speaking, and then asked in an even tone: "Do you mind if I ask why? What have I done that merits getting fired?"

"All newspapers, all companies, have policies and procedures in place so that business can be conducted in an orderly way," Richardson said, lowering the volume of his voice. "When members of the newspaper team follow the policies and procedures, our business runs smoothly. Nick, it's very obvious from your conduct that you don't want to be a member of the team. You want to do things your way. I'm afraid that's just not going to work. It's time to move in another direction. It's time for you to go your own way completely."

"OK, then," Nick said, his voice and temper rising as he looked back and forth between the two editors. "Tell me this. Please tell me that you're canning me because I pissed off a prominent member of the community. I suppose I can handle that kind of reasoning. But please do not tell me that you're ending my journalism career over a goddamned necktie. That's something I don't think I can handle."

"Nick, let's not allow ourselves to get out of control. That benefits no one," Richardson said, dropping the volume of his voice even lower. "Let's stay focused. Your journalism career is not over, not by long shot. You're a good reporter. You won't have any trouble finding another job. But you working here is simply not a good fit. It's not working, and it's time to move on. We are prepared to make you an offer that will help you during the transition between this job and your next one."

With that, Richardson placed Nick's personnel file on his oak desk and opened up the manila file. In it was Nick's kiss good-bye – some walk-away money. The *Blade* offered Nick six months' salary and continued health-care benefits on the condition that he sign a waiver, which required him to agree not to sue the company or make a big stink about his departure. No interviews with local television or radio news reporters. No demonstrations of outrage.

Just quietly walk away with his jeans full of cash. This is what's known in the industry as the clean break. All parties involved go their own ways without leaving a nasty, ugly mess along the side of the road. The newspaper pays out some cash and gets to hire someone who is a better fit for the company, and the fired employee gets a nice soft, cushion to land on while he or she searches for new employment.

"You have the weekend to think about it, Nick," Richardson said. "In the meantime, please give me your door key and parking pass. Drayton will go with you to pack your things. Please leave all company materials on top of your desk. You can put your personal effects in this empty box."

Without saying a word, the three men stood up and stepped away from the table and away from each other. Nick's heart pounded. His breathing shortened to quick gasps for air. He felt dizzy. Nick grabbed the cardboard box and headed for the newsroom. Clapper walked behind him. They did not speak or make eye contact while Nick emptied out his desk. By this hour on a Friday, no one was left in the newsroom save two members of the cleaning crew. It was as quiet and somber as a cemetery. The only thing missing was a bugler playing taps for a fallen soldier. Nick was devastated.

Clapper was crestfallen. "I'm sorry this happened, Nick."

Nick finished packing and left the building without speaking to Clapper or the two older women emptying trashcans in the newsroom. As he drove away from The *Blade* parking lot, he was certain that this had been one of the darkest days in his life. A single tear crawled down his left cheek. It suddenly hit him. This was the first time he'd been fired. It also was the first time he had been unemployed since his sophomore year in high school.

Nick thought about what had happened as he drove toward home. It had to get better because it sure couldn't get any worse. Earlier, he'd made plans to meet Tanya and Dave at O'Hare's. Things were different now. He needed time to think. He called Dave on his cell phone to tell them that he would not be joining the usual Friday evening revelry. He was in no mood to celebrate.

"Hi, Nick. What's up?" Dave fumbled with the tiny cell phone and tried to keep it pressed against his ear as he bumped his way through the growing and raucous crowd at O'Hare's. He sat down at a table in the corner where Tanya was doing her best to hold onto her chair and two others. Dave pointed at the phone and indicated to her that Nick was calling. She smiled. "Hey, man, I'm heading home right now. I'm not going to join you," Nick said.

"Why? The beer is cold, the crowd is hot and the music is loud. Come on over, man," Dave said, as he slid into the chair across from Tanya. "We're waiting for you."

"I can't, Dave. I just got… fired at The *Blade*." The word "fired" almost didn't come out. It got hung up in his tightened throat like a speeding car gets bottled up in heavy freeway traffic.

"What? Say that again. We must have a bad connection." Dave pulled the cell phone away from his ear and stared at it in his hand. Tanya could see the stunned look on his face.

"I got fired. They called me in and dumped me." Nick said. "I'm just going home. I need time to think and sort things out."

"OK, we'll be right there." Dave clicked off his phone, gulped down the contents of his mug in three large slugs and motioned for Tanya to follow him. "Come on, Tanya, we've got to go to Nick's. The bastards at The *Blade* canned him."

Nick walked into his apartment and clicked on the living room light. He kicked off his shoes and looked around the place he called home. He was alone. The place was as quiet as a church on Monday morning. It was also a total mess.

"What a shithole," he said out loud, even though no one was present to hear his despair. "I live in a dump. I just got fired. My refrigerator is empty and my baby is almost out of gas. What the hell am I going to do now?"

As he tossed his jacket onto a dining room chair, the former reporter ambled into what he called his living room and slumped into the couch. In minutes, the quiet was pierced by the familiar thumping sound from the rusty exhaust on Dave's pickup truck as it pulled up in front of his apartment building. Nick could hear muffled voices approaching. Then his front door wobbled under the heavy thud of Dave's balled-up fist.

"Hey, Nick. It's me and Tanya. We come bearing beer and good will. Let us in." Dave and Tanya stood on the front step, waiting and hoping that Nick would respond. They were not disappointed. The door swung open.

"Thanks for coming over, but I don't want to spoil your night," Nick said, holding the door for Tanya and Dave as they burst in to his entryway. Tanya reached up and threw her arms around Nick, pulling him close to her as she stood on her tiptoes. "Nick, I'm so sorry. I can't believe they fired you."

"Me either. I knew I screwed up, but I didn't think I would get the company death penalty for it," he said, wrapping his arms around her and hugging her like a cheap suit clings to a used car salesman. After a minute or so, but what was not nearly long enough, Nick let her go and turned to his friend, sticking out his right hand.

Dave did not reciprocate. "Hey, don't I get a hug, too?"

"I don't think so," Nick said with a laugh. "You probably haven't bathed this week. Let's stick to a handshake." The two friends shook, then quickly embraced. Dave patted his pal on the back.

"Don't worry about it, man," Dave said. "We'll get this figured out. Trust me. It will all work itself out. Now, tell me what happened. And, here, have a beer."

The trio cracked open ice-cold cans of beer and sat in Nick's living area. He spilled out his story and they listened intently. Telling his friends what happened made Nick feel better. Suddenly, it wasn't the end of his life.

"This is just a bump in the road, man. We will ride high again, my friend," Dave said, as he drained his second beer and let the resulting belch escape into his sleeve and the back of his hand. "Yes, we will ride high again."

Tanya ignored Dave's lack of manners and raised the question no one in the room had yet brought up. "What about the story? How does the story get out now?" The room was silent. The trio traded glances.

"The story is dead," Nick said. "I don't have a way to tell it now. I'm out of the newspaper business."

"Oh, no it isn't." Dave stood up to declare war. "We've got to find a way to finish this story. We can't let it go now. It's got to be told. Too many people have been hurt. Too many lives have been ruined. We owe it to them to get this story out before the public. We have to help them find some measure of justice."

Nick was impressed. The beer was working. Dave was on a roll, but swaying, slightly, as he stood defiantly in the middle of the room, blurting out lofty journalistic platitudes.

Now, Tanya stood up and grabbed three fresh beers from the evaporating 12-pack. "We don't need the newspaper. Let's publish it online. You write it, Nick, and then we post it on the Internet. The bloggers will go wild. To hell with The *Blade*." She tossed a beer to Nick and Dave, cracked open the one in her hand and raised it in the air for a toast.

Nick jumped to his feet and hoisted his beer in the air to join his friends. Their cans clicked. They swigged the golden liquid and hugged in a tight triangle. "To hell with The *Blade*," Nick said, pulling his friends close.

"You're absolutely right, Tanya. Let's get the story published online. Will you two help me finish it?"

"Damn right," Dave said. "We'll jump on it the first thing in the morning. But first, let's finish this beer." Nick picked up his cell phone and ordered pizza. The three friends would drink, eat and lay out their plans to finish reporting and writing a story that they each believed had to be told. Their next step would be taking the Johnson and Pepadowski medication to Doc Sheffield and asking him if it was what he prescribed for the two deceased educators.

Suddenly, a bright light now illuminated an otherwise very dark day.

# Doc Sheffield knew something was wrong, and what to do ...

### SATURDAY MORNING

At 9 a.m. sharp, Nick pulled into Tanya's driveway and waited for her to come dashing out of her home. She appeared in the front window and waved at him. While he waited for her, his mind raced ahead. He and Tanya were going to Doc Sheffield's home, but he had decided during his morning walk that they should go to the Joselyns' first.

"Good morning, Nick," Tanya said as she slid into the Firebird's passenger seat. "I told my mom that we were going to see Doc Sheffield this morning, and she said that he usually goes golfing on Saturday morning. Daddy used to be one of his golf buddies and they never missed a Saturday – especially in November when every Saturday could be the last outing of the year."

Nick started the engine and pulled out of the driveway. "That's OK. I think we should go by the Joselyns first anyway. I feel like I should at least tell them about our suspicions. I know he's a pretty miserable S.O.B. and he probably got me fired, but I feel funny about not alerting them. What happens if his medication has been changed, too? It wouldn't be right to not tell them."

"Well, what are you going to say?" Tanya turned in her seat and flipped off the music that played quietly in the background on the car's radio. "How do you tell a person that you suspect that someone is trying to kill him?"

"I'm not sure how I'm going to go about it. My interview with him on Monday ended pretty badly. When I left, he was grumbling and threatening to sue me. He was so pissed that he called the publisher to complain. You can bet that he's probably not going to be real excited to see me standing on his front doorstep. If I were him, I'd call the cops if I saw me."

"Maybe we should call him then," Tanya said. "I don't like simply showing up at the door. Are you sure this is the best thing to do?"

"No, I'm not sure. I'm flying by the seat of my pants here. You can stay in the car. I'll bang on the door and see if anyone answers. If he doesn't want to talk with me, that's OK, too. But at least I will have tried to do the right thing and alert him to possible danger."

The Joselyn neighborhood bustled with activity. It was a sunny and cool morning. Heavy winds overnight had knocked most of the leaves off of tall maple and ash trees that lined the street. Families were already outside raking leaves into huge piles. As Nick pulled up to the Joselyn home, he watched a handyman carrying storm windows from a backyard storage shed. That's good, he thought, because it might mean that the Joselyns were home. He shouted "Morning," to the handyman as he walked to the front door. The doorbell announced his arrival. After several minutes, the big front door swung open. Mrs. Joselyn smiled when she saw Nick. He was relieved it was her and not the nasty old bastard who got him fired.

"Good morning, Doris. I'm sorry to bother you so early."

"Hello, Nick. That's OK. What's on your mind?"

"I was wondering if I could talk with you and Mr. Joselyn. It will only take a few minutes."

"Well, Charlie is not feeling well. He's still in bed. Would you like to come in?" She held the door open for Nick and waved him into the home's entryway.

"Is he just having a bad day?"

"To tell you the truth, he hasn't been very well since you were here last Monday. He was quite upset after you left, but he didn't want to talk about it. He went into a kind of funk for a couple of days. On Thursday, he said he didn't feel very good. Since then he hasn't eaten much and he's spent most of the time in bed."

"I have to ask you something. When I was here last Monday, I overheard you say that you were picking up a new medical prescription for him. Did you get that prescription from the Easy-Med on Center Avenue?"

"Yes, I did. Why do you ask?"

"Has Mr. Joselyn been taking the medication since Monday?"

"Every day. Why? What's going on, Nick?"

"The medication is really the reason I came here today. I wanted to let you know that there may be a problem with it."

"A problem? What kind of problem?"

"The prescriptions may be messed up. Tanya Johnson and I are going to see Doc Sheffield this morning. Could I take Mr. Joselyn's medication with me to show him?"

"Doc Sheffield prescribed the medicine for him. He already knows what it is."

"I understand that, but I'd like to show Doc Sheffield what Mr. Joselyn is taking. Show him the actual pill bottle. I know it sounds kind of crazy, but I think it might help answer some questions."

"I guess it would all right. Wait here a minute while I go get it. It will take a few minutes. He's taking so much these days."

When Mrs. Joselyn returned, she was carrying four pill bottles. She handed them to Nick, who pulled a large plastic resealable bag out of his jacket pocket.

"Thank you, Doris. I promise I will get back to you today on these. I'll show them to Doc Sheffield and if everything checks out OK, I'll have them back to you in no time."

"I took his dosage for today out already. But we'll need them back by tomorrow."

Nick hustled back to the car and Tanya. He tossed the plastic bag of pills into the backseat. It landed right next to plastic bags containing the pills of the late George Pepadowski and Robert Johnson. Nick fired up his machine. "Let's go find Doc Sheffield."

By now, it was just after 10 a.m. Nick and Tanya went to the Sheffield residence, but the doctor was not back from his morning session of golf. His wife said that on Saturdays, he usually golfed in the morning and stayed at the country club for lunch and then an early afternoon swim. He would not be home until later, particularly if Michigan State University football was on television.

The Bay City Country Club was not actually in Bay City. Its rolling hills and lush greens were right outside the city limits, but still within easy reach of ritzy East Side residents and the well-heeled executives from General Motors, Dow Chemical, and S.C. Johnson who lived in the posh suburb of Essexville. The club was not a playground for Nick and other working stiffs. He had been to the club for Christmas parties and other special company events. But this visit was not for pleasure. He and Tanya needed Doc Sheffield, and they needed him right away. Even though they were not members or patrons, Tanya and Nick walked through the country club like they owned the place. They were on a mission. They had to find Doc Sheffield and interrupt the elderly medical doctor's day of leisure.

"Now, you know you're going to have to do most of the talking," Nick said as he held open a door that led to the club's Green Room, the place of comfort where duffers gather after they play to lie about their games that day. "I've never met the guy, but he knows you. You've got your father's pills to show him. He will talk to you, but not to me because of privacy issues."

"No problem. I'll get us started with my dad's medication, and then I'll show him the other pills we have."

As they walked to the back of the Green Room, an older gentleman with rosy cheeks, a white handlebar moustache, and thinning gray hair stood up from his chair as soon as he caught sight of Tanya. Doc Sheffield opened his arms and his face lit up with a smile as big and appetizing as the fruit in a banana split.

"Tanya, my dear. How nice to see you. You look wonderful."

The Johnsons' only daughter slipped into the physician's outstretched arms and planted a kiss on the cheek of the doctor who helped Isabelle Johnson bring a baby girl into the world 32 years ago. Nick stood back and watched the two embrace tenderly.

"Hi, Doc. I'm doing fine. It's so great to see you. Mother said to say hello. She sends her best. I hoped we would find you."

"Oh, you're here looking for me? I thought this might be a chance meeting and it was my lucky day."

"It's always great to see you, but I need your help. But first, let me introduce you to my friend, Nick Steele."

The two men shook hands, exchanged pleasantries and Tanya quickly added that her buddy was a journalist. The doctor invited them to join him at his table. "What's on your mind, my dear? You look troubled."

"I am, Doc. I want to show you something and ask your opinion," she said, pulling her father's medication out from a large handbag she'd brought just to haul the prescriptions around. "These are the pills daddy was taking when he died. We were wondering if you could look at them."

The doctor looked first at Tanya, and then Nick, as if to try to read their minds. Then he held the pill bottles up to the light and looked at the wording on the labels. Then, he grunted and looked back at the young people sitting at his table. "What's this all about?"

Nick spoke up for the first time. "Doc, we have reason to believe that the medication for Mr. Johnson may have been tampered with. That's why Tanya and I came to you."

"Well, you know, young man, that I cannot speak with you about one of my patient's treatments or medications. That would be completely out of line."

"Yes, I know that. But we were hoping that you would speak

with Tanya about it. And her mother knows we are here. It's very important."

"Let me ask you this. I've seen your byline in The *Blade*. Are you working on this for your paper? Am I going to read about this in The *Blade*?"

Nick tried to dodge the question. "This is part of a much bigger story that we're working on. Right now, I don't know exactly what's going to get published. We're trying to get to the bottom of this, and we're hoping that you can lead us to the truth."

Doc Sheffield turned away from Nick and looked directly into Tanya's eyes. "I can tell you this, sweetheart. My memory is not as good as it used to be, but I don't believe I would have prescribed this for your father. But I must qualify my answer by saying that I will have to check his medical records, and I'd be happy to do that for you on Monday."

"Thanks, Doc, but we really need your help today."

"Why? What do you mean, child?"

Tanya reached down into her handbag and pulled out two more plastic bags containing several pill bottles. "We've also got these."

"My Lord. Before I go any further, I need some explanation."

Nick stepped in again. "Doc, we have reason to believe that this medication was tampered with, too. One bag holds the medicine you prescribed for George Pepadowski six years ago, and the other contains your prescription for Charles Joselyn, which I believe you wrote for him last week."

Doc Sheffield again studied the faces of the two seated with him. He then opened each bag and pulled out its contents, holding each pill bottle up to the Green Room's natural light. The doctor placed the pill bottles on the table in front of him. He shifted in his chair and cleared his throat. Then, he looked at each bottle again, carefully examining each container and gently rattling the contents around in a swirling motion. He drummed the fingers of his right hand on the table while he held his formidable chin with his left.

Nick and Tanya watched every move without saying a word.

Finally, after the passing of what seemed like an hour, but was only several minutes, the doctor spoke. "Again, I can't really speak with either of you about these two prescriptions – doctor/patient confidentiality. But I will say this. Right now, I am going to make three telephone calls and you are welcome to sit here and overhear what I have to say."

Tanya and Nick were puzzled by Doc Sheffield's answer, but the mystery was solved as soon as he made his first call. The doctor held the cell up to the light and punched in a number and waited as it rang.

"Hello, this is Doctor Sheffield and I would like to order an ambulance for Charles Joselyn. He lives at 3366 Park Avenue. In a minute, I will call and tell his wife, Doris, that you are coming. He is an older patient and he will require careful attention while you are transporting him to the hospital. I will meet you in the Emergency Room. I believe he may have acute internal bleeding. He may be a little ornery. Try not to let him get too agitated. Thank you."

Doc Sheffield reloaded his cell phone with another number. "Good morning, Doris. This is Doc Sheffield. I do not want to cause you undue alarm, but I want you to know that I've ordered an ambulance to come and pick up Charlie."

The doctor paused while Doris spoke. He looked at Tanya and then at Nick, who could hear the elevated tone of Mrs. Joselyn's voice through the cell phone receiver. She was, indeed, alarmed.

"I can say with certainty that the pills you gave Tanya and her friend this morning are not what I prescribed for Charlie last week. If he's been taking the medication since then, then I would bet that he's quite ill – very listless, no appetite, and extraordinarily grumpy. The ambulance and hospitalization are precautions. I want to get him checked out, straighten out his medication, and then get him back to you. I'll probably only keep him a couple of days. Thanks, Doris."

Doc Sheffield hung up. His eyes danced between Nick and Tanya. He didn't say anything. He didn't have to. His actions spoke louder than anything he could possibly say to them directly. He poked more numbers into his cell phone. This time, he pointed the phone toward Nick and Tanya so they could hear who answered the call. "Bay County Prosecutor's Office…"

"Yes, this is Doctor Sheffield, and I need to talk with the prosecutor right away. Yes, I know it's Saturday morning but please have him call me immediately. Better yet, tell him to meet me at my office in one hour. I have to make a quick stop at the hospital, but then I will be going to my office. I have some records to show him that I know he will be interested in. We're probably going to have to bother a judge to get a search warrant this afternoon, too. Thank you."

The doc hung up his phone and put it on the table. His day of leisure was pretty much shot. He looked down at his shoes for several minutes and then spoke without looking up.

"I don't know exactly what's going on here, yet. But I plan to find out right away. What you've demonstrated is that the medicine of three of my patients has been tampered with, and two are dead. Another patient is gravely ill. This is very serious business and I won't rest until I have some straight answers. I thank you for bringing it to my attention."

Nick and Tanya thanked Doc Sheffield for trusting them before leaving the country club. They walked to the parking lot in silence, trying to absorb all that had just occurred. In a matter of minutes, Doc Sheffield had confirmed most of their deepest fears.

Even with her suspicions, Tanya was stunned to hear that her dad's prescription had somehow been altered – either by accident or on purpose. It left her feeling sick and empty. She was suddenly overwhelmed with the sense that her dad might still be alive if the mix-up hadn't happened. What would she tell her mother and her brothers? How could she explain it? So many questions were still unanswered.

"What do you think, now, Nick? I'm thinking that my dad was taken from us before his time."

Tanya and Nick walked through the country club and out to the parking lot in silence. They were too shocked to speak. Their worst fears were upon them, consuming them like a hot flame licks the edges of a piece of paper before swallowing it whole. It was finally sinking in with Tanya. Her father did not die from natural causes. Someone had poisoned him by screwing up or by changing his prescription and medication. She felt ill. Her stomach churned and her head ached. A feeling of dread swept through her body. She had to tell her mom and her brothers that the most important person in their lives had been poisoned. The next few days were going to be awful. She believed it would be like having the funeral and wake all over again.

"Nick, what am I going to say to my mom? What do I tell her?" Tanya kept walking toward Nick's car with her head down. She was trying not to wet the sidewalk with tears. "Do you think they'll want to exhume the body and do an autopsy?"

Nick kept stride with Tanya and tried to comfort her. "That would be my guess. Now that a question has been raised about his death, they'll want to find out exactly what he died from. You should probably get your mother prepared for that. It could happen fairly soon."

"As hard as this is going to be on her, I know she would want the truth to come out. If it was Gus Phelps who poisoned daddy, or if it was an accident, then we need to know. What about Gus, what happens with him next? Will they arrest him and question him?"

"They've got to investigate. Once they seize the computer files, that should tell them when and how the prescriptions were altered. It won't take too long for them to figure out who did it. Gus had the motive and opportunity to take out your dad, Mr. Pepadowski and Charlie Joselyn. It might take a few days, but, when it's all over, I think all the fingers will be pointing at Gus. I've got to try and interview him before the cops start sniffing too close."

"Confront him?" Tanya stopped dead in her tracks and turned

to face Nick. "He might be a cold-blooded killer. If what you think is true, he plotted and executed elaborate plans to kill two people, and had a third one on his way to the funeral home. Confronting him is risky, don't you think?"

"Well, once the cops come in with a warrant to search computer files, he will either clam up completely and not say anything, or he may decide to run. Besides that, I'm ready to start writing my story. I don't want to wait for the cops. I could have the whole thing ready to publish by the time they arrest him."

Nick and Tanya climbed into the hotrod. Nick took Tanya home. She wanted to talk with her family about what was going on. She needed to be with them for a while, but she also had one other goal for the afternoon that she did not want to share with Nick. Not just yet, anyway. She would catch up with Nick later.

When they parted, she reached up and grabbed Nick's shoulders and pulled him within reach of her lips. She pecked him on the cheek. "I know I'm not supposed to kiss you, but I can't help it. Thank you so much for unraveling this whole thing. Thank you for my family. Nick, I…"

"Tanya, no, no. Don't thank me. I haven't done anything yet. We're figuring this all out together. I'm still not done. We've got a lot to do. Thanks for sticking with me through everything. You know, I am, after all, an unemployed bum. I was pretty damned low when you and Dave came over last night."

Nick gave Tanya a gentle hug and wanted to return the kiss, but was afraid to cross the line. Even though he no longer worked at The *Blade,* he was still a journalist. He still had his standards and values. He knew that there would be a time for a kiss, perhaps many kisses, another day.

"I'll see you later, Tanya," Nick said as he released her and spun around to find his Firebird. It was at times like these that he wished he'd figured out a way to train the Firebird to come when he whistled. Now, that would have been a really cool trick.

# The blind masseuses' hands told him everything…

SATURDAY AFTERNOON

No one was home when Tanya swooped through and peeked into each room on the first floor of her mother's house. She had hoped to find her mom and brothers so she could tell them what she had learned from Doc Sheffield. But all Tanya found in the house was a note taped to the fridge in the kitchen: "Tanya: The boys took me to the mall. What a surprise! Call me if you need us, otherwise we'll see you later in the afternoon. Love, mom."

Tanya smiled at the note. The three of them were having a good time. Her mother didn't get that kind of quality time with both of her boys together very often. It was a great day for her mom. Tanya decided that the heavy news about her dad that she was ready to bring down on the family could wait a little while longer. There was no need to rush. It would come quickly enough. Instead of interrupting their day, she decided to try and achieve her other goal for the afternoon. Tanya grabbed her jacket and purse and headed for the Emergency Room of Bay Medical Center.

The hospital was just a half-dozen blocks away from the Johnsons' East Side home. Once there, she searched the public waiting rooms for Doris Joselyn, but had no luck. Finally, after about 30 minutes of scouting the halls, she stopped an attendant that she thought she recognized from Central High School.

"Excuse me. I'm trying to find someone who I think is here with her sick husband," Tanya said, gently touching the arm of the young, female attendant. "Do you happen to know Doris Joselyn? Have you seen her?"

"Oh, yes. If you went to Central High School, then you know Doris and Charles Joselyn. You went there, too, didn't you? I thought I recognized you. I'm Susan Herndon."

Tanya was stunned. Darrin Appleton's third victim was standing before her. It had been several years, but she knew it was Susan as soon as she heard the name come out of the young woman's mouth.

"Oh, hi Susan. I thought I recognized you, too. I'm Tanya Johnson. It's been so long. Nice to see you again. Have you been working here for awhile?"

"Two years. I absolutely love it. I run into people I know all the time."

Tanya wanted to find out if Susan knew of the band director's fourth victim. She wasn't quite sure how to bring it up delicately, so she decided to simply plunge ahead. "Sue, I have to ask you something I've been curious about for some time."

"What is it, Tanya. I don't have much time to talk right now, but go ahead, ask."

"Do you remember Candace Phelps and Sarah Evans from school?"

"Oh, yes. They were real sweethearts, and poor Candace. What a tragedy. I still think of her from time to time. But I haven't seen Sarah in several years."

"Well, I talked with her last week, and the subject of our old band director came up. Sarah told me some shocking things about him. I had heard he was involved with Candace, but I had no idea about him being involved with others."

Sue's facial expression drooped. Suddenly, it looked as though she'd eaten something vile for lunch and it was just now catching up to her. Instantly, the smile vanished from her face. Deep creases lined her forehead. Her eyes flashed with anger.

"You don't have to tiptoe around it," Susan said. "I'm a big girl. Yeah, I was involved with the bastard, too. But he only got inside my head, not my pants."

"Oh, no, Sue. I'm so sorry."

"Don't be. He hurt me, but not as badly as he hurt some of the others when he was here. He had only started giving me personal instruction – you know, the private sessions in the band room with the door locked – when he bolted from town. I remember being crushed, but then I found out about Candace and the others… What a son-of-a-bitch he was. He played with us. I felt like such a fool."

"I heard there was a fourth girl, do you know who she might be? I wouldn't ask, but it's really important to find out now."

"The fourth girl was Amy Simpson. She was in our class, too. In fact, she and Candace were good friends. They used to hang out together, but Appleton got between them. I didn't find out all the details until much later, but each wanted his undivided attention. I think they were actually trying to outdo each other – out perform each other – with the romance, if you know what I mean."

"What became of her? I remember Amy, but I don't think I've seen her in years."

"Like everyone else, she was wiped out when Candace killed herself, but Appleton stayed in touch with her. He fed her a whole bunch of bullshit, saying Candace was mentally ill and how he had nothing to do with her death. I heard she ended up following him down to Florida. The last I knew, she was going to have a baby. And get this, the prick still never married her. He always talked the big game with us, but never delivered. All that was a few years ago, though. I have no idea what's up with her these days. Her folks still live in town. They moved into one of the new condos down on the riverfront. Of course, they were devastated by what happened, but I bet they could give you more details."

"Oh, thanks, Sue. I really appreciate it. Let's get together and talk more. I have someone I want you to meet. He's a journalist and he's trying to find Appleton."

"Oh, wow! Sure, I'd talk to him. Two questions: Is he good looking and is he available?"

"He's an absolute dreamboat, and I'm doing everything I can to make him mine. I'll introduce you two, but remember I saw him first."

Both women laughed, and Sue said she had to run.

"I gotta get moving, let's get together again. See you. Oh, and you'll find Mrs. Joselyn in the chapel down the hall. When I saw her last, she was in there all by herself."

"Thanks, Sue. I'll catch up to you later."

Tanya turned away from her old schoolmate and hustled down the hall to the chapel. She slowly and quietly opened the door. Mrs. Joselyn was sitting by herself in a wrought-iron pew with a big, lush seat cushion. It was up near the small altar in front of a wall of brightly colored stained glass. A single, tall candle burned atop the small wooden platform on the altar.

"Mrs. Joselyn, excuse me, but could I talk with you for a moment?"

Doris turned and motioned for Tanya to come forward. The two women, separated by 40 years, still had plenty in common. They loved two men who had shared much through the years at Central. They talked quietly.

"It sounds like Charlie is going to be OK, but it was a close call," Doris said, turning her handkerchief to find a dry side. "Doc Sheffield left a little while ago. He said we got him here in the nick of time, and I really do mean the Nick of time. Your young man saved his life. We certainly owe him a debt of gratitude."

"Mrs. Joselyn, did you know that Nick has been fired by The *Blade*?"

"What, why? What did he do?"

"Well, it sounds like he broke some of the paper's policies, and when the publisher found out that Mr. Joselyn did not like the interview Nick conducted, it was all over," Tanya said, her hand resting gently on Doris' arm. "They let him go yesterday. Nick was devastated by it, but he felt like he had a responsibility to contact you this morning. That's why we stopped at your house."

"And I'm so glad you did. Doc Sheffield said Charlie would not have lasted more than two or three days if we hadn't gotten him in here today. Nick should get a medal, not the shit house. Why, it's not right."

"They fired him, but Nick is still working on the story. He's at home right now, putting his notes together in his computer. Mrs. Joselyn, your husband's poisoning was probably not an accident. Nick thinks it's linked to my father's death and Mr. Pepadowski's death."

"Well, we can't have Nick being fired," Mrs. Joselyn said. She looked down at her wristwatch. "I know the publisher of The *Blade*. Let's go. Charlie's resting pretty easy right now. We've got to help Nick."

The two women scooted out to the parking lot. Doris Joselyn directed Tanya to drive her to the Downtown Day Spa, a ritzy, posh hideaway for the city's wealthy elite. It was exclusive and its impressive facilities were divided evenly for both men and women. Mrs. Joselyn thought she knew exactly where to find D. McGovern Givens. By this time of the day, the publisher would be naked and getting a massage by one of the spa's fabled blind, muscular, male masseuses. It might have been true that a blind male masseuse saw nothing, but his hands told him everything.

With Tanya in tow, Doris burst through the spa's steam room and marched directly up to the massage tables where Ms. Givens was getting a hot and heavy rubdown not unlike the working-over that a filly would get after a heated run in the Kentucky Derby.

"Diane, I must have a word with you right now." Doris did not wait for a response. She moved around the massage table and waded right into the nut of the story. "I am here to right a terrible wrong. You fired a man yesterday who saved my husband's life. Please, may I have a word with you?"

"Doris, can't it wait? I'm in heaven right now," the publisher said. "This is costing me a hundred bucks and I want my money's worth."

"No, I'm afraid it can't wait. You may be in heaven, but you've unjustly put a journalist through hell. I'll give you the hundred bucks. Now, come on. Get your ample ass up off that table. Tell the hunk to take a hike and rub some flesh down the hall."

The massage ended abruptly and Doris threw the publisher a towel. She said the two women would wait for her in the spa locker room. When the publisher appeared, Doris introduced Tanya and the three women sat down to talk. For more than an hour, Doris and Tanya yakked back and forth, each stopping only to catch their breaths. Diane mostly listened. When it was over, Diane Givens made no promises to the two women, but she said she would call her editor and they would talk about the situation that day.

Doris and Tanya left the spa feeling that they had at least chipped away at the wall between Nick and The Bay City *Blade*. At just about the same time that afternoon, another attempt to knock it down was well underway in The *Blade's* downtown newsroom.

# Reporters are a dime a dozen and Nick wasn't worth the grief...

## SATURDAY AFTERNOON

Saturday afternoons in The *Blade* news office were usually about as lively as the open banter you'd hear in a public library. Normally, the place was empty until skeleton news and sports crews assembled in the evening to push out the final, last pages for the Sunday newspaper early in the morning.

But this Saturday was different. Drayton Clapper drove into work to catch up on tasks that did not get completed during the chaos of Nick's late afternoon firing. The dismissal upset Drayton so much that he could not finish his work or even look at his dinner when he finally arrived home Friday night. He spoke briefly to Carolyn, his wife of 26 years, and the two then uncorked a large bottle of California merlot and retreated to their library, holding hands and quietly discussing what had happened. Only a small candle and tiny flames lapping at a log in the fireplace lit the room. Carolyn could not remember the last time she saw her husband weep, but big tears splashed down on the collar of his shirt that night. She knew he had been hurt by what had happened to Nick. Even worse, he said he had felt totally powerless to stop it. If it hadn't been for the merlot, the local news editor probably would not have gotten any sleep that night.

So, Saturday was catch-up day at work for Drayton Clapper, but his heart was clearly not into it. Things didn't get any better when he heard a familiar whistle and banging coming down the hallway to the newsroom. Before the door even swung open, Drayton knew that his day was going to get a little dimmer. He looked up just in time to see Dave rolling into his old haunt with his usual bluster.

"Hey, where is everybody? You guys running another fire drill or something? Is this place on lockdown again?" Balz said, his voice rising to near echo level in the empty room. "You know, Drayton, there's a lot of people around town who would like to take you out. You really ought to watch your step. Snipers are everywhere out there."

"Well, now my day is made. Balz afire." The editor flipped his ink pen up in the air and let it hit the floor as either a sign of relief or surrender. "Things aren't much different these days. You still pretty much come and go as you please. How did you get in here, anyway?"

"I'm retired, man. And when you're retired, you're never late for anything. You get to come and go as you please. My clock ticks with a different tock these days. And, the security guards still love me. They worship the ground I walk on. You ought to know that, Drayton. Hell, they used to let me sleep here and bring in visitors to party."

Advancing age and general fatigue were the only things that kept the two from brawling on the floor of the newsroom. They had never gotten along. Some said it went back to a story that Dave developed and Drayton killed, supposedly without reason. Others said their working relationship went sour when Balz started dating Clapper's sister. The editor never forgave him for showing her the dark and slimy side of the town.

Regardless of which tale rang true, the two were about as friendly with each other as a bullfrog and a mosquito. But, on this day, their differences seemed pretty small when compared to what had happened to Nick, a man that both of them felt close to in different ways.

"Drayton, what can we do for Nick?" The veteran reporter

plopped down in a chair near the editor's desk. "How could you fire him over such piddly shit? I can't believe it, man. He's one of the best reporters I've seen come through this newsroom in the last 20 years."

"I didn't fire him. Morton and the publisher did." The local editor fell into his own chair and stared out the window as he talked with his former reporter. "Nick simply rubbed them the wrong way. They didn't like his style, his brashness. They thought he was going to continue being a pain in the ass, so they dumped him when Nick gave them the opening.

"In their view," he continued, kicking his heels up on his desk, "reporters are a dime a dozen. They come and they go. The J-schools are always pumping out fresh, young new ones who will do what they're told and work for next to nothing. Papers all over the country are cutting their staffs, downsizing. Lots of good people out there are begging for jobs. So, in their minds, Nick wasn't worth the aggravation."

Dave leaned ahead in his seat, placing his elbows on his knees and his chin on the top of his rolled up knuckles. "But why wouldn't they keep him on long enough to at least finish this story? That's what I don't get. It's an absolutely great story. We're so close to pulling this whole thing together, and Nick is determined to finish it – with or without The *Blade*."

"I told Morton everything I knew about the story," Clapper said, moving his right hand to massage the side of his head, which was still aching from the Friday afternoon newsroom tension and the empty bottle of merlot he found on his bedroom floor in the morning. "It rolled right off of him, like it didn't matter. I did everything but beg for Nick's job, and now I'm wishing that I'd done that. I drank myself to sleep last night asking myself why in the hell I'm still working for a company that would take a dump on somebody like Nick, somebody who is as good a person as Nick. When I woke up this morning, I still didn't have an answer."

"This is sometimes a really crappy business," Dave said. "Instead of focusing on the news and telling the story, it always gets bogged down in the politics. I don't know how I lasted in it long enough to retire."

"To be honest, I don't know how you did, either," Drayton said, and then both men laughed out loud. It was the only sound in the whole newsroom. They were about to continue their philosophical conversation when they heard a door swing open and close. The two men jumped up as if burglars had entered the newsroom.

Instead of thieves, con artists strolled through the newsroom. Reynolds and Givens did not look toward Clapper's office on their way to the editor's corner office. The editor and publisher walked into Reynold's office without speaking. The door closed behind them. Balz and Clapper looked at each other in amazement. Neither of them had ever seen the publisher and the editor in the office on a Saturday afternoon. Something big was up. Clapper wondered if his job was safe, and Balz immediately thought of his pension – could they get their hands on it or cancel it?

# You do evidence, I do news.
# There's a difference...

SATURDAY NIGHT

The nightlife in Bay City on Saturdays focuses on the town's robust tavern industry. With one of the highest number of bars per capita in America, the city nestled next to Saginaw Bay worked hard to maintain its reputation as a hard-drinking, hard-partying, hangover-loving community. Revelers prowled the bar districts as soon as the sun disappeared from the sky, drinking heavily while dancing to a variety of live music – rock, blues, country – at more than a dozen booze joints. The drinks were cheap, the crowds were friendly, the music was loud, and the local cops looked the other way.

But on this Saturday night, Nick was not hunting for a wild party. As he weaved among young drunks swaying from parking meters and vomiting into the gutters along Midland Street, he worried about how Tanya and her family were handling the news that the head of their household had been murdered. When Nick checked in with her by telephone late in the afternoon, he could hear Isabelle Johnson crying softly in the background. He promised Tanya he would connect with her later – before calling it a night.

Right now, the reporter was looking for his friend, Mickey Davidson, the assistant county prosecutor. The two had talked around 5 o'clock right after a search warrant was issued by a circuit judge for the records and computer files of the Easy-Med on Center Avenue. They had agreed to meet at O'Hare's around 9 – just before uninhibited drinking usually takes its toll on party freaks and all hell starts to break loose in the district's bars. Fistfights. Flying beer mugs. Pushing and shoving. Groping and fondling. Crashing chairs. Dancing on tables. Bleary-eyed fools trying to wrestle the microphone away from lead singers to take a shot at warbling their own mangled lyrics.

Nick and Mickey needed to talk before mayhem would make it impossible to communicate in the bar. Nick bumped and elbowed his way through the O'Hare's crowd, looking for the one member of local law enforcement that he could trust. Finally, he spotted the assistant prosecutor in his usual spot, leaning against the bar, nuzzling a young blonde. In one hand, he held a scotch and water. The other held the blonde close to his hip. She squirmed lightly, each side of her round fanny pumping up and down like churning pistons. She emitted a few high-pitched squealing noises, pretending that she wanted to break free of his one-armed embrace.

"Gosh, I hope I'm not interrupting anything. You two should really think about getting a room," Nick said, wedging himself between a bar patron and Mickey on the opposite side of the blonde. He signaled to Sally behind the bar for his usual – a draught beer. "I'm only going to be here for a few minutes. I've got a big day tomorrow."

"Well, at least you didn't chase her off with a smart-assed remark about the wife and kids. I thank you for that," Mickey said, before whispering to the blonde. She smiled and nodded at Nick before whisking off toward the ladies' room. The lawman watched her sashay away and then turned to face the journalist. "Are we going to have a problem?"

"What do you mean, a problem?" Nick sipped from his beer and wiped the foam from his moustache with a quick flick of his tongue. "I'm just doing my job, chasing a story."

"And I'm trying to do my job, too. You're not making it any too easy for me, either. Doc Sheffield tells me that you're right in the middle of this thing at the pharmacy. How about filling me in on what's going on?"

"Mickey, I told you awhile ago that I was working on a pretty good story. It's all coming together right now."

"What's your story going to say? Something about an error at the pharmacy almost killing Charlie Joselyn?"

"Charlie Joselyn is only part of the story. He's a big part, but it all goes back eight years. I can't tell you everything I know because the information I have is still sketchy. The pieces of the puzzle are still falling into place. When I've got it all locked down, I'm going to write a story about it. You can read all about it."

"Look, I told you before. If you've got evidence that a crime has been committed, then you've got to come forward with it. It sounds like Charlie Joselyn was poisoned. This is serious business now. I can't play around with this."

"I don't have any evidence. That's your thing. Mine is information. I'm gathering it to write a news story. You do evidence, I do news. There's a difference."

"Don't play games with me, Nick. Where is this going? And don't give me that, 'You can read all about it' crap. Don't make me or my department look like a bunch of fools on this thing. What's going on?"

"All right. Here's my theory in a nutshell. Go back in your files eight years and look up a suicide by a Central girl named Candace Phelps. Like most teen suicides, it was all hush-hush. Everybody just wanted to look the other way and forget it. That's where I think this started. Her dad is Gus Phelps. He works at the Easy-Med on Center, the place you raided this afternoon."

"That's the connection? He tried to poison old-man Joselyn?"

"Yup. I think so, but I'm still piecing it together. It's dangerous to jump to conclusions. I won't say it's a sure thing until I've got it all nailed down. But there's more. I think he my have poisoned two others."

"No shit. Two others? Who are they?"

"They're dead. I'll tell you more when I get more information. I've got one more interview to do, and then I think I'll have it."

"OK. Keep me posted. In the meantime, we'll be checking the Easy-Med records. We'll see if there's a paper or digital trail leading to your Mr. Phelps."

"When you're checking files, also take a look at the files for George Pepadowski and Robert Johnson and see where they point. See you later." Nick finished the last gulp of his beer, nodded in Mickey's direction and headed for the front door.

About halfway there, the young blonde from the bar was making her way back toward Mickey. She and Nick pushed through the crowd. They crossed paths. She faced him and let patrons in the crowded bar push her into him. She pulled her elbows back and let her breasts brush across Nick's chest. She smiled up at the reporter. "Excuse me."

"No problem." Nick turned and bounced through the door. As he headed out into the cool November night, he thought of Tanya. She would never do anything like that. She had too much style, too much class for that kind of behavior. It was another reason he started thinking he loved her.

# I watched two die slowly, but I'm not a murderer ...

## SUNDAY MORNING

Nick and Dave met for brunch at the Paddock Restaurant and Lounge on North Henry Street on the city's West Side. It was their favorite place to get a meal that would last the whole day. They would heap their plates with scrambled eggs, rib-eye steak, sautéed hash browns, fresh grilled Polish sausage, fruit salad, and homemade rye bread that had just popped out of the oven.

But even more important than the food at the Paddock was its individual private dining tables and booths. The comfortable accommodations would give the two newsmen a chance to fully discuss the story that was quickly coming together. It was time to update on the band director and Gus Phelps, the suspected central characters of what soon would become a compelling story that would shock and anger local folks right through to their bone marrow.

Nick asked Dave what was new in his pursuit of the band director.

"I called his apartment yesterday, and there was no answer," Balz said, as he tore through a dripping piece of sausage. "'Scuse me. I hate to talk with my mouth full, but this is good stuff."

"It's OK. I've seen you without your pants on, which was really gross. So, don't worry about being polite. Please, continue."

"Yeah, right. *Ahh...* there was no answer at his place so I called the apartment manager and asked him to tell me about tenant Darrin Appleton."

"Wait a minute. How did you get Appleton's telephone number at his apartment and the number for the apartment manager? We're talking Florida here. It's not like you could pick that up by walking across the street."

"I was afraid you might ask that. When I didn't connect with him on Friday, it made me a little nervous, being so close but not actually connecting. So, I called the school secretary and told her I was with the Michigan Department of Lottery. I told her that Appleton had hit a big five-digit game, and the payoff was 50 grand, but time was running out on his ticket and he had to claim it by Saturday or it would go back to the state."

"You, dirty dog, you."

"Yeah, but it worked. She gave me the numbers. Anyway, the apartment manager said Appleton lives alone, but he sometimes had some of his students over for private music lessons. I asked him if any music actually got played during the lessons. He laughed at that. He knew what I was suggesting."

"How did you leave it?"

"I told him the bit about the lottery except for the Saturday deadline part, and said I would try back on Monday morning. What about Gus Phelps? Where are we going with him?"

"I want to run by his place this afternoon. I'd like to talk with him if the situation is right. I've got to get him before the cops come nosing around. My guess is that Mickey will be all over him by Monday. Are you still up for going with me over to Gus Phelps' neighborhood?"

"I wouldn't miss it for the world." The two friends finished eating, exchanging small talk, mostly. Dave did not volunteer what he had seen in the newsroom on Saturday afternoon. He didn't want Nick to know that he'd gone there to urge Drayton Clapper to reconsider Nick's firing. And he didn't want Nick to know that he'd seen the publisher and editor in the building for some kind of Saturday afternoon confab.

Dave turned the conversation toward the Johnson family. He asked how Tanya was doing. Nick said he had talked with her before bedtime last night and then again in the morning after his walk. She was doing better, she said, and her mom had actually slept through most of the night. Nick was relieved that Tanya was rebounding nicely from the stunning developments of Saturday morning at the country club. She told Nick that she was not going back to school in Ann Arbor right away. She wanted to stay close to her mom and brothers. She asked Nick to call.

The younger journalist paid the bill for brunch, and the older one left a generous tip on the table. They left the Paddock, hopped in the hot rod and headed toward the Phelps neighborhood on the East Side.

As they drove down Center Avenue, the sun poked through a gray sky, warming the November air. A light breeze gently shook the huge maple limbs that stretched out over the five-lane thoroughfare. Yellow, red and gold leaves fluttered softly around the street machine as it rumbled along. Nick wondered if Gus Phelps spent his Sundays at home.

They turned right on Grant Street and took it south to Second. As they rounded the corner at Second, they saw Gus Phelps dragging a huge, blue tarp toward the street with his right hand. His left held a yard rake and he used it like a walking staff. The tarp spilled leaves as it bounced across the grass in his front yard. Gus gave the passing Firebird a quick glance as it slowly drove by the home he had lived in for the last 25 years.

"What luck," Nick said as he looked up into his rearview mirror just in time to catch the handyman dumping his load of leaves into the gutter. "He's doing yard work. This is our chance. I'm going to wheel around the block and go up and talk to him. Are you with me?"

"Yup, but make sure you go easy. I doubt that he'd be doing yard work with a 9 millimeter tucked in his belt, but you never know in this neighborhood," Dave said as he scanned the small, wood-framed bungalows that lined the street.

One home's front yard was the resting place for an old Buick sitting on cement blocks. Another sported a smoldering fire pit, its chairs turned upside down amid a couple dozen empty beer cans.

"Just be real careful with this guy. We know he's a little whacked," Dave said. "If he spills my guts with a pistol shot, it's not going to be pretty on this full stomach."

After circling the block, Nick parked his machine in front of the house next to the Phelps residence. The two got out of the car before Gus looked up and spotted them heading his way. He continued with his work, briskly whisking the leaf rake. Dead foliage flipped up into the air and fluttered toward a brightly colored pile in the center of the yard.

Nick and Dave walked toward Gus. They kept their hands out of their pockets so that they would be in full view. They talked quietly and smiled, not wanting to alarm the homeowner as they slowly approached. Gus stopped his sweeping motion and stood up straight, planting the rake squarely in front of him and gripping it with both hands. He cleared his throat and looked directly at the men now in his front yard.

"What can I do for you?"

"Are you Mr. Phelps?" Nick slowed and stuck out his right hand.

"That's right," Gus said, pulling his work glove off his right hand and sticking it in Nick's mitt. "What's your name?"

"I'm Nick Steele and this is my buddy, Dave Balz. We're journalists. I was wondering if we could ask you a few questions."

"What about?" Gus pulled his hand from Nick's grasp and stuck it in Dave's outstretched paw.

"We wanted to ask you about what's going on at the pharmacy. Did you know that the police were there late yesterday afternoon?"

"They were coming in just as my shift was ending. I saw them talking to the manager as I was leaving. There's not much to tell from what I know."

"Well, we understand that the police were there with a warrant to search the pharmacy's records and computer files. Are you familiar with them?"

"I'm just a handyman at the pharmacy. I don't have anything to do with the medical records."

"How long have you worked at Easy-Med, Mr. Phelps?"

Nick decided to go back in time to see if he could put Gus Phelps at ease. It was pretty obvious that questions from two strangers on a Sunday afternoon were making him edgy.

As Nick prodded Gus Phelps, Dave stood by quietly. He surveyed Phelps' meticulous place. It was one of the better-kept yards on the street. Dave also made a mental note of something a little odd. A clothesline stretched the length of the backyard. It was full of women's clothes. Blouses, skirts, stockings, undergarments. It made him wonder if women were now actually living with Gus.

Gus pushed the rake into one hand and stuck the other on his hip. "I started working there about nine years ago. Part-time at first. It was a second job. My day job was over at the Chevy plant on Woodside Avenue. I was trying to put away some extra cash for my daughter. She was almost ready for college."

"Sure, Candace would have been about an eleventh-grader at that time, right?" Nick watched Gus' eyes carefully.

"Yeah, how do you know about my daughter?" Gus stood up straight and glared at the reporter.

"She was a friend of someone I know – Tanya Johnson."

"Oh, yeah. Tanya's a nice girl. Then you know what happened to Candace?"

"Yes, Mr. Phelps. I'm very sorry about your loss."

"Not a day goes by that I don't hurt for her. She was the sweetest thing in the world. Why, I would have worked three or four jobs for her if she needed it."

"Well, I can see why you hooked on at Easy-Med. You said you were a handyman. Is that what you did at GM?"

"I did all kinds of things at GM before I retired, but I ended up working in computer systems. I kept track of the parts inventory – what was getting built, stored and shipped. It was good pay, but I was glad to get out of there. I hated being a shop rat."

"You wanted more for your daughter, right?"

"Doesn't everybody want something better for their kids? Of course I did. She was smart as a whip. She could have done anything. But..." Gus stopped himself and started working his rake against the leaves again. "I need to get back to work here, it could snow anytime and I want this yard cleaned up."

"Mr. Phelps, your wife, Ellen, says hello."

"You met my Ellen? When did that happen? Why were you talking with her?"

"We talked with her the other day. She told us about Candace and the band director. We're doing our best to track down Darrin Appleton right now. What he did was dead wrong. Ellen says she thinks of you often and hopes that you're doing well."

"Appleton? She told you about that dirty, no good son-of-a-bitch?"

Gus stopped talking and started whacking at the leaves with his rake. His breathing became heavy, almost a pant. His obvious agitation scared Nick a little. The guy definitely looked like he had a short fuse.

"I won't take much more of your time, Mr. Phelps. But I wanted to ask you if you knew about anyone tampering with the computer files – the medical records – at Easy-Med."

Gus stopped raking. "No, I told you. I don't have anything to do with the records."

"Yes, but you are familiar with the computer system at Easy-Med and how it works, right?"

"I just do maintenance on the system. I update the software and make sure it stays bug free. They sent me to school for it."

"Did you know that Charles Joselyn uses the Easy-Med?"

The mention of Joselyn's name put rage in Gus Phelps' eyes. He started working his rake again, this time furiously whipping it through the leaves. "I think I've seen him and his wife come in the store once in awhile."

"Mr. Phelps, the cops think somebody poisoned Charles Joselyn. That's why they're searching the records."

"What happened? Did Joselyn die?"

"No, he didn't die. I alerted his doctor that his medication had been altered. Doc Sheffield sent an ambulance for him. He's in Bay Med right now. They say he's going to be OK."

Clearly, this piece of information was too much for Gus Phelps to handle. He stopped raking and squared up in front of the reporter. "You? You stepped in and told his doctor? Who said you could get involved? I think you might have stuck your big nose in the wrong place this time."

"Yup. I did it to save his life. You're the one who changed his prescription, aren't you?"

"You bastard," Gus said as he pulled the rake up over his head with both hands and swung it at Nick. "Damn you."

The metal end of the rake hit Nick squarely in the side of his head, knocking him to the ground. Gus Phelps moved toward the sprawling reporter and cocked his right leg with the intention of delivering a nap-inducing blow. But Dave stepped forward and pushed the older man back before he could deliver a second, more decisive blow to Nick's head.

Dazed, Nick rolled over and got partway up on his hands. "You did it, didn't you, Gus? You tried to avenge your little girl's death, didn't you."

"You're goddamned crazy. I'm not a killer. But Joselyn and his two flunkies deserve anything that happens to them. They left my little girl at the mercy of that rotten prick band director. They did nothing to help her. The cops did nothing. Nobody did nothing for my little girl. When they're all dead and in hell, I'll be happy. I watched two of them slowly die, but I'm not a murderer."

Nick was back on his feet just as Gus lunged at him, trying to knock him back to the ground. Dave moved in between the two men and absorbed most of the blow. The three of them clutched at each other in the front yard. Even at 63, Gus was still a very strong man. Plus, he was enraged now. He continued to rant as he wrestled with the reporters.

"You should have let Joselyn die. You had no right to step in. I want him dead."

"Gus, old man Joselyn is dying anyway. He's all wore out," Nick said, pushing back at the handyman.

"I don't give a damn about that. When he's finally dead, my little girl finds justice."

The three men rolled across the ground in a heap of whirling arms and legs. Steele and Balz were on top, mostly. A passing car stopped and its passengers were watching the melee like it was a hockey game without the ice. A neighbor came out of his house and yelled from his front porch, wanting to know if Gus was OK.

"It's OK," Nick said, breathless and sucking in huge gulps of wind. Blood trickled down the side of his cheek from the rake wound on his head. "I'm calling the cops right now. Everything is going to be OK."

As Nick punched in 9-1-1 on his cell phone, Gus moaned and gasped from beneath the pile. He said he couldn't breathe. "Get off. Get off, you big fat bastard."

"Sorry, buddy, but you're not going anywhere till the cops show up," Dave said. "You're too damn strong." Before long, a squad car pulled up. Two of Bay City's finest brushed Krispy Kreme crumbs from their bulging shirts and walked up the driveway. The three wrestlers got up from the ground.

"Officer," Nick said to the first cop, "I'd like to file assault charges against this man." Nick pointed at Gus Phelps, who was still down on one knee and trying to catch his breath. "He hit me with that rake and knocked me down. I've got witnesses. I want you to arrest him."

After questioning the three men for a few minutes, the cops did just that. They put handcuffs on Gus and placed him in their vehicle. Nick was relieved. Gus was in custody and wouldn't hurt himself or anyone else. They could hold him for 24 hours, and that would probably be enough time for the authorities to figure out who tampered with Charlie Joselyn's prescription.

Nick and Dave brushed the leaves and dirt and grass off of their clothes and climbed back in the Firebird. Nick wanted to call Mickey Davidson. Dave wanted a stiff drink.

"Maybe I'll join you later," Nick said, as the friends parted ways in front of Nick's apartment. "I want to rough in an outline of the story so that I can start writing in the morning. And I've got to call Tanya, too. At some point, we're going to have to break all this to Mrs. Pepadowski. I know it will be really hard on her."

"All right. See you buddy," Dave said, walking toward his vehicle. "I'll call on the band director in the morning and let you know what I find out.

"And one more thing," Dave said over his shoulder.

"What's that?"

"The next time you need someone to go with you on an interview, take one of the young guys, OK? I'm getting too damned old to be out rolling around on the ground."

Nick got in his car, but something nagged at him. Gus Phelps said he didn't do any killing. Guilty men rarely admit to crimes when first questioned, but Nick thought it was odd that Gus freely acknowledged he wanted to see the three school officials dead and had watched two of them die, but that he was not a killer. It made Nick wonder. If Gus wasn't the executioner, then who was?

# What's that filthy creature's name – Harry Balz? ...

## SUNDAY AFTERNOON

As Nick walked up the front steps of his apartment, he punched the memory button on his cell for Tanya's phone number with his right thumb. She answered before he could get through his locked front door.

"Tanya, how are you? Is everything OK at your house?" Nick talked and walked into his living room at the same time."

"We're doing much better today. We all went to church this morning, and we just finished eating dinner together. I think everyone is handling the news about Daddy pretty well. What about you?"

Before Nick could respond, he caught sight of the telephone message recorder blinking. "*Ahh...* Things are going very well on this end. Dave Balz and I interviewed Gus Phelps this afternoon. It was kind of scary, but the whole thing went OK. I'll tell you all about it later."

"Are we getting together later?" she asked, her spirit lifting at the prospect of seeing Nick again.

"Well, I was wondering if you'd go with me to Mrs. Pepadowski's place later. I feel like we should tell her what's going on, and what really happened to her husband before this all ends up in the news or the cops come banging on her door. She's such a sweet woman that I'd hate to see her hurt needlessly."

"Sure, I'll go with you. What time?"

"Give me a couple of hours. I need to shower and get out of these dirty clothes. I'll give you a buzz before I come over. Is that alright?"

"See you later, big boy."

Nick smiled as he clicked off his cell. He just loved it when she teased him like that. He looked forward to seeing her again. He couldn't get enough of Tanya. He knew he was falling for her big time.

But first, he had to find out who had called and left a message. He reached over and clicked it on. The voice and the message surprised him: "Nick, this is Morton Reynolds. I hate calling you on Sunday, but something has come up and I'd like to speak with you today, if possible. I'm sitting at my desk in my office. I will wait here for your return call. Thank you."

Now, that's pretty wild, Nick thought to himself. What a change in his tone, and why in the hell is he in the office on a Sunday afternoon? Maybe he got wind of the story, now that it was spilling out into the public. One of his country club pals probably heard about the search warrant at the Easy-Med. Or perhaps he was told that Doc Sheffield ended up calling an ambulance for Charlie Joselyn.

Nick decided to end the suspense. He picked up the phone and called his former boss back. The editor answered on the first ring by saying, "Hello, Nick. Thanks for returning my call."

"How did you know it was me?" Nick responded.

"Nobody else would be calling me here at this hour on Sunday. Believe me, it had to be you."

"What's on your mind?"

"I'm calling to see if you could come up to the newsroom and meet with me and the publisher."

"Right now? Is she there, too?"

"If it's not too inconvenient, we'd like you to come up now. If you agree, I'll call the publisher and she'll probably be here before you arrive. She asked me to set up this meeting, so I know she wants to meet right away."

"Well, OK. But first, let me ask you this. Do I need a lawyer for this meeting? You know, I didn't fare too well the last time we met. My rear end is still stinging from that little encounter."

"No, Nick. You won't need a lawyer. We want to straighten some things out with you, turn things around. And the publisher would like to do it in person."

"I'll be in the newsroom in 20 minutes. But you'll have to let me in the front door. I don't have a key anymore, remember?"

"Yes. I'll make sure someone is down there to let you in. Please, come right up to my office."

Nick decided to change clothes quickly. He didn't want to meet with the editor and publisher after rolling around on the ground in the leaves with Gus Phelps. Grass stains on his jeans and a torn pullover just wouldn't cut it. Nick decided to cleanup, but there was no way he was going to put on a necktie for this meeting.

After changing, washing his face and combing his hair, he jumped into his hot rod and dodged in and out of slow-moving Sunday traffic. As much as Nick respected his elders, he never understood why they all drove so-o-o-o slow. He tried hard not to think about the approaching meeting. Nick figured the publisher and editor were fearful that he was going to post the story on the Internet and decided to try and stop him. What other purpose could this meeting serve?

A security guard greeted Nick at the front door of The *Blade*. "Hi ya, Nick. Glad to see you back in the building."

"Thanks, Jimmy, but I'm just visiting today. Don't wander off too far, I think I'll be going right back out very shortly. This is probably not going to take long."

Nick took the elevator to the third floor. When he stepped out into the hallway, he could see a dim light coming from Reynolds' office. The door was half opened. He also could hear muffled voices. He walked up briskly, just as he'd been instructed, and rapped his knuckles against the oak trim on the doorway.

"Nick, please come in," D. McGovern Givens said. "I beat you here, but only by a couple of minutes. Thank you so much for joining us on a Sunday. I know this is a bit unusual, but I think you'd agree that we have a pretty unusual situation on our hands."

"Well, yes. I guess you could say that. I was pretty surprised to get your call this afternoon. Now, what's up?"

Without speaking, the publisher looked at the editor, who was sitting in his chair behind his desk. He got up and walked toward Nick, stopping squarely in front of the reporter. Their eyes locked.

"The reason I called you, Nick, is because I want to offer you your job back," he said, just a tad sheepishly. "I also want to apologize for what happened here on Friday. We were wrong to dismiss you like that, and I'm sorry for the way it was handled."

Nick opened his mouth, but no words came out. He looked over at the publisher, who was standing just off to the side of the two men, and then back at the editor.

"I... I don't know what to say," Nick said. "Hiring me back is almost as stunning as the way you fired me on Friday. I'm shocked. What happened to change your mind?"

The publisher stepped into the conversation. She started with her own apology, saying that she had not been fully informed of the circumstances surrounding the dismissal. Before continuing, she gave the editor a quick glare that would have instantly turned a bowl of water into a block of ice.

"Frankly, I screwed up," she said. "Though your style and techniques are a bit unconventional for most businesses today, you're obviously good at what you do. Nick, I want good people working at The *Blade*. I want people who have compassion for our readers and passion for their work. And you've handled yourself well under very difficult circumstances. You've touched a lot of people in this building and in this community. Doris Joselyn thinks you're the greatest, and your girlfriend, Tanya what's-her-name, is obviously in your corner."

CHAPTER 34

"She's not my girlfriend, and her name is Tanya Johnson. She's part of the story I'm working on just like Mrs. Joselyn is. I had no idea they talked with you."

"To put it simply, Nick, we want you working for The *Blade*. Will you come back to work for us?"

"Yes, but only on one condition."

"What's that?"

"Will you promise to meet with responsible people in our building to talk about your personnel policies? Believe me, you can improve morale and productivity by merely becoming reasonable."

The publisher and the editor looked at each other, and then back at Nick. Reynolds walked back to his desk and sank into his soft, cushy leather chair. He fell into it so that at a quick glance only his head, arms and legs dangled from its center.

The publisher turned and faced Nick. "I'm willing to discuss this, Nick, but there are some things you need to understand before we go down this path. I maintain high standards here for very important reasons. First and foremost, Nick, this is a business. We're here to make money and be successful."

"I understand that," Nick said. "But we're also a newspaper that our readers depend on. They count on us to keep them informed. They want us to sort out the bullshit and give them the facts. They want us to chase the truth. That's why we're here."

"Yes, Nick, you're right. Those ideals are very important for all newspapers. But this is not the college newspaper. To achieve those lofty goals, we must be a going, profitable concern. We have to make payroll every seven days. I've got 200 families in this building counting on us to make sure they get a paycheck every week. We've got 200 families who are counting on us to provide health care and dental and vision benefits. We've got 200 families who also are expecting us to put a little money aside for their retirement. And, Nick, let me remind you that we are not like most companies in this country today – your pension is fully funded and it will be there when you need it. And, one more thing, Nick, let's not forget our owners. They are expecting us to return at least a reasonable profit on their investment.

"That's why we have to be a viable business," she continued, as if conducting a seminar for one person. "We're an institution in this community and it's part of my job to protect our standing. That's why we have strict personnel policies, conduct policies and, yes, a dress code. I expect everyone who works here to look and act like a professional. Ties and slacks for men, skirts and stockings for women. That's an important part of doing business in this town."

"We can be professional without wearing pinstripes, can't we? Do we all have to dress like him," Nick said, using his chin to point at the editor, who sat in his swanky chair wearing a dark, thousand-dollar suit with a monogrammed handkerchief dangling from the jacket pocket, a tailored, pink shirt with cufflinks and patent leather shoes. Nick thought he looked like a pimp.

"Please don't tell me we've got to look like that," Nick continued, walking a very thin line once again. "I'd rather be tortured than look like that in public. Nobody in this city dresses that way – talk about being out of place. We can be professional without looking like bankers, don't you think? Why not trust us to act and behave like pros? I think a little of that would really go a long way with the people who work for you."

"Well, Nick, yes, trust is a wonderful thing. But I've learned over the years that you can't always count on everyone in this business to carry themselves in a professional manner – especially you folks in the newsroom. You always want to stretch the rules and go your own way – you know, that freedom of expression thing? Just look at that filthy creature you hang around with all the time, what's his name? Harry Balz?"

"No, his name is Dave. He is pretty hairy, but his name is actually Dave Balz. I suppose you're right in his case, though. He could clean up a little."

"A little? I'm so happy that I didn't get downwind of him

yesterday. What's his name again, Dave? Dave is much better than Harry. Harry Balz – believe me, that's some unsettling imagery that I really don't want dancing around in my head. But no, Nick. Mr. Balz is not going to be the standard around here. I can assure you of that."

"But will you at least discuss the issue?"

"Yes, I will." Diane Givens looked at her editor, then suggested that he have Drayton Clapper set up a committee from all departments in the building to study and make some recommendations on personnel policies, including the dress code.

The publisher then cautioned Nick.

"If you want to be a crusader, start your own newspaper or find another way to get published," she said. "But this paper is not going down that path."

"Well, we actually did think about printing this story on the Internet," Nick said, looking at the publisher and then turning in the direction of the editor. "The Internet is the wave of the future. You can reach a lot of people online."

The editor added his two cents to the conversation, dismissing Nick and the notion of the Internet becoming a viable distributor of news.

"Nick, the Internet is just another flash in the pan," Reynolds said. "We fought off radio and we beat down television news. We'll do the same thing to the Internet. Newspapers are an integral part of everyone's lives. We'll be around forever."

"Gee, Morton, I think you're wrong. This is not the 1930s when radio was big or the 1950s when TV kicked in. It's 1998. More people are getting more information in unconventional ways. Look at what happened with the Gulf War a few years ago. The U.S. swept into the Middle East and defeated the Iraqi army and nobody paid any attention to newspapers. All our daily reports were old news by the time they got into living rooms. We were essentially irrelevant. People don't need us any more. They can get their news elsewhere."

"Well, Nick, I guess that's why you're not running this paper,"

Reynolds said, straightening and tightening the knot in his necktie. "When the Internet has come and gone, we'll still be around and we'll still be the biggest game in town."

The publisher interrupted the discussion between Nick and Morton because she obviously had somewhere else to be.

OK, you two can renew this debate another time," she said, glancing at both men. "Now, Nick are you back on our payroll? Are you ready to be part of our team?"

"Yes. I'm back, and I'm delighted to be back."

With that, the publisher slipped on her jacket and snapped her fingers in the direction of the editor. He rocketed out of his cushy chair so quickly that it made a sucking sound, almost like the noise a plunger makes when it's pulled from the water after unclogging a toilet. Fitting, Nick thought. The editor said nothing and did not make eye contact with Nick. The publisher continued, doing all the talking.

"All right then. Report for duty in the morning. I hear you've got one hell of a story to write. Doris and your girlfriend simply blew me away with it. I look forward to reading it. When do you think it will be ready?"

"A couple of days maybe. I only have to make a few more contacts. I need to double-check some things that don't make sense. I'm almost ready to start writing."

"Good. It's been a while since we shook up this whole town. Make sure you've got every angle nailed down. Keep Morton, here, informed. I will expect a full report on it from him in three days." She reached over and pulled the editor's necktie and cuffed him lightly on the cheek with the back of her right hand. "And don't you screw up again or I'll have your ass back down in the mailroom."

As the two executives walked out of the editor's office, Nick now fully understood how she got her nickname. No doubt about it. She was, in deed, the Castrator. He didn't know if he should sit down or check his groin to make sure he was still in working order.

He actually felt sorry for Morton. She treated the editor like he was her bitch.

On his way out of the newsroom, Nick stopped by his desk. It was just the way he left it Friday afternoon. He picked up the phone and called Tanya.

"Hey, guess what. I got my job back," he said. "I'm on my way to pick you up. I'll tell you all about it on our way to Mrs. Pepadowski's house."

As Nick drove across town to Tanya's, he thought about how amazing the last three or four days had been. He couldn't remember a time in his life when he had been on such a rollercoaster ride. So many things had changed in such a short time. He was working on a great story. He was fired. He probably saved Charlie Joselyn's life. He confronted Gus Phelps. He went face-to-face with the Castrator and came away with all his parts in working order. He got his job back again. And now he was picking up Tanya to spend a little time with her before another week unfolded before him on Monday morning. Suddenly, everything seemed right with the world again.

# Gus Phelps had no right to take my Georgie…

## SUNDAY EVENING

Tanya zipped up her heavy jacket to ward off the cold November breeze that blew across the city from the bay. She waited for Nick at the edge of her driveway. She was eager to see him. Things had been pretty grim around her house all day. Her outlook brightened considerably when his machine rounded the corner and swept up along side of her.

"Hi, Nick," she said, as she swung into the passenger side of his rumbling wheels. "I called Mrs. Pepadowski a few minutes ago to let her know that we were coming."

"That's perfect. Enough time to be ready for us, but not enough time for her to whip something up in the kitchen. I love her dearly, but that woman would surely turn me into a fat man if I were around her much more."

Nick touched Tanya's left hand as it rested on her knee. Instinctively, she flipped her hand over and squeezed his paw tightly before letting it go. She'd hoped for a kiss, even a little peck on the cheek, but understood that intimacy would have to wait. Instead, she was grateful for his tender touch and warm smile. She enjoyed simply being with him.

"Thanks for taking Mrs. Joselyn to see the publisher yesterday," Nick said. "What a shocker. You didn't tell me what you were up to. I had no idea."

"Doris came up with the idea," Tanya said. "I found her at Bay Med and told her what was going on with you and your story. She insisted that we go see your boss. You ought to see Mrs. Joselyn in action. What a fireball. She is really a great lady.

"Oh, and I've got something else to tell you," Tanya continued, touching Nick's hand as it gripped the machine's shifter. "I ran into Sue Herndon at the hospital. We had a great talk, and she told me about Appleton's fourth victim."

"No kidding. You were really busy yesterday afternoon, weren't you? Do you know the fourth person?"

"Only distantly. Like the others, she was older than me. Amy Simpson. But Sue said she followed Appleton down to Florida. Supposedly, her folks still live here – in the new riverfront condos. They both work in the medical field. We can probably find Amy through them."

"Good going. Tanya, I gotta tell you, hey, you know – I think you'd make a great reporter. You have been so super on every aspect of this story. I can't thank you enough."

"Well, remember, I've got a stake in this, too. Looks like Gus killed my dad, and the band director hurt my friends. I want to see justice served. I want to make this right. My dad and Mr. Pepadowski didn't simply die of heart attacks, they were killed. Maybe what they did was wrong, but they shouldn't have had to pay for it with their lives. I'm glad to help, and I want to see it through to the end."

In a matter of moments, the Firebird swept through the East Side neighborhood to Mrs. Pepadowski's house. She was waiting at the front door for the duo and eagerly invited them into her home.

"Hello, Tanya and Nick," she said. "Please, come right in. I started some hot water for tea. I also made fresh chocolate chip cookies this afternoon. I'm warming a few for us right now."

Nick shook his head. You could take this woman out of Poland, but you couldn't take Poland – especially the warm, hospitable side of her homeland – out of her. And, really, he was glad. What a sweet woman, he thought, as he took off his jacket. He searched his mind for the right words. He wanted to deliver the bad news in the least hurtful way possible.

"Mrs. Pepadowski, thanks for letting us come over so late on a Sunday. We really hate to intrude like this, but there are some things – some pretty unpleasant things – that I feel I must tell you."

"Why, Nick, what is it? What's the problem," the older woman said as she studied Nick's and Tanya's faces for clues. "You both look so serious. What on earth is troubling you?"

The three of them sat down in the dining room. Mrs. Pepadowski poured steaming water from a small kettle into their cups. They bounced tea bags up and down in the water and quietly eyed the plate full of cookies. Finally, Nick started revealing what they'd come to talk about by asking Mrs. Pepadowski if she remembered them rummaging through the attic looking for her husband's medicine.

"Oh, sure I do," she said. "I'm getting up there, but I'm not so old that I can't remember something that happened only a few days ago. What did you find out? Is it something bad?"

"Yes, I'm afraid it is bad. Mrs. Pepadowski, it looks like your husband was poisoned. He probably died of a heart attack, as you had been told, but his medication was altered. The combination of pills he took was lethal."

The sunshine disappeared from Mrs. Pepadowski's face. Veins pushed against the underside of the skin in her neck. Her face reddened, and her eyebrows danced across the top of her head as she spoke.

"What? How can that be? George was under Doc Sheffield's care, and he prescribed that medicine for George. I don't understand."

"Gus Phelps blamed your husband and Tanya's father for the death of his daughter," Nick explained in an even tone, "and it appears as though he decided to take revenge by changing their medications and making it look like they had heart attacks."

"Oh, no, no, no." George Pepadowski's widow buried her face in her hands and began to gently rock back and forth in her chair. Tanya stood up and stepped close to hold the older woman in her arms. She began to wail. "No, no, not Georgie. He didn't deserve that. He didn't deserve to die. He was a good man. He did so much for so many. He helped so many kids. Oh no-o-o-o."

Tanya tried to comfort her. "I know how you feel. I lost my dad when I didn't have to. Gus took him from us, too."

"No, you don't know how I feel," Mrs. Pepadowski said, breaking free of Tanya's embrace, anger now overwhelming her sorrow. She walked over to the bureau that stood against the wall of the dining room. She picked up an 8 x 10 black and white framed photograph of the two when they were much younger, but no less in love. She pressed it close against her bosom with both arms. "I've been alone all these years, without my Georgie. He could have been here with me for all those Christmases, all those summers, all those evening walks. He could have been here for our boys and our grandchildren.

"I can't believe it," she continued. "Gus Phelps had no right to take my Georgie, no right to hurt us like that. What did we do?" She fell back down into her chair, still clinging to the picture and crying loudly enough to alarm both Nick and Tanya.

Tanya stepped into the kitchen and called her mother on her cell. Isabelle Johnson had offered to come to the Pepadowski residence if she was needed. "Hello, Mom. You're needed. Can you come right over? You were right. This is not going well."

When Tanya stepped back into the dining room, she saw Nick pull his chair along side Mrs. Pepadowski's. He put his hand on her back right between the shoulder blades. "I'm sorry to be the one to tell you this, but I wanted you to hear it from friends – not the cops, and not on the news."

Mrs. Pepadowski stopped crying and looked at Nick through red and swollen eyes. "No, I'm crying for the loss of my husband, not because you told me about it. Thank you for figuring this all out, Nick. Now, we finally have the truth. At the time of his death, I had a funny feeling that it didn't seem right. He had been sickly, but it wasn't enough to end his life. I knew something wasn't right about it but the doctors in emergency were sure it was a heart attack.

"Now, what happens to Gus Phelps? How does this end for him?"

"He was arrested this afternoon on an unrelated charge," Nick said. "While they hold him, the prosecutor's office is investigating. Doc Sheffield has been alerted. He has acknowledged that his prescriptions were tampered with, and he's contacted the authorities. In the next three or four days, they'll have this whole thing figured out.

"But I also want you to know that I plan on writing a story about what happened to your husband and Tanya's dad and Charles Joselyn."

"Oh, no. Did he get Charlie, too?" Mrs. Pepadowski's mouth hung open as wide as a bear trap. She looked first at Nick and then back at Tanya. "Gus killed three people?"

"No, we stopped him before the altered medication took full effect. Mr. Joselyn is in Bay Med. They say he should be OK."

The doorbell rang. It was Isabelle Johnson. Everyone in the house was glad to see her arrive. After Nick let her in, Tanya's mother threw her coat on the living room sofa and marched up to Mrs. Pepadowski. The two embraced in the dining room. Mrs. Johnson told Tanya and Nick to leave if they wished. She would remain at the house as long as necessary for her friend – even if it meant staying the night.

The couple gave Mrs. Pepadowski a hug goodbye, and then made their way out into the night. They were both exhausted. It had been a draining day for each of them. They did not speak as Nick drove Tanya home. He squeezed her hand and gave her a quick hug goodnight. It was a somber conclusion to an otherwise exhilarating day.

# Prosecutor: Nick, your assumption would not be wrong ...

MONDAY MORNING

When Nick rolled into The *Blade* newsroom at 9:30 a.m. Monday morning, he found a big basket of fresh fruit sitting on the edge of his desk. It was wrapped in bright green plastic. A huge yellow bow kept its contents from spilling onto the floor. Two notes were taped to its side.

Nick opened the biggest one first. It was from Doris Joselyn: "Charlie is doing fine. Doc Sheffield says he'll be back to his ornery self by the end of the week. I can't thank you enough for what you've done. You saved his life, and for that I will always be grateful. If there is ever anything – and I mean ANYTHING – you need, please do not hesitate to ask. Thank you so very much. Sincerely, Doris."

The second note was smaller – simply a sheet of paper folded in half with just a few words on it. The brief missive was from Charlie Joselyn: "Thanks, but I still think you're a smart aleck potlicker. – C.J."

Nick flipped the notes onto his desk and laughed. By the sound of it, Mr. Joselyn was already back to being his old ornery self. He opened the basket of fruit and placed it on an open table in the middle of the newsroom.

Reporters and copy editors descended upon it like a pack of hungry wolves feeding on an injured lamb. Lots of growling and slurping noises. Pushing and shoving. An occasional belch. And in about 15 minutes it was all gone – except for a couple of banana peels, an apple core and the frayed top from devoured pineapple. Nick was surprised that the last feeder wasn't licking the dish and the desk where it was placed.

One by one, reporters and editors stopped by Nick's desk to welcome him back and congratulate him on pulling the big news story together. The youngest members of the newsroom heaped on the biggest amounts of praise.

Nick thanked each and then offered a little jab. "Gee, it wasn't that long ago that you were referring to me as the Old Fart."

Before Nick started anything, he wanted to check in with Doc Sheffield. He dialed the doctor's office number. A female voice answered. "Good morning, Doctor Sheffield's office. This is Maria Simpson. How may I help you?"

Nick held the receiver to his ear but could not respond. The word "Simpson" froze him in his tracks. He couldn't say anything.

"Hello, Doctor Sheffield's office. How may I help you?" the female voice repeated.

"Hi. Yes, I'm calling to speak with the doc. Is he in the office?"

"No, he won't be in for another hour or so. He had to stop at the hospital this morning. May I take a message?"

"No, I'll call back. Excuse me, but did you say that your name is Simpson?"

"Yes. I'm Maria Simpson."

"I thought that's what you said. You wouldn't be related to Amy Simpson by any chance would you?"

"Amy is my daughter. Do you know her?"

"We've never met, but I know some people who do know her. Just thought I'd ask. It's really a small world, isn't it?"

"Yes, I guess it is. Good bye."

"Bye." Nick hung up the telephone. He dug through the pile of papers and books on his desk and found the old Central High School yearbook that Mrs. Pepadowski had given him. He flipped through its pages until he found a picture of a group of cheerleaders, which included Candace Phelps and Amy Simpson. A caption identified an older woman among the young girls in the photo as Maria Simpson, the cheer squad's parent sponsor.

"Amy Simpson was Appleton's fourth victim and her mother works for Doc Sheffield," Nick said out loud. "*Hmmm*, I wonder if she would she have access to the prescriptions?"

Nick grabbed his notebook and his keys and headed for the parking lot. "If anyone is trying to reach me, I'm headed for the hospital to find Doc Sheffield. I'll be back later."

Doc Sheffield walked toward his car in the medical center parking lot. Nick pulled up a long side the aging healer.

"Doc, I got a question for you," he said.

"Hello, Nick. What's on your mind?"

"Doc, I just talked with Maria Simpson in your office. I'm curious. Does she have anything to do with patient prescriptions? Would she have access to them?"

"Maria is my office manager. She handles everything in the office. But I can't talk right now, Nick. I've got to run to the office. I'm meeting people from the prosecutor's office this morning. They finished their search of the Easy-Med computer files yesterday and they want to talk."

"What did they find out? Did their search of the files implicate Gus Phelps?"

"No. They said they released Mr. Phelps this morning. It sounds like he didn't do it. I'll find out more when I meet with them."

"If it's not Gus Phelps, then it's got to be Maria Simpson, Doc."

"What? Maria? Why Nick, she's been with me for 20 years. Why would she tamper with prescriptions?"

"Doc, her daughter was victimized by the band director at school. Candace Phelps was, too. Candace took her own life. Amy Simpson moved to Florida and had a kid with Appleton, who then dumped them both. Sounds like revenge to me. I'm going to call Mickey Davidson and see if I'm on the right track. Talk to you later, Doc."

Nick called the assistant prosecutor on his cell phone as he headed back toward The *Blade* newsroom. The lawman answered his cell as he walked into Doc Sheffield's office.

"This is Mickey."

"Mickey, Nick Steele here. I heard that you released Gus Phelps this morning."

"Yup, that's right. He's not our man."

"Then who is?"

"I can't say Nick," Mickey said, then added with a laugh, "You can read all about it in the indictment."

"Very funny, Mickey. If it's not Gus, then it has to be Maria Simpson. Is that right?"

The assistant prosecutor did not respond. The cell phone was silent.

"It's not like you to be speechless, Mickey. Your silence tells me you're looking at the killer right now in Doc Sheffield's office."

"Like I said, I can't say. But I can say that your assumption would not be wrong."

"Thanks, Mickey. I owe you one. I'll get back to you after you make the arrest."

Nick pulled his machine back into the newspaper parking lot and sat in his car for several minutes. Wow, what a turn of events, he thought. It wasn't Gus after all. It was an office secretary who altered patient prescriptions before they got to the pharmacy.

As Nick made his way back to his desk, two large figures came at him from different directions. Drayton Clapper bounded from his office toward Nick's corner and Dave burst through the door marking the newsroom entrance.

"Nick!" each said at once, signaling the first time they'd been perfectly aligned on anything in about 15 years. Nick looked in each direction, and then responded to his boss first.

"Yes, Drayton, what's up? Are you glad to see me?"

"I got a call from the publisher last night. Good to have you back. Now, I hope you're ready to get to work on this story," Clapper said as he sat on the empty desk across from Nick's work area. "We've got a lot of stuff that has to be fleshed out here, plenty of double-checking. You're going to need some help if we're going to get it ready for the weekend. Plus, I want to get graphics and photo involved this morning. We need to map the whole thing out."

"Sounds good. I'm ready to dive right into it," Nick said. He then turned and looked in his friend's direction.

Immediately, he could see that his partner in rhyme was troubled.

"What's the problem, Dave?"

"We lost him."

"Lost who?"

"The band director," Dave said, sitting on another desk next to Clapper. "Appleton bolted. I just talked with the apartment manager down in Florida and he said he checked on the band director's apartment yesterday. The place was empty and the door was open. The keys were on the kitchen counter."

"What about a forwarding address for the deposit on the apartment?" Nick said as he stood up and stepped closer to the two journalists. "Did he leave a number or an address to get his deposit back?"

"Nope. I asked. He just up and took off. He must have freaked when I called on Friday and mentioned Candace Phelps' name. Damn, I botched that one."

"No you didn't. The guy's a rabbit. He knows we're onto his game. He knows we figured it out, and that he'd be in trouble as soon as we started asking questions at his school. That's why he took off. He couldn't risk getting found out. The guy is about two steps away from the slammer and he knows it."

Clapper raised his hand to calm the two reporters who were becoming visibly agitated.

"Just take it easy. We've still got a good story here," he said. "I'm not quitting on the guy. Eventually, we'll catch up to him. We'll track him down again. Sooner or later, we'll find him. He'll pop up somewhere, taking advantage of more young girls. Guys like him always do."

"Drayton, I'm delighted to hear you say that," Dave said. "This guy is scum. No telling how many kids he's hurt. I'll keep hunting for him and I won't charge you a thing."

"Good. That's music to my ears," Clapper said with a big smile. He turned and faced Nick. "Dave will chase Appleton and I want you to stay focused on pulling this story together. How long before I can see your first draft?"

"I'll start writing this morning, but the story has changed directions again," Nick said, capturing the full attention of Clapper and Balz. "Turns out it wasn't Gus Phelps who poisoned the school officials. It was a lady in Doc Sheffield's office. She's being arrested right now."

"What? That's a shocker," Dave said.

"What lady," Clapper said. "What's she got to do with it?"

"Revenge. We just found out that her daughter was one of Appleton's victims. Now, it all makes sense."

"What a great story," Dave said.

"Yup. That's why it's so dangerous to jump to conclusions," Nick said. "That's why you have to get all the facts before you start writing the story. I'll start writing it this morning, and keep working on it tonight. I'll have something for you to look at by tomorrow afternoon. I want to be finished writing by Friday."

"Why Friday?" Clapper said as he stood up to head back to his office.

"Because I'm going to pick up the telephone right now and make a date for Saturday night and I want to have this story all wrapped up before then."

"Friday is good for me," Clapper said, walking away from the two reporters.

Dave turned and headed for the newsroom door. "Nick, I'll catch up to you later. Maybe you can buy me a beer and make up for leaving me stranded at O'Hare's last night."

"OK, Dave. I was really beat last night. I promise I'll make it up to you. Now, go find that band director. He's going to be our next story. I've got to tell Tanya, the Joselyns and Mrs. Pepadowski what's happening. "

Nick sat down at his desk and picked up the telephone. He dialed Tanya's number. Isabelle Johnson picked up the phone.

"Hello, Mrs. Johnson. This is Nick Steele."

"Nick, I'm so glad to hear from you. It's been a very rough weekend at our house. I was hoping you would stop by. I wanted to thank you for everything you've done."

"Oh, Mrs. Johnson, you don't have to thank me."

"No, Nick. If it weren't for you, we would never have found out what really happened to Robert. We needed to know, Nick. And Robert, he needed this to come out right. I can't thank you enough – from our whole family."

"Well, thanks, Mrs. Johnson. I appreciate it."

"I take it that you're calling for Tanya, right? You didn't call here to shoot the breeze with me? Am I right?"

"Yes, Mrs. Johnson, you're right. If it's OK, I'd like to stop by your house at noon today. I've got some interesting news for you and your family."

"Sure, Nick, you can stop by any time. Do you want to talk with Tanya? Just a minute. She's in the next room."

Nick could hear Mrs. Johnson call out Tanya's name. In less than a minute, she was on the line. Nick was always glad to hear her voice. They exchanged small talk for a few minutes and then Nick got to the heart of the matter.

"Say, Tanya, do you have any plans for Saturday night?"

"Wait a minute. Hold on. Is my hearing going bad? Now, this sounds like you're really asking me out on a date. Is that what you're doing, Nick Steele? Are you asking me out on an official date? This is not more information gathering, is it?"

"Well, as a matter of fact, I am asking you out on a date. I'll be all finished with my story by Friday. So, I wanted to know if you'd like to go out with me on Saturday. There's a new show opening at the State Theatre downtown. Or we could go see the Bay City Players over on Columbus. We could go to dinner and catch the show or the play. Your call. What do you say?"

"Gee, I don't know. I'm pretty busy. Let me check my schedule. I'll have to think about it and see if I can work you in. Call me later. Bye."

She hung up the phone and Nick sat there with his headset on listening to a dial tone. A big smile spread across his face. That was another reason he loved her. She was just so damned feisty.

— 30 —

Made in the USA
Charleston, SC
14 August 2012

# PIVOT

EMPOWERING YOURSELF TODAY TO SUCCEED IN AN
UNPREDICTABLE TOMORROW

## RAVI HUTHEESING

RAVI UNITES, INC.

Ravi Unites, Inc.
info@raviunites.com
Please visit our website: RaviUnites.com

ISBN (paperback) : 978-1-7357441-4-8
ISBN (hardcover) : 978-1-7357441-5-5
ISBN (e-book) : 978-1-7357441-6-2

Special editions may be available. Please contact the publisher for more information.

All photos are used by permission or under a commercial license.

Sun/Give Peace a Chance logo is a trademark of Ravi Unites, Inc.

*World Peace is Possible if We Make it Profitable* is a trademark of Ravi Unites, Inc.

10 9 8 7 6 5 4 3 2 1

First Edition

# CONTENTS

# WHAT PEOPLE ARE SAYING ABOUT PIVOT

*"A journey of self-discovery, noting the need for cultivating and developing one's strengths, social responsibility, communication skills, and desire for lifelong learning. Ravi's Pivot makes for a compelling read with tips for fostering these strengths in yourself today."*
— Mary Beth Pelosky, K-12 Principal & Global Ed. Specialist

*"Pivot combines fascinating life experiences, cross-cultural connections, and core values to create a foundation for success. As entrepreneurs, we benefit by better understanding humanity while developing our ability to pivot for success."*
— Mark Bonnell, Technology Entrepreneur, CEO of Modyo

*"Author Ravi Hutheesing has written a timely, essential book, Pivot, that emphasizes 'cultural competence is the pathway to equity, equity is the pathway to equality, and equality is the pathway to world peace.'"*
— Terry Spradlin, School Boards Association Executive Director

"We don't offer enough opportunities to explore, experience, struggle, and fail—a natural process of learning that helps develop curiosity, self-confidence, grit, and a sense of accomplishment. Pivot has many practical uses and also thoughtful insights on how to champion success."
— Paul Blanford, K-12 School Superintendent

"I would like my own children to read Pivot. It's a good example of what a successful life in 2020 looks like—today's world is rarely picking one profession and sticking with it for life."
— Robert Moje, Entrepreneur, Architect, Founder of VMDO Architects

"It is a choice to pivot and remain relevant. Change can be exciting, and it is an opportunity to look at where we are now, where we need to be, and how we can implement strategies to hit our new goals. Ravi's book is the perfect mindset reminder that we are in control of the choices we make that impact our futures."
— Jennie Norris, Entrepreneur, Owner of Sensational Home Staging

# FOREWORD, BY JENNIE NORRIS

We live in a world that is growing larger while also becoming more intimate. Despite a global population in the billions, technology allows us to connect in personal ways that were unimaginable to most thirty years ago. Social media, cell phones, etc., provide instant access to parts of the world that many will never see in person, and we can experience these cultures and see how others live.

It is through connection that we learn about others and gain a better understanding of our world and ourselves. It is through connection that the world shrinks from a massive sea of humanity to people with similar interests, goals, desires, and dreams. Babies are not born with negative opinions of others. Biases and negativity are learned and can be overcome by showing that we have more in common than differences that divide. It starts with connection.

As Chairwoman of the International Association of Home Staging Professionals® (IAHSP®), it is my responsibility to think globally and act locally. With thousands of members spread throughout the world, we serve others to help them succeed while facing language, cultural, economic, and geographic differences. However, we also share commonality by being entrepreneurs in the real estate industry, helping others, and working towards success. When we focus on what ties us together versus differences that pull us apart, our entire mindset shifts. These "obstacles" no longer represent inaction or inability but become challenges that we overcome by working together.

Home Staging is part of the Real Estate Industry and one of the last services to make "house calls." We deal with the interpersonal workings of homes, families, and people. Our members have had the privilege of learning about cultural diversity and inclusivity from Ravi Hutheesing, where he shared his approach to unifying people from countries and cultures who are normally at odds politically, culturally, and/or spiritually. His work is inspiring, and it is proof that the normal human condition is not one of hate and war, but one of finding common ground and joy.

Remaining viable in a changing world is at the forefront due to recent global issues. When change is required to remain solvent, some panic and shut down while others rise to the occasion and *pivot*. It is a choice to pivot and remain relevant. Change can be exciting, and it is an opportunity to look at where we are now, where we need to be, and how we can implement strategies to hit our new goals. Ravi's book is the perfect mindset reminder that we are in control of the choices we make that impact our futures.

*Jennie Norris, IAHSP® Chairwoman, President & CEO of Stagedhomes, and Owner of Sensational Home Staging*

*In memory of my parents, Ajit and Amrita, who empowered me to take ownership of my education, and pivot.*

1974

1989

# PREFACE

I wrote the majority of this book during the COVID-19 pandemic, between March and August of 2020. It was a pivotal time for almost everyone on the planet, and for me, it could not have been more unusual. I was near the end of a three-week vacation in Valparaiso on the coast of Chile when the border closed, and all international flights were suspended. That trip became six months long, during which I remained quarantined as a guest of close friends.

Having no children of my own, being recently divorced, and indefinitely postponing my keynote touring schedule, I was in no rush to get back to the United States where Coronavirus infections and deaths were outnumbering any other country. Additionally, with the suspected racially motivated killing of George Floyd in Minneapolis, Minnesota, combined with a cantankerous race for the White House between the sitting president, Donald Trump, and the former vice president who won and became President Joe Biden, social tensions were hitting extremes. This was the perfect opportunity to stay put in South America and complete my book while watching the sun sink into the Pacific Ocean every evening.

What made my experience even more unusual was that my host family had four children, ages 13, 15, 19, and 21. We were all quarantined in the same house while they attended school and university online each day. As someone who was getting used to living alone whenever not traveling among strangers, I was surrounded by the daily challenges of a typical family during such an unprecedented situation, and most of those struggles revolved around working at home while also ensuring that the children are getting a decent education.

As for completing this book, spending each day in that environment was a research project in and of itself. It gave me opportunities to test the theories that I highlight, discover aspects of learning and family engagement that I might have otherwise not considered, and confirm many of the concerns or beliefs I had about traditional schooling, technology, cultural competence, and the relevance of an entrepreneurial mindset. It reassured me that not only is there a role for *all* forms of education and mentorship in each person's life, but there is a *necessity* for all forms of education and mentorship to exist to create a "lifelong learner."

I am grateful that you have chosen to travel with me on this journey, and I hope the lessons I have learned along the way will empower you to be the greatest lifelong learner you can be, whether it be as a student or entrepreneur.

*"Life is like a game of cards. The hand you are dealt is determinism; the way you play it is free will."*

—Jawaharlal Nehru, first prime minister of India

# PREDICTABLY
# UNPREDICTABLE

———〜〜〜———

When I began thinking about this book, the world was relatively calm, with strong economies and no major conflicts. With technology rapidly evolving and impacting the future of jobs, the education industry was deeply engaged in debates about how to best prepare students for an unpredictable future. As a keynote speaker who has delivered speeches to thousands of education leaders at conferences, including the International Baccalaureate Global Conference and AASA's National Conference on Education, answering this question has been a cornerstone of my message. Creating cultural competence and equity in education (fairness, regardless of differing values and beliefs), and implementing technology and personalized learning, are common themes because while the future may be unpredictable, educators help shape the future by how they prepare students.

Then the unthinkable happened. The Coronavirus Disease

of 2019-2020 (COVID-19) shattered global economies, flipped education upside-down, and caused all of humanity to make the most significant pivot in a lifetime. For much of 2020, ninety percent of the global population lived in countries with some degree of travel restriction, 1.7 billion people were ordered to stay at home, and the rest either found their everyday lives severely curtailed given the mandated closures of non-essential businesses or were encouraged to self-quarantine while working and learning from home.

Classrooms and conference rooms pivoted immediately from physical to virtual. Wedding receptions, birthday celebrations, and funerals soon followed. The global shutdown accelerated the implementation of technology into education, the workforce, and social interactions practically overnight.

The absence of traditional schooling for at least one semester was probably the most significant disruption for most families. Ninety percent of the world's students found schools closed or were sent home from colleges and universities, sometimes without even the time to pack their belongings. Educators went into a panic as they attempted to bridge a gap that turned into a chasm. School systems everywhere involuntarily accelerated the adaptation to online learning with varying degrees of success. While digital learning had already been increasing in classrooms, it quickly became apparent how much disparity it creates without structure and guaranteed access to computers and highspeed internet. Moreover, since many families depend on free school lunches, creating a system to distribute box lunches often took precedence over solving the challenges of delivering education to the home.

Just as the world was beginning to find its rhythm, a second event stopped us in our tracks. George Floyd, a black man in Minneapolis, Minnesota, USA, suspected of committing a minor offense by using a counterfeit twenty-dollar bill, was killed by the excessive force of the arresting white police officer. While the virus had, in some ways, united the globe in the effort to contain a common enemy, people were also reaching psychological breaking points from being kept in figurative cages. Riots quickly erupted in cities across the United States, often evolving from peaceful protests into violent clashes with police. Then, like the Coronavirus, the protests transcended borders, spreading to Europe and beyond as the world's attention pivoted from overcoming a health crisis to demanding social justice.

The time had come for me to complete this book, which is for all self-directed learners, such as entrepreneurs and proactive students. I believe education is the solution to all the world's problems, but to create "lifelong learners," it must begin as a partnership between parents and teachers and then pivot to one between students and mentors. While it need not always be an active collaboration, each must take ownership of his or her role because education is much more than just going to school. By learning the skills to pivot in the face of constant changes, we are empowered to succeed in an unpredictable future.

My pivots—from a family of politicians and bankers to the guitarist of a world-famous band to a "flying musician" in the aviation industry to a cultural diplomat on behalf of the US Department of State to an arts and education advocate as a keynote speaker—have created an exciting and fulfilling journey made possible by owning my education. The following stories provide examples of how striking the right balance between traditional schooling and real-world education will develop an entrepreneurial mindset that can create successful and socially responsible global citizens, and how that will then help create a socially just future.

My goal has always been to push the education industry to pivot toward a hybrid of traditional and real-world schooling. As a concept, "change" can be daunting, and it can lead to procrastination. If one makes a pivot instead—a shift in direction while maintaining the fundamental principles and strengths upon which one operates—the distance between thought and action is reduced considerably. Whether it is an individual or an entire industry, the ability to pivot is the difference between staying relevant and becoming redundant.

In education, the call for reform is nothing new. It is part of every political platform worldwide. For over four decades in the United States, politicians have campaigned that education must get "Back to Basics" because we are "A Nation at Risk," and there must be "No Child Left Behind." More recently, parents have been taking matters into their own hands by getting vouchers to use public money to enroll their children in charter schools (some of which are for-profit), giving them "School Choice."

Yet, a significant change has been slow to come, possibly because, despite this negative narrative, statistics tell a different story. In the United States, the numbers of high school graduates, college enrollments, and employees (other than in recession years) have consistently risen. While the latest PISA (Programme for International Student Assessment) scores rank American students as average, and behind many other advanced industrial nations, once you dissect these scores further and isolate schools with fewer than 25% of students receiving FRLP (Free and Reduced Lunch Program)—those eligible for Title 1 funding—the USA is close to the top of the list. In this regard, one can argue that there is not a public education problem as much as there is a poverty problem, and much like everywhere in the world, the disparity can often be linked to socioeconomic and racial divides.

While disparity has been accentuated during the pandemic due to the lack of equal access to technology, which would likely perpetuate classism and racism, young people around the world are now taking a firm stance on social justice issues. Even during the months before COVID-19 and George Floyd, millennials have started marching on the streets to fight for equality, from Hong Kong to Chile to France to Lebanon. While previous generations have done the same, it is the multicultural and entrepreneurial nature of millennials and their successors, Gen Z, that could produce a change unlike anything we have seen before.

Moreover, nature appeared to heal, even if only temporarily. While humans were quarantined, wild animals were found grazing in cities for the first time in most of our lifetimes, with dolphins swimming closer to Italy's southern shores in the less polluted waters, and pumas descending from the Andes onto the unusually quiet streets of Santiago de Chile. Air pollution vanished over Beijing and New Delhi, and while household energy consumption increased worldwide, it was being offset by the reduction in businesses' use.

Many found that working from home increased their productivity while companies saw office expenses disappear from their bottom lines. Given the need for social distancing, the recent surge in coworking spaces reversed, but the rise in home delivery benefitted shipping companies and online retailers. Some hotels that depend on tourists found new business as places for travelers to quarantine for the fourteen days most governments required. Just about every industry has been forced to pivot in one way or another.

Are these events and reactions all connected, and if so, how? What are the cause and effects? Who are the winners and losers? Questions like these are ones that tomorrow's leaders should be asking and answering. If self-directed learners do not perpetually capitalize on current events as the basis for curriculum, it would be a great detriment to lifelong learning.

To prepare for an unpredictable future, the most important thing one needs to master is how to learn. The world will always have more to teach than the classroom; therefore, the primary goal must be to become a lifelong learner. COVID-19 and George Floyd's death are excellent examples of world events that yield lifelong lessons, and both history and the future will provide a plethora of others.

The pillars for learning are simple to identify but perhaps more complicated to implement. It comes down to four concentrations: inspiring curiosity, recognizing and nurturing talent, provoking critical thinking, and fostering communication. If we focus on these four, we need not question our own education. Instead, we must embrace every educational opportunity and make lifelong learning impervious to however unpredictable the future may be. In other words, we must perpetually absorb and act upon the lessons of an ever-changing world.

PriceWaterhouseCoopers reports that nearly 40% of jobs will

be automated in the next decade. No matter when you read this, the rate of change is a startling reference. Those who argue that jobs will return are speculating at best. There is no telling whether there will be new jobs created or if our jobs will cease to be the primary focus of our lives. The "ice-breaker" question of the future may no longer be "what do you do?" but rather, "how do you feel about...?"

Outsourcing of labor is nothing new, and less expensive options will always be sought. However, jobs that used to be outsourced to humans in third-world countries will now go to first-world technology. The benefit to companies that employ robots over people will become increasingly apparent—no need for payroll, healthcare provisions, pensions, workman's compensation, etc. Moreover, artificial intelligence will likely evolve faster than job creation, and at some point, predominantly create jobs for other robots.

We are seamlessly incorporating Amazon's Alexa, iRobot vacuums, Thermomix kitchen assistants, smart TVs, and other automated devices into our homes. Most of us already have more power in our pockets than NASA had in the Apollo spaceships 50 years ago, and the next device you buy will offer more power for less cost. Technological deflation—the diminishing price of technology—will have a significant impact on future economies and job markets, and if that is combined with the ability to provide equal access to highspeed broadband internet, the impact on humanity should ultimately be positive. Nevertheless, to stay relevant, one must be able to pivot.

With the rising cost of traditional universities combined with the array of higher education options now online, even the future role of traditional higher education is unclear. University students worldwide have now completed at least one semester of studies online due to COVID-19, and they may be reluctant to return to classes as usual. Professors who initially found adapting their classrooms to online formats challenging are also discovering the ease with which they can now have a visiting lecturer from the other side of the world (or visit students on a different continent without leaving their homes).

Either way, if we may no longer be defined by jobs and careers in the future, why is becoming "college and career ready" still the most relevant objective? As I often say to my audiences, we must prepare students—not for *our* future but *theirs*—and I believe there is now more than ever a higher purpose for education.

## Pivot Points

- Understand your educational role. To educate yourself and become a "lifelong learner," education should begin as a partnership between parents and teachers and then pivot to one between students and mentors.

- Pivot instead of change. As a concept, "change" can be daunting, and it can lead to procrastination. If one makes a pivot instead—a shift in direction while maintaining the fundamental principles and strengths upon which one operates—the distance between thought and action is reduced considerably.

- Emphasize learning over achievement. To prepare for an unpredictable future, the most important thing one needs to master is how to learn. If self-directed learners capitalize on current events as the basis for curriculum, one will be able to continue learning independently of formal education long after one leaves school.

- Concentrate on four pivotal areas. These are to inspire curiosity, recognize and nurture talent, provoke critical thinking, and foster communication. By doing so, lifelong learning will make one impervious to an unpredictable future.

- Think ahead. Prepare for your future.

# 2

# WORLD PEACE IS POSSIBLE IF WE MAKE IT PROFITABLE™

In 2017, I spent a month in the Middle East, serving as a cultural diplomat on behalf of the US Department of State. I traveled to Iraq and Lebanon to conduct what I now call "Songwriting Safaris," which are multi-week workshops creating songwriting collaborations between students from traditionally opposed cultures and religions. It was my first time in the region, and other than knowing that this part of the world has been decimated and demoralized by wars for longer than I have been alive, I knew little about these countries.

For most citizens of Western nations, the very notion of going to Iraq conjures up images of terrorism and war. ISIS terrorists (Islamic State of Iraq and Syria; its official name is ISIL for the Islamic State of Iraq and the Levant—the Levant being the part of the Middle East closest to the Mediterranean Sea) were still quite dominant in the region. However, my memory was of television news reports showing Scud ballistic missiles flying over Baghdad during the Persian Gulf War almost three decades earlier.

Like most frequent international airline passengers, I watch movies to pass the time when I fly. On this trip, however, I was focused on the moving map displaying our location. I would glance out the window, look at the seatback screen, and then gaze into the dark sky with faint lights twinkling from the ground. My heart raced as I triangulated landmarks trying to identify the West Bank, Damascus, Baghdad, Kirkuk, and other war zones as we turned north toward our destination.

Upon landing in Erbil in the Kurdistan Republic of Iraq (KRI), I breezed through immigration with smiling officers who made me, a US citizen, feel more welcomed than the Canadian border patrol does, and met the hotel manager who came to pick me up. For the next two weeks, I taught songwriting and cultural entrepreneurship to a mix of Iraqis and Kurds, two cultures that have been at war for a long time.

The former president, Sadaam Hussain, is still remembered as a strong leader by many Iraqis, but most Kurds have a different memory of the dictator. Hussain and his Ba'athist government did not support the Kurdish efforts to reclaim their independence, which began following World War I when the British created Iraq out of three former Ottoman provinces, including the Kurds in the north.

In the late 1980s, Hussain launched multiple attacks known as the "Anfal" campaign, killing between 50,000 and 100,000 civilian Kurds (according to Human Rights Watch), including chemical attacks that sent many fleeing to Iran for safety toward the end of the Iraq-Iran war. In 2003, the United States successfully captured him during the US/UK post-9/11 attack on Iraq (based on false reports of his having weapons of mass destruction). The Kurds became close US allies, and many migrated back from Iran to Iraq. Their fight for independence continues today through voting and negotiations between the KRI and Baghdad (ironically, the government in Baghdad is now supposedly heavily influenced by the government in Tehran, Iran).

While the goal of my trip was to build a musical bridge between the Iraqis and Kurds, my attention shifted to primarily working with four millennial Iraqi Muslims whose needs were greater than any of the other students. Their entire home city of Mosul had been taken over by ISIS three years earlier and effectively turned into a prison for its 1.5 million residents. ISIS managed to overthrow the Iraqi army in six days, and they seized control of the city and airport (a regional hub for US military), including its helicopters.

According to my students, the terrorists initially charmed locals by providing ample quantities of cigarettes, technology, sim cards, alcohol, and other pleasures, only to later make them illegal, confiscate them, and sell them back on the black market at exorbitant prices. They also restricted all freedoms of expression and communication, including participation in the arts. A violation of these laws had severe consequences, possibly even execution. As ISIS was being defeated in the global war on terrorism, Mosul was slowly liberated section-by-section. My students regained their freedom just days before I arrived, and while it was anything but smooth, they managed to cross the

Iraq/KRI border with the help of the US Embassy to spend a couple of weeks studying and writing music with me.

Mosul was a jail under ISIS, and Khalid, Hakam, Mouhammed (Hamood), and Ameen were prisoners. During that time, they were forbidden to play music, and they told me they would likely have been executed if caught doing so. Each of them has unforgettable stories. Through our work together, I lived their horrors vicariously and, in some way, became part of their collective story.

One week into the program, Khalid asked if he could cut my hair. I did not understand at first, but he had been a professional barber, and since it had been made illegal under ISIS for men to cut their hair or shave their beards, he had not worked for three years. This was not about money, however. As Mosul was slowly being liberated, the men started cutting their hair and shaving to celebrate their newfound freedom (and to give ISIS the proverbial middle finger). Khaled was inviting me to share in his freedom.

This was an incredible honor because, after their birth, the actual day of their freedom from ISIS has become their most celebrated day—they essentially celebrate two "birth" days each year. So, one morning in his hotel bathroom, he gave me an Iraqi style haircut (short!). The other three arrived with their instruments and serenaded us while I was in the chair!

Hamood's story is heartbreaking. He was alerted that ISIS soldiers were conducting surprise inspections in his neighborhood, so he took his violin outside, found a shovel, and buried the instrument in the garden. Moments later, there was a knock on his door. The soldiers did not find anything musical, but for unknown reasons, they believed he was a spy.

14

They blindfolded and kidnapped him for 28 days. During that time, he was hung from his wrists for hours at a time and had electrodes placed on the most sensitive areas of his body. He was tortured repeatedly. Once his captors realized he was not a spy, they released him into the woods, blindfolded. Hamood found his way home only to discover that his parents had regularly watered the garden throughout, and his violin had been destroyed.

Hakam was also alerted that soldiers were approaching his doorstep. He quickly removed a panel from his ceiling and hid his guitar up there. It stayed there for three years, and he keeps the accumulated dust under the strings as a reminder of what it means to lose your freedom. However, Hakam overlooked something that could have cost him his life. He left his guitar-shaped key chain sitting on the desk. The soldiers found it and questioned him, but his quick wit came through, and he convinced them that the shape was of a chicken leg! When I left Erbil, he gave me that key chain to remind me of the value of freedom.

Ameen's story took a different turn. He was caught off guard when the soldiers arrived at his home. As they began to confiscate his instruments, they were suddenly called away, but they warned him not to leave because they were coming back (presumably to take him as a prisoner). He then quickly grabbed the one violin which they had not found, escaped, and traveled 400 kilometers to Baghdad. Feeling safe, he discovered that his true calling was to fight rather than flee.

Ameen became part of the resistance, and he returned to Mosul. Every time ISIS destroyed a temple or a monument, he climbed atop the rubble to play his violin in defiance of

15

terrorism and radical ideology. He was a soldier with a violin as his weapon. Putting his life at risk every time, major news organizations worldwide covered his brave resistance, and each time, he wore a homemade T-shirt displaying the name of the destroyed monument upon which he stood. His most famous protest was on top of what was the Yunis Temple, and the day I left Iraq, Ameen gave me the "Yunis" T-shirt he wore so that I would always remember the power of music. It hangs in my office today.

Their stories not only overwhelmed me but also made an impression on my Kurdish students. Jezhwan, a talented young Kurdish music teacher and performing singer-songwriter from Erbil, spent a couple of days with Ameen composing a song together. As I was helping them develop a storyline and write lyrics (which were a mix of Arabic and Kurdish), they initially clashed based on their interpretations of freedom given the history of their people and experiences with both ISIS and Hussain. As they worked through the verses and choruses (at times, the conversation became a little tense), I was impressed by their growing appreciation for each other's personal views. This was a great example of how empathy can grow organically if a forum is created.

However, what makes me most proud is what the four from Mosul did afterward. They returned to their beloved city and performed in the streets. Now that it was legal, they could introduce music to children who had never heard it before. They also played concerts that raised money and brought books back to the library that ISIS destroyed.

These four Muslims, for the first time in their lives, went into Christian churches—ones that ISIS used as classrooms to indoctrinate young soldiers and then subsequently destroyed—to help clean up the destruction and play music to encourage Christians to return. If this is not cultural competence, I do not know what is. They transcended the most severe religious divides in one of the most complicated regions of the world. To me, they embody the words of Gandhi: "Be the change you wish to see in the world."

In between my songwriting safaris in the Middle East, I flew back to the United States for three days to deliver a keynote address, along with Dr. Jill Biden (current first lady and wife of President Joe Biden), for the Colorado Association of School Executives. It was exciting to reinvent my speech by opening with these untold stories of Khalid, Hamood, Hakam, and Ameen. With many rural school districts represented in the audience, I knew this would catch them off-guard and grab their attention.

More important, I felt it was relevant to share these stories because radicalization can happen anywhere (it was ramping up in much of Western Europe), and the only antidote is education. While ISIS had not been significantly recruiting from rural America, socioeconomic disparity, racial inequality, white supremacy, and extreme political ideologies were on the rise, creating fertile ground for radicalization. Everyone must understand the mindset of radicalization and terrorism because working against it and in favor of peace is, in my view, a fundamental responsibility of a civilized society.

After a short 72 hours in Colorado, I flew back to the Middle East to conduct a similar program in Beirut, this time to unite Lebanese and Syrians. Due to Syria's political unrest and humanitarian crisis, causing a mass exodus, more than 25% of

Lebanon's population were Syrian refugees. Such imbalance creates fertile soil for conflict.

It was my first time in Lebanon, but my parents had vacationed in Beirut when it was known as "Paris of the Middle East" before the civil war in 1975. I had heard stories of nearby picturesque Byblos, which is a well-known UNESCO World Heritage site. However, despite also boasting this designation, the city of Baalbek on the opposite side of the Beqaa Valley was more of a mystery, and it was said to have the most impressive Roman ruins outside of Italy. While it was easy to visit Byblos, and I did several times, I also very much wanted to see Baalbek. I asked the locals if they could help arrange a trip, and the response was almost unanimous: "You are crazy, don't go!"

They said the road to Baalbek was patrolled by Hezbollah, and the ancient city itself was a mere ten kilometers from the ISIS front line along the Syrian border. It certainly did seem unwise, but I continued to ask around until I was given the answer I wanted. A senior staff member at the university where I taught my program assured me things were currently calm and that "most likely," nothing bad would happen. He agreed it was worth the trip but advised that I hide I was an American. There was a remote possibility I could be sold out and taken hostage.

With his help, I hired a French-speaking driver since I speak the language well enough to get by. He was not hard to find since many Lebanese speak French due to Lebanon having been a French Mandate after World War I (whereas Iraq was established as a British Mandate). My driver was a devout Maronite Catholic Christian and former soldier of the Lebanese Armed Forces, so he highlighted many points of interest along our two-and-a-half-hour drive toward Syria. We stopped briefly to climb several bunkers from which he fought as a soldier in the 1970s during the bloody battles between the Maronite and Palestinian forces, and we drove by Syrian refugee camps that captured the perils of that situation (overcrowding, ghetto-like conditions, poor sanitation, etc.).

As we crossed from the Christian to the Muslim side of the Beqaa Valley, we were stopped by an armed soldier standing on the side of the street. He spoke briefly to my driver in Arabic and then got into the front seat of our car. No one acknowledged me in the back, but I was quickly becoming very aware of the Mother Mary pendant hanging from the rearview mirror as we drove away. These two would not even agree on the same God! My heart pounded rapidly.

They spoke animatedly in Arabic, and I wondered what they were discussing. Did they realize I was an American? Were they negotiating a deal for my being taken as a hostage? Twenty minutes later, we pulled over to a little hut on the side of the street, and the soldier got out. He tapped on my window. I reluctantly rolled it down and attempted to crack an innocent and friendly smile when he asked, "Café?"

While I was trying to determine the best answer, another man approached the car, waving what appeared to be the Hezbollah flag. It turned out to be a Hezbollah T-shirt, which he was hoping to sell me. Who knew these "terrorists" were so enterprising? I gently shook my head, keeping my mouth shut to hide my American accent. By doing so, I politely declined the coffee and T-shirt (which would have been a fantastic souvenir except for the stress of trying to pass it through US customs!), so my driver restarted the car, and the two of us resumed the journey. Sensing my great relief, he made eye contact with me in his rearview mirror and said, "Don't worry. He is Muslim, and I am a Christian. But first, we are both Lebanese."

In retrospect, I believe the solider was just getting a ride from one checkpoint to the next, but this simple yet profound statement of unity encapsulated many life lessons. My own implicit bias, to begin with, had me wondering if I was the subject of a negotiation. Had I been more open-minded, I might have saved my heart from skipping a few beats. Fear can cause irrational behavior, and when the fear is unjustified (as is often the case in racial and cultural conflicts), the consequences can be unnecessarily harmful.

However, the more global lesson is that if such drastic differences can be overcome between Muslims and Christians, why can't Democrats and Republicans remember we are all first Americans? Can we teach this to Hindus and Muslims, Israelis and Palestinians, Iraqis and Kurds, Russians and Ukrainians, Straight and Gay, and Black and White? Yes, we can. Cultural competence can and must be learned, and this can be done by first exploring commonalities and then provoking curiosity and civil conversation about our differences.

We soon arrived in Baalbek, and I felt as if I had stepped into a time machine. This city of massive ruins was nothing short of awesome, yet it was also eerie and uncomfortable because no one else was there. Due to the warnings about ISIS and Hezbollah, Baalbek had pretty much become a ghost town. After two hours of walking and climbing through sweltering heat, I sat alone for almost an hour in the ancient and majestic Temple of Bacchus. Its beauty, size, history, and sheer peacefulness mesmerized me, though I was intellectually aware that I was also in one of the most dangerous parts of the world.

While contemplating the juxtaposition of these two realities, my serenity was interrupted by modern technology—breaking news buzzing on my cell phone. Violence had erupted, but it was domestic terrorism on the other side of the world. Ironically, it was happening in my hometown of Charlottesville, Virginia, USA.

On August 12, 2017, white supremacists from Ohio traveled to Charlottesville to protest the removal of Confederate statues. One of General Robert E. Lee sits in our city's center. The protestors were also gathering to unify the American white nationalist movement when one of them drove his car into a crowd of counter-protesters. A 32-year-old woman was killed, and two responding police officers also perished in a helicopter crash.

Best known for being the home of three American presidents (Thomas Jefferson, James Madison, and James Monroe), along with Jefferson's University of Virginia, "Charlottesville" has now become a metaphor for white supremacy and racial tension. How ironic that I was having one of the most peaceful days of my life in what is thought to be the most radicalized part of the world when radicalism was unfolding on my doorstep at home.

I returned to Charlottesville from the Middle East with three strong beliefs:

- Cultural competence is the most important skill for the future
- Education is the solution to all the world's problems
- World peace is possible

As idealistic as "educating for peace" sounds, it is now pragmatic. I believe we will witness the unprecedented simultaneous rise of Gross Domestic Product (GDP) *and* unemployment as technology replaces human workers, along with some type of Universal Basic Income (perhaps in the form of a zero or negative tax rate) to keep the consumer-driven economy afloat. If anticipated by education and entrepreneurs, the significant amount of human capital released from mundane jobs could be pivoted into creating great value, including world peace. Imagine if everyone who might otherwise pump gas, work in the grocery checkout line, or write code could instead be trained in the arts?

Or imagine if we forget about them altogether. What does society look like if we fail to empower graduates with the ability to pivot when their identity may no longer be defined by their jobs or careers? What happens if your skills are obsolete, and you no longer identify with your education? One might become disaffected, and disaffected people are prone to radicalization.

Education need not struggle to prepare students for an unpredictable future because the future will be shaped by how educators prepare students. Therefore, we need to understand what kind of future we want and accept that this, too, will pivot periodically. Today's students, as tomorrow's leaders, will need to make similar assessments.

To do so responsibly, one must first understand and identify with one's culture, which I define as one's system of beliefs, behaviors, and values. In combination with the four concentrations of inspiring curiosity, nurturing talent, provoking critical thinking, and fostering communication, this creates lifelong learners who are emotionally stable and socially responsible. That is the opportunity for humanity during this technology revolution.

Moreover, as we globally continue to pivot toward a sharing economy (think of businesses like Uber and Airbnb, for example), world peace will pivot from ideal to necessity. We have been moving toward a decentralized sharing economy ever since the internet, Napster music service, and p2p file sharing came to light in the 1990s. Over twenty years later, when COVID-19 forced schools to close and deliver content digitally, we broadly witnessed the decentralization of knowledge as students were directed to multiple sources outside of a physical school. If the shortcomings of highspeed internet access and multiple computers in the home are adequately addressed, knowledge will also be democratized, which is key to creating equity in education and beyond.

Quick adaptation to technology has some third-world emerging markets leapfrogging over the first-world due to their lack of infrastructure—their liability has become their asset, which means what put the West ahead during the Industrial Revolution will now cause it to lag. Today's students and entrepreneurs must recognize that their greatest opportunities may lie elsewhere in the world, and therefore, they must be globally and culturally competent. In places like India, where air-traffic navigation systems were not as advanced as they were in Europe and the USA, newer and efficient GPS (Global Positioning System) was more quickly implemented. Countries uninhibited by centralized systems are just more agile. A similar example can be seen with the growth of cellular phone technology in countries where landlines were not as commonplace. Now with smartphones, people who never had a personal computer can surf the World Wide Web.

When it comes to renewable energy, similar scenarios exist

with solar panels. In suburban and rural areas of Chile, it is becoming normal to see small hotels and middle-class homes with panels on the roof. In rural India, where centralized electricity is not well-distributed, the decreasing cost of solar technology enables a larger percentage of the population to leapfrog over nations that are unable or unwilling to capitalize on renewable energy. Even European nations such as Germany, which are relatively progressive with renewables, must still make a significant pivot given their reliance on traditional sources. This is one area of progress where it may take more time to transition than to build from scratch.

As humans become less dependent on finite resources such as fossil fuels or, even more crucial, find ways to make clean drinking water from waste or saltwater, there will be less for politicians and countries to fight over. It is why world peace is possible if we make it profitable—something I say to every young entrepreneur group to whom I speak. War is profitable for politicians and corporations. Fear drives votes, and destruction requires rebuilding, and I believe that is the only reason why war exists today. However, initiatives such as the United Nations' Sustainable Development Goals, which aim to end extreme poverty, reduce inequality, and protect the planet by 2030, provide ample opportunities to engage in meaningful conversations about making peace profitable.

Cultural competence is the pathway to equity, equity is the pathway to equality, and equality is the pathway to world peace. The engines that drive this equation are education and entrepreneurship. We may not need to reinvent the way we educate, but we do need to redefine the goal.

As Albert Einstein said, "Education is what remains after one has forgotten everything one has learned in school." Indeed, it is the ability to think rather than recall and to create rather than replicate. No one can reach one's full potential in an age of artificial intelligence and globalization until one stops focusing on achievement and starts focusing on learning.

Ravi with his students from Mosul, (L-R) Khaled, Hamood, Ameen, and Hakam, in Erbil, Iraq, July 2017.

Ravi in the Temple of Bacchus, Baalbek, Lebanon, August 2017.

## Pivot Points

- Research global threats. Everyone must understand the mindset of radicalization and terrorism because working against it and in favor of peace is a fundamental responsibility of a civilized society.

- Purposefully learn cultural competence. It can be learned by first exploring our commonalities and then engaging in civil discourse about our differences.

- Use existing initiatives to foster world peace. The United Nations' Sustainable Development Goals agenda is an accessible starting point to engage on some of the most critical challenges facing humanity.

- Put the horse in front of the cart. Education need not struggle to prepare students for an unpredictable future because the future will be shaped by how educators prepare students. A school should not think of itself as a factory that builds followers, but rather, a laboratory that creates leaders. Students and entrepreneurs must think about the future they want and connect with their culture—the system of beliefs, behaviors, and values.

- Embrace global citizenship. What put the West ahead during the Industrial Revolution will now likely cause it to lag. Today's students and entrepreneurs must recognize that their greatest opportunities may be elsewhere in the world, and therefore they must be globally and culturally competent.

# 3

# LIFE IS LIKE A GAME
# OF CARDS

My granduncle famously once said, "Life is like a game of cards. The hand you are dealt is determinism; the way you play it is free will." He was Jawaharlal Nehru, the architect of the world's largest democracy and first prime minister of India. His daughter, Indira Gandhi (my father's cousin), and grandson, Rajiv Gandhi (my second cousin), followed in his footsteps and also became prime ministers. They were all educated in England at either the University of Cambridge or the University of Oxford.

Jawaharlal's youngest sister, Krishna, married Raja Hutheesing (my grandparents), and my father, Ajit, grew up with his older brother in India during his family's long and arduous fight alongside Mahatma Gandhi for independence from British rule. In 1947, India became an independent nation, and about a decade later, my father also graduated from

Cambridge but pursued his MBA (Master of Business Administration) at Columbia University in New York.

With the family internally divided about how to best govern a nation of half a billion people (currently 1.4 billion) with 14 official languages (currently 22), hundreds of dialects, and eight major religions with bloody conflicts between Hindus and Muslims, he chose not to pursue a life in politics. Instead, he pivoted.

Ajit and my mother, Amrita, with their two sons, Nikhil and Vivek, immigrated to the United States in the mid-1960s, and my father launched a successful career in banking. He spent a decade working at the World Bank's International Finance Corporation (IFC) in Washington, DC, and that is when I was born, making me the first American-born member of the entire family. Four years later, my father became one of the first Indians to work on Wall Street, so we relocated to the upscale Manhattan suburb of Greenwich, Connecticut, which is where I grew up.

The path for people like me is typically predetermined. Expectations are high, a university education is assumed, and power and/or financial success typically follows. Like my father, my brothers attended top universities and secured jobs on Wall Street, but my journey took an unexpected twist when I turned eleven.

Soon after my brothers moved away for university, my parents' already troubled marriage completely crumbled. I had no memory of them being happy together, and therefore, I did not see their separation as negative; however, it was a shock to my 11-year-old system when in less than a year, I went from being the baby of a family of five to the man of the house living with my mother who struggled with depression.

While my parents were losing themselves in anger and sadness, I was finding myself in curiosity and creativity. I grew disenchanted with the corporate lifestyle my family represented and started to dream that one day, I would become a rock star. Pleased that I was showing an interest in something, my mother bought me an electric guitar for my eleventh birthday. I was not particularly interested in becoming a musician, but I enjoyed making lots of noise in my bedroom, pretending to be Angus Young of AC/DC on stage in New York's Madison Square Garden.

Between the tensions at home and my new distraction with music, going to school became increasingly unrelatable and unenjoyable. I had friends, but being shorter and browner than average, not to mention having a name no one could easily pronounce, I felt like an outcast. I was bored with classes and probably harbored inner rage toward my family life, which made me increasingly insubordinate in school. Eventually, the principal grew tired of having me sent to his office, so he assigned me to the school psychologist.

This was my "happy place" in primary school—the more disturbed I claimed to be, the more "parole" I received. Playing card games and building battleship models with him was my preferred way to pass the school day. I cannot say he helped me sort out life, but the sessions certainly helped me tolerate it.

Unfortunately, dedicated school psychologists are rare today. School counselors (a title combining both guidance and psychological counseling) are being asked to perform both career/educational guidance and mental health evaluations—two separate specializations requiring different expertise.

As I discovered a few years ago while preparing to give the keynote for the All Ohio Counselors Conference (comprised of about two thousand school counselors and an equal number of clinical counselors), this combined job cannot serve students well enough given today's high degree of social-emotional stress and a rapidly changing career landscape. Students who are facing challenges like I did are more likely to fall through the cracks.

My parents' divorce was finalized three weeks before my 13th birthday, and that summer, my mother and I moved to a much smaller house fifteen minutes away in Old Greenwich. I had to attend a new school, make new friends, and embark on a new and frightening beginning. I quickly made a few new friends in middle school who shared a common interest in music, so we started a band. With this collaboration and camaraderie, my interest in music grew. By the time I reached high school, all I wanted to do was drop out and play music professionally.

I had a good group of school friends, but I was also often bullied by others for being a "headbanger" (I listened to AC/DC, Van Halen, Judas Priest, Kiss, etc.) and was called names like "ravioli" and "Gandhi"—yes, I was apparently already very international! However, the bullying gave me grit, which helped prepare me for the world. While we should not encourage such behavior, we also should not shelter ourselves from the "school of life."

There were two reasons why I did not drop out of high school: Anne Modugno, who taught electronic music and music theory, and Carmel Signa, who was the jazz band director. I was lucky to have them in my life because drugs, cigarettes, and alcohol were often used and abused by my peers to get through the pressures of growing up in Greenwich. For me, music became my drug, and Anne and Carmel were my schoolyard dealers. They recognized, encouraged, and fostered my interest to the point where the escape the school psychologist provided for me in primary school was more than replaced by the music department in high school. I spent every free period and many after school hours with Anne and Carmel, and they always made time for me to learn as much as I could.

I reconnected with them thirty years later when I began giving keynotes for education conferences and reflecting on who influenced my life. They remembered me as a musically dedicated teenager and very much believed in me. Today, I can call them friends. It is remarkable how teacher-student relationships can pivot into adult friendships, and what gives me great satisfaction is that I not only realized how essential they were to my happiness and success, but I have personally been able to thank them. The music department is why I am not a high school dropout.

We must always express our gratitude toward our teachers. Doing so enables one to recognize the value of an education. Even if many years have passed, teachers will still appreciate acknowledgment from their students, especially since they will also then be able to witness the results. Since I taught music for many years, I know how much it means to witness the success of a student and be acknowledged for contributing to it. Teachers generally do not see the results of their hard work because the return on education is rarely evident before ten years have passed.

I also reconnected with my one and only school superintendent. Dr. Ernest Fleishman was hired the year I went to kindergarten, and he retired when I graduated high school (the typical term for a school superintendent is currently only three years). I often refer to Ernie as the "architect of my education," and when I needed to learn more about the education industry for a keynote speech nearly thirty years later, I tracked him down, took him out for lunch, and picked his brain to learn everything I could about public education from an administrator's point of view. During our lunch, he said something that really resonated with me:

"School must provide something for everyone. There must be at least one subject that makes each student want to come to school every day."

I am living proof of how true that statement is. Sadly, arts and physical education are most often the subjects that disappear first when budgets are cut, and to Ernie's point, all of these programs were established as part of the school day for a reason.

There is no benefit to exploring how we can fix education until we take a good look in the rearview mirror to see what we might have broken by removing such subjects. STEM (Science Technology Engineering Math) falls short of educating the whole child. STEAM (adding Arts) is critical because there is nothing else that truly teaches empathy, and there is nothing more essential than empathy to create a peaceful world. As my cultural diplomacy work in Iraq, Lebanon, and elsewhere demonstrates, music is a bridge that unites. It creates unity amidst diversity and can be fostered in any classroom of any school in any part of the world.

Taking it one step further, I often promote the importance of

STREAM. We tend to forget that we are animals with aggressive and violent tendencies. *Recess* is a controlled environment in which kids can safely exercise their violent tendencies in addition to benefiting from the social and "play" aspects. During the quarantines of COVID-19, domestic violence rose among most demographics worldwide. Humans need a physical outlet, and I believe this is a key component to reducing street violence and school shootings—especially when students are quarantined and spending most days in their bedrooms staring into the virtual abyss. Recess is not just an important part of the school day but an essential part of life.

Fortunately, my high school time commitment was not that consuming. While I was not a top student, I did well enough to graduate. Unlike what I see in student schedules today, there was enough time in the day to simultaneously educate myself in the real world. Perhaps in the age of school choice and double-income parents, keeping kids busy at school seems more important than unleashing them into a world filled with experiential learning opportunities. However, I believe this is a great disservice to children, and families and schools must coordinate and collaborate both ideologically and practically to educate the "whole child." Parents should not view school as a potential babysitter, and schools should not view family time as an opportunity to impose homework.

The father of one of my classmates in high school was a record producer. I never hesitated to ask him questions because I was already deeply committed to music. Ronald Frangipane invited me to join him one day in the major recording studios of New York City. I had only seen professional studios in magazines, so I did not want to lose this opportunity. One morning, my mother reluctantly called my school to say I was sick, and I went over to Ron's house. He and I drove an hour to A&R Recording Studios on West 48th Street in the heart of Manhattan. Entering the studio was like walking through the doorway of my dreams. It was beyond inspiring and everything I imagined.

That day, he was recording a "jingle"—what the industry calls a song used for advertising. There were a lot of people involved, including producers, engineers, writers, singers, musicians, and the client—a corporate executive—who dropped by to monitor the progress. I remember it almost as if it were yesterday. The song was catchy, the musicians were stellar and professional, and even just watching the interaction between Ron and the client was a priceless business education.

Following the session, he took me out for a fancy dinner around the corner at Joe Allen's. We went over what I had learned, and he offered that I start a formal apprenticeship under him. This was a huge opportunity for a 16-year-old, and I did not hesitate.

For the rest of my high school education, the sound of the final bell was often my signal to race to the Greenwich Metro-North railroad station and take the next train to the "Big Apple." This was when I learned the benefit of not procrastinating by finishing my homework quickly (not perfectly) before the end of the school day. I generally do not believe in perfectionism because I find that it is essentially a form of procrastination. Ever since high school, I have focused on *doing*. If I think about something and then wait to do it, it takes me twice as long. We can learn to be efficient by taking every opportunity to practice good time management. I wanted more time for music, so I had to make it.

Sadly, Ron died at age 75 in April of 2020 from the Coronavirus. Due to the pandemic and quarantines, the memorial service was held online, which was a first for everyone in attendance. Sitting in front of my computer with thoughts drifting into memories, I was able to distill exactly what he had taught me. Ron showed me what it meant to be a professional musician, or more to the point, what it meant to be a professional. He helped me determine if I had "what it takes" to be in the music business and gave me a real-world education that was more relevant than anything I was studying in school.

During my junior year of high school, I built a recording studio in my mother's basement. It began as a basic setup with two cassette decks and a tiny mixer from Radio Shack, but it was good enough for me to start writing and recording music at home. With the techniques I was learning from Ron, I was able to generate pretty good results despite having minimal equipment. In fact, I think my talents and creativity developed further due to having fewer resources.

In Chapter 6, I talk about my flight lessons, which had similar constraints. I trained on a short 2500-foot-long by a narrow 40-foot-wide runway (an airliner typically uses one that is at least 6000 x 100) and in an airplane that had just a stick, rudder, and the minimum number of instruments required. When I took my license test (check ride), the examiner commented on how refined my skills were and confirmed that this was likely the reason.

In any learning environment, having less can produce more. Today, we have so much in terms of tools and devices that problem-solving and creativity are stifled. You can stimulate your own creativity by occasionally restricting the available tools.

As I upgraded my recording studio, I was able to start a teaching business by posting flyers on grocery store and train station bulletin boards. With a handful of private guitar students coming for lessons, I began recording their songs as well as attracting local musicians as clients. A rather odd market I cornered was editing music for figure skating routines of local kids, and it started with the sister of one of my students. Another was transferring old ceramic 78 RPM records to cassette tapes—I happened to have a three-speed hand-me-down record player from my parents. I was invoicing clients, keeping books, and developing business policies and customer service. However, none of these skills were being taught to me in school.

In addition to giving me a guitar for my eleventh birthday, my mother signed me up for lessons with John "Ratso" Gerardi—a local musician who had a great reputation as a teacher and performer. As I mentioned earlier, my interest in music began as superficial as I had no real desire to discipline myself to learn the guitar properly. However, Ratso saw I needed something that went far beyond music.

If you know him, you know he is much more than a teacher. For me, Ratso was and still is my dear friend and mentor. I made little progress on the guitar for the first three years, but he kept showing me different things to see what would resonate. My failure to practice and a bad habit of showing up to lessons without my books could have bumped me off his schedule, but instead, Ratso made each lesson an exploration into a new direction.

This is how I discovered songwriting when I was only 14 years old. I may not have practiced my scales, but I showed up each week with a new original tune that he helped make better. Ratso had a small recording studio in his house where he taught lessons and recorded songs with his band and other local musicians. Clearly, my own business in high school was trying to model the way he ran his as a professional.

Ratso taught me so much. I often say that what means the most to me is what he taught me "between the notes." It was his example that influenced me more than his lesson plans. He had a full teaching schedule and was often running late because in between students, he had to return calls, book gigs for his band, and double-check with the printer and newspaper on his advertising. He was a one-man operation as a local business, and by watching him, I learned to be an entrepreneur.

Like Ron, Ratso taught me the importance of professionalism, but in a different dimension. It had less to do with what you do and more to do with who you are. Ratso taught me "goodness," which no one was teaching me in school or at home (my mother's goodness was too often overshadowed by her depression and anger, and my father's only began to show as he mellowed with age). It sounds basic, but it is not; goodness—being universally kind, naturally doing what is ethical, searching for the best in others, etc.—is at the very heart of what makes a decent human.

Ratso also gave me two great pieces of business advice: "If you want to be paid like a professional, you need to act like a professional," and "It is better to be prepared and not have an

opportunity than to have an opportunity and not be prepared."
These principles guide me to this day.

One could say it was lucky to have had a classmate with Ron
as a father or that my mother came across Ratso. I do believe in
luck, though my definition has evolved. Early on, it was driven
by my passion. I was lucky to have a mother who believed in
me and allowed me to occasionally skip school to pursue an
alternate form of education, and I was also lucky to have a guitar
teacher who saw my passion through my distractions.

It is essential that we have the opportunity to experience
boredom and hardship so that we discover our passions early.
Passion is infectious, and parents, teachers, and others are likely
to support and invest in a child's passion. As I once told the
parents of a dedicated and talented student who wanted to
pursue music professionally, "He's going to do it whether you
support him or not. But if you support him, he has a better
chance of becoming successful."

As a young adult embarking on a career, I pivoted to the
definition of luck provided by the philosopher Seneca: "Luck
is the moment when preparation meets opportunity." Great
opportunities surround each of us all the time; however, we only
uncover them if we are curious and confident enough to engage
in conversations that may have no clear benefit. Curiosity and
communication are essential skills. Then, one must feel
prepared to seize an opportunity, which is where talent and
critical thinking come into the equation. One either has the
ability to meet the criteria or the belief that with dedication and
commitment, one can rise to the occasion.

Now, as a more seasoned professional, I define luck with the words of Thomas Jefferson, "The harder I work, the more luck I have." There is just no substitute for hard work.

Ravi giving future first lady, Dr. Jill Biden, his grandmother's book at the Colorado Assoc. of School Execs. Conference, July 2017.

Ravi celebrating his 44th birthday with Ratso, May 2015.

Pivot Points

- Embrace gratitude. We must express gratitude toward teachers, even if many years have passed. This is not only encouraging to teachers but also enables us to recognize the value of our education.

- Participate in many electives. Schools must provide something for everyone. There must be at least one subject that makes each student want to come to school every day.

- Focus on the arts. STEAM (Science, Technology, Engineering, *Arts*, and Math) is critical because there is nothing else that teaches empathy, and there is nothing more essential than empathy to create a peaceful world.

- Encourage a family/school partnership. Families and schools must coordinate and collaborate in both ideology and schedules to best educate the "whole child." Parents must not view school as a babysitter, and schools must not view family time as an opportunity to impose homework.

- Prioritize efficiency over perfection. Perfectionism is a form of procrastination. Learn to be efficient by taking every opportunity to practice good time management.

- Focus on less, not more. We have so many tools and devices that problem-solving and creativity are stifled. Stimulate creativity by occasionally restricting the tools.

- Use boredom as a catalyst for creativity. Embrace boredom and hardship to discover passions early. Passion is infectious, and parents, teachers, and others are likely to support and invest in a child's passion.

- Seek opportunities. We only uncover opportunities if we are curious and confident enough to engage in conversations that may have no clear benefit. Curiosity and communication are essential skills. Then, one must feel prepared to seize an opportunity, which is where talent and critical thinking come into the equation. One either has the ability to meet the criteria or the belief that with dedication and commitment, one can rise to the occasion.

# 4

# DON'T CHASE
# SUCCESS; PURSUE
# EXCELLENCE

More than luck, I believe that if you pursue excellence rather than chase success, success will chase you. To be truly successful in any career requires a strong work ethic, and perhaps even more so when one attempts to pivot one's passion into a profession. Much like how Ron taught me about professionalism and Ratso showed me the tools of entrepreneurship, other adults in my life influenced my work ethic.

The more opportunities there are to interact with elders with whom you can develop cross-generational friendships, the better. This is not the role of parents or schoolteachers since they have other clearly defined responsibilities, but sports coaches, private music teachers, and summer camp counselors are good examples. With such opportunities, each of us can learn from the wisdom which only comes with experience—there is no shortcut to wisdom.

When my mother and I moved out of the family home shortly after my 13th birthday, one silver lining was that I was moving into a neighborhood full of kids, parks, and stores. What was now my father's house was far from town, and it had made me feel isolated growing up. This new environment would justify a proper bicycle, so my mother took me to the local cycle shop.

Still traumatized by her failed marriage, and given her lack of emotional stability, she made every effort to protect me while working it out. Tony, the owner of the cycle shop, was a friendly man, so she asked if he would consider hiring a 13-year-old. I imagine she shared her concerns about me because he agreed to it even though I was underage.

For the next two years, I spent all day Saturday plus Monday and Wednesday afternoons earning the minimum wage, which was $3.50/hour—not bad for a 13-year-old in 1984 working 12 hours each week. I began by changing flat tires in the back of the store but soon graduated to building new bikes. In addition to Tony, there were four employees, all of whom were 10 to 20 years older than me. I was surrounded by baby boomers (I am Generation X), but they made me feel like one of them. It was a great opportunity for me to mature.

I had moved from a secluded upscale neighborhood to one that was comparatively crowded and middle-class, and while some of my new friends had typical teenager jobs like delivering the local newspaper, babysitting, or mowing lawns, mine was different. The cycle shop was a fully operational retail business requiring many of the soft and hard skills one is expected to have upon graduating college. Tony taught me how to use the cash register and count change backward, what to say when I answered the phone or greeted a customer, how to track inventory, and of course, the mechanics of building a bicycle. While all this skill-building certainly contributed to my ability to run a business, it was something he once said to me that formed a key aspect of my work ethic today.

I had finished doing inventory with a coworker in the basement, and when I came upstairs, it was to a quiet store. Tony was outside test-riding bikes with a customer, and the others were on break. I did not know what to do next, and there was no one around to give me instructions. After a few minutes, Tony came inside the shop to get an air pump. He turned to me and, in a slightly frustrated tone, said, "Don't wait for someone to tell you what to do. Find something to do and do it."

I felt embarrassed, and I quickly started straightening the tools beside the service station and wiping down countertops. Tony was right. There is always something to do that needs doing. Moreover, I discovered that it is less humiliating if you see it and do it before someone asks you to do it. This childhood lesson not only makes me more efficient today but also more respected by my clients, colleagues, friends, and family. A little embarrassment can go a long way, and we should not be so afraid of our emotions that we forego opportunities to learn the most meaningful life lessons.

Following my sixteenth birthday, I passed the most coveted test for a teenager at the time: I earned my driver's license. One afternoon, I was in town walking toward my parked car when a man in a wheelchair dropped a one-gallon jug of water from his lap. It landed right in front of me, so I picked it up and offered to carry it to his car. On the way, I noticed his wheelchair had special tires that I remembered from the bike shop. I commented on them, and he said he recently had them installed.

Peter had been a regular customer of Tony's for a long time, though I had never met him. I told him I used to work there but quit to focus on music. This caught his ear because he had just bought some musical recording equipment to build a home studio but had not been able to set it up by himself. Peter said that if I could help him, he would be happy to let me record my songs using his equipment. At the time, I did not have much more than those two cassette decks and a tiny mixer, so I was eager to accept his offer. I excitedly jotted down his phone number.

Regardless of whether my mother approved, I now had "wheels" and could go wherever I wanted. I imagine that most parents today would be uneasy with a 30-year-old stranger inviting their 16-year-old child to his house, but it is critical to strike the right balance between protecting one's child and giving him or her opportunities to exercise judgment and assess risk. Overprotecting will hinder a child's opportunity to receive and absorb the lessons of the world. For my mother, sixteen was a reasonable age to use my judgment since I had already been safely interacting with strangers for several years. Her confidence in me paid off in spades.

This accidental meeting turned into a meaningful friendship lasting many years, and it also enabled me to water the entrepreneurial seeds Ratso had planted. Peter was reasonably wealthy and enjoyed dabbling in music as a hobby, but mostly, he liked technology and upgraded his equipment regularly. As such, he would sell me his barely used equipment for a fraction of his cost, for which my mother gave me interest-free loans.

This is what made it possible for me to upgrade my basement studio into a studio business, so I began surveying construction sites and learned how to frame walls. I had also just started working with Ron in the major studios, so I took note of how they were constructed, including how to isolate sound using double windows and floating walls.

Over several weeks, I drove to the local home center to buy 2×4 studs, sheetrock, fiberglass insulation, and plexiglass, and I asked local markets to save their large egg cartons (commonly made from recycled paper pulp) so that I could glue them to the walls and ceiling to absorb reverberation—I could not afford professional acoustic tiles. Every spare moment, I hammered together walls and soldered audio cables. One month later, my after-school and weekend project was a fully-functional home recording studio ready for students and clients. It was not long before I managed to pay my mother back.

Two years later, I graduated high school and wanted nothing more than to *continue* my career in music. However, my parents had other plans because, in my family, you go to college. They were supportive of my entrepreneurial spirit but also conventional in their beliefs and felt that I would be better served with a college degree. I was opposed to this but had already agreed and applied to university to keep my options open. At the very least, they wanted me to give college "the old college try."

I applied "early decision" to New York University because it had a good music program. More important to me, I could then still apprentice in the studios under Ron, study guitar with Ratso, and keep running my studio and teaching business in the suburbs on weekends. I also wanted to keep making money to invest in my recording studio.

NYU accepted me, and I majored in classical music composition. It felt like the best combination of advancing the music theory that Anne taught me in high school and broadening my musical knowledge to create new studio opportunities such as film scoring. Since being on stage had never been my interest, learning to write and orchestrate music seemed to be the best use of my time at university.

However, I quickly became bored with classes and found them to be reminiscent of the high school education I loathed. I was wasting my time, and after one semester, I was done. Having fulfilled my promise to my parents by giving it a try, I told them I wanted to leave school.

While they clearly did not like the idea, my father left the door open by challenging me to write a business plan before making a final decision. I accepted his challenge and wrote a detailed plan on how I would use the unspent college tuition to invest in my studio, grow my teaching business, and continue my education by hiring my college professors to teach me privately. My professors were happy to have me pay them to teach me personally, but I think they also genuinely felt that this was best for me. So, when my father consulted with them, they gave my plan their full support.

No one had ever asked me to write a business plan in school, yet this was probably the most important exercise I had done up to this moment. Perhaps the focus of "college and career ready" needs to pivot to "college *or* career ready" because the goal of every school ought to be to graduate each student into the real world as soon as they are ready. My father was impressed with my plan, and despite some hesitation, he ultimately supported my decision. My story is obviously not the common theme of being the first person in a family to go to college, but I am the first to have dropped out!

In truth, just about every one of my mentors was supportive, but none were really in favor of my decision. Anne and Ron both felt that college was valuable, and Ratso, who did not go to college, believed it was a great opportunity for me. However, it was something Peter said that stuck in my head.

He did not believe college was for everyone but felt that choosing not to go makes life harder. His point was that if you choose to take the road less traveled (to paraphrase the poetry of Robert Frost), you will have to rely on yourself much more. Peter's words of wisdom that he conveyed to me in multiple contexts were, "Do it with conviction or don't do it at all."

Indeed, stability would be harder to achieve, but perhaps so much more worth achieving if you are pursuing your dream. In the words of Confucius, "If you love what you do, you will never work a day in your life."

All of these adult influences were critical to navigating life's most pivotal decisions. Parents and teachers are important, but they are not enough. Unfortunately, we live in a time where youth culture seems to reject the wisdom of elders, but perhaps that is partly because elders often fail to see value in the innocence of youth. If we are to make the world a better place, learning must be bidirectional and cross-generational.

As families become more global, fewer include multiple generations living under one roof or even in the same vicinity. Therefore, creating opportunities for cross-generational interaction is a valuable part of education. There must be occasions created for people of different ages to interact with each other, and for students to interact with teachers who are not their own.

As a 19-year-old college dropout, I started working harder than ever. I studied privately three times each week with my NYU professors plus my weekly guitar lesson with Ratso. Soon, I landed a job teaching guitar at the local music store in Greenwich, and within a few months, had a teaching schedule of forty students per week. Several evenings each week, I taught a classical music appreciation continuing education course for adults at a nearby high school. More clients began recording in my studio (often due to referrals from the music store), and I was also regularly writing and recording my original songs. I started filing copyright registrations with the Library of Congress and put together a band to perform my compositions.

I ran my band like a business, including registering the name with the county clerk as a DBA (Doing Business As) and opening a business bank account. On most weekends, we performed in bars and nightclubs in the suburbs of New York City, and I secured every gig with a written, legally-binding contract. I built a significant mailing list (before the days of email) and sent out hundreds of physical newsletters once a month, folding and stamping them myself while also distributing press releases to local newspapers to promote every show. We rehearsed every Tuesday night, and I held back pay from the next gig if someone was repeatedly late or did not show up. My bandmates, most of whom were older than I, felt that I took it too seriously. However, I was committed and determined to be professional and successful. Over the next five years, I built and ran a small stable local business.

A few months before my 26th birthday (1997), I got a phone call from a former studio client, Rob. He had become the musical director for eleven-time Grammy-nominated artist Vanessa Williams, and he no longer had a need for my home studio. We had not been in touch for a few years; however, that holiday season, I had sent him a Christmas card to reconnect—my mother and Ratso taught me the importance of handwritten notes and keeping doors open. Rob left a message on my answering machine mentioning that an executive at Mercury Records had asked him to recommend a young guitar player. I had popped into his mind.

Could it have been the Christmas card? Probably, but there was something else that has always opened more doors for me than my talent: my pursuit of excellence and professionalism. What Ron and Ratso had taught me was paying off because Rob had never actually heard me play the guitar. He is an excellent guitarist himself and had only worked with me as his audio engineer in my home studio. However, he knew he could count on me to show up on time, be respectful and professional, and ultimately make him look good. As is often said: Sometimes, perception actually is reality.

These are the "soft skills" that employers say are lacking among today's new hires. We must purposefully learn and practice soft skills such as *responsibility* by assigning ourselves responsibilities, *accountability* by recognizing and rectifying whenever failing to be responsible, and perhaps most important, *communication* by proactively engaging with peers and elders who are neither our parents nor teachers—one of the worst lessons we are taught as children is to not talk to strangers. Instead, we should have been learning *how* to talk to strangers.

Rob had already given the record label executive my phone number; he just wanted me to expect the call. However, I wanted to learn more, so I called him back immediately. He did not know anything more, but upon my request, he agreed to give me the phone number of the executive at Mercury. This turned out to be critical because, after a few days, I had not heard from this person, so I decided to take matters into my own hands. What did I have to lose?

As it turned out, he was recruiting for the Harvard Business School of Rock and Roll.

Ravi with his bike while working at the cycle shop, August 1984.

Ravi in the studio that he built in his mother's basement, July 1993.

## Pivot Points

- Do not be afraid to be occasionally embarrassed. We should not be so protective of our emotions that we forego taking risks that yield the most meaningful life lessons.

- Expose rather than protect. Strike the right balance between protecting yourself from the unknown and exercising good judgment and risk assessment. Overprotecting hinders opportunities to receive and absorb the lessons of the world.

- "College and career ready" needs to pivot to "college *or* career ready" because the goal of every school system ought to be to graduate each student into the real world as soon as they are ready.

- Pursue multi-directional communication. To make the world a better place, learning must be bidirectional and cross-generational. Create opportunities for cross-generational interaction, such as going to places to interact with unfamiliar peers or elders.

- Purposefully learn soft skills such as *responsibility* and *accountability* by assigning yourself responsibilities, and *communication* by engaging with peers and elders—one of the worst lessons we are taught as children is to not talk to strangers. Instead, we should have been learning *how* to talk to strangers.

5

# THE HARVARD BUSINESS SCHOOL OF ROCK & ROLL

Being the guitarist of Hanson was the best music industry education money could buy, and I was being paid to learn. In 1997, the dark grunge explosion of bands like Nirvana was beginning to fade, and the world was getting hungry for something different. Nirvana's former manager, Danny Goldberg, saw an opportunity to pivot that many others did not.

The "bubblegum pop" doors had just been opened by the Spice Girls, and Danny, who had become the CEO of Mercury Records, believed there was room for something equally infectious in a boy band. However, Hanson had something that the carefully crafted boy bands of the time (Backstreet Boys, NSYNC, etc.) did not—they were three brothers with raw talent and a great family story. They were also as wholesome and middle-America as one could get. Mercury took a leap of faith and raked in the rewards.

Hanson rapidly turned into a teenage phenomenon. Fans' parents were thrilled to have their kids gushing over something so innocent and pure, and mothers also understood their daughters' infatuation over the band because they had exhibited the same hysteria over the Beatles, David Cassidy, and other heartthrobs of their generation. Between multi-platinum record sales and endorsement deals that included the brothers posing with white mustaches for the famous series of milk ads, and appearing on frozen waffle boxes, they took the music industry and pop culture by storm.

My education at the "Harvard Business School of Rock and Roll" began before the world had heard of Hanson—on the day when I called Michael at Mercury Records. I had waited a few days to hear from him, and when my phone did not ring, I remembered what Tony at the bike shop taught me about taking the initiative. I asked myself, "What do I have to lose?" Even if he had already hired someone else, I would be no worse off than if I did nothing. I only had something to gain, so I pushed myself out of my comfort zone and followed up on this lead.

Michael took my call. He said he was overwhelmed with projects and had not yet gotten around to calling me but appreciated that I called. The soon-to-be world-famous brothers needed a guitarist to perform a showcase of their newly recorded album, *Middle of Nowhere*, to record distributors. It was just one performance preceded by a week's worth of rehearsals.

He asked a few questions about my experience but basically just needed a photo and recording of me playing the guitar. Since he was running behind schedule, he asked that I mail them to his house. Michael lived less than an hour from me, and since I knew he was pressed for time, I offered to hand-deliver them that same evening. He was most grateful.

I was nervous about meeting a major record label executive, but what did I have to lose? I was prepared and had everything to gain. That evening, I stood in his doorway and shook the hand of someone who turned out to be one of the biggest decision makers of my career. The next day, Michael offered me the job.

We discussed the details, but curiously, he did not suggest we sign a contract. I had believed that all my due diligence training as a local artist-entrepreneur would have seasoned me for the big leagues; however, it seemed my training exceeded industry standards. I asked him to send me a contract, and while he did not feel it was necessary, he offered that if I put something in writing, he would sign it. While I was afraid of losing this opportunity by being difficult, I felt it was professional and, at the very least, appropriate to have our deal documented. So, I wrote a one-page "letter of intent" outlining everything we discussed, faxed it to him (before the days of email), and he signed and faxed it back without hesitation.

In March of 1997, I met Isaac, Taylor, and Zachary, who were only 16, 13, and 11 years old. They were three of the most talented kids I had ever met—what they lacked in skill and experience, they made up for in natural ability and personality. Along with two other band members, the six of us rehearsed for a week in a dusty, unused theater in their hometown of Tulsa, Oklahoma. With a road crew of three (this was the first time I had my own guitar technician), we worked hard for eight hours each day, and then I either relaxed at the hotel bar with the crew or, more often than not, had dinner and played laser tag at the local shopping mall with the Hanson family. After a week of rehearsals and family fun, we traveled together to Orlando, Florida, to perform at the NARM (National Association of Record Merchandisers) convention.

Our first concert was a huge hit, and the executives at Mercury were very pleased. I remember our assistant manager coming up to us after we got off stage to share that the producer of *Late Show with David Letterman* had already called, and Dave wanted to be the first late-night talk show host to introduce the band to America. The energy and excitement were almost surreal.

This two-week experience was transformational for me. Having always been the youngest in my family, Ike (Isaac), Tay, and Zac became the little brothers I never had. We bonded quickly as I instantly pivoted from a young GenXer apprentice in a sea of baby-boomers to an old GenXer professional in a sea of millennials—it was almost as dramatic as when I was 11 and went from the baby of a family of five to the man of the house.

I also discovered a new degree of elation from performing on stage. The youthful energy and big-league optimism brought me to new heights, and while the recording studio had always been my "happy place," the taste of being a rock star was exhilarating. It was not just what happened on stage or with the audience (which was a group of corporate executives—hardly the wild teenagers we would soon become accustomed to), but also the roadies, green rooms, first-class treatment, and being the center of everyone's attention. Whether or not it was true, I felt as if I might have finally "made it."

I returned home and resumed teaching at the music store and recording in my home studio. It did not feel like I was going backward because I had a new appreciation for how and to where I could pivot, and I was also pretty confident that this was not the last I would see of Hanson. One month later, Mercury Records called to see if I would be available to play with the band, this time on *The Late Show with David Letterman*.

It was again just a single performance, but from that point on, those calls kept coming. That same week, we also performed on *The Today Show* and *The Rosie O'Donnell Show*, and a few weeks later, at the end of May, during the week of my 26th birthday, "MMMBop" soared to #1 on the Billboard *Hot 100* chart. I remember rehearsing the following week in Los Angeles and thinking, "Wow, I am in the band that currently has the number one song in America, and we are now, at this moment, practicing it." This was the turning point for Hanson and a huge pivot opportunity for me. As far as I was concerned, there would be no going back to being a local musician. I had, indeed, finally "made it."

Hanson wanted to make me an employee, but as a singer-songwriter with a studio business, I had never considered becoming a guitarist for another band. I did not want to quit, so I hired an accountant to give me business advice. He suggested that I remain an independent contractor but said I could set up a corporation and have Hanson contract my company to provide my services as a guitarist. This would give me more independence, create greater distance in terms of limiting any liability, and ultimately help me build value that would last beyond my time with the band. In July of 1997, I filed articles of incorporation and established my very own C-Corporation with Hanson as my first client. From that point on, 100% of my business would funnel through what is now called Ravi Unites, Inc., with me as its sole employee.

School never taught me how to establish or run a company, handle payroll, withhold taxes, create a health insurance program, or even do basic invoicing and bookkeeping. I had to learn by asking questions. My father was a smart businessman, but no one in my family was an entrepreneur or had started a company. However, my parents had often made me, as a teenager, pick up the phone to ask questions directly to store salesclerks, teachers, or movie theater ticket offices rather than calling on my behalf. When I was only eleven, my mother made me call my piano teacher personally to tell her I wanted to quit and switch to the guitar.

These experiences taught me that it is worth risking rejection to gain the benefit of assistance or information. This is arguably the most important characteristic of lifelong learning—to find out what you do not know by asking someone who does. The old saying that "you don't know what you don't know" need not always be true, and in this case, I was as much a student as I was a client of my accountant as he unknowingly taught me how to run my company.

By August, Hanson had outsold every other band in the world that year, and by the end of 1997, I had performed on many major morning and evening television shows, including *Late Show with David Letterman*, *Tonight Show with Jay Leno*, *Saturday Night Live*, *Today Show*, *Good Morning America*, and others. We also played Madison Square Garden (my childhood dream), President Clinton's *Christmas in Washington* celebration, and capped off the year by earning three Grammy nominations. My parents and brothers were very proud, coming to several of our live concerts and recording every television appearance.

However, from the moment this incredible opportunity began, I was thinking about the day it would end. It was not an inability to live in the moment, but I was cognizant that it was not going to last forever. I had to be prepared to pivot into something else.

My mother was an avid diarist (as was my grandmother), and she always encouraged me to keep a journal whenever we went on vacation. I realized early on that Hanson would be some kind of milestone in my career, so I kept a journal from day one. Each day, I would write down the activities, conversations, and my feelings, and I also tried to capture as many photos as possible—we were still taking pictures with film and had to get them developed, so it was not quite as convenient or inexpensive as it is today. I did not know what I was documenting or what I would do with it, but I felt it might be relevant in some way down the road.

On a side note, I once forgot my journal in the back of an airplane seat. About a week later, a Delta aircraft mechanic who had found it called (I had written my name and phone number inside just a few days earlier). I do not know how much of it he read, but he said he thought it was something important and kindly offered to ship it back to me. That was *lucky!*

Since I was not a Hanson brother, I had much more freedom than they did. My security was never at risk, and there was ample time for me to do other things while they were busy with press tours and photoshoots. Moreover, I could step into and out of fame as I wanted—I was a rock star being chased by fans and paparazzi within a few blocks of any concert venue, but outside of that radius, I slipped into obscurity.

Before shows, I often walked through the hallways at concert arenas to greet fans and hand out custom guitar picks that featured my email address. Email was new, and it was not long until I also established my website. This generated fan mail, some of which included personal stories of hardship, broken families, teenage depression, and suicidal thoughts. While I was only famous within this narrow scope, I discovered the power of fame and the potential to use it for good. As you will see in later chapters, I have felt compelled to help youth survive their hardships and pursue their dreams ever since because I see my younger self in many of them.

In January of 1998, I got the dreaded call. The brothers' father, who was also the co-manager, decided to make changes. I was fired. No matter how many times I asked, no one gave me a reason. I wrote multiple letters to the family and management saying I respected their decision; however, I would be most grateful if they would let me perform with them one last time on the Grammy Awards at Radio City Music Hall, New York. This was a performance in honor of three Grammy nominations and a celebration of everything we had achieved together that year, not to mention that it was a legendary venue and ... the Grammys! I never received a response, and that Sunday evening, February 25th, 1998, I sat alone in front of the television, watching Ike, Tay, Zac, and their new guitarist perform at the 40th Annual Grammy Awards.

I was out of a job, had nothing going on at home, and felt tremendously bitter about the industry I loved. It was frightening when at the age of only 26, everything I had dreamed of and worked for had come true and then disappeared so quickly. I started thinking of myself as a "has been before 30." One friend remarked that it is better to be a "has been" than a "never has been," and while that may be true, I also found that the benefit of not yet realizing a dream is that the dream is then still alive. Dreams matter, and they must be encouraged and nurtured regardless of how unrealistic they might seem. They are the fuel that keeps each of us striving for something greater, and they help form our identities.

While feeling abandoned, devastated, and essentially lost, I was also aware that my story was unconventional and one from which fellow musicians could learn. After all, I had become the guitarist of the top-selling band in the world that year—not because of my talent, but because of my initiative, professionalism, and entrepreneurial mindset. This was something I could teach, and it was time for me to stop feeling sorry for myself, and instead, pivot.

I managed to get a commission to write a magazine article about my experience. While I was not a writer, my father and eldest brother were both talented with words, and they helped me craft my written voice—I am pretty sure every member of my family went through the first draft with a red pen! Soon, "published author" became part of my resume, and I began work on a memoir based on the daily journal I had kept.

There were already three books written about Hanson that had made the *New York Times* Bestseller list, but none told the inside day-to-day story. I knew I had something unique, and since I was never an employee and not bound by non-disclosure agreements, there was nothing to hold me back. I researched literary agencies to find out who had made the deals for the bestsellers, tracked down the individual agent, and gave her a call. She agreed to represent me, but after a few months of shopping my proposal unsuccessfully, she decided to move on to other projects.

Perhaps it was simply too late, and Hanson was already passé, but surprisingly, she had not approached Random House or Simon & Schuster—the two biggest names in the business. She said they would not be interested since the others had all declined. Realizing that I was disappointed, she kindly offered me the phone numbers of editors at both publishers. Once again, I asked myself, "What do I have to lose?" as I picked up the phone. To my great surprise, they were both interested. When Simon & Schuster presented the best offer, I hired a lawyer and negotiated the contract.

*Dancin' with Hanson* was released just over one year after I was fired from the band (April 1999). Unfortunately, between the time I signed my book deal and the release date about eight months later, Mercury Records folded when its parent company, Polygram, was sold and dismantled. Hanson's tour had been postponed indefinitely, and there was no telling if or when their new CD would be released.

My book sales were sure to suffer, and to compound things further, the internet peer-to-peer music file-sharing company, Napster, was about to launch and would quickly bring the rest of the recording industry to its knees. Napster was changing the consumer economy to a decentralized sharing economy, and the record industry could not figure out how to monetize it. In some ways, I was lucky to have temporarily pivoted from musician to author. However, any dreams I had of returning to the major labels were quickly shattered. Virtually all my contacts were now unemployed, so my pivot would likely have to be permanent.

After Mercury collapsed, but before my book was released, I went back to my studio in my mother's basement, assembled a band of top New York studio musicians, and recorded a CD. I created an independent record label under my corporation, and in less than two months, had written, recorded, and manufactured thousands of copies of *Beyond the Blur*. I was then able to leverage my Simon & Schuster book deal and publicity tour into a distribution deal for the CD with the now-defunct Borders Books and Music.

Over the next eight years, I rebuilt my career as a performing singer-songwriter, sold books and CDs, wrote over a hundred magazine articles, and began speaking at conferences and universities about creating multiple streams of income as an independent artist-entrepreneur. The rebound was always a struggle because book and CD sales were slow, and performance and writing contracts were not well-paid. However, my business was at least growing until the global economy collapsed in 2008, taking my career with it. While I could have picked up the pieces and put them back together, the most unimaginable personal challenge was about to unravel my world.

Ravi's "diploma" (in the form of a double platinum sales certification) awarded to him for his work with Hanson, August 1997.

Ravi's photo of an empty Madison Square Garden in New York City, which he took a few hours before performing on the legendary stage with Hanson, December 1997.

Pivot Points

- One must learn to assess risk/reward. It is worth risking rejection to gain the benefit of assistance or information, such as asking questions directly to store clerks, obtaining information over the phone (especially in the internet age), and communicating with strangers safely. This is arguably the most important characteristic of lifelong learning—to find out what you do not know by asking someone who does.

- Take the initiative. There simply is no substitute. By doing so, one keeps the most options available.

- Exercise professionalism. Preparation, reliability, and ethics will always prevail, even at times when it may not appear to matter.

- Engage in journaling. The habit of writing, especially by hand, not only develops thought processes but also builds the narrative of one's life story—a valuable resource whenever one has to pivot.

- Focus on potential strengths. When everything collapses, further develop other skills.

- Nurture your dreams. As unrealistic as they might seem, dreams are the fuel that keeps us striving for something greater, and they help form our identities.

6

# WHAT DOESN'T KILL YOU MAKES YOU STRONGER

———❦———

Following the adventure with Hanson and the subsequent release of my book and CD, I fell in love. Marie, a French girl from Bordeaux, was temporarily making her home in New Orleans, Louisiana. She was a registered nurse but enjoyed the music industry and had fashioned a side career out of creating fundraisers to help struggling local artists. In addition, she occasionally worked as a personal assistant to BB King and other big names when they came to town to perform. I met her when I was performing in a French Quarter nightclub where she was the stage manager—she was, in fact, just filling in for someone else for one night only. We were married in Paris one year later to the day, one month before my 29th birthday.

Initially, we made our home in the city where we met, and the spirit of New Orleans reconnected me with music as an art

71

form as opposed to a business. Having come off the tremendous high and low of Hanson, I probably would not have tried to make a comeback without Marie's participation. She was a great supporter of my talents, and she acted as my manager for our first eight years of marriage.

Through her contacts, I put together a new band featuring some of the finest local musicians. She became my partner in life and career though she and most of my friends, family, and clients did not see eye to eye on many things. This was a divide I never could bridge, and while we were rebuilding my career together, the personal relationships I valued most were falling apart.

Marie handled everything from booking concerts to promoting shows to selling CDs and T-shirts from the side of the stage. She also managed my budding speaking career and accompanied me to every conference, clinic, and university. In the process, we explored most of the United States together as we drove coast to coast while taking time to discover the country.

While in New Orleans, I also launched my first non-profit venture, "Sunflowers in the Shade"—a music enrichment program for homeless children. Every Tuesday night, I would give guitar and piano lessons to abandoned "street kids" sheltered at the Covenant House, and I raised money to purchase and donate instruments for their use. I started this program due to a combination of social consciousness, guilt, and business need.

When we first moved to New Orleans, I begrudgingly returned to giving guitar lessons to make some quick money. I say "begrudgingly" because I had no desire to return to my pre-Hanson life in the music industry—it felt like I would be taking a step backward. What made this worthwhile was that I catered to the upper-class (mostly the white population living in "Uptown" New Orleans) and charged above-average fees. Coming from Greenwich, I was used to working with an affluent population and being paid more than most. Now with my "rock star" resume, I could leverage that and command high fees anywhere.

However, while poverty was nearly absent or at least well-hidden in Greenwich, it was rampant and in-your-face in New Orleans. My desire and ability to target the wealthy resulted in my neglecting the larger and more needy communities that I drove by each day. I began to feel guilty because my type of business model was promoting disparity, not just between rich and poor but also between whites and blacks.

Racism and racial inequality are often closely aligned with socioeconomic status. Growing up in the northeast of the United States gave me little exposure to this reality, but as soon as I moved south of the Mason-Dixon line (the division between north and south), racially-based inequality became quite apparent. Living in the south has been an eye-opener in this regard. It is a tragedy that it takes something as violent as the killing of an unarmed black man by a white police officer for the rest of the country to catch on.

Since I also had to make a name for myself in the highly competitive and crowded New Orleans music scene, it occurred to me that choosing to "pay it forward" within the community would be better than exclusively promoting myself. "Paying it forward" is like "giving back," except you give *before* you receive. Since you have not yet received anything, you do not know where or from whom the return will come, if at all. We more often recognize those who give back because the transaction is easier to follow—rarely do we know what non-famous or not-yet-famous people do for others, but when it is a celebrity, we celebrate them for not losing sight of how they got there.

However, I believe in creating a culture of paying it forward because it not only cultivates a more socially-conscious society but also attracts a level of support that lifts one to even greater heights. Call it karma or the law of attraction, but I believe it is less ethereal than either of those. In fact, I think paying it forward is potentially as transactional as giving back, and there should be no shame in gambling for a return on an investment when that investment is for the benefit and betterment of others.

This can be learned. By purposefully exercising this mindset through daily activities that enable one to do nice things for others, it would likely result in doing more good in the world.

I raised enough money to buy and donate instruments while rallying the local community and media to support the cause. Local news covered my fundraisers, and I was soon a well-known New Orleans musician. It was a win-win proposition, and what gratified me most was that each week, I met with a group of inspiring but disturbed teens—typically between the ages of sixteen and twenty—and we created music together.

I had never worked with this demographic, and it was not easy. I dreaded going to the shelter each Tuesday because I never knew what awaited me. Sometimes it was just a guitar that had been stolen, a kid who had returned to the streets, or someone new who was skeptical and confrontational. Sometimes it was more serious. Most of them had undiagnosed psychological problems, and one even pulled out a knife and threatened me. He was trembling with paranoia, but fortunately, I managed to calm him down by talking to him peacefully until he handed me the knife. He then asked me to walk him back to his bed, and he was visibly shaking as I, concerned for my safety and his, carefully monitored his every move.

I had no training or life experience in dealing with disorders such as paranoia or schizophrenia, so I had to learn to recognize and manage them through these experiences. As I had begun to understand when Hanson fans sent me fan mail expressing depression or thoughts of suicide, unstable children, at the very least, need to feel that someone is listening. This was certainly something I could do for the kids in the shelter, but I later discovered that my weekly music class was accomplishing more than I had imagined.

Most of the students were gaining self-confidence by learning to play songs, but because they came to the shelter voluntarily out of desperation, they often returned voluntarily to the streets before getting enough medical and psychological help. There were no legal grounds to keep them against their will, but on average, my program was keeping them at the shelter longer, even if for only one week more because they were looking forward to next Tuesday's music lesson. Extra time meant extra treatment, which could only improve their chances of pivoting back into the community with a healthier disposition and greater stability. Extracurricular activities are the ones that provide the incentive to be present to receive everything that is needed for a complete education.

After three years of living in New Orleans, my career hit a plateau, and I did not see additional growth potential. Marie and I stumbled across a beautiful piece of property near Charlottesville, Virginia, while I was touring in the region, and I bought my first home toward the end of 2003 at age 32. Even though we had no friends locally, my singer-songwriter tours were now primarily on the east coast of the United States, and Louisiana was too far to keep as my home base.

Additionally, Marie had suffered a miscarriage the year before (and never got pregnant again), so we also personally needed to push a "reset" button. I was sad to leave the music scene and felt guilty about abandoning the homeless kids (no one took over my program despite my best efforts); however, as the airlines tell you on every flight, you have to put the oxygen mask on yourself before putting it on others.

While Virginia is clearly north of Louisiana, it is still very much "The South," perhaps even more so. While I did not know it at the time of purchase, the property sits amidst significant American history. My property line extends halfway into the James River, which is known as the "founding river" of the United States since the first permanent English colony of Jamestown was established upon it in 1607. The surrounding areas are marked with placards noting battlegrounds where General Robert E. Lee and his Confederate army fought General Ulysses S. Grant and his Union army until they reached Appomattox (about 30 minutes from my home), where Lee surrendered and ended the US Civil War in April of 1865. History surrounds us all the time. Yet, if one is not intrinsically curious, many of the world's lessons will go unnoticed. Curiosity is a fundamental part of learning.

Three months after I bought the house in Virginia, my mother suffered a complication from emergency surgery and fell into a coma. She was unconscious for about a month, followed by many more months of rehab and skilled-nursing care (she never fully recovered but lived another decade despite her diminishing health and quality of life). Already emotionally fragile, having not found peace since her divorce twenty years earlier, she was now facing an ominous future, which made her more scared and depressed. She asked me to be the primary caretaker for her first few months back at home. No one lived with her for longer than I had, and the idea of having a stranger move in made her question the value of living at all.

Having already spent months with her off and on in the hospital and nursing home, I accepted the role and spent much of my first year of homeownership with my mother in Connecticut rather than with my wife in Virginia—Marie stayed home to take care of our new property, and she only visited me a couple of times. It was hard on our marriage, but we survived. However, the personal relationships with my friends and family continued to deteriorate over the next few years, which added further stress to our marriage. It was mostly my career that was holding us together, so when the economy and my career collapsed four years later in 2008, Marie stopped working with me and, shortly thereafter, moved to France. We were not ready to divorce but were taking the first steps by separating.

A few months after moving, she delivered the most unexpected news. Marie had been diagnosed with throat cancer and, without treatment, likely would not survive more than six months. What made this especially difficult to accept was that she was an all-organic raw foodist who did not believe in allopathic medicine—she grew to reject Western medicine, ironically while working as a nurse in oncology. I was sure I would lose her forever, so I immediately flew to Paris. After consultations, conversations, arguments, and tears, we decided she would undergo radiation and chemotherapy—a decision she would later regret as the permanent damage from the treatment became too much for her to bear. As I have since learned, one must accept that sometimes there is no "right" decision, and one must just make a decision.

For twelve weeks, we spent every morning at a cancer hospital just outside of Paris. These were some of the hardest days of my life, not only because of her pain and unknown prognosis but because I sat in waiting rooms daily across from the most visibly sick head and neck cancer patients, including children, who were suffering and probably would not survive. We coped with this daily existence by visiting museums or going to the movies each day after treatment.

However, she quickly grew weaker, and the last eight weeks were mostly spent between the hospital and her mother's apartment. The radiation caused such severe burns on her face and internal throat pain that it made it almost impossible for her to eat. I bought soup or baby food and put it in a blender, and she would then spoon-feed herself slowly for an hour or more. She often vomited soon after finishing the meal because of the effects of chemotherapy, which negated the benefits of this herculean effort to obtain nutrition. She was slowly withering away into nothing.

Marie suffered terribly, but this was also the most emotionally challenging experience I had ever faced. Nevertheless, it was an essential time of growth for me—someone who had mostly focused on himself and put his career above everything else.

Her cancer kicked me hard, and it was the ultimate test of my ability to give. While I always tried to rise to the occasion, my limitations began to show. I suffered physical ailments such as debilitating back pain, and because I did not yet speak French well and needed my own medical attention, I was at times more of a burden to Marie than helpful. I was also emotionally drained and sometimes could not put her needs before my own. However, I did grow as a person, and we grew closer as a couple.

For the next five years, I put my career second because the doctors said it would take that long to know if she was cured. Therefore, I wanted to focus on our living rather than my working because, as I had felt with my mother's illness and poor recovery, if one does not experience the value of life, one may lack the ability to heal. Tapping into whatever savings I had, we made our home together between Paris and Charlottesville, and we also frequently traveled the world: Spain, Prague, Hungary, Belgium, Turkey, and beyond.

I do not know if the phrase "what doesn't kill you makes you stronger" is always true, but I did discover that if you remain humble and accept lessons from tragedy, one can at least become a better person. There is, unfortunately, no substitute in terms of gaining such perspective. We often try to shield ourselves from hardship, but rather than run from it, we should learn to manage it. Pain can be a gift when repurposed—or pivoted—for growth.

Just before Marie's cancer and our initial separation, I took a break from music to search my soul and explore other interests. As a child in the large Greenwich home, I sometimes created model airports in bedrooms and converted the long hallways into runways. The magic of flight had always fascinated me, and

I had often imagined what it might be like to be a pilot. With the economy in free fall and my music career going with it, I did not know what else to do, so I enrolled in flight lessons locally. Fortunately, my flight instructor was fascinated by my musical career and had always wanted to learn guitar, so we soon started bartering flight lessons for guitar lessons!

At the end of 2008, I earned my pilot license and became part of the local aviation community. Flight training captivated me because I was constantly acquiring skills that had relevance outside of the cockpit. Whether it was learning about hypoxia (biology), calculating headwinds (trigonometry), checking the airworthiness of the plane (physics and mechanics), developing routines and using checklists (management and efficiency), or communicating on the radio (language skills), the cockpit of an airplane was the greatest classroom for me. Yes, someone taught me trigonometry in high school, but I learned it in the cockpit of an airplane.

Life skills, such as decision-making, become refined. As a pilot, you do not always have time to make the "right" decision, especially in an emergency (similar to how I felt with Marie's cancer treatment options). So, you do not try to make the right decision. Instead, you make a decision and then make it right.

One can learn how to do this by understanding that regardless of the result, one can usually still influence the outcome. While one bad decision can lead to others and cause what is known in aviation as an "error chain," incorporating the skill of evaluating each result leads to better subsequent decisions and "course correction." This one lesson has dramatically improved my efficiency, and many others also apply outside of the cockpit. For example, I now regularly create backup plans, adopt and adhere to routines, use checklists, and maintain a greater awareness of my environment and current situation.

The most important lesson I learned was about evaluating data. In the cockpit, you never rely on one instrument to determine what the airplane is doing; you cross-reference a minimum of three. This is data triangulation, and I believe that if we all consulted three sources of information before forming an opinion, we would more quickly overcome atrocities including racism, classism, sexual discrimination, religious conflict, radicalism, and other social injustices. If data triangulation were part of everything we do, there would be no such thing as "fake news."

Furthermore, when the data does not neatly add up, one must defer to common sense. "Street smarts" have as much of a place in modern society as data. Never miss an opportunity to practice common sense as current events and daily activities provide practically unlimited exercises in using good judgment and making smart decisions.

The reason why the cockpit works so well as a classroom is simple: experiential learning is about executing rather than recalling, and when death is a potential outcome, one learns very well! Granted that death should not be incorporated into traditional education, and therefore, we cannot put every child at the controls of an airplane. However, there is nothing preventing one from installing a flight simulator program on a computer and obtaining a ground school course along with it. One might surmise that this is only relevant to those wanting to learn to fly, but aviation truly is one of humanity's greatest achievements. For that reason alone, it applies to everyone and offers an excellent opportunity for experiential learning.

I loved sharing this revelation with everyone and was completely enthralled with how my learning was expanding. One day, I was reading *Flight Training* magazine and thought my training experience could motivate other potential or current flight students—many quit or never start because of the high cost, and this contributes to the current pilot shortage.

I sent the editor an email and pitched my topic. He responded enthusiastically, and in November of 2008, my first aviation article was published. "It's a Car Payment" made the analogy that for the monthly cost of buying a car, one could learn to fly, live a dream, and gain valuable life skills.

With this aviation magazine credential, I was able to secure unpaid speaking opportunities at the two largest airshows in the United States in 2009 (one before Marie was diagnosed with cancer and one after the completion of her treatment). My focus was to help flight schools successfully recruit students like me.

However, I did not make a name for myself in the industry until a year later when I learned of a startling statistic: 49.7% of pilots play a musical instrument. For an industry that was suffering a shrinking pilot population, I wondered: "Could music be the common denominator of aviators and millennials?" Armed with this theory, I approached aviation and music companies for sponsorship.

I had recently seen a California-based company on the entrepreneurship show, *Shark Tank*. They made full-size folding guitars for travelers who could not easily fit a regular guitar in an overhead compartment of an airplane. That got me thinking. There were 600,000 pilots in the USA, of which almost 50%

played music. Based on a study revealing that roughly 60% of musicians play guitar, I concluded that 180,000 pilots could not fit their guitars in the cockpit of a small airplane. This seemed like a great opportunity to create a micro-market of affluent white males (the majority of aviators and guitarists) who would buy a guitar specifically made with their needs (and egos!) in mind. I sent Voyage-Air Guitar a proposal, and they agreed.

About one year later, we had a prototype of "The Raviator"—a sky-blue electric guitar with a cloudy white pickguard. It was perfect for a flying musician. Sadly, it never got into production beyond the prototype because the company, at that time, pivoted its focus from manufacturing guitars to licensing their patented hinge to a larger brand (it functions like a door hinge, enabling the guitar neck to ... pivot!). I was disappointed because it seemed like a perfect niche market, but ultimately, it became one of my business failures. Failures are stepping stones to success, so I chalked this one up to experience.

A German company, which makes audio equipment for musicians and headsets for pilots, was an obvious potential sponsor because I already had an endorsement deal with them as a musician. With Sennheiser's support, I began to generate revenue from the aviation industry, which now included keynote presentations at flight schools around the country as well as performing music on stage (often with fellow pilots) at major air shows. After getting a few more sponsors, I created a middle and high school tour called "You Can Do It" and spoke to students around the country. The schools were in a mix of affluent suburbs and inner-city low-income districts, and I loved getting to know this wide range of students and inspiring them with career possibilities in music and aviation.

My flight school audiences included many seasoned flight instructors, and often, one would invite me to fly "something new" after a presentation. While I was not qualified to pilot anything other than the most basic aircraft, they were certified flight instructors (CFI). I had opportunities to fly a new type of plane several times a month, including sea/floatplanes, helicopters, and "warbirds" (vintage military planes), and even learned to fly aerobatics. This was an amazing way to expand my aviation knowledge, and I took full advantage of every invitation.

I was also hired to be a guest speaker on two aviation-themed Caribbean cruises, and I soon found myself hobnobbing with astronauts, including Buzz Aldrin, and war heroes such as the Tuskegee Airmen. Moreover, I was now earning enough money to cover Marie's and my cost of living and personal travel during her five-year recovery period—my network of pilots became large enough that I could often get low-cost employee airline guest passes. Never had I imagined building a business in aviation, but the opportunity presented itself right when I needed it, so I pivoted.

I am often asked, "How does one know when to pivot?" For me, there are primarily two triggers: when an opportunity presents itself, or when everything collapses. This can be learned, and it requires one essential skill to be developed: the ability to fail. To recognize opportunity, one must first have a tolerance for risk. To have a tolerance for risk, one must be willing to fail. The same holds true for when everything collapses. The only way to get back up is to have self-confidence, and the best way to gain confidence is to fail and recover. As they say in business, "fail fast and fail often," and as I have heard educators say, FAIL stands for "First Attempt In Learning." Unfortunately, failure is not a real option in an achievement-based education system, but we must push ourselves to the point of failure because failures are critical stepping stones toward success. There simply is no shortcut.

After the five years passed, Marie was deemed "cured" but never really recovered. The damage from the treatment paralyzed her emotionally, and it prevented her from building a life she enjoyed. She became increasingly frustrated as each day passed, and this eventually contributed to our divorce a few years later. To compound things, almost immediately after our focus shifted away from her cancer, my health took a turn for the worse.

One morning in 2014, I woke up with the world spinning around me. I had never experienced vertigo, but I could not get out of bed without vomiting and falling over. Marie managed to get me into the car, and with a bucket sandwiched between my legs, we drove to the hospital. I was diagnosed with vestibular neuritis—an inner ear infection had obliterated the right side of my vestibular system, causing me to lose balance. To me, everything looked like a moving walkway. Vertical walls stood still while floors rolled like a conveyer belt.

The doctor first delivered the bad news, which was that my right inner-ear was destroyed, and my balance would never come back. He compared it to a motorboat with two outboard motors but with only one working. I was going in circles. The good news was that my brain would learn to counteract the spinning like a rudder would counter the imbalanced motors.

Most people with this condition go to bed for a few months and never fully recover. He advised me to dance, jog, fall over as much as possible, and do everything I could to train my brain to learn how to counteract the rotation. So that is what I did, but I still felt it would be too risky to try to land an airplane by myself. My career in aviation was no longer viable because it became increasingly obvious that fatigue and stressful situations would put my brain one step behind, and the key to safety in the air, as in life, is to always "stay ahead of the plane."

Aside from learning so much about myself and my abilities, my primary takeaway from aviation was that one of humanity's greatest achievements—the magic of flight—spawned a community that did not represent the scope of humanity. While I initially reveled in the novelty of being the new pilot that had captured the attention of the most seasoned of aviators, I became increasingly disenchanted with having catapulted myself into an industry that is only 5% women and 1% African American. I missed the diversity of the music industry. Fortunately, I had also planted other seeds yet to be watered, so it was once again time to search my soul and plan my next pivot.

Ravi "The Raviator" in the airplane in which he trained and earned his license, September 2008.

Ravi discussing aviation with the astronaut, Buzz Aldrin, April 2014.

## Pivot Points

- Pay it forward. By purposefully embracing a "pay it forward" mindset through daily activities that require one to do nice things for others, it would likely result in doing more good in the world.

- Do not overlook extracurricular activities. These are what create incentives, improve attendance, and enable one to get more of everything one needs.

- Do not shield yourself from hardship, but instead, learn how to manage it. Pain can be a gift when repurposed—or pivoted—for growth.

- Triangulate data. By making it a habit to consult three sources of information before forming an opinion, we would more quickly overcome racism, classism, sexual discrimination, religious conflict, radicalism, and other social injustices. If we practiced data triangulation as part of everything we do, there would be no such thing as "fake news."

- Make efficient decisions. Do not always try to make the right decision. Make a decision and then make it right. Do this by recognizing that regardless of the result, one can usually still influence the outcome. Instilling the habit of evaluating each result leads to better subsequent decisions and "course correction."

- Use common sense. "Street smarts" has as much, if not more, of a place in modern society than data. Never miss an opportunity to use common sense, as current events and daily activities provide practically unlimited exercises in using good judgment and making smart decisions.

- Make learning relevant by using easily accessible tools. Installing a flight simulator program on a computer and obtaining a ground school course is a great experiential learning opportunity. Aviation truly is one of humanity's greatest achievements, and therefore, relevant to everyone.

- Practice failure. To recognize opportunity, one must first have a tolerance for risk. To have a tolerance for risk, one must be willing to fail. Push yourself to the point of failure because failures are critical stepping stones toward success.

# 7

# WHEN PRIVILEGE & POVERTY UNITE

Soon after my 45th birthday, I gave the keynote address for a large education conference in California. I did not mention my family heritage or Greenwich-grown privilege, and in fact, I had never publicized either during my music and aviation careers. It just was not something I found relevant. On this occasion, my full biography was printed in the conference program, and during the "meet and greet" following my presentation, an elderly African-American woman approached me, put her hand on mine, and said, "Mahatma Gandhi, Nelson Mandela, and Martin Luther King all came from privilege. Don't be ashamed of your privilege; just use it for good."

I realized, at that moment, privilege is indeed nothing to be ashamed of despite the general implication whenever racial or socioeconomic unrest erupts. Moreover, if society motivates those who have this tool in their toolbox to use it for good, it is potentially the fastest way to defeat social injustice and change the world for the better. I believe the recognition of one's own power is a stronger force of motivation than the awareness of one's own guilt. Regularly engaging others in conversations that force them to acknowledge their resources and consider how they can use them for a benefit beyond themselves would be priceless.

Back in 1989, when I graduated high school, the Greenwich public school system ranked in the top twelve of the United States—I assume we were number eleven or twelve because otherwise, we would have celebrated being in the "Top Ten." During my thirteen years of public education, I attended four different schools within the system. For most of my classmates and me, this elite foundation enables us to maintain our place in the privileged world. Growing up in such an environment comes with a degree of financial security, but it also establishes a high standard of achievement and promotes the pursuit of *cultural capital.*

Commonly defined as the value society places on non-financial assets that help one move up the social ladder, cultural capital includes quality education, resourceful social networks, and material possessions such as clothes. This, combined with a high value placed on ambition, greatly enhances the potential for financial success. However, happiness and fulfillment may be a different matter. What I failed to recognize in my own privilege as a student practically hit me over the head as an adult, and it was my personal growth during Marie's illness and discontent with the lack of diversity within the aviation community that reconnected me with someone from my past.

The South Asian Journalism Association had invited me to speak on a panel of authors at Columbia University in New

York following the release of my book in 1999. At age 27, this was one of my first professional speaking engagements, and I was sharing the panel with some well-respected South Asian authors. I was clearly the "newbie"; however, since the topic was about being a South Asian published in the United States, I aimed to engage on an equal level since I fit that description.

While *Dancin' with Hanson* did not broach the subject of racial identity, my reality as part of Hanson was as a brown person in a high profile all-white American band. At that time, I was also one of only two or three Indians in mainstream Western pop-music (Tony Kanal of the band No Doubt was another, and perhaps Norah Jones can also be pushed into this category). I was able to pivot my music industry experience into a book publishing-related conversation about ethnic and racial biases, and by doing so, garnered the respect of my fellow panelists and the audience.

An Indian gentleman introduced himself to me after my talk, mentioned he knew my father, and enthusiastically solicited me to come and visit his new school in India for the "poorest of the poor." Abraham George is the founder of Shanti Bhavan Children's Project, a residential (boarding) school on a mission to eradicate poverty. We exchanged contact information, but other than a systematic follow-up from me, I filed him and his school away as a friendly but relatively inconsequential encounter.

Even though *initiative* is part of my DNA, Abraham was more proactive than I. He added me to his email list, and for the next decade, sent pictures of each incoming kindergarten class. In 2010, he sent an additional picture: the first graduating class. While I enjoyed the cute 4-year-old faces year after year, I was now awakened to his incredible accomplishment and had to go to India to see it for myself.

Marie's cancer treatment had come to an end, and by late 2010, she was well enough to stay home alone in Virginia for a few weeks. I needed a break from having been her caretaker, and I managed to secure the keynote speaker slot for the inaugural Indian Music Conference in the former Portuguese seaside territory, Goa, on the western coast of India. It was an expense-only offer, but it was also my chance to visit Shanti Bhavan.

After a few days at the conference, I traveled southeast to Tamil Nadu and spent several weeks living on campus and getting to know Abraham and the nearly three hundred students. I was impressed, and with his help, studied this model, which aims to break the cycle of poverty in India. I have partnered with Shanti Bhavan ever since, and just last year, we named the kindergarten dormitory after my grandmother, Krishna Nehru Hutheesing. My father had created a charitable, educational trust in her name before he died, and my brothers and I chose to donate it to the school. What an honor it is to know that incoming students will begin their educational journey with my grandmother watching over them.

Abraham built Shanti Bhavan in 1997 on a scorpion-infested hill in a remote part of the southernmost state. The site is about two hours by car from the modern tech capital of India, Bangalore. There was no road going to the site of the school, so before construction could commence, one had to be built. Once completed, public transportation could also service nearby villages, giving locals access to the closest economic center situated about 30 minutes away. Next, because the school would be home for a large group of children, a medical center needed to be built. Abraham did that too, also giving nearby villagers access to good medical care.

The sprawling campus is beautiful and spotless. Today, it is mostly energy independent, with about 85% of its power delivered by solar panels. In addition to rigorous studies, the students have cleaning duties, from sweeping the grounds to making sure three hundred plates and cups are cleared and rinsed after each meal. Their donated clothes are washed by staff and students, and full-time cooks prepare five fresh meals (including hearty snacks) each day using ingredients sourced mostly from the organic farm on campus. The farm also employs some nearby villagers, and the students take turns pulling its weeds on weekends.

The day is long but filled with activities, including early morning sports, morning and afternoon academic classes along with arts and music, afternoon sports, and evening homework. Each day features a mid-morning assembly during which Abraham (or "DG" as the students affectionately call Dr. George when he is not present) delivers some words, rotating students read news and current events aloud while offering commentary and answering questions, and several songs are sung. When I am there, I also offer some words of motivation.

About two-thirds of the teaching faculty are full-time, and the remainder is volunteers from all around the globe. While most of these kids will likely never travel beyond their village before they graduate, the world regularly comes to visit them. Through a constant stream of volunteers who typically stay anywhere from a month to a year, the students' exposure to international culture and languages is significant. It creates the perfect blend of cultural and academic stability from faculty and global stimulation and perspectives from volunteers. I find these students to be more globally aware than most of their peers whom I meet in the West.

Shanti Bhavan has strict criteria for the children they accept. The sustainability of the school depends on the success of the mission, and the success of the mission (as well as the flow of donations) depends on the success of *all* students. While it is a Pre-K-12 school, only children under the age of four are accepted to mitigate the damage and impairment of childhood malnutrition, as well as any possible trauma from their living circumstances. Only one child per family can enroll, allowing for more families to be positively impacted by the benefits of education.

The boy-girl ratio is almost one-to-one, and each child is evaluated and accepted based on several indicators, including that the family lives under the standard global poverty line (USD 2.00 per day). Preference is given to single mother/single parent-households because of the greater need and impact, and the family must be willing to keep the child in the program for the entire duration—for example, they cannot pull their daughter out to marry her at a young age or recruit their son to go to work. Finally, no children with severe physical or mental deficiencies are accepted because the school is not equipped to handle such challenges, and there are other programs better suited for those individuals.

As with most residential schools, the students generally only go home during school vacations, but parents also visit the campus from time to time. Finding the right balance can be tricky because to break the cycle of poverty, students must learn to value the opportunity and environment that Shanti Bhavan provides without being lured back to the cultural and systemic norms oppressing their villages.

India's poor poses a herculean challenge. According to the World Bank, roughly 300 million (approximately 20%) live at or below that poverty line of $2/day, and this is down from the estimated 500 million when Abraham first built the school. Imagine having the entire United States living in poverty. Moreover, India is about one-third of the geographic size of the United States, but it has four times the population.

Eradicating poverty is further complicated by the caste system, India's social classification structure. A key difference between a caste and a class system is that in the caste system, there is no social mobility. Neither money nor level of education will reclassify you. In that sense, it is more analogous to racism than traditional classism (and one can probably argue that racism is, in fact, a caste system). You are born into your caste, typically marry within it, and die in your caste.

The roots of this are likely based on religious anthropology; however, the British exploited and enforced the system to better organize and control the massive population in their colony. Even after India's independence in 1947, this social construct remains strong. Brahmins are the priests and teachers, Kshatriyas are the warriors and rulers, Vaishyas are farmers and merchants, and Shudras are laborers. The lowest are the Dalits, or more colloquially referred to as "untouchables." They are, in fact, not even part of the four-tier caste system as they are deemed below the rest, and therefore make up an unofficial fifth tier. All of Shanti Bhavan's students are Dalits.

To break the cycle of poverty, the caste system must be broken. It is now happening organically with the younger generations in India (millennials and Gen Z), but it may take many generations to completely outgrow it. The first few sets of Shanti Bhavan graduates have a major obstacle to overcome despite their "Brahmin" quality education, global vision, and mastery of multiple languages. We want them to be highly successful but also to always remember that the mission is greater than themselves.

I speak to the graduating classes specifically about this when I visit. Their education costs them nothing, but it is far from free. It carries a value and, therefore, a responsibility to make the country a more socially just nation for those who follow. Similarly, students in public education worldwide ought to recognize that their fellow citizens are investing in their future via paying taxes. Therefore, they, too, have a responsibility as part of the social contract to deliver a return on that investment.

It is the collective effort made by students, faculty, administrators, and volunteers that make Shanti Bhavan a success story. The school's data shows that 97% of incoming pre-kindergarten students graduate, 100% of graduates go to university (which is also paid for by Shanti Bhavan), 98% graduate from higher education, 97% go on to work at multinational companies, and all the working post-graduates are the primary or sole income-earners for their families. Moreover, working graduates give back 20-50% of their salaries to their families, communities, and others in need, tackling a variety of issues: basic necessities, housing, healthcare, education for siblings, repayment of the generational debt, and much more. The effect is exponential as each Shanti Bhavan child impacts dozens or perhaps even hundreds of others.

While the school's success is inspiring, "success" means

different things to different people. When I visit the impoverished villages where the students' families live, I often see more smiles than I do on the bustling streets of New York City. This makes me question the primary objective of education, along with the definition of success. Is it predominantly financial independence, or happiness? Shanti Bhavan students are certainly happy and filled with hopes and dreams, and graduates are achieving a degree of financial independence that their families have never experienced before. In the end, one can only hope it brings everlasting happiness as well.

We must always be conscious and careful in how we may impose a set of first-world or privileged beliefs, values, and biases on others. Cultural competence also means being culturally sensitive and culturally responsible. The impact of all forms of charity and volunteerism should be considered broadly and adjusted to create the most benefits with the least unintended consequences.

When Abraham first broke ground, it was difficult to recruit students because villagers did not understand the value of an education. Some also feared this could just be an organ trade/trafficking operation intending to capture and kill their children to sell body parts to the West (kidneys or eyes, for example). Now, more than twenty years later, a second Shanti Bhavan is about to break ground as trust has been established, and the benefits of education have become obvious to the surrounding villages. Netflix even produced a four-part documentary series called *Daughters of Destiny* that follows five Shanti Bhavan girls for seven years, revealing their hopes, struggles, and incredible achievements. It is an intimate, complex portrayal of poverty and the burden it places on children, families, villages, and society at large.

Being involved with Abraham and Shanti Bhavan has helped me truly appreciate the power of an individual and how he or she can create significant change in the world. It is commonly said that if you impact even just one person, you have made a difference. Abraham has impacted thousands directly and also many more indirectly. Each of us has this ability should we choose to exercise it. By instilling this mindset today, the potential for significant change is unlimited.

While I am a Brahmin who grew up in the elite town of Greenwich, Connecticut, I never realized the scope of privilege until age 48. In October 2019, I found myself running from army tanks spraying tear gas on the streets of Santiago de Chile while protestors tossed Molotov cocktails at police. Social unrest was dismantling what had been revered as the most prosperous country in Latin America (following the collapse of Venezuela). Similar riots were simultaneously occurring in Hong Kong, Lebanon, Iraq, India, France, Bolivia, and other countries. For Chileans, they had not experienced this level of violence since the days of President Pinochet, thirty years earlier.

I had only wanted to be a curious observer of a peaceful protest, but everything unraveled so quickly. Without warning, I found myself engulfed in a stampede. My privilege yielded no benefit over those alongside me who were suffering from economic disparity, unaffordable healthcare and education, and few employment opportunities. We were equally blinded by tear gas, and we gagged together as we ran.

However, the following day, I sipped coffee in the plush office of Andronico Luksic, who is one of the wealthiest and most influential businessmen in the country. Despite his social consciousness, sense of civic duty, and track record of philanthropy, he is part of the elite that the Chilean people were confronting. We discussed the current issue as I recounted my frightening experience twenty-four hours earlier on the streets. Obviously, my privilege was still alive and well.

Much of my father's work at the World Bank took place in Chile during the 1970's regime change from Salvador Allende, the world's first democratically elected socialist president, to Augusto Pinochet, the dictator who, as a military general, led a coup d'état and assumed power as president. The United States was motivated to aid in the collapse of Allende's administration because it would prevent communism from infiltrating the Chilean government and, likely more to the point, upend his policy to nationalize copper mines in which several US companies had investments.

My father provided opportunities for Chilean corporations to relocate outside of the country. Presumably, this would help collapse the economy and pave the way for a regime change. In doing so, he built a network of influential friends (almost all of whom he lost touch with following the coup), and on my first trip to Chile nearly 50 years later, I attempted to reconnect him with any remaining descendants I could find. I was only able to track down the son of my father's closest Chilean friend (now deceased), and that is Andronico. Sadly, my father died before they had a chance to meet, but Andronico and I have committed to maintaining the link between our families.

The disparity in running from tanks one day and my conversation with him the next helped me recognize that while masses of poorly connected people can unite and push for change, it is the privileged who have the resources to implement change. As Andronico and I discussed, if we are to create a more peaceful world, it is those of us with privilege who must right the wrongs and embrace our social responsibility before our hands are forced by violence and destruction.

As I saw with my own tearing eyes in Santiago, one cannot wait until the animal within us is unleashed at the point of desperation. Most recently, we saw similar violent responses in the wake of George Floyd being killed in Minneapolis and the systemic racism that was revealed. Andronico "gets it," and perhaps so do Bill Gates and Richard Branson. However, not enough do. If more people with privilege embrace a greater level of social responsibility and direct some of their resources toward reducing inequity, the potential for world peace would dramatically increase. Schools can and should foster critical thinking and classroom discussions around current and historical events that showcase such disparities.

During the Pinochet regime in the 1970s and 1980s, a group of Chilean economists known as the "Chicago Boys" (because they studied at the University of Chicago under American economists Milton Friedman and Arnold Harberger) redesigned and privatized the country's economy. That gave opportunities to those with resources to acquire contracts and build wealth. It also included the creation of a "free market" education system, essentially privatizing schools, which ultimately came at the expense of a public education system that still serves 93% of the country's students.

Public schools in Chile are funded entirely by vouchers (it is possibly the only country that has a universal voucher public education system). About six out of every ten public school students use vouchers to go to charter schools, and the remainder uses them to attend those run by municipalities. Until recent reforms, many of those charters were for-profit entities, and they charged families a premium on top of the subsidized voucher (but much less than the tuitions of non-subsidized elite private schools), and because lower-income families could not justify paying the premium, disparity grew. Charters were also permitted to screen, select, and expel students while municipal schools had to accept everyone.

Moreover, because the national population is only around 18 million and has experienced a declining birth rate for 30 years, there are not enough students to adequately fund all public schools, and no politician wants to run on a platform that promotes closing schools. Today, anyone who can afford the exorbitant tuitions of Chile's private primary and secondary schools does so—it is a higher standard of education but also an important social status symbol.

This disparity in education contributes to the cycle of disparity (growing with each generation) throughout the country. It is analogous to the cycle of poverty, the cycle of racism, etc. As I mentioned earlier, education is the solution to all the world's problems, and as a public education advocate, I believe the most significant way to make any country stronger is to invest in its public education system. However, when classism is ingrained in the culture, one must defeat the ideology, not just the profiteering.

For Chile, I have come to believe that the solution is to first invest in making the 7% of students enrolled in elite private schools more culturally and socially aware regarding their own country's disparity. A 2018 government study showed that the richest Chileans had an income nearly 14 times greater than the poorest, making it the most unequal of OECD (Organization for Economic Co-operation and Development) countries. Like most "third-world" countries, the haves and the have nots are mostly absent from each other's radar, but when you have a population of 18 million Chileans versus 1.4 billion in India, the awareness can more easily grow and the problem then more easily solved. Given the organic tendency for youthful idealism to pursue social justice, raising this awareness may be the fastest way to close this gap.

Next, the 93% in public schools must also be taught that privilege, be it financial, racial, or social, is often inherited. Therefore, they cannot fault those with privilege for having it, but those with such resources cannot abuse those without. For example, the extension of credit to people without sufficient employment to pay it down or the education to understand the terms (not to mention Annual Percent Rates nearing 50%) is a form of abuse. Suppressing minimum wage is another, as is not cultivating a high-quality public-school system for the majority. In a small country like Chile, there may be a greater chance of breaking the cycle of oppression through empathy and cultural competence than there would be in India, where the disparity is so widespread and deeply ingrained in the caste system.

For the United States and Western European nations, there are lessons to be learned from these emerging markets. Any community with disparity can potentially close that gap using one of these two methods (depending on the extreme): focus on the privileged and create social responsibility (Chile) or focus on the poor and create social justice (India). Moreover, privileged families worldwide need to recognize that in a global sharing economy soon to be dominated by technology, including artificial intelligence, suppressing the less fortunate around you may no longer leave the elite with more opportunities.

As egregious as it sounds to purposefully keep someone else's child from attaining a good education so that one's own has less competition in the future job market, teachers have told me that parents occasionally admit this without any shame (such as when a teacher might suggest that a more advanced student helps one who is falling behind). School board members and superintendents have shared with me how certain board members vote against measures that would help disadvantaged students even though these measures would not deprive their own children of any immediate benefit (busing, for example). However, if jobs and careers are not what define us in the future, this advantage is shrinking. Denying advantages to poorer children is not just morally offensive but also socioeconomically shortsighted.

Regardless of class, everyone needs to acquire a greater degree of cultural competence. It is not only cross-geographic but also cross-generational and cross-socioeconomic. Power used to be vertical with the boss delegating from the corner office, but today, it is horizontal with influence forming from diverse teams. Capital used to be mostly financial, but today, it is more often talked about as social—your network is your net worth. We are all in this together, and it is more critical today than ever that the privileged of the world learn that true leadership is about empowering those below you to rise above you.

The system in Chile is one example of disparity perpetuated by education, but most countries with significant social and economic diversity can probably be viewed similarly. The

United States is still mostly grounded in public education, and it is public education where the most diversity exists under a single roof. Even though school funding structures often foster disparity (due to local tax base differences), education leaders can purposefully create programs that unite whatever diverse populations they have. Busing is one example, and I have often pondered the possibility of not just busing disadvantaged students to better-performing schools, but also advantaged students to lower-performing schools. This could be the tide that raises all boats, and at the very least, every student would be empowered with a higher degree of cultural competence. Inclusion and diversity in any form are critical, and technology can help bridge the gap.

After I returned from Shanti Bhavan in 2010, I went to Los Angeles, California, to engage with a foster-child after-school program called Educating Young Minds. The actor Bill Duke (*Predator*) heard from a mutual friend about my trip to Shanti Bhavan and wanted to introduce me to this African-American education organization he supported. I met with the students and told them about my experiences with their peers in India. The kids were so intrigued by my stories, so I asked if they would like to meet the Indian students via video conference. With great enthusiasm on both sides of the world, I set it up.

I scripted a thirty-minute dialogue because I feared they would have nothing to say once the camera was rolling. However, after ten minutes, they were off my script, and ninety minutes later, they were still talking. When the conversation finally dwindled, they began showing each other dance moves. The interaction ended with the kids in India beat-boxing and girls in Los Angeles dancing, all in real-time.

I was stunned by how organically it unfolded. During a press interview that followed, the only thing that came to my mind was, "Wouldn't it be great if we could do this with young Israelis and Palestinians so they could bond naturally before we teach them how to hate each other?" I do not believe kids are born to be racists, classists, or to discriminate in any way, and educators can create opportunities daily to prove and preserve this.

This technology-based interaction sparked a program that I launched while speaking at the International Baccalaureate Global Conference eight years later, in 2018. *Ravi Unites Schools* is a series of real-time audio-video interactions that I host between classrooms around the world. The mission is in the matching. My goal is to not just cross geographical boundaries but socioeconomic ones as well.

I have since matched poor high school students in India with rich peers in Northeast USA, wealthy middle school students in India with poor peers in Southwestern USA, English speaking bilingual high school students in Chile with Spanish speaking bilingual peers in the USA, global high school students in Japan with provincial peers in Midwest USA, and elementary school students in communist China with peers in the democratic USA. The goal is to foster cultural competence, and it works. Much like the initial interaction between Shanti Bhavan and Educating Young Minds, my role is simply to facilitate—the kids create the magic by themselves.

I have often said that the role of a modern-day teacher is not the purveyor of knowledge but the facilitator of experiential learning. Every classroom in the world can create their own video pen-pal interaction, or a "virtual field trip," as one of the participating teachers called it. It requires a network and logistical coordination, which is why I created *Ravi Unites Schools*, but almost any teacher can provide the facilitation to make the experience valuable.

Implementing technology to foster cultural competence and experiential learning is essential in an age of artificial intelligence and globalization. The human connection and development of empathy must be sustained. The ability to connect classrooms around the globe is the perfect medium, and students will also benefit greatly by connecting with peers who live nearby but have socioeconomic profiles that otherwise might not intermingle. While premature integration of technology and limited availability of broadband internet may increase educational disparity (as we saw with the COVID-19 pandemic), it is ultimately a valuable tool to create equity in education and beyond.

Having understood how privilege can be a truly valuable tool, I began to look for ways to use mine in a manner that would give my life greater meaning while making a positive impact in the world. In looking back at the various seeds I planted during my first half-century on the planet, my next pivot would be guided by my intimate experience with the fragility of life combined with the realization that anyone, if given a real opportunity, can succeed regardless of race, religion, or creed. I had to be bold and do something bigger.

Ravi with Abraham George, founder of Shanti Bhavan Children's Project, in his office at the school in India, September 2017.

Ravi unveiling Krishna Nehru Hutheesing House, India, Sept. 2019.

Pivot Points

- Use privilege as a positive force. Motivate those who have privilege to use it for good. This is potentially the fastest way to defeat social injustices. Recognizing one's own power is a stronger force of motivation than the awareness of one's own guilt. Engage others in conversations that force them to identify their resources and also consider how they can use them for a benefit beyond themselves.

- Embrace the social contract. Students in public education need to recognize that their fellow citizens are investing in their future. They, too, have a responsibility to deliver a return on that investment.

- Purposefully expose disparity. If more people with any degree of privilege obtain a greater level of social responsibility and direct resources toward reducing inequity, the potential for world peace would dramatically increase. We can all foster critical thinking by initiating discussions around current and historical events that showcase such disparities.

- Foster social responsibility and/or social justice. Any community that has disparity can potentially close that gap by focusing on the privileged and teaching social responsibility (Chile model) or focusing on the poor to create social justice (India model).

- Be a leader. True leadership is about empowering those below you to rise above you.

- Prove every day that love conquers hate. I do not believe kids are born to be racists, classists, or to discriminate in any way, and we must create opportunities daily to prove and preserve this. The role of a modern-day teacher is not the purveyor of knowledge but the facilitator of experiential learning. Every classroom in the world can create virtual pen-pal interactions using video conferencing tools.

# 8

# BECOMING A GLOBAL CITIZEN

⌇

Losing my balance due to an infection of the right side of my vestibular system was the catalyst I needed to exit the aviation industry. I loved being a pilot, but the community lacked the diversity I valued. However, I had not yet figured out how to pivot into something more meaningful. Gandhi's words, "Be the change you wish to see in the world," served as my guide, but I still needed to discover *more* of the world to figure out exactly what changes I wished to see.

In 2014, NAMM (National Association of Music Merchandisers) partnered with MusikMesse in Germany to put on conventions in Russia and China. NAMM had been a decade-long client of mine as a speaker for their biannual conventions in the United States. They had presented me at least once each year to speak about how music stores can best foster the passion of up-and-coming musicians. I typically discussed everything from how to sell dreams rather than products to making music stores the center of the local musician community to creating lesson programs that increase student retention. However, these topics were centered around the American musical products industry, which I knew firsthand. Russia and China were unfamiliar cultures and business landscapes.

One thing I did know about these countries is that due to the leapfrog effect of emerging markets overtaking the first-world (which I discussed in Chapter 2), both had greater smartphone penetration than the United States. So, I pitched a progressive topic that I believed would engage these international audiences: "Attracting Customers Using Geofencing Technology." I would explain how triangulating cell phone towers could capture spontaneous purchases when customers (and their mobile phones) come within a predetermined geographic radius of a music store.

It was a highly technical subject. However, I had recently hired a startup software developer to build an app and partner with me to test this technology during one of my aviation events. We purchased a geofence (an invisible "fence" connecting three cell phone towers in a triangle) from the local cellular network provider that would surround the airshow where I would be speaking. When attendees with my app installed on their phones were within the fence, they received scheduled "push notifications" on their mobile phones, alerting them about my upcoming presentation as well as digital coupons that could be redeemed at select vendors on the premises (typically my sponsors). Each time one was redeemed, I received a commission on that sale for referring the customer.

In actuality, it did not work that well because I earned only a few commissions, and the cost to set up a geofence was too expensive by comparison. However, the economics were viable for a "brick and mortar" retailer because the cost of a single geofence would be spread out over a month's worth of targeted advertising and sales rather than just one day at a temporary airshow. While this business relationship with the app developer was another of my entrepreneurial failures, I came away with just enough knowledge to give a presentation that could showcase the potential. As my guitar teacher, Ratso, told me when I first began teaching music at 16 years old, "Just make sure you always stay one page ahead of your best student."

Learning how to pivot failures into opportunities empowers one with a valuable life skill. Like any pivot, it requires creativity and critical thinking, and if we can incorporate failure into the school experience, students can practice this skill without any real consequences. In addition to focusing on what one does incorrectly, an equal amount of attention can be given to what one does correctly and then recognizing how those strengths can help one in other situations. By doing so, one will gain more self-confidence, be willing to take more risks, and successfully create more opportunities for oneself.

NAMM and its partner were intrigued by my proposal. They paid me just enough to cover my travel expenses, and they featured me at both conferences. I was still recovering from vertigo, so even though Marie was no longer working with me, I needed her to come along—having pushed her wheelchair through airports for the past five years, she would now have to do the pushing!

Shanghai is an amazing dichotomy that boasts extreme modernity, including the Maglev speed train between the airport and the city (which travels at a swift 400km/hour) juxtaposed with traditional Old Shanghai "Hutongs" (small communes resembling stereotypical "communist" poverty). It is hard to reconcile that one is in communist China when everything about it seems ultra-capitalist. One is always negotiating prices, and practically everything is for sale. Servers in restaurants may even ask you to complete a survey before you finish your meal.

Much like the European-influenced island of Hong Kong (a British colony from 1841 to 1997 before being returned to China), Shanghai is filled with commerce, tourism, and hospitality. What struck me most was the refined hospitality in hotels. No matter where we went (including a five-day vacation in Beijing), the front desk personnel had a friendly, warm style with perfect comedic timing—almost as if the entire country had been trained identically, and I am pretty sure that is exactly what happens. However, I did find my keynote audience to be genuine. While reserved and polite as a group (possibly due to my being assisted by a translator), they individually expressed a great deal of warmth, gratitude, and enthusiasm following my presentation. Many gave me small stuffed animals, which I was told that even between adults, is quite customary in the culture.

It is what happened in Russia that set up my next pivot. We arrived in Moscow, and I saw in the conference program that the cultural attaché for the US Embassy was speaking on a panel the day before my keynote. Not knowing what a cultural attaché was, it sounded important enough for me to find out. I attended the panel and then approached him to introduce myself as the only other American conference speaker.

His actual title was Minister Counselor for Public Affairs, and he had explained to the audience that the embassy's cultural programs typically bring US artists to foreign countries to share American values and promote cultural exchange. So, I asked him if they had ever brought in American speakers to help Russians become artist-entrepreneurs. I went on to express that I believe there is no greater American export than the entrepreneurial spirit, and if he wanted to explore my idea further, I would follow-up with him. Jeffrey Sexton handed me his card, his deputy came to see me speak the following day, and after several conversations during the next few months, he invited me back to Russia as a cultural diplomat to give a week of lectures in Moscow and St. Petersburg.

Communication skills are essential. Just about every pivot I have made was a result of starting a conversation with a stranger. While I often had no idea if there was anything to gain, I was always confident there was nothing to lose. One must take every opportunity to overcome any inhibitions and learn to ask questions. Being curious is important but acting upon that curiosity is the essential step that too many are not prepared to take. It begins by frequently asking yourself, "What do I have to lose?"

On April 4th, 2015, I returned to Russia for my first engagement as a cultural diplomat. This time, I traveled alone, although I was carrying the heaviest of hearts. Just one day earlier, my mother died following her decade-long decline from renal failure. She had been under home-hospice care off and on for many months, and there had been several false alarms in the past. She would even joke that it was embarrassing because she would call her friends to say goodbye but then would not die!

This time, the nurse once again said she believed the end was near. It would have been reasonable for me not to take this one too seriously, given the challenge of my schedule, but I chose to reroute my flight so I could first spend a few days with her in Connecticut. My brothers joined me that week and, perhaps, by having the three of us together, my mother was finally able to let go. Curiously, April 3rd is also the death anniversary of her mother, reinforcing just how powerful the mind is over the body.

My brothers and I were fortunate to spend those final days with her even though she remained unconscious throughout. There was one moment the evening before she died when she opened her eyes and looked at me briefly before drifting off again. I do not know what she saw, if anything, but I will hold onto that moment forever.

Sadly, I was not able to attend her cremation later that week. My brothers were present, and I joined them by video conference while sitting in the garden of St. Basil's Cathedral in Moscow. They placed three white roses, one for each of us, on her heart before she was placed in the chamber. Watching this on my phone from a park bench in Moscow was truly surreal, and possibly it was foreshadowing the way we will now often mourn loved ones in a post-COVID-19 world, as I did my mentor, Ron.

Despite my grief or possibly as a result of it, the lecture tour was a great success. The embassy invited me to a dinner party of dignitaries that the ambassador hosted in his residence. I managed to corner him for a few moments following the meal, and I introduced myself with a business card in hand. I was still using my "The Raviator" cards with a picture of me in a small airplane, and that amused him enough to start a conversation about flying (I do not recall if he was also a pilot, but the picture was often a good ice-breaker).

Having taken the initiative, and now commanding his attention, I had to turn this moment into something that would last for more than just this moment. I thought about the phrase of my Granduncle Jawaharlal Nehru, "Life is like a game of cards. The hand you are dealt is determinism; the way you play it is free will." Never before had I played the family card to advance my career, but now seemed like a really good time to do it. What did I have to lose? So, I told the ambassador about my relationship to Nehru, Indira Gandhi, and Rajiv Gandhi, as well as a little more detail about my family's involvement in the creation of the world's largest democracy. He was intrigued, and he offered to introduce me to the Indian Ambassador to Russia because he thought I ought to meet him.

Ambassador Teft had also given me his business card, so the next morning, I thanked him by email for his hospitality and reminded him how much I would enjoy meeting Ambassador Raghavan. I never heard from him again, but later that afternoon, the Indian Embassy called my hotel to request my presence; however, my schedule was very full, and I had limited options. Of course, the ambassador was also very busy, but his secretary found thirty minutes where our schedules aligned, and the next day, I went to the Indian Embassy in Moscow.

The ambassador was extremely gracious. Our thirty-minute meeting lasted more than an hour over several cups of coffee, and as I was leaving, he asked if he could give me a tour of the embassy residence and gardens. I was getting late for a university keynote, and a US Embassy car and two officers were waiting for me outside. However, I could not decline his kindness because my grandaunt (my grandmother's and Nehru's sister) was Vijaya Lakshmi Pandit—the first Indian Ambassador to the Soviet Union (she later held posts as ambassador to Mexico, Ireland, and Spain, and became the first woman president of the United Nations General Assembly).

In Hindi, "Dadi" means grandmother, but because my grandmother had died before I was born, Vijaya Lakshmi was always my "Dadi." It was a great honor Ambassador Raghavan bestowed upon my family by taking such an interest in my visit, and he personally wanted to show me where Dadi had lived as Ambassador Pandit. I felt that my university audience would understand why I was late, and the story of how this all unfolded turned out to be a great lesson for them on taking the initiative and stepping out of one's comfort zone.

Still living in the United States and part-time in France, I emailed the Indian Embassies of both countries and said I would like to meet the ambassadors. I honestly did not know what I had to gain, but again, I certainly had nothing to lose. To my surprise, they both replied personally, stating they would welcome my visit. I later learned they each called Ambassador Raghavan in Moscow (I had mentioned my visit with him in my initial messages), and he encouraged them to take the meetings with me.

In all these social but high-level diplomatic encounters, I found myself sipping coffee in formal embassy offices discussing globalization, climate change, the North Korea nuclear threat, tensions between India and Pakistan, upcoming world leader summits, and other highly political subjects. It was fascinating, a bit nerve-wracking, and highly educational, but in the back of my mind, a little voice was asking, "Do they know you were the guitarist for Hanson?"

Perhaps they would not have taken me as seriously if this claim to fame had been my calling card. While I am proud of my music career, the nature of these conversations made me realize Hanson, and even music, no longer defined me—I was not just a former rock star in the eyes of a teenager nor a flying musician in the eyes of an aviator. The ambassadors saw me as part of a political legacy, and for the first time, I felt that not only could I be the change I wish to see in the world, but I actually could create it.

The question of exactly what that change would be remained unanswered until a horrific global event revealed my next calling.

Ravi with Ambassador Raghavan at the Indian Embassy in Moscow, April 2015.

Ravi with his "Dadi," Vijaya Lakshmi Pandit, 1974

## Pivot Points

- Learn the value of risking failure and rejection to create opportunities. Creating opportunities requires a willingness to fail. Like any pivot, it involves creativity and critical thinking, and if we can incorporate failure into the school experience, students can practice this skill without any real consequences.

- In addition to focusing on what you do incorrectly, an equal amount of attention can be given to what you do correctly and then recognizing how those strengths can help you in other situations. By doing so, you will gain more self-confidence, be more willing to step out of your comfort zone, and successfully create more opportunities. It begins by learning to always ask yourself, "What do I have to lose?"

- Communication skills are essential. Take every opportunity to overcome inhibitions and learn to ask questions. Being curious is important but acting upon that curiosity is a step that too many are not prepared to take.

- Prioritize relationships. In an ambitious and career-driven society, we tend to forget the intrinsic value of building relationships. Prioritize people over profits because those who feel closest to us are often the ones who do the most for us.

# 9

# UNITING THE WORLD THROUGH MUSIC

On Friday, November 13th, 2015, Paris became the site of the deadliest terrorist attacks France had endured since World War II. The radical Muslim terrorist group ISIS coordinated a series of simultaneous assaults, sending suicide bombers and gunmen to a stadium, nightclub, and multiple restaurants and cafes. What made this especially barbaric was that the targets were French civilians who were killed at random. I was not in France at the time but knew a couple whose child was killed in the nightclub, and my in-laws were now living under a cloud of fear. Paris was still my second home, and no one was feeling safe outside their own door.

I woke up the next morning trying to wrap my head around what had happened. As it turned out, most of the terrorists were European citizens who had traveled to the Middle East and returned radicalized. Of course, this was not discovered until later, but the radicalization of European citizens was becoming more prevalent and frequently covered by international news.

I had not yet been to the Middle East, but after I traveled to Iraq and Lebanon nearly two years later, I began to understand through my students there how such brainwashing occurs. That insight led me to believe education is the *only* way to defeat it. A war on terror cannot just attempt to contain the violence. Much like socioeconomic disparity and racism, we must also defeat the ideology. At the time of the Paris attacks, I was only beginning to speculate about the role education could actively play in counterterrorism strategy.

Europe was experiencing a high level of radicalism, mostly among the rural and suburban populations. In France, the public education system had been focused on creating career pathways from an early age, and combined with a comparatively high unemployment rate, it seemed to me that this combination might be leading to a high number of disaffected youth. Many have likely been educated for jobs that are not available or will no longer even exist (which will become more commonplace in an age of artificial intelligence). Furthermore, the skills they have obtained may be less relevant to the vocations about which they are most passionate and which help form their identities. Add to this a high Muslim immigrant population, and grounds for radicalization seemed fertile.

Could this also happen in the United States? Radicalization, or extremism in any form, often stems from a lack of identity. It does not just have to be Muslim related or even religiously connected. There are also political extremism, white supremacy, anarchism, and others, some of which are on the rise in the USA. Moreover, there has been a push in public education to create a career pathways model that resembles European nations, and there has also been continued defunding of arts programs in schools and a strong push for STEM education (overlooking the value of STEAM). In fact, most of the world is currently moving away from "the middle" and in critical need of empathy and cultural competence. After learning about the tragedy in Paris, I asked myself, "Are we educating youth to rise above disaffection and radicalism?"

While my question was essentially rhetorical, I wanted to pose it to others so I could spark and engage personally in discussions to explore this further. I felt this topic was incredibly important, so I had to reach out to people who knew much more about this than me. The best way for me to learn something new has always been to put myself in a position where I would either become an expert or suffer embarrassment—this is potentially derived from my pilot mindset: learning something new and learning it well is generally the difference between life and death.

At that moment, I decided to pivot my career to keynote speaking at education leadership conferences—a sector I knew little about but believed was more relevant to world peace than anything else. My expertise in formal education was mostly what I garnered from having been a school student, much like how I began speaking in aviation by sharing my observations and experiences as a flight student, or how every parent mostly learns to raise a child based on his or her own childhood. However, that was not unique from a marketing perspective (almost everyone has been a school student), and I was not promoting solutions to any specific problem the industry was facing.

To make myself attractive to education leadership, I focused on my knowledge of the millennial generation, which I acquired empirically during my time with Hanson and then later through my research while helping the aviation industry recruit and retain new pilots. Since public education was facing a teacher shortage, I could help administrators recruit and retain new teachers. I pitched a topic called "Millennial Mojo" to every education leadership conference I could find in an online search, and the New York State Council of School Superintendents hired me for their annual conference in March of 2016.

This is why I tracked down my former school superintendent almost 30 years after I had graduated high school. He gave me a crash course on what it meant to be an education administrator. The attendees in New York gave my presentation positive reviews, and ever since, my primary focus has been on helping the education industry pivot. Today, it is not just in terms of recruiting and retaining teachers but also to create cultural competence (empathy for those who are different) and equity (fairness) in education. I believe that if all schools teach with a vision of global citizenship, we will have a more peaceful world in the future.

In addition to shifting my career focus toward educators following the terrorist attacks in Paris, I thought about the opportunities waiting to be revealed in my contact list that now included diplomats from two of the world's greatest democracies. I decided to send each one an email expressing my sadness over this tragic event and posed the same question, "Are we educating youth to rise above disaffection and radicalism?" What did I have to lose? One of my associates at the US

Department of State replied, asking if I had something more specific in mind. I did not, but I told her I would send a summary within 48 hours.

I racked my brain to see how I could pivot my fears, hopes, and skills into a program worthy of funding. The constant threads—or pivot points—throughout my life had been music and teaching. As different as one might view the music and aviation industries, I really had only transitioned from being a touring musician and music industry speaker/writer to a "flying musician" and aviation industry speaker/writer. While the audiences were completely different, my activities and messages were surprisingly similar. I used to joke that I just kept all the verbs and replaced most of the nouns. Once you identify your pivot points, the actual pivots happen quite naturally.

Given that the State Department has programming and budgeting for cultural programs, I chose to focus my proposal on the power of music. I pitched the idea of a songwriting workshop comprised of students from traditionally opposed cultures and religions. They would collaborate on writing American-style pop music and, in the process, organically discover how much they have in common. I had already created four online music education courses almost a decade earlier, and using the methodology of one of them, "1-2-3 Songwriting," I launched my two-week workshop in Indonesia during the summer of 2016 as part of an existing US Government-funded arts academy.

Indonesia has the world's largest number of Muslim residents and one of the youngest global populations with a median age of only 28 years old at the time. What made this especially interesting was that we would also invite applicants from neighboring ASEAN (Association of Southeast Asian Nations) countries, which would give me a variety of cultures and religions from which to choose. About 75 college-aged students submitted multi-page applications listing their motivations and abilities, along with video auditions.

Only 16 scholarships would be funded by the US Department of State, so I needed to be selective. I chose the finalists by first matching their level of musicianship and talent, then making sure there was collaborative compatibility in their primary instruments (so we could form a band and perform our songs), and finally determining that there were indeed traditionally opposed religious and cultural beliefs among them—which I feel is the key opportunity in building such a bridge through music.

My students came from Cambodia, the Philippines, Timor Leste, and various parts of Indonesia, and they were equally represented in gender. From day one, they all bonded and began playing music together. I began the program by having each of them perform live using the same song they had submitted in their video audition. By discovering each other's talents and personalities this way, they immediately formed duos, trios, and quartets on their own.

Each group wrote one song together over three days, and then I regrouped them to repeat the process. First thing in the morning, right after lunch, and again before the end of the day, we would meet as a full class of 16 to show our "works in progress" to each other and offer feedback and suggestions. The rest of each day was mostly spent writing songs in those small groups. Additionally, I taught them cultural entrepreneurship daily to inspire and empower them to create arts programs in their own countries that could foster the same type of unity through music.

After two weeks, we had a dozen songs, and what truly great songs they wrote! I hope that one day we will be able to come together again, this time in a recording studio, and make professional recordings available for everyone to hear. During the 14 days, we gave one concert for a select group of international dignitaries at the ASEAN ambassador's residence, another at the American Center in Jakarta (inside a large shopping mall open to the public), and a final concert for the public at the arts institute that hosted the two-week program. The audiences were all very impressed, and I could not have been more proud.

The diversity of this group was extreme. I had Christians, Buddhists, and Muslims writing together, and while I could say they put their differences aside, what really happened was they discovered there were no meaningful differences at all. In fact, when I shared with them just how amazing of a cultural breakthrough this was, I almost ruined it. It was the organic nature of it that made it pure, and by acknowledging it, the results might have become forced. That was an important lesson for me.

This was also the moment when I discovered the magnitude of the millennial generation's idealism and just how powerful it could be as a catalyst for social justice. With millennials, we have the greatest chance (so far) to organically defeat human atrocities such as racism, but if we try to "rally the troops" around a cause that is not personal to them (because they really do not see such differences in their own peers), we run the risk of not letting them help us "grow out" of such social injustices.

For example, this generation does not see racial differences like previous ones, but they can identify racial injustice. The conundrum is that by making them more aware of racial injustice, they also start to become more aware of racial differences. Watching my students in Jakarta organically work together, laugh together, and fall in love together as friends for life gave me greater confidence that world peace may really be possible. To this day, they all interact online regularly.

The program was so successful that the government continued to fund it, which is what took me to Iraq and Lebanon. In Erbil, I used music to bridge the divide between the Iraqis and Kurds, and in Beirut, I created collaborations between the Lebanese and Syrians (both of which I discussed in Chapter 2). It was in the Middle East where I began to intimately understand radicalism, the importance of cultural competence, and how education is the solution to all the world's problems.

I believe people all around the world want peace regardless of their nationality or religion. Politicians and corporations benefit from war, which is why it still occurs. Fear secures votes, and destruction requires rebuilding. However, there may be nothing more powerful than music to unite people, and there has not been a more meaningful musical experience for me than creating and conducting these songwriting workshops.

Millennials and Gen Z consume more music than their predecessors, and that is why fostering an interest in the arts through education is more logical and necessary now than ever. We are at a crossroads where greater empathy is needed, and the youth are ripe for cross-cultural engagement. The rest of us just have to create the forums because, in any collaborative and creative art project, it is the participants who make the magic.

Music is not the only opportunity. The more senses that can be stimulated, the stronger the bonds will likely be. Culinary arts is potentially an even greater activity for cross-cultural bonding—I know of no other art form that stimulates all five senses in a single experience. Food begins with the smell, followed by sight, touch, sound, and finally, taste. Experiencing that sequence of sensations with other people creates powerful and lasting bonds. There is a reason why business deals and family celebrations occur over meals. Cooking and eating together is important, and a daily family meal provides cross-generational bonding with all five senses stimulated.

Even if a school no longer has a formal art and music department, music (and food) is still an integral part of almost every student's life. We need to purposefully help bridge social and cultural divides by inspiring passion and developing empathy to those around us—making sure no one gets left behind. If we create the opportunity, the human spirit will take care of the rest.

Ravi with his students in Indonesia, preparing for their live performance at the American Center in Jakarta, July 2016.

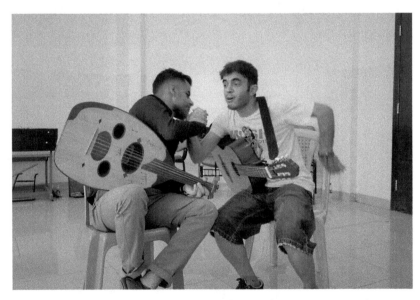

An Iraqi and Kurd writing music together with Ravi in Iraq, July 2017.

Pivot Points

- Purposefully address disaffection and radicalism. Are we educating youth to rise above this? As extremism in multiple forms takes hold worldwide, use the arts to foster empathy and cultural competence.

- Promote global citizenship. The goal is to create cultural competence (empathy for those who are different) and equity (fairness). If we all operate with a vision of global citizenship, we will create a more peaceful world.

- Empower millennials and Gen Z. With today's youth, we have the greatest chance to organically defeat human atrocities such as racism, but if we try to "rally the troops" around a cause that is not personal to them (because they really do not see many differences among their peers), we run the risk of not letting them help us "grow out" of such social injustices. Create the forums for them to come together, and they will do the rest organically.

- Use music as a tool for peace. I believe people all around the world want peace regardless of their nationality or religion. There may be nothing more powerful than music to unite people. Millennials and Gen Z consume more music than their predecessors, and that is why fostering an interest in the arts through education is more logical and necessary now than ever. One just needs to create the forums because, in any collaborative and creative art project, the participants will make the magic.

- Focus on stimulating senses. Music and food are an integral part of almost every person's life. Purposefully help bridge social and cultural divides by inspiring passion and developing empathy in others—making sure no one gets left behind.

# 10

# OWNING ONE'S
# EDUCATION

———◆◆◆———

One's passion and work ethic will ultimately triumph over any business or personal "five-year" plan. However, creating such a plan (as my father required of me) is an excellent exercise that every self-directed learner should do. At the same time, one must understand that nothing is set in stone, and the path to success is indeed a "long and winding road." During that journey, you may never know for sure that the intended destination is ahead; however, if you are consistently and measurably learning throughout, life's unpredictable nature is nothing to be feared. A simple daily or weekly aviation-style checklist to identify new lessons learned and the potential uses or outcomes can help keep one on track.

As an 11-year-old dreaming of being on stage in Madison Square Garden, never could I have predicted the series of events that would ultimately lead me to New York's historic arena at the age of 26. After our soundcheck that cold December morning of 1997, instead of going back to the hotel with the rest of the band, I climbed my way to the "nosebleed" seats (the very top row at the back of the arena) and stared down at the stage for hours.

I had seen many of my favorite bands from this vantage point, and from there, I could soak in the view of the entire empty arena with a seemingly tiny stage far off in the distance. Later that evening, all of those seats would be filled with screaming teenagers, and I would be the one on the stage under bright lights. Not only did I appreciate the gravity of the moment, but I purposefully made sure to feel its entire weight. "Awesome" only began to describe it.

That evening, Ratso, my longtime friend, mentor, and guitar teacher, came with his teenage daughter as my guests, and they watched from the side of the stage—a coveted position typically reserved for close friends and family. He had also often dreamed of performing in Madison Square Garden but never had the opportunity, and he told me afterward how proud he felt watching his student take that legendary stage.

It was only a month later when my unexpected firing from Hanson left me feeling lost and frightened of an unknown future. Amidst my devastation, my parents shared similar concerns and questioned their wisdom in letting me sacrifice a college degree that would have provided a "plan B." I know they were both proud of my success in music, but it turned out to be the lower-profile things I pivoted to over a decade later that really earned their respect.

My relationship with Shanti Bhavan, which began while I was finding my true "purpose" through aviation, is what really established a new trajectory for me. I was now global, socially conscious, and somewhat self-sacrificing. While my mother and I always had a close relationship, this made her particularly proud. She often praised me to others for my interest in working toward poverty alleviation and my willingness to travel to rural India where a warm bucket shower was a luxury (a cold one was the norm in 2010, though today, the campus has hot running water heated by solar power), and she also appreciated my spirit of adventure and commitment to being the change I wished to see in the world.

Sadly, she died just before my cultural diplomacy and keynote speaking career gained momentum, but my father lived another couple of years to see its beginnings evolve. He and I had a relationship that was a rollercoaster of bright highs and dark lows, though it generally rested upon eggshells. While we shared many personal characteristics, including productivity, perseverance, a quick wit and sense of humor, and being the "renegade" of our families, perhaps there was just too much baggage from my childhood that we could never fully unpack.

However, my father enjoyed public speaking and never missed the opportunity to make a toast at a party. In his last few years, he even began giving formal speeches about India's past, present, and future, mostly at social networking events for retired C-suite executives. He was pleased that he could now give me advice on giving a good speech, but I think he was *proud* that he could ask for and accept advice from me. My father made it clear to anyone who asked (and occasionally to those who did not) that he admired my public speaking ability and entrepreneurial mindset. Unfortunately, neither of my parents witnessed me delivering a speech live, and my father only saw some videos. Were they still living today, I have no doubt they would be my greatest fans and supporters.

Everyone's education begins with his or her parents. They are the first teachers in a person's journey, and they must continue by partnering with schoolteachers—one cannot simply hand off the full responsibility of education to a school once the child enters kindergarten. Such a partnership does not necessarily require active collaboration, but it does come with a division of roles and responsibilities that can also be assumed by self-directed students. This division lies within the four concentrations that I believe creates lifelong learners.

**Inspiring Curiosity:** At home, one should be allowed to suffer some boredom and face uncomfortable realities of life while exploring solutions. This fosters creativity and emotional intelligence. Going to museums and cultural events on weekends (online if necessary, but in-person is better) opens minds regardless of how much one might resist or complain. For parents who work from home, allowing children to see what they do during the workday will also generate healthy curiosity.

At school, students should seek out something completely new each day, formulate questions about it, and engage in related dialogue. Access to a variety of electives, including arts and sports, is also essential for exposure to new ideas and opportunities.

**Nurturing Talent:** At home, passions are more likely to show themselves as creativity evolves out of boredom. Through passionate endeavors, talents will begin to surface. Each of us has natural strengths, and they may initially show themselves through what might sound like an unrealistic dream or delusional fantasy, such as becoming a rock star. However, these strengths evolve into the future pivot points that enable lifelong learners to reinvent themselves repeatedly, and long-term happiness and success are more likely to ensue.

At school, teachers must purposefully seek and identify the strengths of students rather than predominantly focus on correcting and overcoming weaknesses. A dangerous trap anyone can fall into is spending most of one's life trying to overcome weaknesses rather than exercising strengths. This may mark the difference between a perpetual school student and an entrepreneur. I believe in focusing on strengths because as we become part of a team—whether it is family, social, or work-related—one can and should delegate weaknesses to others who possess those talents. Learning to delegate is essential because being a team player is an increasingly needed skill in a global sharing economy.

**Provoking Critical Thinking:** At home, it begins with asking questions, but it is not complete until those answers are evaluated by asking more questions. Data triangulation must be incorporated. For every question, a minimum of three sources should be consulted before formulating an opinion. Family dinners are a great opportunity to conduct this exercise because such conversations can be engineered to provide more critical thinking opportunities than an entire day at school. However, each day of school will provide all the needed content to generate meaningful discussions as long as the parents exercise the same skill of curiosity by asking provocative questions and engaging genuinely with their children.

At school, similar exercises can take place between students. The collaborative opportunities in classrooms cannot be equally or easily reproduced at home or online, and face-to-face peer interactions yield lots of social skills and benefits. Additionally, while online interactions have us talking, reading, touching, and typing, it is writing by hand that keeps us thinking. We must continue to write by hand (ideally through keeping a journal) because there is no other activity that slows down one's thoughts to the point where one can fully recognize them. Our thoughts are the basis of critical thinking, self-learning, implicit biases, emotional intelligence, and social-emotional stability. If we take this away, we inhibit our ability to pivot in ways that not only make us more successful but also empower us to improve the world tomorrow.

**Fostering Communication:** At home, one must learn to become comfortable with strangers by answering the phone, asking who is at the door, and engaging with the mailman or a store clerk—especially in an era where so much communication happens online. Asking a person's name and showing personal interest in others (empathy) is the technique that solicits the same level of interest in return. Such conversations help ideas pivot from incubation to execution.

At school, rather than learning not to talk to strangers, learn *how* to talk to strangers. Engage in casual one-on-one exchanges with other students and teachers, as well as peer-to-peer interactions with those from different classrooms (and different ethnicities, religions, etc.). It is a perfect and safe environment to engage with people who are different cross-culturally and cross-generationally, which is the key to expanding one's comfort zone and future circle of influence.

Educators (teachers and parents) must take every opportunity to venture into the unknown and encourage students to do the same. As children discover that adults do not know all there is to know, they will not feel so embarrassed about admitting their ignorance on a given subject. This will give them the confidence to find out what they do not know. The most important closing question whenever seeking advice or information is, "What should I be asking you that I am not?" Often, the expert on the other end of the conversation knows what you do not know.

As one grows and becomes more independent as a teenager, self-directed learning can start to take form. I was determined to control my education by the time I entered high school, even if that meant adjusting the traditional public school imposed upon me, and the higher education later offered to me. While I certainly faced opposition along the way, I was given a chance to prove myself at every turn. When a student *earns* ownership over his or her education (as opposed to it being given), the opportunity to identify one's journey and successfully pursue it increases.

However, student-owned learning must not be confused with having a lack of structure or expectations. These are integral parts of the equation, and it is how the traditional five-year plan can be molded into a self-directed education plan. Each of us can create one and revise it annually. While it should be specific so that it represents a vision, it can begin as something quite simple. If I dissect my educational journey and put it into a basic formula, it looks like this:

- Pre-School: 100% parenting
- Elementary School: 50% school and 50% parenting
- Middle School: 50% school, 30% parenting, 20% self-directed real-world experience
- High School: 50% school 20% parenting, 30% self-

directed real-world experience

- Higher Education: 30% school, 10% parenting, 60% self-directed real-world experience
- Postgraduate: Some degree of structured education in perpetuity with about 25% of my time allocated to lifelong learning in the form of professional and personal development.

The world is more complex today than it was for previous generations, so it may take more time now to progress through the steps of discovering your passions, charting your courses, and committing to your journey. David Sinclair, the director of the Paul F. Glenn Center for the Biology of Aging at Harvard Medical School, says the first person to live to 150 years old has already been born. If that is the case, a prolonged lifespan will require prolonged or even perpetual self-introspection and reeducation.

Moreover, as technology increases the rate of change, there is additional and increasingly contradictory information that one must parse within any given timeframe. Compared to previous generations, this added stimulation and/or distraction reduces the time to become bored. That is unfortunate since boredom is the catalyst to creativity and passion discovery. We will need to be more patient in the effort to create happier and more productive members of society.

Education is not a schoolhouse; it is culture—a culture of lifelong learning. There should be no rush to acquire the maximum knowledge or number of skills within 12, 14, 16, or 20+ years of formal education. Moreover, we must also reign in the institutional agenda to keep students enrolled in formal schooling for as long as possible (including post-graduate studies). The business of education and our culture promotes basking in the glory of one's degrees by proudly displaying institution-branded diplomas above one's desk, but where one studied should not be the badge of honor. Rather, we should be celebrating what our education helps us achieve. One cannot frame a real-world education and hang it on a wall, but one can naturally demonstrate it through financial independence, raising a family, empowering others, and positively impacting the world.

While college was not the right path for me, I would like to see it become a viable option for *everyone*. Perpetual schooling is part of lifelong learning, and it must therefore be relevant, affordable, and equitable for all. To remain relevant, higher education institutions must also prioritize learning over job placement. Unfortunately, this is not the trend, given that today's students have mortgaged their future to obtain a diploma, at which point they quickly need employment after graduation to repay that debt when collectors start coming six months later. Since employers increasingly report that university graduates are ill-prepared to move beyond entry-level positions, the need for higher education to pivot should be obvious. Education, as a whole, must focus more on learning than achievement.

So, how do we prepare ourselves for an unpredictable future? One must learn how to learn, pivot, and positively impact the world. If we are encouraged to believe we can change the world in some meaningful way, we probably will. Without even realizing it, each of us does something daily that causes someone or something to pivot. Whether it is giving advice to a friend, disciplining a child, or simply smiling at a stranger who crosses our path, the energy is altered, and that causes a pivot. When we begin to recognize this as a skill or an ability, it becomes a great opportunity to practice and develop it.

It is often said that if you can impact just one person, you have made a difference. While technically true, I encourage you to aim higher. To paraphrase Michelangelo, "It is better to aim high and miss than to aim low and achieve." Remember, failures are necessary stepping stones toward success. Each of us can responsibly and positively impact many. Professional teachers do this every day as the centerpiece of their jobs, and if more embrace this potential and purposefully use it for good, anything is truly possible.

Furthermore, if we adopt such a mindset and inspire future generations to do the same—or maybe just help them maintain this mindset since millennials and Gen Z seem naturally inclined to be more considerate of each other and the world around them—the exponential effect will conquer many of humanity's most significant challenges, including environmental issues like climate change, and social injustices such as racism and economic disparity. While political and economic forces often propagate harmful ideologies, we can and must learn to defeat them by allowing ourselves to outgrow them, even if gradually, from one generation to the next.

This is why I am convinced world peace is possible *if* we make it profitable. With today's students and entrepreneurs already thinking about the benefits of renewables and not relying on limited resources, there will simply be less to fight each other for in the future. A modern and relevant education must inspire an entrepreneurial spirit that broadens the definition of profit.

Social-entrepreneurship and other forms of conscientiousness will help us build a society that fosters equity and unity.

I became a keynote speaker in education not to provide answers but to prompt more questions. When I stand on stage before a group of professional educators, I am keenly aware that I am not the smartest person in the room; however, perhaps neither is anyone else, and that is why I love what I do. My work unites people, enabling them to think and work collectively. When we work as a team, there is no problem we cannot solve. Education *is* the solution to all the world's problems, and each one of us has a role, responsibility, and opportunity to make the world the best it can be.

# Appendix A: Selected Quotes from Text

**On Change & Privilege**

"Be the change you wish to see in the world."
– Mahatma Gandhi (Chapters 2 & 8)

"If we are to create a more peaceful world, it is those of us with privilege who must recognize the wrongs and embrace our social responsibility before our hand is forced by those revolting in violence and destruction against us."
– Ravi Hutheesing (Chapter 7)

"Recognizing one's own power is a stronger force of motivation than the awareness of one's own guilt."
– Ravi Hutheesing (Chapter 7)

"True leadership is empowering those below you to rise above you."
– Ravi Hutheesing (Chapter 7)

## On Success & Professionalism

"Life is like a game of cards. The hand you are dealt is
determinism; the way you play it is free will."
– Jawaharlal Nehru (Chapter 3)

"If you want to be paid like a professional, you need to act like a
professional."
– John "Ratso" Gerardi, guitar teacher (Chapter 3)

"Don't wait for someone to tell you what to do. Find something
to do and do it."
– Tony, cycle shop owner (Chapter 4)

"Don't chase success. Pursue excellence, and success will chase
you."
– Ravi Hutheesing (Chapter 4)

"Do it with conviction, or don't do it at all."
– Peter, a friend (Chapter 4)

"If you love what you do, you will never work a day in your
life."
– Confucius (Chapter 4)

"It is better to aim high and miss than to aim low and achieve."
– Michelangelo (Chapter 10)

## On Teaching & Learning

"Education is what remains after one has forgotten everything one has learned in school."
– Albert Einstein (Chapter 2)

"Education is the ability to think rather than recall and to create rather than replicate. No education system can reach its full potential in an age of artificial intelligence and globalization until it stops focusing on achievement and starts focusing on learning."
– Ravi Hutheesing (Chapter 2)

"There must be at least one subject that makes each student want to come to school every day."
– Dr. Ernest Fleishman, superintendent, Greenwich Public Schools (Chapter 3)

"I do not believe kids are born to be racists, classists, or to discriminate in any way, and educators can create daily opportunities to prove and preserve it."
– Ravi Hutheesing (Chapter 7)

"Are we educating children to rise above disaffection and radicalism?"
– Ravi Hutheesing (Chapter 9)

"While online interactions have us talking, reading, touching, and typing, it is handwriting that keeps us thinking—there is no other activity that slows down our thoughts to the point where we fully recognize them."
– Ravi Hutheesing (Chapter 10)

## On Luck & Preparation

"Luck is the moment when preparation meets opportunity."
– Seneca (Chapter 3)

"The harder I work, the more luck I have."
– Thomas Jefferson (Chapter 3)

"It is better to be prepared and not have an opportunity than to have an opportunity and not be prepared."
– John "Ratso" Gerardi, guitar teacher (Chapter 3)

"Just make sure you always stay one page ahead of your best student."
– John "Ratso" Gerardi, guitar teacher (Chapter 8)

# Appendix B: Additional Resources

Please visit PivotByRavi.com or scan the QR code below to find the following and more:

- Courses to help implement strategies discussed in the text
- The "Pivot by Ravi" book/coaching club
- Sources expanding on historical and cultural references in the text
- Additional information on Ravi Unites Schools, Ravi's "Songwriting Safaris," Shanti Bhavan, education initiatives around the world, etc.
- Bonus pictures, including color versions of the photos in this book
- United Nations' Sustainable Development Goals
- Information on Ravi's keynote speaking

# ACKNOWLEDGMENTS

*Thank you:*

Anita Simian for the daily encouragement, brainstorming, and unwavering support throughout the writing of this book. She and her family provided the perfect "palette" for me to "paint" this "canvas" while quarantined together for half of 2020.

Marie Séréis, for not only contributing to many of these growth experiences but also selflessly supporting my desire to share them, and offering encouragement whenever "writer's block" set in.

Bob Moje, Mary Luehrsen, Jeffrey Sexton, and Mary Beth Pelosky, for being my advisory board and giving valuable guidance throughout my career.

Paul E. Blanford, Jim Blasingame, Ajit George, Jay A. Katz, Philip Levine, Ronni Levine, and Gregor Polson, for providing detailed feedback and suggestions that made this book better.

The editors, Sarah Barbour, for her effective book coaching and developmental editing, and Charmaine Tan, for her meticulous copyediting and proofreading.

My brothers, Nikhil and Vivek, for always being supportive of my endeavors, and for being the first two to "pre-order" this book!

# ABOUT THE AUTHOR

Ravi Hutheesing is an international keynote speaker who empowers education and business leaders to pivot for success in multi-cultural and multi-generational environments. Born into a lineage of prime ministers and raised by a family of Wall Street bankers, his journey as a rock star, aviator, and cultural diplomat on behalf of the United States Department of State is an inspiring example of how to stay relevant while positively impacting the world.

The first American-born member of the family that created and governed the world's largest democracy for over 40 years, Ravi is the grandnephew of Jawaharlal Nehru (India's first prime minister) and the cousin of prime ministers Indira Gandhi and Rajiv Gandhi.

He became an artist-entrepreneur before graduating high school, but Ravi's worldwide visibility skyrocketed in 1997 as the guitarist for triple Grammy nominee, Hanson. Their massive millennial fan base catapulted them to the White House, Madison Square Garden, Saturday Night Live, and more. He continued performing and began giving artist-entrepreneurship keynotes sponsored by the music products industry.

In 2008, Ravi became a pilot, and aviation manufacturers sponsored his keynotes on millennials to help reverse the shrinking pilot population.

In 2015, the United States Department of State began sponsoring his keynotes and cultural programs in Russia, Indonesia, Iraq, and Lebanon, and in 2018, he founded *Ravi Unites Schools*—a large network of international K-12 schools that participate in peer-to-peer real-time audio-video interactions hosted by Ravi. He believes these opportunities create a path to world peace.

**Published Works by Ravi**

PIVOT: Empowering Students Today to Succeed in an Unpredictable Tomorrow (Educators & Parents edition), and Empowering Yourself Today to Succeed in an Unpredictable Tomorrow (Students & Entrepreneurs edition)
Published by Ravi Unites, Inc., hardcover, paperback, e-book, and audiobook

DANCIN' WITH HANSON
Published by Pocket Books, Simon & Schuster, full-color paperback

1-2-3 SONGWRITING
Published by Truefire, DVD and video course download

LEARN GUITAR IN 21 DAYS
Published by Truefire, DVD and video course download

BEYOND THE BLUR
Published by Suburban Turban, CD and audio download

*To book Ravi for your next event, read his full biography, or learn more about his work, please visit RaviUnites.com.*